ART
AND CRAFT

ART
AND CRAFT

OLIVIER BERNIER

Seaview Books
NEW YORK

The people and events described or depicted in this novel are fictitious, and any resemblance to actual incidents or individuals is unintended and coincidental.

Library of Congress Cataloging in Publication Data

Bernier, Olivier.
    Art & craft.
      I. Title. II. Title: Art and craft.
PS3552.E7316A88   813'.54   81-50314
ISBN 0-87223-719-2   AACR2

Design by Tere LoPrete

To Sherry Huber,
my editor,
whose advice and encouragement
helped me immeasurably.

ART
AND CRAFT

ONE

The seat belt sign came on and Poppea Vlassoff strapped herself in, never interrupting her chatter. After the night spent in the plane, she looked worn and soiled. Her short black hair was greasy and disarranged; the circles under her eyes had turned a dark yellow. Her left hand, which had worked itself out from under the airline's blanket, looked soiled, dirty; but the spots spattered from knuckles to wrist were due to a permanent darkening of the skin. "I'm going to buy a skirt," she said. "Yes, really, I used to wear dresses when I was with Fred, even long gloves when he took me to charity balls."

The man sitting next to her laughed. "You, Poppea, in a dress! Oh, come on. I've never seen you out of pants," and he winked, to Poppea's obvious delight.

"And I also want to buy a bag," she went on. "I know a shop on Via Montenapoleone where they have perfect copies of Hermès, but for half the price. Milan's a great place. Let's go out right away. You don't want to sleep, do you? Let's hit the galleries as soon as we've checked in."

"Okay," Jack Griffenbaum answered, "let's see if you can sell my Léger today."

"Sure I can," said Poppea. "I know them all here, and I'll even introduce you to some collectors. I mean, like there's Vittorio Malamonte, who's got a fabulous surrealist collection—Magritte, Klee, Miró, Ernst—why don't we but it from him? I bet you could get the whole thing for half a million."

Her companion laughed. "Half a million!"

"Well," Poppea replied, "if you sell your Léger you'll get a quarter of a million, and I'll bet we could get Frank Levinson to put up the rest if we gave him a forty percent profit over six months. And I know at least two dealers who'll take anything from the collection off our hands whenever we need liquidity."

"Maybe," Griffenbaum said vaguely, looking out of the window.

Jack Griffenbaum was short, dark, wiry, precise. His traveling suit—perfect attire for the "now" man—consisted of a purple-pink battle jacket worn over a pink open-necked shirt and matching purple-pink trousers. As he looked out over the clouds, he was thinking of his accomplishments. He had started with just $100,000, an inheritance from his grandmother, and, with that and the constant exercise of an exceptionally sharp business acumen, he had made a fortune in the commodities market, working his way up to being a full partner of the firm he had started with. He had left, he remembered with satisfaction, a number of casualties along the way. Five years ago, he had been told it was time he progressed socially; the other three partners, well launched into Manhattan's social whirl, scarcely relished being associated with a raw boy from the Bronx. Buy paintings, they had said, that'll start you on your way in.

So Jack had spent $1,000,000 on a big Léger, three little Picassos, a Matisse studio scene, two Chagalls, and a brand-new Frank Stella. And it had paid off—soon. At one of the sophisticated parties he had begun to attend, he met a slim, fair, elegant young woman whose father was in real estate. He invited her to see his collection, courted her assiduously, and finally proposed. She would, he said, have a co-op in the city, a house in the Hamptons, and be the wife of a famous collector; and he loved her, too. They were married that spring.

Then, just three months ago, he had realized that the art dealers he knew were richer than he himself was; he left the commodities market to become an amateur collector-dealer (so much more elegant and "now," his wife had said; just another kind of commodity, he had thought); so he was using his collection for stock. Determined to make even more money than before, he thought that Poppea Vlassoff could be an ideal instrument: She knew a little more than he did and could lead him to people he hadn't met; on the other hand, she was penniless and not all that smart. The lure of his money would keep her in line, always ready to be used—or discarded.

The plane was circling now over the airport, just under a layer of gray clouds. Poppea Vlassoff started to comb her hair. "I look like hell," she said, absorbed in her task, and Jack Griffenbaum turned around to look at her. "I need to lose weight," she added. "Maybe I can go to a fat farm if I make money."

"You look good to me," Jack whispered, staring at the abundant breasts shown off by Poppea's T-shirt.

"Oh, come on. Your wife's very thin. Maybe I should ask her how she does it."

"Does what?" Jack asked, staring at her. Poppea laughed and licked her lips.

As they stood waiting at customs, Jack looked Poppea over again. She's sexy, he thought, messy but sexy. Her tight dungarees and high heels emphasized her curves; her very lushness had a real appeal, and Jack began to feel he should take advantage of this stay in Milan. He thought of his wife in New York and remembered her questions. "Well," he had answered, telling her about Poppea, "she just appeared six months ago. She was living in Italy before, I think, although she was born in Caracas of Russian émigré parents; she's got no money, is trying to make it as an art dealer, and doesn't know anything. She's crude, vulgar, brash, but nothing stops her. She just walks in everywhere and introduces herself—that's how I met her. I was talking to Stephen Muller in his gallery, and she just walked up to us and said, 'Hi, I'm Poppea Vlassoff. I've just become an art dealer and I hear you have a Picasso cubist drawing. I want to show it to some privates.' "

"Some privates?" his wife had asked.

"Yes, private collectors. Anyway, Stephen gave her the drawing for two hours, and by the time she brought it back she'd shown it to every dealer up and down Madison. I don't know if she really has any clients, but she's so pushy that some people give her things, not that she knows anything about art; she couldn't tell a Rothko from a Monet."

So, when Poppea had said she was stopping in Milan on her way to the Basel Art Fair, and that she had lived there for two years and knew everyone, Jack had decided to go with her. After all, he had nothing to lose.

They took a taxi to their hotel, Jack carefully letting Poppea split the $20 fare with him. She'd reserved rooms at the Hotel La Scala, explaining that she always used to stay at the Grand, but the Scala was much less expensive and very pleasant. And, in fact, Jack felt a thrill as the taxi crossed the piazza in front of the Teatro alla Scala and let them off, in the midst of a terrific din of traffic, streetcars, and news vendors. There was no porter at the door.

"Sorry, Signore," the receptionist said, "the personnel is on strike; you'll have to carry your own bags."

"Let's just leave the luggage, and we can have a cup of

coffee next door," Poppea said. "Real coffee, not like that shit they give you in New York."

Ten minutes later, Poppea Vlassoff and Jack Griffenbaum were coming down the stairs, his tidy, precise look in striking contrast to Poppea's blowsy appearance.

"Okay," Poppea said, once they had sat down and ordered two *cappuccinos,* "let's make our plans. I know everybody here and they just love me. We can make at least three galleries before lunch." And leafing through a soiled gallery guide, she added, "Let's go see Schwarz. He's loaded. He'll buy your Léger."

"Schwarz?" Jack asked. "But isn't he the Dada specialist?"

"Sure," Poppea answered.

"But then he won't want a Léger. And the other photographs I've brought with me are all Picassos and American paintings."

"He buys everything," she said flatly. Waving wildly, she added, "Oh, look, there goes Roberta Boxer; you know, the dealer. I hear she's raking it in." And, sharing the check, they walked off to the Via Montenapoleone.

By the time Jack and Poppea returned to the hotel, his confidence had been somewhat shaken. Schwarz had refused to see them ("Sorry, Signor Schwarz is with a client") three times. The next dealer, Levi, had indeed seen them, been most pleasant, sent out for coffee, looked at Jack's Léger deprecatingly, and tried to sell him a late Max Ernst for twice its value. The two brothers at the big Galleria dell'Oriente had looked at all of Jack's transparencies without a word, offered him $100,000 for his Léger (when his asking price was $250,000), smirked at Poppea's photographs, and looked thoroughly bored. When Jack asked them whether they had anything, they showed him a small cubist Braque, asked $500,000 for it, and said disdainfully when Jack suggested a trade, "We never do trades."

At two other galleries, the owners were out of town. At none did Poppea get the kind of reception she had apparently expected. "They're just upset because business is bad," she had explained unconvincingly. "Just wait until we hit the privates. I know a *principe* who has a villa between here and Turin, and a fantastic collection. I'll take you there tomorrow."

The best part of it was Milan itself, the narrow streets full of elegant, stylish shops where Poppea maddeningly priced everything without ever buying anything. Taxis were infrequent, so they walked, all the galleries being in the center of town. Soon Jack discovered that the city's greatest charm was carefully hidden: The facades of the palazzi, heavy, gray, and grim, hid charming gardens with pavilions, courtyards full of flowers and fountains. And then there were the Italians themselves. Unlike those rather unpleasant dealers they had been visiting, the pretty girls and elegant young men, the chic older women, even the street sweepers were part of a stylish pageant, polished by more than two millennia of unceasing civilization. The very movement of a woman getting into her car was full of an age-old, almost weary kind of grace; the idle young men sauntering along the streets expressed a sophisticated and ambiguous eroticism; and Jack, although the last man to pay attention to mere environment, could not help being charmed.

They had lunch in a crowded, expensive restaurant. "All the stockbrokers have lunch here," Poppea said. "My boyfriend Emilio and I ate here every day."

Jack, who had been "into" food and wine for almost three years now, ordered melon and prosciutto; then *piccata* of veal, the thin slices of meat melting into the buttery, lemony sauce; and a wonderfully fresh salad, along with a bottle of Verdicchio. "Deliciously green," he said to Poppea, and felt like a world-weary epicure. Becoming an art dealer had definitely been the right move.

By the late afternoon, Poppea's face was yellow and shiny, Jack's drawn and tight. "We won't go out tonight," Poppea said. "I'm flaked out." Jack went on to his room, thinking he would try to make Poppea the following evening.

When his phone rang the next morning, at nine-thirty, he had already breakfasted on *cappuccino* and fresh, crusty rolls. The hotel strike was apparently over.

"Why don't you join me?" Poppea said. Her room was piled with clothes, folded, unfolded, crumpled, bras here, panties there; open pots of makeup littered the table, next to used Kleenex and lists of names. Boots and shoes were strewn all over the floor. Poppea was unexpectedly dressed. "I've been working," she told him, without a greeting when he arrived. "I spoke to a runner—he's got access to some of the best collections in Milan and, anyway, I know his girl friend, who's a model. He's called Francesco Tevere and he's got a fantastic Picabia he inherited from his father. Anyway, he's rich and he'll be here at ten-thirty. Then, after lunch, we'll go see Malamonte—he's the collector I told you about, he's got all those surrealists, maybe he'll buy your Léger . . . and I made an appointment with Schwarz for twelve. I bet you can buy something from the Sardine."

"The Sardine?"

"Yes, that's what I call Malamonte. He's from Sardinia, or, anyway, he has a factory there, so I call him the Sardine. Let's go out and have a cup of coffee. Francesco won't be here for an hour yet."

So they went and sat at the café opposite the Scala; the sun was already warm and the palaces on the square, grimy as they were, seemed to glow. Poppea Vlassoff kept up a

steady monologue ("We'll sell your Léger—we'll buy a
Magritte or a Klee—I'll bet Schwarz will be interested in
your Americans; you could make an exchange. . . .") while
Jack, barely listening, began to relax. Soon, a typically
Italian young man walked up to their table: He had a
charming, sensual face, was dark, thin, short, and dressed in
a suede jacket, open-necked beige silk shirt, and tight, bell-
bottom pants. Jack noticed he was wearing a Cartier watch.

"*Sai*, Poppea," he said, and rattled away at great speed.
Poppea stopped him, introduced him to Jack, and went back
to Italian. After five minutes, she turned to Jack while
Tevere waited.

"Francesco says he has a client for your Léger, a multi-
millionaire, you'd better give him a transparency, and he's
bringing me three Ernst oils this afternoon." Jack waited
another ten minutes while the dialogue went on; then
Francesco left. "He's been telling me about his girl friend.
She's a model, like my friend Zaza. You'll meet her tomorrow—Zaza, I mean."

    That evening, Jack began to feel he understood why
Poppea, though endlessly talking of buying million-dollar
paintings, never had any money. They had returned to
Galleria Schwarz and met its owner, who had spent five
minutes with them and looked bored. None of the other
dealers had shown the remotest interest in either his or
Poppea's transparencies. Since Jack hoped to do business at
the Basel fair, he wasn't really upset; and since Milan was
a waste of time, he decided to concentrate on what he
hoped would be pleasure.

    When Francesco Tevere reappeared at six, he was carry-
ing a large paper bag; and there, on Poppea's bed, he took
out four Max Ernst oils on paper. After he had spoken to
her, Poppea turned to Jack. "They're the Arizona period.

Francesco says he got them from a friend of his father and he only wants twenty-one *millioni*, that's thirty thousand dollars, for each of them. Of course," Poppea added, looking wise, "they've been restored, you can see where the paper is damaged. I think you should buy them; they're a steal. Francesco doesn't understand English, but they're really cheap," and when Jack declined on the grounds that he knew nothing about surrealist painting, she went on, "Well, I'll call Vincent Germain, he's in Paris, I'm sure he'll come over. You know him, don't you? His father's very rich and, anyway, he knows Ernst and I'm sure he'll buy them. You want to go dancing tonight? I can get us into the chic discothèque, I used to go every night with my boyfriend, he was a big industrialist."

Poppea came into the lobby at eight-thirty that night wearing a tight silk blouse and black velvet pants, also tight; she was tottering on enormously high heels. She had washed her hair, made up her face, and looked sexy. Putting her arm through Jack's, she automatically moved her left hand backward so that he couldn't see its scattering of spots, and they went off. The restaurant was in the courtyard of an imposing neoclassical palace; a cluster of tables was covered with peach-colored tablecloths and lit with candles. There were scattered trees growing out of pots, and boxes of bright flowers.

"I told you it was nice," said Poppea, and Jack was indeed impressed.

"Tonight's my treat," he answered, looking her straight in the eye, and he spent the whole dinner trying to find out who she really was. When they left, he only knew that she had gone to a college that remained nameless. She had left Caracas at the age of six and moved to Florida; her parents were dead; she had spent three years in Italy with several boyfriends; most of her girl friends were models; before going to Italy she had lived with a man in New

York and they had split up after two years. Adding it all up, and accounting for gaps, she must be about twenty-nine, he thought, and thoroughly experienced.

He ordered brandy, and wondered about having her. By now, she was talking about her two current boyfriends, one a South American ("He's got fantastic connections and I'm going down to Argentina and sell paintings to all the millionaires there"), the other an Italian newspaper correspondent in New York ("He's helping me put together material. I want to start an art fund, but it's all got to be really documented, and he's very good at financial reporting"). Slowly, it dawned on Jack that the way to her bed was through her greed.

"Art fund?" he said. "I could really help you with that. I know some big investors."

Poppea immediately caught fire and, within five minutes, was talking about charts and average profits and the normal yearly rise of the art market. Her eyes sparkled; she was almost panting—and Jack realized he would have no problem. "Let's go and dance," he said, and soon they were knocking at a closed door. A little panel opened, and a man peeped through.

"*Sono io*, Poppea Vlassoff, *l'amica di* Federico Treponti..." and the man let them in. They walked downstairs into a silver and plastic room full of people sitting at tiny tables and dancing on a small platform. They made straight for the platform and Poppea started wriggling in front of Jack, now and again waving and saying, "That's my friend Francesca, she's a big model," or, "That's Enrico, his father's an industrialist, and he has three factories."

When the disk jockey put on a slow song, Jack held Poppea tight against his body. Her left hand, resting on his shoulder, looked like a dark brown stain, but he couldn't see it. Her breasts were squeezed against his chest, her belly followed his, and when he whispered, "You really turn me on," she just moaned a little. It was less than a half hour before they went back to the hotel. Jack said nothing, but when they stepped out of the elevator, Poppea asked him to come in for a while. "Yeah," Jack answered, "I'd like to," and followed her in. As soon as the door closed, he hugged her again, kissing her this time. She responded violently and, leaving his arms, began to pull her pants off; a minute later, they were in bed and Jack was pleasantly surprised by her ardor. Once it was over, he turned around and almost laughed as he thought, well, she didn't talk about the art market for at least a half hour!

The next day began very grandly: A large black Rolls-Royce pulled up to the hotel, but, to Jack's surprise, it was driven by Francesco Tevere. He looked at Poppea. "Oh, yes," she said, "Francesco often does errands for the Sardine, so I asked him to come and fetch us this morning." The big car started to glide silently through the narrow streets while Poppea and Francesco talked without pause; finally, Jack asked where they were going.

"Well," Poppea answered, "it's really not far, just we have to drive around because of the one-way streets. Anyway, we're going to the Sardine's office, you'll see, he has paintings there, and then we'll go home with him." And turning to Francesco, "I call him the Sardine . . ." but her joke was either lost in Italian or, Jack thought, vastly overfamiliar.

They drew up before a deep doorway made of huge blocks of gray stone and capped with a bearded head; but the door was of glass and chrome, obviously brand-new, as were the hallway and the elevator. They rose quickly to the fifth floor and came out in a little reception room. Poppea asked for Signor Malamonte, the secretary spoke into a pearl-gray phone, and they were ushered into Malamonte's private office, a large room with windows looking out over a garden.

The furniture was modern and quite beautiful: the desk an oval slab of marble on a pedestal; the chair, two huge leather cushions held together by bands of chrome. There were globes of opaque, milky glass hanging low from the ceiling. Malamonte himself, short, square, and paunchy, had gray hair and tiny eyes set deep in a seamed and pitted face. He got up, almost scowling.

"So it's you again," Jack understood him to say in Italian, but failed to follow the rest of an apparently very unpleasant speech.

"What's the problem?" he asked, when Malamonte finally stopped.

"Oh," Poppea said airily, "I took one of his pieces, a Magritte, with me when I was here the last time, and he's angry because he hasn't been paid for it, but it doesn't have a certificate, and my client in Philadelphia hasn't given me a check yet," and, after another question, she added, "Yes, a a fairly long time, about a year."

Poppea launched herself back into Italian and Jack looked around the room, noticing a Picasso drawing, a Chagall gouache, and a Max Ernst oil—quite a promising beginning to the collection. After what seemed like an endless time, Jack took advantage of a lull to ask Poppea whether Malamonte wanted to see his Léger. The resulting burst seemed even more violent than the earlier ones and, finally, Poppea said, "Well, he says he's not buying another thing until he's been paid for his Magritte; but he might be willing to sell several pieces from his collection. We'll go home with him in a few minutes."

Right then Malamonte spoke into the phone and Poppea added, "Well, no, he has to stay here, but Francesco will bring us the paintings he wants to sell." The wait seemed to go on and on, and Jack reflected that since his arrival in Milan, he had spent most of his time waiting for Poppea to finish speaking; between her loquacity, he thought, and the Italians' speeches in response, I'm likely to spend the rest of my time here sitting and listening to a language I don't understand.

Finally Poppea got up. "Let's go," she said.

"But what about the paintings?" Jack asked.

"I'll explain later," she answered quickly and, nodding to Malamonte, they walked out.

"Francesco will bring us the pieces at the hotel tonight," Poppea said, as they strolled toward a restaurant. "It's just as well, really, because by then Vincent will have arrived and maybe we can sell him one on the spot. I could use the commission."

"Will he pay you one?"

"Well, he won't know he is; I can easily outsmart him. I'll say I'll take my commission when the painting is sold— ten percent of the sales price—so he'll be more willing to buy, but I'll put ten percent on top of Malamonte's price so I can have some ready cash. Also, we really don't have to pay Malamonte right away. If we see something interesting, we could buy it with the money we get from Vincent —but it should be something we can resell within a month, say, and then we can make a double profit and pay Malamonte when we have resold the other piece."

Jack felt himself reeling. "You can get yourself in a lot of trouble, you know."

Poppea laughed. "No, I can manage it. All I have to do is tell Malamonte he'll be paid in thirty days and then he won't expect money before that and we can sell whatever we buy here at Basel—it'll be easy."

Jack just smiled and shook his head, but there was no stopping Poppea, and, even as they entered the restaurant, sat down, and were given menus, she was continuing her speculations until finally Jack said, "But, Poppea, this whole edifice that you're building in your mind is based on selling one of Malamonte's pieces to Vincent Germain—and he hasn't even seen it yet!"

Vincent Germain was due at the hotel at eight that evening, and Francesco was to come by at ten-thirty bringing two Klees and a Magritte. Poppea and Jack spent another unsuccessful afternoon going from gallery to gallery, while Poppea remained as optimistic as the day they had started. The more Jack pointed out that, so far, they had done no business, *none*, the more Poppea returned to her fantasies of future deals to be successfully concluded. By then, Poppea had called Eve Lamarque, a Paris gallery owner, and offered her one of the Ernst oils on paper brought the day before by Francesco; Mme. Lamarque had been interested and had told Poppea to bring it to Basel; Poppea had quoted a price of $45,000 for it, conditional on the work's being authentic, and spent a good part of the afternoon speculating about what she could do with her $15,000 profit—well, $14,000, because she was really buying some clothes and shoes and a pocketbook or two.

"If you've asked her for forty-five thousand dollars, how much do you suppose she'll sell it for?" Jack had asked.

"Oh, probably eighty thousand," Poppea had answered airily, leaving Jack to wonder about a system where the price of a painting could grow from $30,000 to $80,000 in the course of two transactions made, probably, within a month.

As they walked back into the lobby of the hotel, Jack realized that he had had his fill of useless visits and Poppea's castles in the air. "Let's go to my room for a while," he said, holding her hand, and she smiled and agreed.

When Vincent Germain arrived two hours later, he

found a message from Poppea asking him to call her in Jack Griffenbaum's room. She sounded rather remote. "Let's meet in the lobby in a half hour," she said. "We'll go on to dinner. I want to take a shower first."

Vincent Germain was French, but in New York, where he lived, people always thought he was English. "You're not French!" they would exclaim. "How can you be French? You talk just like an Englishman." Hiding his exasperation (it must be the ten-thousandth time) he would explain, mendaciously, that he had learned English in England; or, if he was in a good mood, he would smile and answer, "I don't know why I talk like this; it's just a mistake of nature."

Still, as his wife, Sarah, would sometimes tell him, he didn't behave like a Frenchman: Everything about him really did seem English; or, at least, like the outmoded Englishmen you read about in certain stereotyped novels. He was tall and slim, with brown hair and a light complexion; he dressed in English clothes; he was cool, reserved, sometimes almost withdrawn, so that he struck people as being standoffish, even supercilious. He didn't have the warmth of a real Frenchman, Sarah would say, and he would answer that most Frenchmen are anything but warm. He knew she had a point, though, even if it was a little wrong: He was not cold, really, just absent, living more in a separate world of books, paintings, and gourmet food, a world to which he was usually unwilling to admit anyone else. Above all, he shielded his emotions from the public glare—or thought he did. For many years he had taken pride in never letting his face reveal what he felt, so that he developed two almost distinct personalities: one for outsiders and one for himself. Even with his friends, he kept himself secret: He could have intellectual discussions that went on for hours—he's so intelligent, everyone said, so cultivated—but he never talked about himself.

He was cool, distant, formal, so people assumed he was always in control; and, as an art dealer, he seemed to fit another stereotype, that of the cosmopolitan always flying to Europe, of the connoisseur whose trained eye enables him to spot the painting that can be resold at a profit. Nothing, people said, could have been more natural, more appropriate. But in fact, or so Vincent was beginning to think, nothing could have been more wrong.

It was Sarah who had been the first to realize how deceptive that particular set of appearances might be. At first, like all the others, she had thought Vincent was doing just the right thing, and he would confirm it. "After all," he would say, "I love paintings. I enjoy having money. And I'd be miserable if I didn't get back to Europe several times a year. What could be better for me than dealing in art?" But even before they were married, when they had been living together just a year, she had noticed that he became very tense before meeting a client or another dealer; that he came back from those meetings exhausted and angry, even when they had been successful; that, most of all, he hated the bargaining that unavoidably went with the job.

At first, when she mentioned this to him, he simply denied it. "I don't mind it," he would say. "By now I'm used to it. And look at the advantages. How else would I get to Europe? How else would I make all this money? Besides, what else would I do?"

"Teach," she would say, "or write. You like books so much. Why don't you write one?" But he would always push her suggestions away. You needed a doctorate to teach, he would say, and did she have any idea how difficult it was to get a first book accepted? What would they live on while he wrote it? No, no. He liked being an art dealer.

Half an hour after his arrival, Vincent was sitting in the hotel lobby, waiting for Poppea Vlassoff. "He's very knowledgeable," Poppea was telling Jack at that very moment. "He really knows art and he's got a lot of connections; but he's not very sharp in business. Anyway, he's really useful; he can tell a fake when he sees one and he has access to major paintings. I've done business with him before."

"He lives in New York, doesn't he?" Jack asked.

"Yes," Poppea answered, "his family's French, but he lives in New York. He went to Princeton and then worked for Iris Johnson. You know, the gallery. Anyway, last winter I sold a big Miró for him to a dealer right here in Milan. It's the biggest sale I ever made." And with that, they went down and joined Vincent.

Dinner that night was startlingly similar to every other night's, Jack thought. Poppea had led them to yet another good restaurant, indoors this time; the pasta was famous and he ordered *tagliatelle* Alfredo while Vincent had ravioli; Poppea, characteristically disregarding her own advice, was eating risotto; but, as always, the conversation was monopolized by Poppea and her anticipations. First, she gave glowing descriptions of the Ernst oils (and their certificates) and told Vincent that Eve Lamarque was buying one and he must buy the other two—to which he replied that he wanted to see them before he could say anything. Then she went on at great length about the Malamonte collection, telling Vincent about her delayed-payment idea and how much money could be made. Jack, watching it all, felt that Poppea had far less influence on Vincent than she thought. There was a remoteness about the other dealer that he didn't quite like. Vincent was scrupulously polite, but there was something subtly wrong; Jack couldn't quite put his finger on it. Perhaps it was Vincent's manner, his English accent, his formality: The man almost dressed like a banker, or perhaps it was that quiet assumption of superior knowledge about wine, food, the local customs. Also, there was his obvious lack of enthusiasm, but, then, Poppea certainly gave him good reason for a measure of disbelief. Still, Jack missed the easy camaraderie of the other dealers. It wasn't even as if Vincent were that important, that successful: He had no reason to put on airs.

Jack returned to the conversation just in time to hear Poppea say that there was another private collection, a well-known one that belonged to Giacomo Barolo, and that she would take him there. Vincent seemed more interested but said firmly that he could only stay in Milan for two days. "Can it be arranged?" he asked, and looked unconvinced when Poppea announced that there was no problem. Jack sympathized, or felt he should, but he could not help being irritated by Vincent's aloofness, and then, with a jolt, it all came together: That guy is slumming, he said to himself.

They walked back to the hotel together after dinner, Vincent asking questions about Francesco Tevere and his reliability. Poppea told the story of the Picabia inherited from his father and swore he had fantastic connections. When Vincent said, "You mentioned certificates?," she answered that, indeed, there were certificates, and that she was sure they could get more from Mundberg, the well-known author and critic who lived in Paris.

They found Tevere waiting in the lobby when they came in. "Let's go to your room," Poppea said to Vincent. "We'll look at the pictures there," and soon the different works were spread out on the bed. First, the Ernsts Poppea had ordered; taking them from a red leather case, Francesco put them down on the counterpane. Vincent looked at them carefully, lifting them to the light, then looking at the backs.

"Well, they're interesting," he said, "but where do they come from?"

"They belong to Francesco," Poppea answered earnestly. "He inherited them from his father. You see, his father was an artist who knew Max Ernst, and they made an exchange more than twenty years ago, and they've got certificates," she went on, turning to Francesco who produced black-and-white photographs, each bearing on its back a typed inscription certifying the work in question as a genuine Max Ernst, and, a little lower, an illegible signature over a round seal consisting of an ornate "E.C." and the name "Prof. Dot. Ernesto Credibile."

"This won't do, you know," Vincent said. "I, for one, have never heard of this Credibile, and I very much doubt anyone else has, either."

Poppea didn't even let him finish. "It's okay, it's okay, Mundberg will give certificates. Francesco has already shown him these works and he loved them. Look, I'll join you in Paris, take them to Mundberg myself. Then will you buy them?"

Vincent was silent for a moment. "Well," he said, "if you do get certificates, I'll buy one and take the other on consignment. I can sell it in New York easily enough. But I won't pay forty-five thousand dollars; offer Francesco forty thousand dollars and tell him it's my last word. I assume you'll take your commission on resale."

"Oh, yes," Poppea shouted, "I will, and he'll take it."

"But hadn't you better ask him?"

"Oh, I'll talk to him later and get him down. It's a deal."

"Subject to there being certificates," Vincent repeated.

"Oh, sure, sure," Poppea said, "no problem. Now let's look at the other things."

Francesco untied a large bundle that contained two framed Klee watercolors and, behind a sheet of cardboard, a 30" x 26" Magritte canvas representing a marble head decked with flowers and floating above a landscape.

"Let's see the Klees," Vincent asked, and Francesco put

the two watercolors on the bed while Poppea exclaimed that they were top quality, and fantastic, and could be sold at Basel in ten minutes. Francesco started explaining that both works were of the best period, 1924 and 1926, and in perfect condition, never restored, and that they were reproduced in the Klee literature. Vincent looked at them carefully, then handed them on to Jack, who whistled.

"What's the price?" he asked.

Poppea, after consulting with Francesco, answered, "Fifty thousand dollars a piece." Vincent grunted, and Poppea said excitedly, "Well, what do you think?"

"They look all right, and the price is reasonable, but I'd like first to see the books in which they're reproduced," he replied.

Poppea turned to Francesco and spoke to him. "He says he'll bring them tomorrow."

"All right," Vincent replied, "we'll see tomorrow. Now what about the Magritte?" Francesco handed it to him, and Vincent looked at it carefully. "It's been heavily restored," he said. "Look, here, the flowers around the head have been repainted and the nose is touched up, and that whole section of the sky is a different texture from the rest. I'll bet you that canvas has had a tear." He turned it over and saw a sheet of cardboard nailed to the stretcher and covering the canvas. "Well," he added, "it's pretty obvious. This is just the ghost of a painting; it must have been torn and then relined with a new canvas; there's almost nothing left of the original. *Questo e troppo restorato*," he went on, turning to Francesco. "*Non e il quadro originale, non vale niente.*"

Poppea looked shocked. "I didn't know you spoke Italian," she said.

"I don't really, just a few words." Vincent smiled and Jack realized why: He had probably understood things Poppea had not meant him to know.

Francesco immediately started to defend the painting, saying that many Magrittes were relined and that there was a certificate by Mme. Magritte dated just two weeks earlier. Vincent drew himself up and, in a disdainful voice, answered that relining and tears were very different things; and that Mme. Magritte's certificate meant nothing. In response to Francesco's argument that, as the artist's widow, she alone was entitled to give legal certificates, Vincent pointed out that no one accepted them; that she could hardly remember every painting her husband had ever done; and that, unless the painting were reproduced in the big Magritte book or had a dazzling provenance, no one would touch it.

Poppea intervened then and Jack, who had watched the whole scene almost as a spectator, suggested they go down to the bar for a drink. Vincent agreed, adding, "All right, now we have it straight: Poppea, you bring me the Ernst certificates in Paris and Francesco will appear tomorrow with the Klee book." As they went downstairs, Poppea started figuring out how much her profit on the Ernsts would come to once they were resold, and what she'd buy with it, and what they could make on the Klees; they walked into the bar, sat down, and ordered without once interrupting Poppea's logorrhea.

The next morning, Francesco walked into the lobby and found Poppea, Jack, and Vincent waiting for him. He was empty-handed. "Where are the books?" Vincent asked and was told, through Poppea, that Francesco hadn't been able to get them, but that he was going to the bookstore now; Vincent must come with him and he would show him the books. Somewhat reluctantly, Vincent agreed and walked out with Francesco, who stopped in front of a mini-Fiat. "It belongs to a friend," Francesco explained, and both men squeezed in. Five minutes later, Vincent was sitting, waiting in the double-parked car.

It seemed like a very long time before Francesco reappeared, holding a book on Klee, which he opened to the right pages. Vincent looked at the book, which had been published in New York three years earlier; and indeed, there, on pages thirty-two and fifty-four, were the two Klees in question. Francesco pointed them out, emphasizing the fact that these two had been selected for a book devoted to Klee's best works.

"Very nice," Vincent said and looked up the list of illustrations to see if the two watercolors were listed as belonging to the Malamonte collection. He soon found the first; the dimensions and year were right, but it seemed to be in the Yale University Art Gallery; and the other was listed as belonging to the Chicago Art Institute. "When did Signor Malamonte buy these, do you know?" he asked Francesco.

"Oh, years ago, at least ten years ago; they were among his first purchases. That's why I can give you a good price on them; he paid so little at the time."

Vincent smiled. "I must think about this," he said. "I'll let you know."

Francesco clearly didn't understand. "Why don't you want them? The price is so low, and they are in the book, so they are authentic."

"I'm sorry," Vincent replied, "but I'm just not ready to commit myself yet."

"But they'll be gone if you wait. At that price, they'll sell right away."

"Then I must take the chance," Vincent said shortly, as they drew up before the hotel.

Poppea was waiting for him in the lobby. "Did you buy them?" she asked excitedly.

Vincent smiled. "No."

Poppea looked as if she would burst. "Why not? Why not?"

"Because they're almost certainly fakes."

Poppea's mouth fell open. "Fakes?"

"Yes, if you look at the listing here, at the back of the book, you'll find that as recently as three years ago one belonged to Yale and the other to the Chicago Art Institute. Since your friend Malamonte is supposed to have owned them for more than ten years, and since it is most unlikely that either museum sold these Klees—though I will check when I get back to New York—it seems pretty certain that the works we saw yesterday were fakes."

Poppea looked appalled. "Fakes," she repeated, clearly making an effort. "Well, you know the Italians. The Sardine must have bought them years ago without knowing —but please don't tell him. In fact, I'll say you can't buy them because you just put all your money in a big Miró."

"Tell him anything you like," Vincent said drily.

Poppea had arranged a visit to a well-known private collector, Giacomo Barolo, for the next day. She didn't know whether he'd sell anything, but he had a major collection of nineteenth- and twentieth-century paintings it would be interesting to see; and he was a good contact. Poppea kept emphasizing, time and time again, that no one else, no other dealer, would be so generous. Others kept their acquaintance with collectors carefully to themselves, but Poppea wasn't like that; she was willing to introduce Vincent and Jack to people and merely expected her 10 percent on any business that might transpire. She didn't see, she said, what all the mystery was about. Other art dealers would never give the names of people they dealt with, for fear someone might steal their clients; but she trusted Jack and Vincent and was perfectly straight with them.

Vincent remembered with amusement that just a few months earlier Poppea had called, full of excitement, to say that she had a sensational 1914 Léger that was in a private collection and had never yet been on the market, and was reproduced in all the books. When Vincent had asked for a description, she had been vague but offered to bring it right over, adding, "I'm at the private's now. I can just get into a cab," and sure enough, she had appeared within the hour with a Léger; but it was a painting that belonged to a dealer, had been on the market for over a year, and was unsaleable because it had been heavily restored after being in a fire.

Vincent had recognized it right away and, smiling, had said, "Are you sure it's never been on the market?"

"Never," Poppea had answered with fervor. "Never! I just took it off the wall of these collectors myself."

And so, as he listened to Poppea's paean, it occurred to Vincent that the visit to Barolo might not be altogether what it seemed, although it certainly looked as if Poppea had produced the goods with the Ernsts.

That night, they had dinner with one of the six young women Poppea referred to as her best friends; they were all models. As they drove to the restaurant, Poppea raved about her friend Zaza's beauty, the money she made as a top model, and the fact that she was engaged to the heir to a real-estate fortune. It was a kind of relationship, Vincent realized, that depended purely on externals: It wasn't that Poppea liked Zaza or had anything much in common with her; she simply admired her glamour and, probably, worshipped beauty because of her lack of it.

Still, when they arrived, Vincent was pleasantly surprised. Zaza was indeed ravishing: tall, very thin, of course, with a very pale complexion and huge dark eyes. Her face hardly seemed made up; her dark brown hair was pulled back from her forehead and gathered into a bun at the back of her head; even her nails, though long and obviously cared for, were covered only with a transparent polish; and her clothes—a cream-colored silk blouse, a Hermès scarf loosely tied at her throat, and dark trousers—were part of an overall image of great simplicity. But it was the natural look that made Vincent realize how very beautiful she was, and the message came across clearly: She needed no enhancement, no trickery; her triumph owed nothing to art.

It was fascinating to watch Poppea that night. The two men were frankly taken with Zaza, unable to look away from her, agreeing with her, trying to please her, as if giving themselves up, for the moment, to her beauty. But Poppea's behavior was quite different: She alternated between showing Zaza off—how much she made an hour, how many covers she was on, how popular a model she was, how hard she had to work—and an odd kind of flirtation, teasing Zaza about boyfriends, impressing her with all the deals she, Poppea, was involved in, the expensive pictures she handled.

It was no longer the standard monologue. Poppea, for once, was interested in someone other than herself, but the result was an attempt on her part almost to incorporate the other person into herself by making her life seem desirable to Zaza. It was not that Poppea was seduced by Zaza's beauty, or even her success; nothing could have been further from her than any physical desire; rather it was as if, through Zaza, Poppea could stop being that overweight, blowsy girl with the spattered left hand, an art dealer who knew nothing about art, a woman whose lovers meant nothing to her, someone who had to impose herself on people who didn't really want her. Zaza was sought after because of her looks, and as Poppea talked to her, she started to become Zaza, to receive all the things she was always yearning for.

That evening, Poppea seemed more human, more attractive, in fact, because she was more real than ever before; and Jack suddenly thought she was good for more than just sex, while Vincent, much to his surprise, began to feel real sympathy.

As they went off the next afternoon to see the Barolo collection, Vincent Germain was feeling quite embarrassed: Although he would try to disassociate himself from Poppea Vlassoff, he felt it was more than awkward to be visiting a man of that caliber in Poppea's company; in the taxi, he quickly reviewed the mutual acquaintances he could claim. He had asked Poppea a little earlier how she had first met Barolo. Her answer was obviously cautious: It had been at a party and they had immediately felt a rapport, so he had invited her to see his collection; but something in her manner that was already familiar to Vincent permeated her explanations, and, with a little shock, he realized it was akin to the way she behaved with Jack, that this was the attitude she assumed when dealing with a lover. He thought about it now: What a way to meet Barolo, he kept repeating to himself. And when they had been led into the living room by the butler, and Poppea had introduced him, Vincent quickly said: "I'm so glad to meet you finally after hearing so much about you. We have many friends in common."

"Yes," Barolo answered, "and one of them will be here later today. You're related to André Germain, aren't you?"

Vincent felt his heart sink; his father was always bad news. He barely had time to smile and answer before Barolo started his tour of the collection: several Nabi-style Vuillards, all of exceptional quality; a sensational Gauguin, ablush with warm color; a fiery early Signac; then, in a room by itself, a major cubist Picasso, a man with a pipe, dated 1912.

Poppea could hardly contain her excitement. "It's worth a million," she enthused, to Vincent's horror.

Trying to make up for this, Vincent asked Barolo how long he'd had the picture and was rewarded with a complete story. They went on to the next room where a curiously stiff Chagall was hanging next to a Matisse portrait and a Braque still life; then came a superb Juan Gris.

Poppea could contain herself no longer. "If you want to sell any of this," she said breathlessly, "I can get you the top price anytime. . . . In fact, I'd get you a record-breaking sum."

Barolo smiled. "I am thinking of selling one or two pictures, but I'm afraid I've already spoken to someone else —your father, in fact," he said, turning to Vincent.

Poppea blushed. "But when I saw you last year, you said you'd give me business."

"Yes, yes, I even mentioned you to André Germain. I thought you might work together, but apparently it isn't possible. You see, Poppea, you're so new to all this. I asked André how long you'd been in the business, and he didn't even know you, he said. . . . Well, in fact, Poppea, you don't know museum people, do you?"

"Sure I know them, and, besides, I have lots of privates, the richest people in New York!" Poppea almost shrieked.

"I am so sorry," Barolo said politely. "Another time, perhaps, we can do something together."

It was a great relief to Vincent when they began to leave. "I'll tell your father I saw you," Barolo told Vincent as they went out.

"Fine," he answered. "Give him my greetings."

When they arrived at the hotel, it was obvious that Poppea had decided, after a struggle, that Vincent was innocent of the double cross. They discussed the collection, and Vincent remarked he found the Chagall so peculiar that, were it not part of such a good collection, he would think it a fake.

"Well," Poppea said absentmindedly, "he bought all his pictures from the Fornetti brothers, and I don't think there can be anything wrong." Then, launching herself into her real theme, "I know he's your father, and I don't mean to offend you," she began, "but it's disgusting the way he stole Barolo from me. It's just stealing. He bad-mouthed me, that's obvious, but I know as many collectors as he does, I'll get even. He won't be able to show his face in New York, I can tell you. I'm going to do a job on that bastard! He's not so clean himself. I look nice but I can really fuck people up. He'll see. . . ."

An hour later, she was still raving, and Vincent, while amused at the violence of her resentment, did not think her altogether wrong.

The complaints went on all through dinner that night, and Vincent bore the brunt. To Poppea's astonishment, Jack had gone on ahead to Basel early that morning, saying he would rather try to do business in Switzerland than meet Barolo. But, as dessert was brought to the table, and Vincent was bracing himself for another bout of Poppea's rage, Francesco ran into the restaurant and up to their table. He sat down, barely nodding to Vincent, and started to speak very fast, gesturing violently.

Poppea looked shocked. "Would you believe," she said breathlessly, "they've arrested the Sardine!" After a few minutes, she went on to explain that he had apparently embezzled a large sum of money, so that he couldn't even get out on bail.

"No wonder he was anxious to be paid," Vincent answered, laughing. "And now the poor man has nothing but fakes!"

TWO

Vincent Germain decided to stop for the night in Paris on his way back to New York. "I won't meet you at the airport," his mother had said on the phone, "because I have the flu." Still, he was a little surprised when a nurse opened the door of the apartment; he thought nothing of it and nodded politely as he opened the coat closet; and then, irresistibly, the memory came back of a day a few years earlier when, at that same gesture, a mountain of empty liquor bottles had come cascading down into the room. At first, he had frozen in shock; then, briefly, he had told himself: If she drinks, that's her business; but, still motionless and surrounded by the gin bottles, he had decided he couldn't just ignore the incident.

Now he looked up to see the nurse walk away, and he realized that, obviously, his mother didn't have the flu; it must be one of her periodic alcohol-induced illnesses. Quickly, he decided not to say anything about it: He had long lost his illusions and knew that nothing would stop her. Besides, they were just friends. He picked up his suitcase and took it into his old bedroom, but, as he put it down, the past once again assaulted him. It was a little like watching a movie: He could see himself at the age of ten, stealthily dressing under his robe, then sneaking down the back corridor, through the empty kitchen, and down the back staircase, then running through the streets to his father and saying proudly when he opened the door: "I've escaped!"

He shook his head and smiled wryly at the memory. That deadly enmity he had been sure would endure as long as he lived had only lasted a few years. Then, his mother had become a friend, someone who shared Vincent's interest in books and politics. He looked forward to seeing her whenever he came through Paris; he even thought that, at last, she had come to feel affection for him; so he felt rather offended, that night, when she seemed anxious only to be left alone.

When he walked into her bedroom, she hardly greeted him, and let the conversation drop after asking him how long he was staying. "Just for a day," he answered. "Are you feeling very unwell?"

"Yes," she said drily. "It's very painful."

"But what is it? What does your doctor say?"

She pulled the sheets a little higher. "Nothing," she answered.

"Well, he must have told you what disease you have. Is it really the flu?"

"Yes. The flu," his mother said. "Vincent, I've taken a sleeping pill. I'll see you in the morning," and with that she closed her eyes.

Still, he wasn't worried; but the next morning at seven, just three days before Christmas, the nurse woke him up. "Quick," she said, "your mother is much worse. Call the doctor."

"What's the matter?" he asked, still half-asleep.

"Just call him quickly," the nurse answered. "She's unconscious. I'll try to give her an injection."

And although he was now fully awake, Vincent found himself in the middle of a nightmare. The doctor was out; his service said he was in surgery and could not call back for at least two hours.

"She won't last two hours," the nurse answered when Vincent told her.

He saw his mother lying motionless, her eyes closed, moaning softly.

"What is it?" he asked.

The nurse, not answering directly, simply said: "She's not responding."

So Vincent called the police and asked them to send a doctor. "It's an emergency," he said coolly. "My mother is dying," and then he realized what he was saying, realized his mother was actually dying, there, behind that door, in the familiar room.

"She's going," the nurse said when he went in to tell her that a police doctor would soon be there.

"Going?"

"Your mother is dying," the nurse said firmly. "I'm experienced. I know. She won't last more than ten minutes."

Paralyzed, Vincent stood at the foot of the bed: There, right where he could touch her, his mother was dying. He was still wearing pajamas and a robe; he thought, this is no way to be dressed at a deathbed. He looked down at his mother's face; it had become ivory-colored. She was breathing more heavily now; and he didn't know what to feel, except a little embarrassment, as if by standing there he were somehow being indiscreet. And then his mother opened her eyes and said his name.

Quickly, just as if he had been trying to smooth over a socially difficult situation, he smiled and asked how she felt.

"It hurts," his mother said.

In the corner of the room, Vincent saw the nurse preparing another injection. "I've called the doctor," he said.

"He'll be here any minute." He looked away as his mother murmured, "No more injections"; but already the needle had gone into the vein. "The doctor can give you something for the pain," Vincent said, feeling incredibly foolish.

His mother stared at him. "Don't let them take me to the hospital," she whispered slowly and distinctly.

"I promise," Vincent answered, but already she had closed her eyes.

The nurse was holding her patient's left wrist now, feeling her pulse. "She's going," she repeated, and still Vincent, standing there, didn't know what to do.

"Take her hand," the nurse said.

Gratefully, Vincent crouched down by the bed and took his mother's right hand in his; it was warm and limp. Still, he felt nothing. His mother was there, dying under his eyes, but he could only think of what it would be like when he told Sarah, as if somehow the situation weren't real. "So I got down by the bed," he could hear himself saying into the future, "and took her hand." "You mean she was dying?" Sarah would ask, unbelieving. "Yes," he would say—but, with a start, he realized that, anticipating, he was about to say ". . . and she died."

Shaking his head, he looked at the nurse, who said in a competent voice, "Minutes."

Vincent felt a flood of anger. "What can that doctor be doing?" he muttered.

"It doesn't matter anymore," the nurse answered. "It's too late," and, just as she spoke, he felt a slight movement of his mother's hand. Quickly, he looked at her face, but her eyes were still closed. "She's gone," the nurse said, and put down the wrist she was holding.

"Gone?" Vincent repeated.

"Yes, deceased," the nurse answered with a touch of impatience. "Do you want to say a prayer?"

Vincent just shook his head.

"Then," said the nurse, "you'd better leave the room. There are things I must take care of." So, still feeling nothing, Vincent walked out into the living room and stood by the window. I should get dressed, he thought, I should call my aunt. I should call Sarah and tell her. And again, he heard himself saying: "Hi, Sarah, you won't believe it, but my mother just died."

Although he felt he must talk to someone—and, under the circumstances, he could hardly ignore Sarah—Vincent, when it came to it, was hesitant to call her, so much so that he first dialed a friend's number by mistake. Still, there was no choice, so he started again, firmly pushing all hesitation from his mind.

It was easy: After all, he was used to it, since his job and his marriage were the two topics he was never willing to think about. He would ponder the workings of our society, the nature of mental illness, or the real causes of the French revolution of 1848; but the art world must be endured and Sarah indulged. That their marriage didn't make much sense—that much, at least, Vincent knew. Perhaps she wasn't a good painter, but, he was beginning to think, a painter she was nonetheless, and she should be left alone to pursue her vocation. Everything had changed since the day, five years earlier, when Sarah had asked him whether she could join him for the summer in Europe. He had answered he'd be glad if she came, but only on the understanding it was just for the summer. "I've been badly hurt by another girl," Vincent told her, "and I don't want to get involved again. You must understand that."

"I understand," Sarah had said, and they'd been together ever since, but almost unwillingly. Sarah complained constantly about the way they related: She wanted love, she would say, romantic love, and Vincent would laugh at her. That, in fact, was how their fights usually started.

At first, Vincent could not quite understand why they stayed together; after all, they were hardly committed to each other. Perhaps it was laziness. Sarah was attractive and already there; continuing to live with her was surely the line of least effort. Still, not a week ever passed without some violent but random confrontation.

The scenes surprised them both: It took so very little to get them started. In his calmer moments, Vincent sometimes found them funny. They were so absurd.

"Can you believe we had a fight yesterday about whether to reorganize the books?" he said to Sarah one evening, in an amused voice. "Honestly!" and he walked over to kiss her; but, her face closed, she turned away.

"What's so funny?" she asked, her eyes flashing.

"Can't you see? Fighting about how the books should be arranged! Surely it's not that important," he said in a more serious tone.

There was a brief silence as Vincent realized what he had done. "Why shouldn't we fight?" Sarah said furiously. "Why should I put up with your laziness and your neglect? You may not care if the books are disorganized, but I do! I'm not going to live in a pigsty—"

"Pigsty!" Vincent interrupted, nervously stroking his face. "Oh, come on!"

"That's right," she answered, pale with rage. "You may not care how the house looks, or pretend you don't, anyway, because you're too lazy to do anything about it—"

"Lazy!" Vincent exploded. "Goddamn it, I forbid you to speak to me like this!" He, too, was now shouting, and realized with dread that there was no getting out of this fight about a fight.

Still, after a while, they made up; they always did. Perhaps the fights were no more real than the coming back together. Perhaps, also, Sarah had her own use for them: Like most women, she seemed solidly grounded in the real world, and yet . . . It took Vincent a while to realize it, but Sarah, too, was unconnected, floating, unsure of where and who she was.

Just as Vincent affirmed his desire to be an art dealer and lead that kind of life, so did Sarah explain her goals and ambitions. Years passed before Vincent began to see the gap that separated announcement and achievement. When Vincent had first met her, Sarah had been deeply split. Educated and trained as an art therapist, wanting to do good, to help, to improve, she found herself growing increasingly unhappy, or so she thought, with her supervisors: They were rigid bureaucrats, for all their psychological training, and wanted to force her patients into standard categories, stereotyped therapies divorced from any human reality.

With a wrenching effort, she had left art therapy and gone to work at the Iris Johnson Gallery, where Vincent had met her; and that was her dilemma: She loved art, painting, just as passionately as she loved helping people. What was she to do? Of course, as an art therapist she had no time, no energy for painting, and that, she said, was clearly wrong; but she needed to work with children; she could not be satisfied unless she did. And so, after a year, she had gone back to art therapy; but then she felt she had to paint, had to become an artist. That was her goal, her need, her desire. She said so frequently, eloquently.

Now, three years later, Vincent was beginning to have doubts. Sarah had left art therapy again, but did not quite become a painter. It wasn't that she was idle: She had free-lance jobs now and again, designing catalogues or layouts, but she had become such a perfectionist that each design took forever. Somehow, very few paintings got started; fewer still, finished.

It all came to a head one day when Vincent complained about his work. "You don't work," Sarah answered, "you just sit around waiting for something to happen."

There was a brief silence and Vincent began stroking his face. "You should talk!" he finally said in a shrill voice. "I don't notice you turning out masterpieces, exactly."

Carefully, Sarah put her brush down. "You *would* say that," she hissed. "How can I paint? All you do is criticize, criticize. I hear you all day, judging everything you look at. I'd have to be Picasso for you to like my work and, even so, I'm not sure you would have liked Picasso before he was well known. Don't you think I ever listen to you? 'A bad work, the wrong period, a poor example,' " she went on, mimicking him.

"But I *like* your work," Vincent answered, trying to control his anger. "You know I do. Those tulips, the other day, I told you I thought they were ravishing—"

"You don't think I believed that, do you?" Sarah interrupted savagely. "You were just lying because you were afraid of a fight!" And when Vincent shook his head, she went on: "Don't try to tell me you consider me a great artist! I'm just one of those third-rate painters you're always putting down, so don't lie to me!"

And Vincent, realizing she was right, moved into a new phase, one in which he earnestly looked for the positives in Sarah's work and praised them, thinking that she might then be able to work more often, more effectively.

That didn't do either. Now, Sarah accused him of being insincere. Even when he praised a particular line, color, or composition, his comments only pleased Sarah for a minute; soon, she would be repeating her leitmotif: "You're only saying that in order to avoid a fight."

The point was, Vincent eventually realized, that—sincere or not, encouraging or critical—he remained the great obstacle in Sarah's way: She would be a professional painter if only he weren't there, if only he weren't a dealer. Sometimes Sarah would even point out that most great artists were unmarried or bad spouses. Art is too demanding, she would say, it leaves no energy for marriage, for another person. If she lived alone, she could be a successful artist.

It's just like her weight, he often said to himself. She wasn't fat, but she was short—about five foot three—and always ten pounds too heavy. She minded, so she often bought clothes one size too small because they would fit as soon as she had lost a little weight; she often dieted, busily counted calories; yet, somehow, none of it worked. First, Vincent had told her it didn't matter. She was beautiful enough to carry it off; and he was right. Sarah shone with a dark, exotic beauty that made people ask her if she was Italian or Spanish; her long, dark brown hair, huge brown eyes, high cheekbones, and elegant blade of a nose made her stand out at any party. The lines of her face, the curve of her nose, the roundness of her chin, set off by a creamy, dark complexion, were so perfect that they seemed almost untrue: You could not help looking at her.

Still, Sarah did not think she was beautiful. A pretty girl, she felt, must be blonde and pink and snub-nosed. She worried about being too heavy; and while, perhaps, her ankles were not quite slender enough, the added weight gave her great voluptuousness because she had an hourglass figure. Only, according to her, this extra weight was due to an awful curse: She breathed fattier air, perhaps, or absorbed calories by osmosis; she would point out to Vincent, at great length and very convincingly, that she ate almost nothing, that she had not had more than five hundred calories a day for a week now. Then she would decide it was meat, or bread, or sweets, or even vegetables that made her fat, and swear off whatever it was, always apparently with miraculous (but invisible) results, so that the size ten dresses would remain hanging in the closet. At first, Vincent, who never gained weight himself, thought Sarah's was a problem capable of solution: It was not, after all, as if she were obese. But the years passed, and Sarah, too heavy despite all efforts, accused her metabolism (which was quite unlike anyone else's), or even a mysterious fate (I eat nothing but I don't lose a single pound), so Vincent began to think of all this as another manifestation of that peculiar distance that seemed to separate them from the real world. She would never get thin, she would never really paint. Only, to his surprise, she spent more and more time at her easel without talking about it or complaining.

Now, naturally, within a half hour of his mother's death, Vincent was calling Sarah and saying, just the way he had in his fantasy, "You won't believe it. My mother's dead." Even as he poured out the story and listened to Sarah's shocked questions—"You mean you were there when she *died?* You were actually holding her hand?"—he felt conscious of a withdrawal. He had to tell her, just as much as before, only now he wasn't sure he wanted a response, or even sympathy. Perhaps it was one more connection between himself and the outside that was fraying, but he didn't really care when Sarah empathized or pitied. His first real reaction came when she asked whether he wanted her to fly right over.

"I could get on the plane first thing in the morning," she said, "and I'd be there to help you."

Instantly his whole being recoiled. "No," he replied, "you can't really help. I'll just be speaking French all day."

"But what about the nights?" she insisted. "I can be there for dinner and the evenings. I can help you to bear it all." And he knew that he desperately wanted her to stay in New York; that, for all her good intentions, she would be a weight, a constraint. So they went on talking until he finally said it had been almost an hour, think of the phone bill, and she didn't come.

Later that night, as he sat up in bed thinking about the day, Vincent was shocked at his feelings. He, who always needed Sarah, who was tied to her by that strange indissoluble link, did not want her at his side; but, when he wondered how it would feel if she weren't there in New York to greet him when he came out of the plane, he realized that he still couldn't live without her.

It was also becoming plainer to him that he hated to do business. Within hours of his mother's death the phone had rung. Vincent had expected it to be a call for his mother; instead, it had been for him.

"Hi," Poppea Vlassoff had said, "I hoped I'd find you," and started to talk about the Ernsts.

Of course, Vincent said he couldn't talk, that his mother had just died; and Poppea, after a few perfunctory words, rang off; but he knew quite well that it was all just a pretext: He could have discussed business if he had wanted to. Quickly, he pushed the thought away. What he had told Sarah so often was still true: What else could he do? And in that sense, his mother's death was a boon, a situation in which he could act decisively and escape the powerlessness that usually haunted him. Besides, a death, a mother's death, was a real event: It took him outside the unreal world of business, the closed little circle of his marriage. Parents die; funerals are organized. It happens to everyone; and, though he didn't feel much grief, Vincent thought he was rejoining the rest of humanity.

Then he realized with a jolt that he was actually rejoicing, so he tried to feel regret for his mother's death; but, remembering those bottles, he began to wonder (though he himself hardly drank at all) whether he wasn't, like his mother, trapped in a cell of his own devising from which there was no escape.

It was a great shock when, a week later, Vincent saw Sarah waving at him from the other side of the customs barrier at Kennedy; she seemed smaller, different, foreign. She hadn't changed, even her dress was familiar, but she had become an outsider, someone you might notice in a crowd, not the wife he lived with every day. The feeling lasted only as long as it took him to reach her, to smell her familiar perfume, to kiss her. His hand quickly found her waist again; seen so close, now, she was herself again; and, immediately, he was answering her questions.

As soon as they were settled in the car, on the way back to Manhattan, Sarah produced what Vincent promptly recognized as well-thought-out, deliberate, meritorious good behavior, and he responded with appropriate but equally contrived warmth and gratitude. They must have a Christmas, Sarah was saying, and not let themselves be cheated: They could have it on New Year's Eve instead, with presents and decorations. She hadn't bought a tree, she went on, it would have been too heavy to carry, but she had managed something nonetheless, he would see. He must rest tomorrow, she would take care of him, and he must talk to her: It must have been so hard for him to go through it all alone.

Vincent agreed, gratefully; he was touched, or knew he should be, when he opened the front door of their apartment and found it festooned with Christmas lights. In the living room, silver garlands floated across the maroon walls, multicolored bulbs twinkled, and an ornate tree, made of glitter on a huge sheet of green, velvety paper, hung from the mantelpiece. It was a comfort to see the familiar room again, to be sitting on the low couch, to be home. Sarah smiled happily when he said: "You know, the room has never looked prettier. We really have to photograph it. This is all so pretty we should have a record of it."

"Well," she answered, "I thought we should have a Christmas."

Opening his arms, Vincent beckoned to her. "It's a perfect welcome home," he said.

Soon, she brought in black bread and smoked salmon, a bottle of cold white wine, and a plate full of little strawberry tartlets. Vincent, feeling himself bathed in a glow of mutual goodwill, interrupted only when Sarah told him how she wished she could have been with him in Paris. Then, of course, he remembered he hadn't wanted her there; but even that recent feeling seemed to belong to an earlier era that had ended this night at the airport. Later, when they went to bed, he held her close, her head on his chest, and felt joy at this moment of pure affection.

THREE

In Paris, the Galerie Voir, together with the offices of *Voir*, the art magazine, occupied the ground floor of an imposing seventeenth-century house on the Left Bank near the river. As you walked up to the door, you noticed a big window partly curtained by a profusion of tropical plants; this was André Germain's office. Two windows away, a door opened into a large, square room; the silk-lined walls were hung with six small, brilliant gouaches by Delacroix, while several stone cycladic figures, stark and geometric, were displayed on the shelves in the alcove. The only furniture was the receptionist's modern glass desk, her Saarinen chair, and a small couch upholstered in the same beige silk as the walls.

Vincent had come to see André Germain and was still standing there, having just been told that his father was busy, when the door at the far end of the room opened and Thérèse Vendel-Malnoury came rushing through, scowling. She was a tall, excruciatingly thin woman. Her dress was obviously elegant but drooped from her narrow figure. Her short, straight brown hair and her brown eyes were the only spots of color in her chalk-white, classical-looking face. She was clasping a handkerchief in her very red hands and sniffling.

She stopped in front of the receptionist and nodded at Vincent. "Well," she barked, "is Monsieur Germain in yet?"

"*Bonjour*, Thérèse," the receptionist answered warningly. "Yes, he came in five minutes ago. How are your sinuses?"

"Awful," Thérèse answered as she marched through the archway into the next room. "Infected again," and she sniffed with renewed vigor.

André Germain, with his wife, Viola, was not only the publisher of *Voir*, the best-known art magazine in Paris, but also the director and, ostensibly, the proprietor of the Galerie Voir. He was sitting in a leather-covered, mahogany Regency chair in front of a large Directoire desk. The wall behind him was lined with books, while a big Vuillard pastel of the Place Vintimille in summer hung in the center of the wall opposite him. To his left, tall green plants growing out of a trough of earth recessed into the floor were lit by spotlights installed in the top of the arched window. Tapping his foot, he shouted into the phone: "No, Marie-Claude, it's impossible. How can I run a magazine when no one does their work properly? I told you we were publishing the article on the Castello Sforzesco this month. . . . No, I didn't . . . It doesn't matter what you think I said, you finish that article by tomorrow. It's really incredible how lazy and incompetent you all are. . . . No, I don't care if you have theater seats." His dark, rather good-looking but pudgy face flushed with anger. Opening the door, he shouted: "Thérèse! Thérèse! Now where has she gone to? Thérèse!"

"She's coming, Monsieur," Jeanne, the receptionist,

shouted back. Germain returned to his office, slammed the door, and resumed pacing.

André Germain paced whenever he was angry. He was a rather short, thickset man in his fifties, with black, wavy hair and hard, brown eyes. His suits, always dark, were a model of propriety and hinted at Germain's care always to maintain the right social facade. He was able, for very short periods, to display great charm and was generally considered intelligent and cultivated.

While his wife always asserted he could be really nice, she seemed almost alone in this opinion. Vincent had made it a practice, some years earlier, to supply his father's favorite rejoinders whenever he found himself the target of one of André's interminable discourses. "I know," the son would finally say as the older man's face darkened with anger. "I'm interrupting. I should let you finish. But then, I'm just one of those idiots you're surrounded by." The first time Vincent had tried this trick, Viola, who was present, had dared to laugh. A prolonged scene ensued, liberally sprinkled with "don't interrupt me" and "why must I always have cretins around me"; but then, as Vincent later pointed out to her, at least this particular eruption had a reasonable pretext. "And then," he added, "it did stop the monologue."

André's name seldom came up when Vincent was present, but he knew what people said. One day, at a party, he overheard Justin Berg, the Philadelphia collector, say: "André Germain? He's quite odious. Very intelligent, of course, but so unpleasant. We'd never see him if it weren't for Viola."

"What's the matter, André?" Thérèse asked rather tremulously as she came in.

"Marie-Claude, naturally. She can never get anything straight. It's incredible! She thought we were not running the Castello Sforzesco article in this issue! Why must I always be surrounded by incompetents! You know what would happen to this magazine if it weren't for me! They're all the same. And as for Viola!" He paused. "As for Viola. She can't even run the household properly. The silver hadn't been polished last night. And now that she's off to Barcelona for the Miró interview, it's going to cost a fortune again."

Thérèse gave a thin smile. "But you had said, you know, about the Castello article—"

André exploded: "What! You too! Now you're going to tell me I didn't say we needed it right away. It's unbelievable! I thought I could count on *you*, Thérèse, at least!" This time, Thérèse kept quiet. André continued pacing up and down, muttering, "Unbelievable! Unbelievable!" now and again. Finally, he sat down at his desk and Thérèse, who had been standing all this time holding a notebook tightly clutched to her bony bosom, sat down also.

"I need to talk to you about Barolo," André said.

"Yes." Thérèse answered. "Did it work?"

"Oh, yes. I thoroughly destroyed that woman, that Poppea Vlassoff—what a name!—and we'll get the collection: just two or three pictures now, but more in the long run, I suspect. I offered him seventy-five thousand dollars for the fauve Signac, and a hundred and twenty thousand dollars for his Braque still life, cash down in Geneva. He's supposed to call me tomorrow, but I don't think we'll have a problem, especially since I pointed out to him that both paintings are in terrible condition."

"Are they?" Thérèse asked.

"No, but it worked." There was a pause while André twiddled his pencil. Thérèse began to look worried. Finally, she spoke.

"But, André, we don't have one hundred ninety-five thousand dollars."

André exploded. "What do you mean, we don't have one hundred ninety-five thousand dollars? We just sold Pierre-Paul's Renoir; that's ninety-five thousand, and those two Klees we got from the Bergs; that's another ninety thousand; so that's one eighty-five, and we have some money left in the Berne account."

Thérèse looked even more worried. "Yes, but Pierre-Paul will expect to be paid soon; after all, you told him his Renoir was sold; and so will the Bergs; they've already been complaining."

André stopped to think. "Well," he said, "it's easy. We'll tell Pierre-Paul his Renoir needed restoring and that the client won't pay until it's finished. That'll give us three months or more if we stretch it. And if the Bergs ask, we'll just say that the Klees are out on approval for a while."

"Yes," Thérèse answered, "but what about the printers?"

"They can wait."

"Not much longer. The last month we paid them for was January, and that's five months ago now."

"That's enough, Thérèse. You know very well they've made their name with *Voir*. They're lucky to have us."

"But, André, they're getting very unpleasant. I tried to tell you yesterday, but you didn't want to talk about it. They say they won't print the next issue unless we give them at least partial payment, say twenty thousand dollars."

André exploded again, and raged for ten minutes. Thérèse just sat motionless looking down until, finally, she started to cry. Appearing rather pleased with himself, André turned to her and said: "It won't do any good to cry. We'll just sell one of the Vuillard pastels to Strauss this afternoon. We'll get at least thirty thousand dollars."

"But what about the consignment price?" Thérèse asked. "We have to pay thirty-two thousand."

"It doesn't matter," André replied. "There's no need to pay for it soon and we'll make it up somewhere else. Now, stop wasting my time with all this nonsense. I have something serious I want to talk to you about."

At that point the phone rang. "You answer it, Thérèse," André shouted. She picked up the phone. "It's Barolo," she said.

A triumphant smile appeared on André's face. "Yes, *cher ami*," André said smoothly, "I'm delighted to hear from you. . . . No, not at all, this is a perfect time. . . . Yes, of course . . . the price we agreed on. . . . Oh, you are coming . . . yes, about the conditions, then . . . absolutely . . . in three days, perfect. *A bientôt.*" He hung up, gloating, and turned to Thérèse. "This is much bigger than you think." He was almost murmuring now. "You see, there's a third picture we'll be selling, in six weeks or so. Barolo would rather wait a little. A Chagall." He paused for effect. Thérèse looked blank. "And I'm quite certain it's a fake."

"A fake?" Thérèse repeated. "But then we don't want it."

"Oh, yes, we do. Try to use your head for once. I know it's a fake, even you might know it's a fake, but those idiots in America won't know it. I'll tell you exactly who will buy it: the Bergs. They're completely green, they want to make a big social splash in Philadelphia with their collection, and, if I tell them it's the gem of the Barolo collection, they'll snap at it. You see, Barolo agrees that the picture is stiff, and, generally speaking, a poor Chagall. He only paid sixty thousand dollars for it and is willing to get back no more than he paid. If it were real, it would be worth one twenty-five. We'll sell it to the Bergs for a hundred ten thousand, tell them they're getting a bargain, and make fifty thousand dollars. Nobody will know enough to question it or even have doubts, because it has such a good provenance. And our fifty thousand dollars is only the be-

ginning of it. Just look: Barolo bought all his pictures from
the Fornettis, and they knew just what they were doing,
you may be sure, when they slipped him this fake. So we'll
confront David Fornetti with it. He won't want it known
he sold Barolo this fake: Who knows what others he's sold
as well, and it only takes one to make everything else suspect. So we'll have a handle on him, and that should open
up almost endless possibilities."

Vincent Germain was in an excellent mood; he always
enjoyed returning to the city of his childhood; though he
lived in New York and liked it, he still missed Paris. Even
unpleasant chores became easier for Vincent when he
walked through the streets of the Left Bank. Rome, he felt,
was more spectacular, but also more like a theater set. Paris
was full of moderation, more real, ultimately more beautiful. Then there were all the antique shops, full of delectable
objects. He stopped now at the window of the autograph
store on the rue Bonaparte to read the letters on display:
a love note from Victor Hugo, a royal command signed
by Louis XIV, a poem in Verlaine's own hand. Then there
were the fashions, artfully displayed and fun to see; the
pastry shops, with their rows of tempting cakes; the cafés,
in one of which he stopped for a few minutes, asking for
an *express* and getting a tiny demitasse of strong, tasty
black coffee. It was a pleasure to be speaking French again,
to be reading a French newspaper, to be eating French
food.

He had come to Paris, not just for business, but also to
settle matters connected with his mother's estate. As he
made his way to the notary's office, he felt he could be living in a Balzac novel, so little had things changed in a century and a half. The legal phrases remained the same; the

laws, indeed, had hardly changed; it all seemed a part of the continuity of Paris, in spite of the newly erected Maine-Montparnasse skyscraper's reminder that this was 1974.

Vincent's mood was shattered, however, as soon as he walked into the offices of *Voir*. With a sinking stomach, he remembered his father's awful rages, the times when the older man said with gusto: "I consider it my duty as your father to tell you how wrong you are and how badly you're doing this." Now, with Vincent's move to New York and his complete independence, an uneasy half-peace prevailed, based more on Vincent's withdrawal than on André's improved temper. When, a few years earlier, Vincent had gone into business for himself, André had promised help in the form of consigned paintings that had signally failed to materialize. Having escaped ruin, Vincent had kept his distance and derived mild enjoyment from his father's unsuccessful attempts to find out just what he was doing at any particular time.

Now the moment had finally come. "*Bonjour*, Jeanne," he said, "is Monsieur Germain in?"

"He is," the receptionist answered. "I'll call to say you're here." Vincent nodded and smiled, then walked through to the gallery's main room, a large salon with French doors opening onto the courtyard. Here, too, the walls were covered with silk, but there was no carpet. The floor was paved with big, square flagstones, and paintings were stacked against the walls, ready to be hung: The Galerie Voir was soon to have an opening. The show was entitled "Les Peintres Embusqués" ("Draft-dodging Painters") and consisted of the works of several major painters who had *not* fought in World War I.

Marie-Claude de Lantignac, the researcher, article-writer, and general drudge of the magazine, was waiting there. She greeted Vincent and added, "I'm waiting for Thérèse."

At that moment, the door opened and Thérèse walked out. "*Tiens,*" she said, "it's you, Vincent. You're in Paris." "As you see," Vincent replied. "Is my father free?" "No, he's on the phone. Give him another minute," and turning to Marie-Claude, who was nervously caressing her moustache, she barked: "Why isn't the Castello article ready?"

Marie-Claude looked as if she were about to cry and muttered, "But, Thérèse, you know very well that Monsieur Germain didn't want it in this issue. You were there when he said so."

"Nonsense," Thérèse answered viciously. "You don't know what you're talking about. You'd better get it done, and fast."

"Yes, Thérèse," Marie-Claude answered submissively as she walked out.

Vincent said nothing for a while and quietly enjoyed the show, remembering his friend Jacques's comment: "Thérèse?" he had once said. "Everybody knows that she's odious to everyone except your father, and that she lies as a matter of principle." Gathering himself up, Vincent turned to her. "How is Igor?" he asked. Thérèse's face started to glow as she gave details of the achievements of her eleven-month-old son.

Aside from her obvious intelligence, the decision to have this child, her first, at forty-two was the one thing about Thérèse that Vincent admired. She was not married, not even living with anyone. When he had heard from André that Thérèse was pregnant, and, though unmarried, had decided to have the child, Vincent had written her a long letter praising her for her courage and wishing her all possible luck; and when he had seen her, shortly before she gave birth, he had encouraged her anew and been told that the father was an old lover, now married, whom she had met by chance at a ski resort, and who had no idea he was responsible for her pregnancy. Vincent had written her again, when the baby was born, to congratulate her, and Thérèse had seemed touched. Her obvious love for her son was the one human emotion Vincent had seen her display—except for suffering. Suffering, in fact, was the keynote of Thérèse's conversation. It was usually enough for Vincent to say: "*Bonjour,* Thérèse. How are you?"

"Terrible," Thérèse would say. "My sinuses are infected. I have the most awful headache."

"But what does your doctor say?"

"Oh," she would answer with a martyred look, "he wants to cauterize them—without a painkiller. And then, there's my stomach."

"Still sore?"

"Yes. All I can eat is almost-raw steak and, naturally, your father makes fun of me."

"Then tell him it's not funny."

"I did once," Thérèse answered with gloomy satisfaction. "But then he got angry and that made me cry, which is bad for my sinuses." Now, the door opened again and André waved to Vincent.

"Come in, come in," he said. Then, less amiably, he asked, "What are you doing in Paris?"

"Settling some of my mother's estate," Vincent answered to his father's obvious annoyance, "and doing some business.'

André's dark skin turned distinctly yellower. "Doing business?" he asked. "And with whom? What are you dealing in?"

Vincent smiled. "I'll tell you once it's concluded. I can't really talk about it now. What about that suite of Léger drawings you were going to give me on consignment?"

André sat back with a smile. "I can't give them to you

for a while—I can't quite explain it to you, but they have to remain here."

"Really? How surprising! And I expect you have nothing else at the moment?"

"No, nothing. Such a shame. You know how much I'd like to work with you."

"I certainly do," said Vincent, smiling.

There was a pause. "I'm having lunch with Thérèse. Why don't you join us?" André finally said.

"No, I can't, I'm busy for lunch," Vincent answered.

His father looked curious. "Oh, yes? Who with?"

"No one you know. A friend. In fact, I have to go."

"Very well," André said, coldly. "You'll come to the opening, I suppose."

Vincent got up.

"Wait," his father said, more urgently now. "You were just in Milan, weren't you?"

"Yes, I was."

"And you met Barolo. You know I am selling some paintings of his, I expect."

"Yes? Which ones?" There was another pause.

"The Signac, the Braque still life, and the Chagall."

"The Chagall?" Vincent repeated in a surprised tone. "Did you actually like it? I thought it was awfully stiff."

André's face purpled. "Stiff! Stiff! What do you know about Chagall? What gives you the right to say it's stiff? Are you a Chagall scholar? How many Chagalls have you sold? Just tell me that! Stiff! It's a very fine work of that period and it will go straight into an American collection."

Vincent smiled. "The Bergs, I'll bet. They'd buy it just for the name."

André didn't answer. "Did Barolo tell you where he bought it?" he asked. "And who is this Poppea Vlassoff?

What does she have to do with Barolo? What does she know about his collection?"

"No," Vincent said, "Barolo didn't tell me about the provenance [but Poppea did, he thought to himself]. And Poppea Vlassoff is a new runner who doesn't know much but works very hard. I think she might have been Barolo's mistress when she lived in Milan some time ago."

To Vincent's surprise, André looked relieved and became more amiable. "Well," he said, "be sure to come to the opening on Tuesday—and to the party we're having at home afterward. There will be lots of interesting people."

"I will," Vincent answered, and walked out.

It was quite a while before Vincent calmed down. At first, ignoring his feelings and holding himself tight, he strolled about aimlessly. When he finally sat down at a café terrace, a flood of unpleasant memories assaulted him. "You'll be a failure," his father was saying smugly. "You'll never have any friends. . . ." Impatiently, Vincent shook his head, but the voice went on. "I should have known you'd be in a slum," it was saying, and Vincent saw his father's disdainful expression as he looked around his office. "A slum. You'll never get clients to come here." A slum on Madison Avenue and Seventy-fifth Street, Vincent thought bitterly. It was so grotesque he shouldn't mind, but he did; and for the next ten minutes he sat smoldering.

Later that afternoon, Vincent was sitting in his mother's apartment on the rue de Verneuil when the phone rang. It was Poppea Vlassoff. "Well," she said excitedly, "here I am! I've got the Ernsts and the certificates. I just flew in from Milan this morning, called Mundberg as soon as I got to my hotel, went to see him, and got the certificates. When can I bring them to you?"

Vincent groaned silently. It was bad enough that he'd had to see his father; he really could do without Poppea Vlassoff the same day. "How about tomorrow morning?"

"Why not today? I can bring them right over."

"No," Vincent lied, "I have an appointment, and then I have to go out for dinner. Let's make it tomorrow."

"All right," Poppea answered, obviously disappointed. "Maybe you could come to Vitruzzo's with me."

"Who's Vitruzzo?"

"Oh, an Italian dealer. He's got a gallery on the rue Jacob and he has a Mondrian gouache for sale."

"All right, we'll go tomorrow morning. Why don't you come here at about eleven?" and giving her the address, he hung up.

Restlessly, Vincent started pacing up and down the apartment. It was being sold, and he knew this was the last time he would stay there. After his mother's death, he had decided that it should be sold. The decision made sense, but it was no less sad for all that. He stood now in the doorway of the big living room, with its tall windows and yellow brocade curtains, and sighed, then went out onto the terrace, which was a mess of dead bushes, scattered earth, and broken pots. He sighed again and made his way to the kitchen. It was almost time to go out again.

The walk over to Esther Pfalzman's did nothing to ease his melancholy. "Well, Esther," he said as she let him in, "I'm glad to see you again. How's business?"

She was a small woman, quite ageless. I wonder if she still has a lover, Vincent said to himself as they walked into her study.

"Business?" she repeated, with a trace of a German accent. "We do no business here. It's not like you rich New York dealers. What are you looking for?"

"What do you have, Esther?" Vincent asked with a smile.

"Nothing, I tell you. It's all dead here. I make no money, I sell no paintings." Her eyes strayed to a pile of canvases leaning against the wall.

"I'm looking for Picasso drawings," Vincent said in encouraging tones; but Esther was obviously not listening.

"How's your brother?" she asked suddenly.

"Luc?" Vincent answered. "He's fine."

"No, not Luc, the little one, Igor."

It took all Vincent's self-control to show no emotion and answer, as if all were normal, "Oh, doing very well, Thérèse tells me," but Esther was pushing on: "Don't you think your father should officially recognize him?"

"It's nothing to do with me," Vincent said drily. "As you know, we're not on the best of terms."

"I know," said Esther, "but you're still his heir. You'll have to share, of course, if Igor is recognized legally."

"Of course," Vincent answered, and the conversation flowed back into its usual channels. But as he walked away and thought about it, he grew angrier and angrier. Not to tell me, he kept saying aloud to himself, after I was so nice to her and encouraged her. Lying to me like that and letting me find out from Esther. And he realized he might have found out from anyone since, clearly, the fact was already so well known. I wonder whether Viola knows, he went on, thinking now of his stepmother. "If she does, she can't like it." And he went back to being angry.

As soon as he got home, he sat down, took out a piece of stationery, and wrote quickly:

Dear Thérèse,

I have just heard, as a piece of common gossip during a conversation with a dealer, that Igor is, in fact, my half-brother. After my letter to you when I heard you were pregnant, considering what I have said to you since and the fact that my attitude to you has always been purely encouraging, I find it upsetting, indeed sad, that I have had to hear the truth in this way. When all the world knows the name of Igor's father, did you really have to lie like this?

With deep regret,
Vincent

He folded the sheet into an envelope and, setting off in a taxi, dropped it off at the Galerie Voir.

When Poppea Vlassoff appeared the next morning, she was clearly in the best of moods. "Guess what?" she said jubilantly as soon as Vincent opened the door. "I sold the Klee."

"What Klee?"

"Malamonte's Klee. You know, the one you said belonged to Princeton."

Vincent gaped silently. "But, Poppea," he finally exclaimed, "you know it's a fake."

"Who knows which one is really a fake? Anyway, it doesn't matter; it'll never come on the market again. I know this dealer in Boston, Mark Spence, and he sold it to a rich doctor who's just starting his collection, so it won't come out for years, and if it ever does, I'll have the money to buy it back by then, so it won't matter."

"You can't do that, Poppea, it's really dangerous. If it comes out, you'll be completely finished. Nobody will deal with you anymore; and besides there are laws, you know, against this kind of thing."

Poppea was clearly getting annoyed. "Don't worry about it," she repeated, "I've got good news for us too," and unwrapped the two Ernst oils Vincent had seen in Milan. "And here are the certificates."

It was true; there on the back of each photograph was the certificate: "I certify that I have seen the work photo-

graphed here and that it is a genuine Max Ernst oil on
paper of the Arizona period," with Max Mundberg's signature and the date underneath.

"You can't do better than that," Poppea remarked.
"After all he's done a book on Ernst, and one on Magritte,
and has written plenty on the other surrealists."

"Yes, that's true. But you can do better, you know.
There is the artist."

"He really shouldn't be bothered," Poppea said, and
Vincent didn't altogether like her solicitude. He knew he
was getting a very good deal but felt somehow uneasy. "I
should be glad," he said to himself, as he made a pretense
of looking at the Ernsts, "I can make a great deal of money
from these, and they really are good" . . . but still, something—he didn't know what—was bothering him.

"What's the matter?" Poppea asked.

"Nothing. It's okay. I can give you the first thirty thousand dollars within a week, and the balance in a month."

"That's good," Poppea replied, licking her lips. "Now, I
want to do it in Switzerland. If you pay me at my bank
at Chiasso, then Francesco can just drive over the border,
pick up the money in dollars, and drive back. That way, he
won't have to pay Italian taxes. And I'd like my commission in Switzerland, too. No need for the IRS to know anything about it. Why pay taxes, right? I've got a numbered
account. You do too, don't you?"

"That's *my* secret," Vincent said, smiling, "but, sure,
we'll do it that way." And feeling still somewhat disturbed,
he went out with Poppea.

As soon as he got home again, Vincent called a client in
New York. Charles Morgenstern had been a successful
manufacturer of women's shoes; he now spent his days investing his money, and his evenings worrying about it.

The Ernst was to be their second venture. Vincent
reached him easily, told him he could expect to double his

money, and was assured that $40,000 would await him in
New York. Putting down the phone for a moment, Vincent
quickly lifted it again and this time called Sophia Lyon,
knowing he could count on her greed. "Hi," he said, "this
is Vincent. Listen. I'm in Paris and I have just the kind of
Ernst you said your client wanted. Is he still in the
market?"

"Yes," Sophia answered, "but what is it like and how
high is the price?" After Vincent described the painting
and quoted a price of $55,000, she said she would call her
client to let him know and asked Vincent to bring the
painting in as soon as he returned. Vincent agreed and
rang off. Quietly, he looked at his hands; they were still
clean, but he went into the bathroom and washed them
carefully; then, as he was drying them, he said to himself,
well, it's a quick fifteen thousand, but the thought failed
to cheer him. With a deep sigh, he started to change for
the opening.

There was already quite an elegant crowd assembled at
the Galerie Voir when Vincent walked in at seven. A
large table covered with a pink and silver cloth had been
set up in the main room, and two waiters were busy dis-
pensing drinks to people gathered around them. Three
maids in uniform circulated among the assembled guests,
carrying trays of hot hors d'oeuvres: little Roquefort
cheese puffs, pieces of chicken liver wrapped in bacon, tiny
meat pies, and small anchovy tarts. The men, most of whom
were wearing dark, well-tailored suits, looked as if they
had become all outward sophistication, probably as the
result of relentless socializing; here and there, less carefully
brushed hair, a lighter-colored suit, unshined shoes, or, in
one case, the complete absence of a tie denoted the presence of an artist. The women, their hair carefully and
fashionably coiffed, were dressed in couturier models (or
copies good enough to be convincing); there was a lot of

pink, a lot of brocade, a lot of pearls; and, now and again, a big stone, diamond or emerald, glittered on a finger or in a brooch. The noise was deafening, and absolutely nobody looked at the paintings on the walls.

Vincent made his way slowly to the bar, greeting a few people along the way. As he came out of the middle room, he ran into Thérèse, dead white as usual, and scowling. Vincent recognized her black cocktail dress as an Ungaro, but, in spite of the good lines and the beautiful bouclé wool, it hung so loosely on her that she managed to make it look like something off the rack.

Thérèse gave a little start when she saw him. Vincent nodded, and she quickly said: "I received your letter, and I understand what you mean, but it's not the way you think. I'd like to explain it to you. Can you come by tomorrow?'

"At ten?" Vincent asked coldly.

"Yes, at ten," Thérèse confirmed, and added, rather wildly, "I'm sorry," but then turned immediately and, addressing a well-known critic, started barking: "Well, have you seen the paintings?"

Vincent continued to push his way through to the main room and, near the bar, spotted Viola Germain rushing to greet Emmanuel Weinstein, the famous cellist.

"Darling Manny," she said enthusiastically, "I'm so glad you could come. Such *luck* your being in Paris! We just can't wait for your concert tomorrow. . . ." Viola was looking her best that night: tall, elegant, her brown hair carefully and becomingly waved; her Dior cocktail dress, fashioned of red printed silk, was the new longer length and was adorned near the shoulder by a clip made of lapis, turquoise, gold, and diamond rays emanating from a black cameo representing the face of a ringleted god.

Vincent merely waved to her and continued on toward the bar. Once he had a drink in his hand, he turned around and, finding himself next to a French political writer he knew, started to talk about the coming presidential elections, the chances of the Left, and the disarray of the Gaullists. Soon, he felt a touch on his shoulder and turned to see Katia Crompton, the still young widow of the famous English novelist. Vincent, feeling pleased, kissed her on both cheeks.

"You are coming to the party tonight?" Viola asked when she joined them. "We never get to see you anymore, and we can have a chat there. It's too much of a crush here, and there will be lots of people you know—like Pierre-Paul, and Immy de Raguse. It's a small party, we'll only be about forty," and she bounced off to greet a new collector.

Vincent started to wend his way toward a painter he wanted to speak to, but was stopped by a compact group of unknown, polished people. "Of course," one man was saying, "everyone in Paris knows Germain is simply living on Pierre-Paul Sanche's money—"

"Oh, no, darling," a woman interrupted, "he's trying to get in more solidly with the Goldschmidts. That's why he's having an affair with Coche del Mancha. You know, she's Laure's best friend, and Marguerite told me that André is divorcing Viola to marry her."

Another woman interrupted: "Well, Viola's here tonight."

"Yes," the first woman replied, "but that doesn't mean anything; it's all business. She doesn't want to be ruined any more than he does."

Only in Paris, Vincent thought with amusement as the guests continued slandering their host.

"Of course," the woman was continuing, "it's all Laure de Goldschmidt's scheme—you know what she's like— thinking all that money gives her the right to arrange her friends' lives. If you ask me, she means to go in for paintings now. That's why she wants Coche to hold on to André."

At that point, a movement in the crowd allowed Vincent to walk past, only to get stuck right behind a man he recognized as Jacques Pernet, one of the most successful dealers in Paris. Pernet was saying: "Of course, I don't do business with him, you know how dishonest he is, always cheating everyone. You can't rely on his word at all. He's capable of anything. And, after all, most dealers won't touch him with a ten-foot pole; just the other day, Pearlstein was saying to me, 'Stay away from André Germain. You'll only get your fingers burned if you don't.' "

Vincent smiled to himself with pleasure, moved on, and, although he soon found himself in the middle of a conversation, continued to feel deep satisfaction over his father's poor reputation.

It was only a ten-minute walk from the gallery to André Germain's apartment, through Saint-Germain-des-Prés and over to the rue de Varenne. The night was warm, the café terraces full of people watching other people walking back and forth. Though he didn't stop, Vincent noticed one world-famous author, two actresses, a couple of transvestites—betrayed only by their hard, masculine faces—several unisex couples, and a man strolling about, holding a lion cub in his arms.

The Germains' apartment occupied the top two floors of an eighteenth-century house that had belonged to Mme. de Genlis, the author and educator; but when you came out of the small creaky elevator, you walked directly into a gigantic living room with huge panoramic windows overlooking the Eiffel Tower and the golden dome of the Invalides. Both monuments were lit up that night, and the effect was striking. If you walked up to the windows, you could look down on the gardens of the prime minister's official residence, formal and dotted with statues.

Vincent felt a pang as he walked in. He was always aware of an unpleasant taste in his mouth as he remembered the long evenings spent listening to his father's monologues, the scenes, the desperate unhappiness. It looks wonderful, he thought as he stopped at the door, his right hand stroking his face nervously. But he wished he weren't there.

The huge room, which took up the whole top floor, was pointedly devoid of paintings; the walls were covered with a beige burlap stamped in a palm motif. There was a white stone Louis XVI chimney at one end of the room, an alcove with a silk-covered couch at the other. Almost as striking as the view, two eight-foot-tall New Hebrides fern-wood sculptures looked menacingly toward a large Louis XV commode, on the marble top of which a green Polynesian tiki glared back from amidst a surrounding of pre-Columbian objects.

As Vincent moved to the windows, he noticed the room was already crowded. *"Bonjour*, Jacques," he said, smiling to the butler. Mixing with the crowd, he came up against his father. André immediately put on a display of affection.

"At last!" he said. "We've been looking for you. We hardly see you these days."

Vincent felt his stomach contract and made a deliberate effort to keep his hands open and hanging at his sides. "Well, here I am now," he replied, "and tell me, how is little Igor?" He saw his father start. "You know, now that I think of it, he does look a little like you." And smiling nastily, he turned aside and greeted a woman wearing a 1920s embroidered and beaded dress. "Jane!" he exclaimed. "I'm so glad to see you! How perfectly stunning you look! And what a divine dress! Tell me, is it Poiret?"

When dinner was announced, Vincent went down with his Poiret-clad acquaintance and held her plate as she heaped it high with duck pâté, roast beef, mimosa salad, and a wonderfully runny wedge of Camembert cheese.

When, later, the plates had been cleared, the butler and four waiters hired for the occasion started passing around cassis sherbet and cookies. Vincent went toward the bedroom to make a phone call, but, as he was about to enter the little sitting room that led into it, the sound of voices stopped him. He immediately recognized them as belonging to his father and Pierre-Paul Sanche and, quite unashamedly, stood still and listened while keeping an eye on the corridor. His father was speaking.

"But I assure you, Pierre-Paul, as soon as the restorer is through—"

"Yes, more delay. You've had that picture for over a year, and I need the money. I mean, André, it's absolutely ridiculous. I could have sold it faster if I had just walked into Wildenstein's. Can't you hurry it up?"

"I'll try, but you know restorers—"

"In any event, I also wanted to talk to you about *Voir*. After all, you know, I have put a great deal of money into it, and I get no return. Besides, now that I am settled in Paris, I'd like to give it some of my time. How would you like me as your codirector?"

There was a pause; then André started to shout. "It's impossible, completely impossible. What arrogance! What makes you think, Pierre-Paul, you're capable of doing anything on the magazine? You're untrained. We'd have to teach you everything. And even if I wanted to, I wouldn't have the time." There was a silence.

"Well," Sanche said timidly, "maybe I could work with Thérèse."

"Thérèse! She's just as busy as I am. It's simply not possible. Besides, Pierre-Paul, this isn't your idea. Nini put you up to it. Let me tell you, she's very much mistaken if she thinks she can push me around!"

"But, André, it's true, she has a point. After all, it is my money, and I should—"

"Your money! Your money! Don't you have any manners? How dare you talk to me about your money!"

There was another pause and, when Sanche spoke again, his voice was much firmer. "We can stop talking about it as soon as you give me that accounting you've promised me for two years. I mean it, André. If I don't have it within a month, you'll have to deal with my lawyers. I'm holding them back as it is. . . ."

Vincent, hearing a step on the staircase, hastily withdrew. As he walked up the stairs again, he passed Thérèse, who was coming down. She stopped and reminded him of their appointment. He nodded coldly and went over to Viola. "I'm leaving," he said. "Such a successful party." And with that he walked away.

At one-thirty that morning, in the sumptuous bedroom of an apartment overlooking the Seine, a fight was in progress. Nini Sanche's feathered dress was flung over a chaise longue, and her pin, necklace, and rings thrown down on a bedside table. "I just don't understand," she was saying heatedly. "I mean, it's your money, and what good does it do us? You're known as an idler, an incompetent. What can I say when people ask me about *Voir*? It's too humiliating. We should run that magazine ourselves. I won't be known just as a society woman; besides, if we ran the magazine, we could meet all the intellectuals, and that's always a help socially. Also, I've been hinting for too long that we were taking it over; I'm beginning to look ridiculous."

"But, Nini," Sanche meekly replied, "we don't know how to run a magazine. I wouldn't have any idea what to do."

"I don't care," Nini shrieked. "You're not rich enough to be idle. I want that magazine. And I can tell you something else: It's the last time I'm going to the Germains' parties. Let people see I can't stand them! Why, Viola is actually patronizing to me, as if I didn't know the Tout-Paris better than she! And anyway, it's all our money."

She paused, and Sanche, clearly trying to buy peace, said, "All right, Nini, I'll do my best. I'll go over to *Voir* tomorrow and talk to André. I'm sure we can arrange something."

"You'd better," Nini answered menacingly. As Pierre-Paul put his hand on her shoulder, she recoiled. "No, not tonight, Pierre-Paul. I'm really not in the mood."

"But, Nini, it's been almost a month."

"I don't care. If you can't be a man in business, then you can't be one in the bedroom either."

"You know how much I want you," he whispered. "I'm dying for you, Nini, for your lips, for your breasts," and, coming closer to her, he suddenly hugged her, pressing himself against her.

"I mean it, Pierre-Paul," Nini hissed, pushing him away. "I mean it. If you touch me now, I'll scream and wake the servants up. I don't care how much you want me. If you can tell me tomorrow that you have finally put Germain in his place, then I'll say yes tomorrow night." Pierre-Paul bit his lips and, turning away, muttered: "You'll regret this, Nini, I swear you will."

The next morning, Vincent came into the Galerie Voir at ten and asked to see Thérèse Vendel-Malnoury. He was immediately told to go to her office and found her, pale and haggard-looking, sitting at a desk piled high with papers. Behind her was a bookcase filled with back issues of *Voir*; she faced a French window into the courtyard.

Vincent, feeling deliciously vengeful, sat down and asked: "Do you really not have those Léger drawings? Or is it simply that you don't want to give them to me?"

There was a pause. Thérèse, looking very gloomy, hesitated.

"Oh, come on, Thérèse," Vincent said, laughing, "tell me the truth."

Thérèse looked stung. She answered, in a low voice, "Well, your father wants to keep them here for a while."

"I realize that, but I'd like to know why."

Thérèse looked even more upset. "All right. He doesn't want to give them to you because he thinks you're working with Poppea Vlassoff to try to get the Barolo pictures away from him."

Vincent laughed. "Really, Thérèse," he finally said, "that's the weakest excuse I've heard in a long time. Almost as bad as the one about the old friend you met at a ski resort."

At that, Thérèse started crying, much to Vincent's satisfaction. He had often seen her upset, but it had only made her unpleasant. A sobbing Thérèse was a new experience, and Vincent almost began to feel sorry for her. He watched as she blew her nose, still crying.

"It's not my fault. I wanted to tell you the truth, I really did. I told your father a thousand times it would be better, but he wouldn't let me, he absolutely forbade it. He even invented that story about the old friend."

"But why?"

"He just didn't want you to know. You know how much he loves you. He's always telling me how proud he is of you." Vincent shook his head impatiently and clenched his hands.

"Yes, he's always saying that, I know. It's a shame there is such a discrepancy between his words and his behavior. I certainly can't see any proofs of his supposed caring. Any-

way, that's not the question, and I don't think his telling
you to lie to me is an excuse. Surely you're old enough to
make your own decisions. You know how friendly I've
always been to you, how I praised you when you decided
against an abortion. At least you could have told me the
truth instead of letting me find out accidentally from a
dealer I was visiting. You can imagine how pleasant that
was for me!"

Thérèse started to sob violently as Vincent, enjoying his
revenge, looked at her. After a minute or two, she finally
said, with difficulty: "You don't know how unhappy I am,
Vincent. I'm sorry I had to tell you that phony story, but
your father forced me to. And now he's having an affair
with Coche del Mancha. He sees her all the time, and I'm
the one who has to remind him to call the florist or to leave
himself free time to see her. And he hardly ever comes to
see Igor." The sobbing grew worse again.

"Then break with him," Vincent said, "if he makes you
so unhappy."

"I can't do that," Thérèse answered quickly, sobered
by the very suggestion. "You know how much he depends
on me."

"All the more reason. I mean, if you really mind being
so unhappy." Vincent paused, swept by a wave of disgust.
"Well, Thérèse, it's your problem. But you can tell my
father this from me. I'm fed up with his deceit, his unpleasantness, and the way he keeps trying to trip me up
in business. You know he said he was holding the Légers
for me to pick up when I came to Paris. On that basis, I
showed the photos to a client, who then made me a firm
offer. Now I have to tell him he can't have them, and I
have no good reason to give him. I can assure you that,
the next time, he'll go to another dealer. And this is hardly
the first time I've been double-crossed." Vincent's face
was almost drawn. "If you like to suffer, Thérèse, that's

your business. I don't. And I don't like to be treated like this. So please tell my father from me that, for a while at any rate, I prefer not to see him. I won't return his calls. I won't answer his letters. I won't have anything more to do with him. And I'm going to let people know just what the situation is."

Thérèse, calmer now, looked aghast. "But you can't do that. He'll be dreadfully upset."

Vincent smiled and got up without speaking. "About time," he said as he walked out.

His heart was beating fast, but this time it was with pleasure. Nothing would annoy his father more than a complete break and the resulting gossip, he knew; just the threat of it would be effective. For the first time, Vincent felt in control of their relationship.

An hour later, Viola walked into one of André's blasts. "Naturally," he was shouting, "you never do anything. Everything rests on my shoulders. I have to carry every burden. Why did I have to saddle myself with an incompetent wife? All you do is spend money! You think you can just go to Balenciaga's and get yourself that suit you're wearing, but who has to pay for it? Not you! I'm the one who has to keep producing money. And your Pierre-Paul! It's all your fault, getting us involved with him! Now he thinks he can run the magazine! Well, let him! I'll just leave it to him. Let him see how easy it is to run a magazine!"

"But, André," Viola answered in a tense, even voice, her elegant face wan and tired-looking, "you know you told me to go to Balenciaga and get a suit. You're the one who's always telling me to keep up appearances, and that I must be well dressed. I would be just as happy going to Marie-Martine or to the Balmain boutique—"

"Yes," André shouted back, "and I also told Pierre-Paul to demand the money for his Renoir!"

"But haven't you sold it, André?" Viola asked patiently, as if talking to a naughty child.

"Don't talk to me as if I were crazy and had to be indulged," André shrieked at the top of his voice. "I never told you I had sold it."

"Yes, you did, André. You told me you had sold it to Etienne, just last weekend."

"Well, he hasn't paid me yet, and Pierre-Paul can bloody well wait."

Viola's patience was clearly faltering as she said in a tight voice: "I don't know why you're shouting at me about Pierre-Paul's Renoir. Look, André, if only you'll be calm for a moment, we ought to talk about his wanting to run the magazine. I know exactly what's going on. It's Nini. You know how ambitious she is and how she always wants to shine in Paris. Pierre-Paul told me all about it. He's always complaining to me about Nini, and how difficult she is."

André was listening carefully; his face, which had turned purple as he was shouting, was going back to its usual olive color. "That little bitch Nini," he said reflectively. "I'll fix her."

Viola continued. "I made sure he understood it would be the end of the magazine if he tried to run it. He said he was coming to see you today—"

"Yes, any minute now."

"Well, I'm sure if you tell him the same thing, he'll understand, but maybe you should give him a title of some kind so as to appease Nini—"

"Never," André said viciously. "Never. But I'll take care of her."

"Be careful, André," Viola implored. And seeing his face darken again, she quickly changed the subject. "Now, since

Vincent is in Paris," she began to say, but André interrupted her.

"You know about Barolo. Well, I'm selling several of his paintings—I'll tell you more in a minute. They're all good except the Chagall, which is quite awful, but I think the Bergs will buy it. They're going to be in Paris in two weeks, and we'd better give them a party. You know what snobs they are."

"A dinner?"

"No, just a cocktail party."

"They're so common," Viola said, "but if it's necessary we'll do it. Are we going to the country this weekend?"

"I'll tell you later," André replied. "You'd better leave me now. I have to get all my figures straight for Pierre-Paul."

Viola stood up, looked as if she were about to say something, thought better of it, and opened the door; then, unable to resist, she said: "I thought Coche del Mancha looked terrible last night. That dress she was wearing! It may have looked very well on Laure, but it was not made for a brunette." And, before André could answer, she walked out, closing the door after her.

She had hardly left before Pierre-Paul Sanche walked in. His hesitant, shy manner was in painful contrast to his looks: This tall, broad-shouldered, darkly handsome man, who was also rich and intelligent, behaved like a frightened child. As usual, he opened his conversation with André by complaining: "My life's so difficult, André," he said, "you have no idea. I've just lost ten thousand dollars on the stock market, and we're redoing our dining room, but the carpet hasn't come on time, and now, frankly, I'm having trouble with Nini. She thinks I should be publisher of *Voir*, and you should be editor-in-chief. Well, she has a point, you know. I mean, it is my money—"

André promptly interrupted him. "I understand your difficulties, Pierre-Paul," he said with a look of sympathy, "but, after all, you can't let Nini, charming as she is, run your life. Of course, I'm perfectly willing to have you become publisher of *Voir*; but let's look calmly and quietly at what would happen then. You know that I have twenty years' experience running a magazine. I may not be the most brilliant of men (here, Pierre-Paul shook his head to indicate dissent), but I do know what I'm doing. Now, if you were to take over, what would happen? You know how close we always are to losing money. Well, are you prepared to finance a large deficit, say ten thousand dollars a month, for a year or two? Do you know the advertisers? Do you know why *Voir* sells as well as it does? Think carefully, Pierre-Paul. Can you take all these risks? After all, as you say, it's your money!" André stopped and there was an awful silence.

"But, André," Pierre-Paul finally stammered, "I never meant to actually run the magazine. It's just that at home—"

"And are you prepared," André continued relentlessly, "to be here every day at nine-thirty and to stay until seven or eight if necessary?"

Pierre-Paul's face was now flushed a deep red. "No, André, I'm not. But couldn't I at least have the title of publisher? I wouldn't have to bother you, really, you'd still run *Voir*; but then, you see, Nini—"

André drew himself up. "What do you take me for, Pierre-Paul? No, if you want to be the publisher of *Voir*, go ahead, but my name comes right off the masthead, and I walk out of this office. It's your decision. And you must tell me now."

Pierre-Paul was almost in tears. "Of course, you must stay," he choked out, "but what will I tell Nini?"

André relented. "Tell her we're discussing the creation of a whole new book-publishing organization called the Editions Voir, of which you'll be the head."

Pierre-Paul sighed, unconvinced. Then, with a return to his earlier manner, he asked, "And the Renoir, when will I be paid for it?"

"Oh, nothing to worry about. In three or four weeks, as soon as the restorer finishes with it. It's all settled."

Pierre-Paul reluctantly stood up. "Well, André," he mumbled, "I don't know what to say."

"Don't worry, things are often easier than they seem," André replied as he led Pierre-Paul to the door.

That night, shrieking with rage, Nini abused Pierre-Paul for his credulity. They were the laughingstock of Paris, she said. Everyone knew how they'd been taken in by the Germains. And after an hour's vituperation, she finally ended with a venomous: "Don't think you can touch me, Pierre-Paul. I meant what I said. You won't make love to me until you run *Voir*."

FOUR

A week later, Vincent Germain was sitting in his Manhattan office. It was, as he often explained, no gallery: He was a private dealer; people came by appointment only; but the big room, on the parlor floor of an East Side brownstone, was arranged so as to make paintings look their best. Vincent was proud of it. Taste—superior taste—seemed to him not just an achievement but a symbol; it set him apart from the other dealers and gave him the only unalloyed satisfaction of his professional life. At a time when most New Yorkers had plain white walls, his were a dark, tobacco brown, and the shiny parquet floor was a darker brown still. There was very little furniture, very little distraction; just a huge fur rug, white with brown markings, two white and orange modern armchairs, and a small table between them. The big, round glass and chrome table in the corner was always clear when visitors came to see Vincent. And, seemingly afloat in mid-air, hanging on invisible nylon wires, the paintings stood out, stark against the dark walls. Even the light was carefully planned. During the day, transparent white curtains filtered out the sun's glare while, at night, each painting was bathed in the golden glow of its own picture light. It was lovely, and it worked.

When Vincent had walked in that morning, his assistant, Olga Kourakin, was waiting for him, and, although he was glad to to see her, he felt a curious twinge: She was on his side, in his employ, but he still had to keep up a mask as an enthusiastic dealer when they were together.

"I'm exhausted," he said after greeting her. "I still feel as if I'm living on Paris time."

"You'll get over it," she answered drily. "We have a lot of work to do."

"Yes, I know; but, Olga, let's have coffee first. Be an angel and phone down for it, would you?" He looked at her as she made the call. She was wonderfully fair, with long, full, golden hair, huge blue eyes, a snub nose, and a fresh, silken complexion. Even the grace with which she moved seemed to confirm her origin. She was not very tall, but no one noticed: She was also slim, sexy, radiant. And even though she certainly had no private income, even though she was unmarried and barely twenty-five, she always dressed far more elegantly than her salary could possibly allow. That enigma, however, was easily explained: Any of her many friends would have smiled knowingly and mentioned her lover, an enormously successful painter whose social ambitions, most people thought, were more important to him than his work. Still, John Partridge and Olga Kourakin made a perfect New York couple. They were socially apt, gave wonderful parties in his huge downtown studio, knew everyone—well, almost everyone—and looked spectacular together: she, small, lithe, golden; he, tall with cropped black hair, expensive clothes, and ingratiating manners. It didn't hurt, either, that he was twenty years older than she, since it allowed people to make those deliciously scandalized remarks.

"How did you find Sarah?" Olga asked when they were

sipping their coffee. "I had dinner with her while you were gone and she seemed very depressed."

"Did she?" Vincent asked, playing with his pencil. "Perhaps it's her painting. She's not producing much, and I rather think she blames me."

"You're right, she does. She says you don't care."

"I do," Vincent replied, feeling stung. "I'm always trying to encourage her; but if I criticize she says I'm too harsh, and if I praise she says I'm insincere. I'm wrong whatever I say."

Olga shrugged. "Perhaps she senses you don't take her seriously."

"Perhaps. But honestly, should I? I mean, you're her friend. Do you really think she's a painter?"

"How can I tell?" Olga said with a grimace. "I just know she's unhappy and you should do something about it."

There was a brief silence. Then, sitting up straighter, Vincent said: "I know what I'll do. I'll look at her stuff just as if I were still running Iris Johnson's." He paused. "God," he went on, "do you remember?" Olga, smiling, nodded.

Vincent had met Olga several years ago when they were both working for Iris Johnson, and Vincent had quickly found out that she was not, in fact, what her name implied. She came from California, not Russia, and her father had been a successful tax lawyer, not a Russian general. Her mother still lived in a canyon house in Los Angeles with Olga's younger brother; and Olga had moved East to forget an unhappy love. It had certainly been a courageous move: New York is a hard city to crack. It's often closed and frightening, even for the very young.

Olga, however, didn't hesitate for a moment. She came and, within a week of her arrival, had found a cheap apartment and a job at Iris Johnson's. After a few months as the receptionist, she had convinced Iris to let her organize a

print department and had done very well at it. It was, perhaps, a little difficult to tell whether her clients were devoted collectors or devoted admirers. Still, the result was
the same: The new department was a success.

Olga's social life was a success, too. She wanted to please,
to attract people. It was easy. She was pretty, bright,
charming. Best of all, she had that quality of energy that, on
the screen or off, always seems to attract people. Besides,
she was free. She could go from man to man, enjoying each
on his own terms. So there was a young Norwegian sculptor, as fair as she was, with whom showers became a new,
sensual experience. There was a painter, a complicated,
flawed man of forty whose brief moment of success was
over; he was a kind of con man, really, not without pic-
torial talent, but his real gift was an ability to get money
out of people by almost any means With him, a whole
new sexual realm opened; he was sometimes impotent but
loved women and made kissing go a good deal further than
it usually does. And, even better, he belonged to that whole
group of second-generation abstract expressionists who
were just then reconverting to a new, more fashionable
style, and he helped Olga meet that stratum of New York's
art world. There was even a collector who was dazzled by
the golden girl and, during their brief affair, introduced
her to a whole new group of moneyed people. And
through it all, Olga always avoided giving her men the
feeling that she was after anything—nor, in a sense, was
she. She chose her lovers quite spontaneously; yet, somehow, they all added something to her life, so that, after
three or four years, she had become a well-known young
woman about town.

Vincent had not been among the elect, a fact he sometimes regretted, even though he was married to Olga's best
friend, a woman as different from her as night from day;
but he had watched, sometimes with amusement, as Olga's

life expanded. They had become friends, were accustomed to working together, and often talked about Iris Johnson's eccentricities. "We should write it down," they kept saying. "We really mustn't forget what a book all these stories would make." And like most people who say that, they went no further: Olga was far too busy, Vincent too unaware of himself to know he might find satisfaction in writing a book.

During their last year together at Iris Johnson's, Vincent had told Olga that he meant to leave soon, that he wanted to be in business for himself. Iris's son was coming back from Germany to work with his mother and would be a permanent nuisance; besides, there was so much more money to be made as an independent dealer. At first, Olga had just listened and encouraged him. Soon, she became more directly interested, and eventually asked Vincent if she could come and work with him. He had thought it a good idea: Her new contacts, her way with clients, it could all be put to good use. She would bring in new collectors and be well worth her salary. They would both leave Iris Johnson's in July, they decided, and start working together in September. The summer didn't count. The art world seemed to go to sleep at the first hot days.

In January, though, that scheme almost fell apart. Olga's new love, John Partridge, was one of the mainstays of the Iris Johnson Gallery. Tall, powerfully built, handsome, Partridge was a curious combination. Reared in Utah, he had come to New York as a young man, not quite sure whether he wanted to design clothes or paint. He had finally settled on the latter and moved to London where he had produced dark, brooding abstractions esteemed by connoisseurs. And then, one day, intent on financial success, he had changed his style. Brilliant splashes of fiery reds, yellows, greens, and purples raced across the canvas. The connoisseurs didn't like them quite so much, but it didn't really matter to Partridge: They began to sell like hotcakes, and he discovered a whole new set of goals. So he made more of them and was soon earning a huge income, as much or more as the most famous American artists of the time.

The more canvas he covered, the more the critics shuddered. He had lost his originality, they said with contempt; he had sold out; but, as he made more and more money, as his carefully cultivated social connections continued to expand, he simply smiled. Of course, he deeply resented the contempt with which the art world was treating him; perhaps he even knew that his work was not what it ought to be—that might be the reason why, without being a drunk, he often drank a little too much; why, above all, he could never bear to be alone; why he could not spend a single night without a woman in his bed.

Partridge was married, but that didn't make much difference. At first, for a few weeks, his affair with Olga was a dead secret; they were supposedly just friends, and the front they put up was so effective that even Mrs. Partridge soon became a great friend of Olga's. When the news leaked out, to a small circle at first, Mrs. Partridge took it quietly: After all, she was used to her husband's promiscuity. She was a sculptor, and had always kept her own studio and apartment. Now, she stayed there, and Olga moved in with Partridge—it was all very hush-hush. By the end of the first year, the affair was official. Partridge and Olga were invited everywhere together, as a couple. It was all very glamorous—she was so young, so attractive, and he was so successful—though, perhaps, not quite as blissful as it seemed.

Partridge had never been an easy man. He was generous, in a way, quite ready to give Olga beautiful clothes, a fur coat, anything that would make them both look good; after all, he much preferred to be seen with a chic young woman. Still, he never considered changing his life in the least: It was up to Olga to adapt, to make her life fit into his. And since he was a man to whom success meant so much, he had learned to pursue it in every possible way. Olga was more charming, and soon more popular, than Mrs. Partridge; it didn't hurt him socially to have her along. Even better, she could be his eyes and ears inside the gallery; he could count on her to push his paintings, to make sure that he was treated better than any of the other artists. Still, he really loved her, really needed her. It was just that everything must dovetail with his own plans.

It was about two years after the start of the affair that Vincent and Partridge had clashed. Two floors of Iris Johnson's gallery, which occupied a whole brownstone, were devoted to exhibitions. Upstairs was for paintings, downstairs for smaller works on paper. That January, Partridge was to have a watercolor show downstairs. Vincent, who ran the exhibitions, had spent the day with him, arranging the watercolors on the floor, along the walls, to see which went together and which clashed; then, with the help of the gallery's handyman, they hung them and adjusted the lighting, just enough to make the colors sing. It was a little after five when Partridge announced that he would bring in a large painting the next morning to hang on the upstairs landing, the one you saw from the street through the big glass front.

There was a pause before Vincent asked in a surprised voice: "Upstairs?"

"Yes," Partridge answered, "that way people will know right away that I'm having a show."

"But they'll know anyway, John," Vincent said patiently, "and they come in downstairs, you know."

Partridge hardly listened. He almost seemed to be talking to himself as he answered: "It doesn't matter. I need the leading spot as well."

"Look, John," Vincent said more firmly now, looking him in the eye, "you know that's not possible. Blackwell has the upstairs. We can't just put one of your paintings in place of his; besides, you agreed to have your show downstairs. There was never any question of anything else."

At that, Partridge had exploded. Screaming, shaking his fist, he demanded the leading spot, shouting he was the gallery's best seller, that he was famous, that Vincent would have to get up very early in the morning before he could cross him like this. Then, goaded on by Vincent's disgusted look, he bellowed: "This isn't your gallery, you little shit. You just work here. Don't you dare tell me what to do!"

Stiffening, Vincent turned away and answered almost in a whisper, as he started up the stairs: "Very well, let Iris make the decision"; but when he came across Olga on his way into Iris's office, he had stopped and hissed: "You really ought to teach your boyfriend some manners."

"It's nothing to do with me," Olga answered quickly. "I'm not responsible for him." And even though Partridge had expressed regrets the next day, the very way in which he had done it had, in Vincent's eyes, made everything worse. To be sure, the artist had said he was sorry there had been a misunderstanding; but he had done it the way an old friend might, as if there had been an inexplicable pause in an otherwise long and warm relationship, when, in fact, the two barely knew each other. Vincent had pretended to be satisfied; but the phony friendship, the hypocrisy of Partridge's behavior had repulsed him quite as much as the artist's rage of the evening before. Nor, in Vincent's eyes, was the situation improved when Partridge went on behaving as if they were close friends. It wasn't just that Vincent had never much liked him, and now found him to be a pretentious bore; he resented the pretense, the falsely implied existence of a warmth between them. Ever since then, although they appeared even to Olga to be on the best of terms, Vincent had nursed his grievance; it never quite ceased rankling.

He was reminded of it yet again, as he and Olga sipped their coffee, when Olga asked him to a party she and Partridge were giving down at his studio. Vincent accepted, feeling he had no other choice, but groaned inwardly: He didn't like large parties, and he didn't like Partridge. So he quickly turned the conversation to business. Pushing his chair back from the table and crossing his legs, he said, in a puzzled tone: "You know, something very peculiar is happening with Barolo and my father. I wrote you I went to see his collection with that awful Poppea. Well, it's everything you might expect except for one Chagall that, just between us, looks to me like a fake."

"In the Barolo collection? A fake?"

"It happens to the best of people," Vincent answered drily. "But the really curious thing is that my father has bought it from him, and that he's about to sell it to the Bergs—or, at least, I think he is. Now, that just doesn't make any sense. The Bergs may not know a Matisse from a Raphael, but they're shrewd enough when it comes to money; and, besides, you know there will be at least one dealer who will be happy to question the painting. Now, my father can't need to make a sale that badly; the Bergs are good clients. So why is he doing it? There must be something else going on."

That same morning, Jack Griffenbaum walked the two blocks from his penthouse to Poppea Vlassoff's apartment. She had called the evening before, asking him to come and discuss the next week's auction. "I'll explain it to you," she had said smugly. "It's all fixed anyway."

Poppea's apartment was an amazingly accurate reflection of her personality. She often wondered, as she walked through it, why it failed to give the image she wanted. That day, she was sitting and staring at it resentfully. On the top floor of a converted brownstone, in the sixties between Fifth and Madison, it should have had immense charm. As it was, the living room was a large, square room, with tall, sunny windows and a fireplace. Only, the windows were blocked by dead or dying plants. "They always croak on me," Poppea would say, puzzled. "I water them, but they croak." There was very little furniture; the long, modern couch, imported at great expense from Italy, would have been beautiful if its gray suede had not been marred by several grease spots. The glass coffee table, again Italian and expensive, had a chipped corner. Then, there was a wicker chair—but the bottom was coming out. The fireplace had andirons in it, brand-new, but they were too big, and so couldn't be used. Poppea felt puzzled as she looked at them: She had exchanged an ivory snuffbox a former lover had given her for them—a smart move, she thought at the time. And now they were no good after all. In the corner, the mirrored screen had lost one of its panels. But, most curious of all, there wasn't a single painting on the walls. You could see at once that Poppea had intended to hang several things —the nails and cracked plaster made this abundantly clear— but the walls remained bare while a whole stack of paintings, their backs turned to the room, sat on the floor near the fireplace.

When Jack rang, it was a while before she opened the door. Tucking her blouse into her dungarees, she exclaimed breathlessly, "I was on the phone." Shouting, "Oh, fuck!" as it started to ring again, she motioned him into the bedroom. It was a fairly small, very dark room, so Poppea had painted it yellow. But it looked dirty somehow, not sunny, and Poppea often said that she couldn't understand why the paint had come out such a shitty shade. "Perhaps the chartreuse rug doesn't help," Vincent had suggested once, but Poppea had just shaken her head. Now, she sat down on the unmade bed as she grabbed the phone, directing Jack to a wicker chaise longue, the only other piece of furniture, its lurid cushions thickly piled with hastily discarded and obviously dirty clothes.

Jack shook his head and smiled as he listened to Poppea saying feverishly, "Yes, yes, Zaza, but not this week. . . . I never said two months. . . . Oh . . . well, that's not till next week. . . . No, I don't even have the money to pay my rent. In fact, I still owe for last month. . . . No, I borrowed the money from the janitor. I told him he should go into art. . . . Yeah, soon. . . . Look, Zaza, I'll sell it. Just give me a little time. I mean, it's not a big deal, only five thousand. . . . Okay, look, I'll try for next week. . . . Yeah . . . Yeah . . . sure, it's a good investment."

"Trouble?" he asked, as Poppea put down the phone.

She grimaced. "Well, it's just that I told Zaza that she should invest in art; so she gave me five thousand, and I bought a Marcoussis from Harry Pearl, and I'm sure I could sell it today for at least sixty-five hundred." She paused.

Jack smiled. "Why don't you, then?" he said.

"I can't. Harry won't let me have it. The thing is, I sold him a Léger that he resold to one of his clients. Only, some jerk said it was a fake and his client returned it and now he wants his money back, and I can't give it to him because I only took a commission, so he's holding the Marcoussis, but I can't tell Zaza because she'd hit the ceiling, and I don't have enough money right now to pay her back." As she spoke, Poppea unconsciously allowed her left hand to come up to her face. The spattering of dark brown spots looked flushed, as if it had been fruitlessly scrubbed. Jerking around, she stood up. "Let's go into the other room," she said more quietly. "I want to talk about the auction."

Jack followed her, watching the sway of her hips in the tight jeans. Suddenly he laughed. "Poppea, you're impossible," he said. "Your friend is just going to call you back next week. And then, what will you do?"

"Oh, don't worry," Poppea answered as she slouched down onto the couch. "I'll just sell something else and give her the money. Now, about the auction. The ring will be in control."

"The ring?"

"Yes, all the big dealers get together and agree on prices beforehand. Only, the public thinks auctions are open, and that the final prices really show where the market is. It's all fixed, really. Even painters bid on their own work. Take John Partridge: He's very successful, but everyone knows his paintings never sell at auction, so he's got people bidding on them."

"It must be expensive," Jack said, smiling.

"Oh, sure, but a lot less expensive than having his whole market collapse. I mean, look, he can tell his clients that his work is doing well at auction; then they buy more. Anyway, a lot of others do it, too."

"It's lucky Matisse, Léger, and Picasso are dead," Jack interrupted. But the irony was completely lost on Poppea.

"There, it's not the artists," she went on, "it's the dealers. They've got to keep up the market. So, for some pictures, they get together and bid them up; but, for others, they see that nobody bids on them. Then, they get them really cheap, sit on them for a year or two, and double their price."

"But they can't stop other people from bidding."

"Sure they can. Look, this friend of mine, he's a dealer, and he had sold a cubist Juan Gris to one of his privates. So, after a year, the private wants to sell it again, and he has my friend put it in one of these auctions. Well, he goes to Russell and Company, shows it to them, and puts it in their October sale, the big one. And they agree on a reserve of sixty thousand dollars, you know, so it can't be sold cheaper than that. So then, he goes away for the summer, and when he comes back, he hears everyone saying it's a fake. Well, he calls up Russell's and they say, 'Sure, three of the big dealers came by and said it was a fake.' So naturally he denies it, and at Russell's they say they don't believe him and they want a certificate. Well, the only people who can give a certificate for a Juan Gris are the people at the Leiris Gallery, and they're in Paris. Of course, it takes time for my friend to get a photograph over to them, and then they have to check their archives and send it back. So, three weeks later, my friend goes back to Russell's with the certificate, and they admit the painting is real. In the meantime, everybody's heard there's something wrong with it, so nobody's going to be interested. Then, the day before the auction, the guy from Russell's calls my friend and says, 'Look, you'd better lower the reserve because the market's down and anyway your painting is not really desirable anymore.' So naturally my friend realizes there's something going on, and he says, 'Not on your life. The reserve stays.' "

"But how could those people say the painting was a fake if it wasn't?" Jack asked.

"Easy. Look, they say it's a fake, and everybody believes it's a fake, right? So then, nobody bids on it. Of course, they know it's good all along. So anyway, naturally, this Gris doesn't sell at the auction. The last bid is fifty thousand, which is just what Russell's had wanted to lower the reserve to. Then the next day my friend gets a call from the auctioneer who says, 'Look, now that your painting hasn't sold, it's burned. Nobody's going to want it for years, but, luckily for you, I've got this client who's kind of interested in it and he'd be willing to buy it at forty-five thousand, less our commission, of course.' Well, my friend, who understood that it was one of those other dealers trying to get it cheap, said, 'As a matter of fact, the price has just gone up to seventy thousand and you can tell your client that's my last word.' "

"You mean he never sold it?"

"Oh, sure he did, a year later in Paris, and for the full seventy, to a French private. But anyway, you see how it works. So you have those dumb privates everywhere, thinking they're so smart, checking the auction prices, and all they're getting is what the dealers want them to think."

"So, then," Jack said slowly, "you really need to be part of that group of dealers if you want to make big money. But how do you do that? Do you know any of them, Poppea?"

Instead of answering, Poppea suddenly stood up, raising her hands to her head. "Oh, Jack," she cried, "you should have told me. I forgot to comb my hair before you came. I must look awful!" and she stared him straight in the face. Jack stood up also and, walking over to her, silently put his hands on her breasts. Poppea sighed, linked arms with him, and turned to the bedroom; but, as she was unbuttoning her blouse, she added, "I'll bet Vincent could get us into the ring. He knows all the big dealers."

When Vincent rang the bell, forty-five minutes later, Poppea was dressed again. As soon as she opened the door, Jack, with a greeting to Vincent, walked out. "You're doing business, I see," said Vincent with an ironic smile, as he watched Poppea run her fingers through her hair. "Well," he went on, "I've been working, too. I think I have a client for that second Ernst you showed me in Milan. If you can give it to me for a day or two, I'll let you know for sure."

Leading him into the living room, Poppea dropped on the

couch, looking pleased. "Oh, yeah? How much did you ask?"

"Fifty-five. That's what we agreed on."

"Yeah," Poppea repeated, as if lost in thought. "Yeah, I need that money."

"Poppea, it's not sold yet."

"Oh, it'll sell. Does your client pay quickly?"

"Fast enough," said Vincent drily. "You wanted to see me?"

"Yes, about the auction. Look, I know all about those big dealers," Poppea began, before she was interrupted by the phone.

With a grimace, she lifted it off the hook. "Yeah," she went on, speaking into the mouthpiece. "Oh, it's you. . . . So . . . so. . . . No, I told you it's good. . . . Sure, it has a provenance . . . yeah, the whole history of the painting, all it's earlier owners . . . sure it does. . . . Yeah, it's even in a book. Yeah. . . . Who told that jerk it was a fake? Sure, there are lots of fake Klees, only this one isn't. . . . You know where I got it. I told you, from an Italian private. . . . Yeah, the Sardine, and let me tell you, he wants to be paid. . . . So you gave me a third. That's not enough. I want the rest of the money. Look, I know I told you he was in jail, but he'll come out, and he's got a whole collection. No, of course not. . . . No way. I'm not giving you that third back. What do you take me for, your fairy godmother? No way . . . no way. . . . Look, you fucking bastard, you come up here, and I'll have the cops on you. . . . That's right, for assault."

She hung up violently and, breathing hard, turned back to Vincent. "I don't want him here," she almost shouted. "He's got a terrible temper. One time last winter he punched me in the stomach."

"Oh, come on," Vincent said, looking shocked.

"Yes, he did. Anyway, I sold him that Klee later."

"You know, Poppea, you shouldn't be dealing with people like that. And anyway, are you so sure you actually sold it to him? Instead of giving it on consignment, I mean?"

Poppea laughed. "Sure, I sold it to him. And he's never getting his third back. Some jerk in Boston said it was a fake. Well, he bought it, so he owes me."

"Is it, Poppea?"

"A fake? How should I know? It came from a private in Italy."

"It came from Malamonte, didn't it?"

"So?"

"Poppea, if it's like those other Klees, then you know it's a fake. You'd better think seriously about returning the money and taking the picture back. You could be in a lot of legal trouble; and besides, I assure you, if this gets around, absolutely nobody will do business with you anymore."

Poppea scratched her head, then waved her right hand. "Oh, I'll be okay," she said. "I can always arrange things. Now, what are you buying at the auction?"

"Nothing, probably."

"Listen, I hear your father flew in for it."

"Yes," said Vincent, "so do I."

Poppea stopped for a second, looking a little surprised, then went on. "So we can go together."

"I don't think so, Poppea. I've already said I would go with other people."

Now Poppea really looked thoughtful." You know the big dealers, don't you?" she asked, almost in a whine. "I mean Copley and Weinstein and the others. Couldn't you introduce me to them?"

"I don't think so," Vincent answered. "They're very busy, you know, and very difficult. Why don't you just let it happen naturally? Maybe one day you'll have something to offer one of them. Look, Poppea," he added quickly,

"I have to go. But I'll probably see you at the auction tomorrow."

"Yeah," Poppea answered thoughtfully, "yeah, I'll see you there. I think I might go with Roberta Boxer."

At lunchtime that day Vincent and Olga stayed in the office, and, as Vincent unwrapped his sandwich, he saw Olga take out a very small container of cottage cheese. "You're not on a diet, surely?" he asked with a smile as he looked at the slender girl sitting in front of him.

"Sure I am," said Olga seriously. "I have to lose five pounds."

"You! Oh, come on! You're already so thin."

"No. Well, not my derrière. I don't like the way it looks in skirts."

"What about exercise, then?" Vincent asked. "Katriona says you do her exercises better than anyone else."

"Oh, I do. I have no flab anywhere. Here, feel," she added, raising a leg.

Vincent felt her calf. "Yes, iron-hard," he answered, adding, "and you're still going to your judo classes, aren't you?"

"Twice a week," Olga said proudly. "Down in the Village. It's really a high. The master says I'm his best student. I have only studied with him for six months, but I have already reached the level of a second-year student. You really should try it, it gives you such control over your body. John has begun to go, too, and he loves it."

"Oh, I'm sure it's good for you," Vincent answered, "but, really, I think I'll just stick to Katriona. I feel so much better since I've started to take her exercise class. Besides, I don't have the time for anything else."

"You could make the time," Olga said, and, noticing that Vincent was staring at her suit, "Yes, it's new. It's from the Saint-Laurent boutique. John insisted on buying it for me."

"He did?" Vincent asked with a smile. "Tough!"

But Olga didn't smile back. She paused for a moment, frowning, her blue eyes almost hidden. "I don't like it," she murmured.

"What, the suit?"

"No, the suit's very nice. Only, I don't like being treated like a harem girl. John is always buying me things I don't ask for. And I don't like him to spend all that money."

"I daresay he can afford it," Vincent remarked drily. "And, after all, if he wants to give you presents, why shouldn't he?"

"They're not presents, they're bribes," Olga said, looking quite angry. "I have to do everything he wants and then he gives me a dress or a coat. I'm getting tired of organizing his life, arranging parties, and being pleasant to people I don't like."

"I only wish Sarah had this kind of complaint," Vincent said with a sigh.

"No, you don't. And I've had it with all those people."

"Oh, come on," Vincent interrupted. "You know how good you are with people. Of course, they like you."

"No, they don't. I'm too young and, besides, they're really friends with John's wife, and they don't like it when he brings me around."

"I can see why the wives might not like you at first," Vincent said quite seriously, "but, obviously, the husbands will. And if you really can't stand that sort of socializing, I expect you should talk to Partridge about it. Surely he'd understand."

"Maybe. But that's not the worst part. Look, I work while he's painting and, when I get back to the studio, he expects me to be ready to have fun with him. Well, I understand that, but when do I get to do my own thing?"

"What is your thing, Olga?" Vincent asked. "What would you really like to do?" On an impulse, he stroked her cheek. There was a long pause. Olga was toying with her spoon, looking down at her feet.

"I'm not sure," she finally answered, almost sullenly. "Maybe I'd like to work with children."

"Well, you couldn't do that at night. Would you rather have that kind of job?"

There was another pause. "I don't know," Olga said finally. "I don't know. It's just that with John I have no life of my own. Everything always centers on him, his work, his shows, his friends, his parties."

"What about your own friends? Surely you still see them?" said Vincent, with real concern in his voice.

"Yes, but not as often, and John doesn't really like it when I do."

"What about your life-style?" Vincent asked, feeling like an analyst. "Surely you like that? The studio, the trips to Paris, the openings? It must be fun."

"Yes," Olga said slowly, "yes, it's fun. But, you know, I sometimes feel like an extension of John's personality. When I was in college, I always thought I'd lead a creative life, that I'd write, or teach, or design. . . ." Her voice trailed off. There was a silence. Then, with a visible effort, she changed the subject and asked: "What about the auction? You've seen the big Magritte they're making such a fuss about?"

"Yes," Vincent answered. "It's been so heavily restored that it's practically a new painting. It'll never set a new record, as they say it will; in fact, if they keep the reserve high enough, it just won't sell. They're really taking chances, trying to sustain the market with stuff like that. You know, this is what I don't like about the business, this feeling that the public is being fooled, again and again, while a few dealers get rich. I mean, even if the prices can go up indefinitely, which I doubt, at least you have to have quality work to sustain them. And, not even counting the Magritte, most of the paintings they're selling are at best second-rate. Still, you can be sure that in two days the *Times* will have a headline saying a new record was set; the dealers can't afford to have the prices visibly dropping."

"What about the Léger gouache?"

"It's quite nice—a big flower. I think it must be a study for one of the ceramics. By the way, guess who I met in front of it?"

"Your father?"

"Yes. How did you know? And he was extremely amiable. He must be up to something very shady, or he wouldn't have been half so pleasant."

"Maybe he just made a big sale?"

"Maybe. But I wonder where he is right now, and what he's doing there."

FIVE

André Germain, as he stood outside the door of David Copley's Fifth Avenue house, could hardly contain a sneer: The address (the best in New York), the discreet wood door concealing a metal panel, the tiny brass plate bearing only a number—all was carefully calculated to make you feel Copley's importance. It said here is a sanctum of art, too important even to need a name. If you didn't know David Copley, you had no business being there. And the success of "that little peddlar," as André called David, always maddened him when he talked to Thérèse about this despised yet essential dealer.

André never tired of recounting Copley's story: how he had started in a little basement shop selling coins; how he had chanced on some old master drawings and, unloading them at a profit, seen a new way; how eventually he had moved from that hole in the wall to a little gallery uptown. André usually stopped his story at this point. There was no enjoyment to be gained from describing the success of a man he considered his inferior. Of course, he ascribed that success to chance and the ignorance of most American collectors; André never tired of pointing out that, general opinion notwithstanding, Copley was nothing but a common little man with neither knowledge nor discernment; and Thérèse knew better than to ask how such an ignoramus had managed to accumulate a dazzling collection of old master drawings at a time and in a place—New York—where it was hardly the fashion to do so.

André Germain had abundant reason to hate Copley: It wasn't just that the American was so successful, so respected, or even that he was so rich (wealth was something André rarely forgave in others). The worst of it was that André needed Copley. It had long been established among André's little entourage that André was a giant surrounded by dwarfs: He was more intelligent, more cultivated, had a keener eye, understood painting and everything else better than anyone; and, curiously, there was just enough truth in this to make it plausible. André was, in fact, sometimes brilliant. And yet he never seemed to do much with all his talents. *Voir* was a good magazine, most of the time. It was respected, talked about, quoted, but it never seemed to sell much and limped about from one financial crisis to the next. As for the gallery, its shows were often interesting and original. Many of the paintings and drawings that made up the stock were first rate, but, despite all Viola's charm, they didn't sell as well as one might have expected. And that was why André continued to court Copley.

There were other dealers with whom André did business (dealers often seem to spend more time trading with their colleagues than with that adversary, the client). The drawback was that when one dealer sells a painting to another the price must stay well below the market so that the painting can be resold at a profit. And so, while André was often forced by an urgent financial crisis to sell to another dealer, it really was not very profitable for him to do so. Nor could he complain to Viola about that: She had a maddening way of replying, "Well, André, it's your own

fault. You should hold out until you get a private client."
This was more than André could bear, and he made sure
it didn't happen often; but although Viola, knowing what
to expect, usually refrained from uttering the provoking
remark, she made it plain through her lack of sympathy
that she didn't think much of André's way of running the
business.

Her attitude, unfortunately for André's pride, was not
devoid of importance: It was Viola, after all, who had
convinced Pierre-Paul Sanche to invest, first in the magazine, then in the gallery. Almost worse, Copley respected
André for his intelligence and his keen eye, but it was
Viola who kept things going smoothly. Business was business, and this particular business seemed to require a lot of
social intercourse: dinners, lunches, weekends when Viola's
charm was expected to work its magic. Luckily for André,
Viola understood just why they both needed Copley.

The reason was simple enough: Copley, who had a
plethora of clients, would sell paintings at the highest
possible price. And, instead of simply buying André's stock
as cheaply as possible, he would often share paintings with
him. This made all the difference. André could buy twice
as many pieces and, in some cases, that meant a collection
would go to him instead of another dealer. More important
still, Copley sold the paintings they owned together, ena-
bling André to make the kind of profits he dreamed about
but usually seemed unable to make on his own.

Still, this arrangement had a major drawback: It made
André dependent on Copley. "When I think," he would
say to Viola as he paced, "that I have to put up with
David's ignorance! The man has no sense of quality, no
instinct, no culture. He can't tell a masterpiece from a
third-rate work. Oh, of course, he's a good salesman, as if
it mattered. But, you know, he might just as well be selling
underwear, for all he understands about painting! And if

it weren't for me, for my knowledge, where would he be, I ask you, *where?*"

Viola always refrained from pointing out that Copley had become the most successful private dealer in New York well before André ever met him. Still, it rankled. André could hardly forgive a man he needed so badly, a man who had the gall to be much richer and more powerful in the art world. Nor did it help that André was unable to right his grievances: After all, he could hardly make the kind of scene that regularly reduced Viola and Thérèse to tears; he could not tell other people that Copley was a dolt, since that might have unfortunate consequences. It was altogether unbearable.

Luckily for André, a new plan had recently been born of all his rage: Ahead of him stretched a long and sunny vista in which vast profits were compounded by Viola's final, complete humiliation. He could hardly contain himself, really, as he stood before that plain wood door: The hour of triumph was at hand. André's satisfaction grew even more complete as, having rung the bell, he was ushered into the central hall dividing the house in two: On the right was a large living room with double doors while, on the left, two offices sheltered files and secretaries. As he waited, he looked about smugly and felt sure, yet again, of his superiority. Copley, with the help of the best decorator in New York, could only produce a cold, dull, conventional interior while he, André Germain, whose taste and decorating skills were nothing short of superb, could have made it into a real showpiece.

He wasn't completely wrong, either. There was something awkward about all this cold luxury. The floor's white marble squares linked with green lozenges looked institutional, not Venetian. The pale gray silk on the walls, chosen with enormous care, managed to be both expensive and very dull: It might just as well have been paint. The doors into the living room and offices had been specially ordered and were meant to have a Louis XVI, neoclassical look; but they reminded one of nothing so much as a papier-maché door in a theater set. The sconces, three on each wall, and the chandelier, hanging uneasily from the low ceiling, were made of gilt-bronze and crystal. They had been copied from eighteenth-century models, but they too looked wrong somehow, and, instead of precious materials, one saw only a clumsy copy.

The walls of the entrance hall had been left bare of ornament, but in the living room, where André now waited, masterpieces glowed on every side. Over the fireplace and along the whole wall hung half a dozen Giandomenico Tiepolos of the Pulcinella series: Here, Punch had become a father and was surrounded by half a dozen smaller replicas of himself; there, he relaxed in a carriage driven by another Pulcinella; elsewhere still, he was escaping the rage of a jealous husband; and, always, the line was full of wit, of the melancholy grace of the 1790s. A little farther along, Giambattista Tiepolo had drawn a swirling ceiling decoration that gave its sheet of paper a monumental look and reminded one of a Venetian palace. Near the corner, you could see a sad, smiling Watteau lute player sitting gracefully next to a woman and brought to life by a few red chalk lines. A Carracci water carrier strolled next to a Degas dancer; and a cubist Picasso head stared at a Corot landscape. Elsewhere, a huge, colorful Matisse offered its odalisque, reclining on a welter of striped silks, while a solemn, almost geometric Courbet of two women by the ocean answered to a very famous contrast-of-forms Léger, full of facets and gaiety.

Not even André's self-absorption stopped him from looking at the drawings and paintings, although he derived very little pleasure from them. They should have been his, not Copley's: That upstart had no right to do so well for himself. As he looked around the room itself, however, André's good humor quickly returned. It was an unwieldy hodgepodge of styles, full of expensive antique furniture standing on rare carpets, of inlaid tables covered with rare bronzes, of old coins and *objets de vertu*. Yet the Empire desk, beautiful as it was, clashed with the Victorian petit-point rug next to it; the comfortable beige silk Bloomingdale's armchair looked clumsy and dull near the Riesener sewing table; the two rococo Venetian chairs seemed less flamboyant than merely vulgar. To be sure, everything here had cost a great deal of money; and yet, as André said to himself with great satisfaction, it all looked like a jumble sale. The attempt at mixing styles and periods—something André knew how to do with unparalleled success—completely failed to convey the intended hint of easy sophistication. Instead, confusion reigned; every object detracted from its neighbor.

Just as André reached that happy conclusion, the double doors opened and David Copley came shambling in. Tall, rather heavy, with pale blue eyes, he looked like an athlete slightly gone to seed, or perhaps a professor in some midwestern university who had, in his youth, played on the football team. Copley's fair hair was shaggy, slightly unkempt. His straggly beard belonged to the overall look of amiable, slightly distracted intellectualism. Even Copley's suit, no doubt cut by the best London tailor, looked almost slept in; he held a snuffbox as if a sudden burst of thought had made him forget he carried it. His shy smile, his serious look, all helped to make you feel comfortable, in control; there was nothing to remind you that the shrewdest of art dealers stood before you. And, in fact, Copley's image, convenient as it was, corresponded to a reality: He liked to think of himself as an art historian, an intellectual who condescended to make money.

At first they smiled across the room at each other with

surprise. Then Copley raised his right arm and, almost shouting, said, "André! You came! How wonderful to see you!" while André, his head thrown back and his arms extended, answered, at the very same moment, "At last, David! It's been so long, much too long!"

Still, each stayed in his corner, smiling, until Copley moved forward with great urgency and said, "You've been kept waiting!"

At that, André also started toward the center of the room, exclaiming, "No, no, not at all, only a few seconds," until the two men finally met. They shook hands, and, amiably staring at each other, stepped back, as Copley said, "You had a good trip, I hope! Those awful planes..."

And André answered, "Yes, yes, a good trip. And, besides, I thought of seeing you and so it was nothing."

There was a brief pause. Gesturing to a chair, Copley said, "Such a pleasure, André, such a pleasure," before reminding him of the last trip they had taken together.

André bided his time. Now Copley was taking him over to the drawings, showing him his latest acquisitions, something that never failed to madden André all the more, since it forced him to put on a look of admiration as Copley pointed out the vividness of the Tiepolo, the subtlety of the Watteau. This time, however, André forgot to be angry. As he pretended to look, he was rehearsing the sentence that would change this particular relationship forever. "Let's change the subject for a moment," he would say, "do you remember the big Braque still life you bought in half-shares with me . . ." But his thought was interrupted brutally as Copley moved back toward the chairs.

"You've found something new?" Copley was already asking as he settled himself down and took a pinch of snuff from a little gold box ("Snuff!" André often said in disgust to Thérèse. "Snuff! The pretentiousness!").

André, sitting in one of the Venetian chairs, responded

eagerly. "I wouldn't call a Chardin something new," he said in perfect English. "After all, David, it's one of his best-known still lifes. The Louvre has been ogling it for twenty years now and if it weren't that I know Jean de Montigny so very well—"

"Is it in good condition, though?" Copley asked rather roughly.

André, his fingers drumming on the arms of his chair, his face darkening, answered: "In excellent condition. You know very well, David, that the picture hasn't been moved from its wall since it was painted."

There was a silence. Copley, looking distracted, took another pinch of snuff. "It's an important work," he finally said.

"Of course it is," André retorted. "We're damn lucky to have a chance to buy it. And we never would have had, if I hadn't been at that dinner the other night. Jean wants to build himself a modern house at Granmont and move out of the castle—even he can't afford to keep it up any longer. He's asking Philip Johnson to do the new house. I arranged it. 'André,' he was saying to me, 'I wish one could find the right architect.' Well, Philip was coming through Paris, so we gave him a little dinner, we asked Jean, and there you are."

Copley smiled. "Yes," he said, "here we are. We'll buy it in half-shares, of course. And very discreetly, since that's what he wants."

"I thought of organizing a show around it at the gallery, but Jean would be furious. It must be just between the three of us and the eventual buyer. No museum, of course. That would be much too public."

"Yes, naturally," Copley answered. "I'd like to see it—"

"Impossible," André interrupted. "Jean would be furious if I brought someone else in. And besides, you know, David, if we don't act fast—"

"You've made an offer?"

André looked shocked. "An offer? Really, my dear David! Not before talking it over with you, of course. But we must make one as fast as possible. I really should call Jean tomorrow morning."

"Yes. Well, what do you think?" Copley paused as he took another pinch of snuff, then turned the gold box around in his fingers. "Half a million?"

André flushed. "Half a million! David! Surely you realize—"

But before André could launch himself into a long tirade, Copley interrupted: "A million, then?"

"Or more. If we make what Jean considers a low offer, we'll lose the picture. And after all, my dear David, a historic Chardin!"

Copley half rose and resettled himself in his chair, pushing his hair back from his forehead. "All right, then, André," he said with a smile. "One million two. I think I might have someone for it at a million eight or two million."

André relaxed visibly. "A million two would do it, I think. And if you have someone—"

"I do," Copley said firmly, and was about to continue when he was interrupted by a knock on the door. He looked down at the paper handed him by his secretary, then looked up at André apologetically. "I'm so sorry," he said. "Could you wait just five minutes? There's a client I've been trying to reach all day and I really must talk to him."

André waved his hand amiably. "But naturally, David," he said. "Do you mind if I use this phone to make a quick call myself?"

Vincent and Sarah were right in the middle of a violent argument when the phone rang.

"Goddamn it," he shouted. "There goes the phone again. How can I speak to people when you upset me like this?"

Sarah laughed nastily. "I! Upset you! You're the one who upset me! So don't answer, then!"

"How can I not answer?" Vincent hissed over his shoulder as he walked over to the little table on which the phone sat. "This is a business, you know," and muttering, "I'm fed up," he picked up the receiver.

"Oh, it's you," he said coldly, after a short pause. "No . . . not tonight. I'm busy. . . . That's right, it is more important. Tomorrow, if you want . . . no, not for lunch. Eleven-thirty? At your hotel? All right." Banging the receiver down, he turned to face Sarah. "That's just what I needed. First, you make a scene; now my father's in town. I just can't go on like this!"

The lull following the death of Vincent's mother had, of course, quickly run its course, and now he and Sarah were again engaged daily in a debilitating round of bickering.

Sarah had never been willing to work with Vincent. She would discuss business with him, reluctantly and seldom, but she had given him good advice about how to handle specific people on several occasions—for example, Sophia Lyon. Vincent, when faced with hysteria, simply withdrew, and thus fueled the flames. Sarah had advised him to fight back but in a calm, practical manner, and it had worked beautifully. Then, too, she was good about remembering people's feelings: Vincent thought only of the business relationship, but Sarah could see the man or woman who needed a little flattering attention. Now all that had stopped.

"It's obvious," she told him, "that you're in the wrong profession. You were never meant to be a dealer at all. You're no good at bargaining, it makes you uncomfortable, and people feel it. Besides, if you can lower yourself to the point of doing business with Poppea Vlassoff, then I will have nothing more to do with any of it."

"Uncomfortable or not," Vincent answered, "it's where we get our income. Look, the more money I make, the

freer we'll be. In fact, Sarah, there's a deal I'm not sure
about and—"

"Don't talk to me," Sarah said angrily. "You pay no
attention to my work; I won't pay any attention to yours.
And don't pretend. I know I'm not Picasso, so how could
you be interested? You just go back to Poppea Vlassoff!"

Now, as their fight resumed, Vincent realized with a
sinking feeling that it was getting close to dinnertime. A
morning fight might be settled by lunchtime, but now, even
if they tired of the argument (and Vincent, to his surprise,
was beginning to feel bored rather than enraged), it would
promptly be revived when the problem of dinner came up.
Whenever Sarah was in a bad mood, she became absolutely
contrary, defending her often shifting stance with a string
of interminable good reasons. So, even before asking,
Vincent knew that if he suggested going out to dinner, she
would say either that she was too unwell or that she was
too upset to sit in a restaurant. This last argument, Vincent
had come to realize, was among her very best, since it
provided her with a richly varied choice of ways to make
him miserable: She could refuse to go out (and then what
would they do about dinner?), or she could reluctantly
agree to go. The conflict then shifted to the choice of
restaurant.

"Chinese?"

"No, we went there last week."

"Italian?"

"You just want me to eat pasta so I'll get fat."

"All right, then, French?"

"I won't go to an expensive restaurant when you've put
me in a bad mood."

"I see. What about a cheap French restaurant? You want
to go to the Café du Soir?"

"The Café du Soir! You know you hate it. I'm not going
to sit there while you complain about the menu!"

Even if they finally agreed on one particular place, Sarah's choices were still wide open. She could sit there stone-faced, making it perfectly plain to the waitress or waiter that she was one of those martyred women you read about; she could start a whole new argument ("You're always forcing me to go out when I don't want to, and then we'll get home too late for me to paint"); she could discover that her chair was the wrong kind for her back, so that every minute spent on it during dinner caused her excruciating pain; or she could complain about the final choice of restaurant ("I never wanted to come here!" "But you said you did." "I only said that because I knew you wouldn't want to go where I wanted.").

In his calmer moments, Vincent almost admired the incredible versatility of Sarah's maneuvers. They worked no matter what and could be repeated almost endlessly since, after all, one eats dinner every night. Once again, Vincent felt it was all too much. His life had become all of one piece, the increasing difficulty of doing business merged into the impossibility of living normally. It seemed as if pleasure had vanished, as if the hours were only to be endured. And that night was worse than usual: Even the fact that he had felt goaded beyond endurance completely failed to palliate Vincent's shame.

When Sarah had launched into the usual "I don't want to go out" routine, Vincent had begun to feel unbearably sorry for himself—so much so that, before Sarah's puzzled eyes, he had actually lost interest in their argument. Then, after a moment of silence, he had exploded, shouting that he didn't care about the dinner or anything else, that he was fed up, that his life was too difficult. When Sarah had started to answer, he had told her to shut up; that she was no wife, no help; that all she thought about was that fifth-rate painting of hers (and even as he had said those words, he had known they would come back to haunt him);

then, further maddened by her interruptions, he had rushed over to her and, taking her by the shoulders, shaken her violently, relishing the look of fear on her face as he hissed, "Shut up! Shut up! Shut up!"

That had only lasted a minute, of course. As soon as he let her go, Sarah had run upstairs and violently slammed the bedroom door. Vincent, who was following, opened it just in time to hear the bolt being pushed shut on the bathroom door. Sure enough, when he tried it, the door wouldn't open. The evening now sank into final, irretrievable disaster. Sarah refused to open the door or even speak, so Vincent was left alone to cope with the full burden of his rage. He was not quite furious enough to break down the door, but he couldn't just sit down and pick up a book either.

It did occur to him that he was likely to pay dearly for all this: Sarah would once again become sick, and it would be his fault. Finally, after pacing for a few minutes, he returned to the bathroom door and announced, in an icy voice, "I've had quite enough of all this. I'm leaving!"; but when he found himself in the street, full of anger and self-pity, he realized he had no place to go.

For quite a long time, he stood at the street corner, unable to decide what to do next. He wondered about a movie, but the thought of sitting in the dark watching a film he cared nothing about was simply repugnant. Still, he couldn't just keep standing there; he started to walk down Madison Avenue, passing several restaurants. He didn't stop; he had always disliked sitting in a restaurant by himself. Finally, he walked into a hamburger joint, a little place with a long counter and two tables in the back, and, as he sat, then ate, he realized with sickening certainty that, no matter how unbearable he had felt it all was before, things would be much worse now.

First, even though the fight with Sarah would have to be

resolved, the solution could only be pretense. Nothing would improve, that was certain. The current level of hostility between them would only be raised a degree, and Sarah would withdraw further still. There would be a long period during which she would not speak to him. She would refuse to cooperate at home, and thus every meal would become a problem. She would sleep late on the day the maid came so as to create an embarrassing situation. And, of course, she would refuse to go to the auction, leaving Vincent on his own to face people he either disliked or actually dreaded. He suddenly looked at the almost raw hamburger he was eating. Carefully, he put it back down on his plate and, leaving some money on the counter, walked out into the night.

André Germain would have been delighted, had he been able to see his son disconsolately walking down Madison Avenue. As it was, he had reason enough to feel pleased. As soon as he had left Copley, he had headed straight back to his hotel and, stopping in the lobby to call her, had gone up to Thérèse Vendel-Malnoury's room. He knocked and, without waiting for an answer, walked in. Thérèse, her face chalk-white as usual, sat writing at a table, her thin legs stretched out sideways.

"Oh, it's you," she said gruffly, but already André was speaking.

"A triumph, Thérèse, a triumph," he said with an expansive gesture and, interrupting himself to call room service for a bottle of Dom Pérignon, went on. "I told you it would work. I only wish you could have seen David's face when I finally brought the subject up. That little peddlar, he thinks he's so clever, so rich, you should just have seen him. Oh, and by the way, I can't wait until you visit his new establishment, Thérèse. It is simply grotesque.

He has no more idea of style or decoration than he does about manners. I tell you, if it weren't so sad, it would have made me laugh. When you think he's supposed to be the most successful dealer in New York. . . !"

"Yes, I know," Thérèse said anxiously, "but what happened?"

"Don't interrupt," André snapped back. "Can't you ever let me finish a sentence? Well, first, we talked about Jean's Chardin, and we agreed to offer a million two. Remind me to call Jean tomorrow morning and offer him a million one. We can use the extra hundred thousand for Barolo. Then David was called to the phone, so I had a good look around the sitting room. When I think of what I could have done with the money he spent—"

"Yes, but André—"

"Then he came back," André went on, raising his hand, and I told him I wanted sixty percent of the Bonnard profit. After all, I found it and sold it; he only provided half the money. We had quite a discussion and he wouldn't agree, so I smiled and said there was something else to discuss. I asked him if he was still on the list of Internal Revenue Service appraisers for works of art. He looked puzzled and said he was. Then I went on and said everyone knows how heavily the Art Dealers' Association relies on him, and what a pleasure it is to deal with someone who enjoys such universal respect. I could see he wasn't sure why I was complimenting him, and then I asked him if he remembered our Swiss arrangements, and whether the IRS and the Art Dealers' Association would think well of them."

"Oh, André, I wish you hadn't," Thérèse moaned. "You'll see, he'll manage not to work with us anymore."

"Be quiet," André answered savagely just as a knock came on the door. "Ah," he went on, "the champagne," and, tipping the waiter, he opened the bottle and poured. "To Fortune," he said, holding his glass high. "Well, you should have seen his face. He took a big pinch of that snuff of his and said he didn't understand. So I explained that I had copies of all the papers relating to our transactions in Switzerland, and that, if I were to make them public, they might prove embarrassing for him, Mind you, he did try to fight. I'll give him that. He said, well, he could offer the same information to the French tax people, but I answered I very much doubted he has the kind of documentation we have and that, besides, I was thinking of moving to New York anyway, where none of it would make the slightest difference. Oh, come on, Thérèse," he went on after a pause. "Don't look so glum. This is a celebration, you know."

Thérèse tried to speak, but again he held up his hand to stop her. "Later, later," he said impatiently. "When will you learn not to interrupt!" and, swallowing, he leaned over and poured more champagne.

At that moment, the phone rang. "It's Paris," Thérèse said.

"Now what?" André asked impatiently as Thérèse listened. She went on to give instructions about little Igor while he gestured furiously at her.

"I needed to know about Igor," Thérèse said, more firmly than usual, as she put down the phone.

André waved the topic away, and continued as if there had been no break. "So I said to him that I was perfectly willing to keep it all quiet, that I was far too good a friend to want to destroy his reputation, and that I looked forward to doing business with him in just the usual way. Then, when I could see he was completely puzzled, I said, 'By the way, David, I may have to be a little late with my half of the money for the Chardin. If it should become necessary, I assume you would not object to putting up the whole sum for a few weeks?' Well, it took him a while, but he finally understood. I tell you, Thérèse, I could have laughed out loud. Of course, he agreed; he had no choice. And we're going to make a very pretty profit without investing a penny!"

André stopped to sip champagne while Thérèse underwent a remarkable transformation: Her usual glum, worried expression vanished and was replaced by a shy, tender smile. She looked at her great man with admiration and, hands almost fluttering, patted her short hair into place. The jacket of her suit fell open as she leaned forward and almost whispered, "Oh, André! You did it. You were right," and, watching the satisfied smile now spreading over his face, she added, "You're so brilliant!"

"Come, come, Thérèse," André answered, looking modest. But before he could continue, she interrupted:

"Yes, André, yes, brilliant. When I think of what you've achieved, the magazine, the gallery . . ." Her usually white face was flushed now, an unbecoming shade of red; her flat chest heaved visibly under her tan silk blouse. André put down his glass. He had only to reach out to her. Coming over to him, she closed her arms around him with a little moan. "Now, André, now," she whispered into his ear and, moving back a step, she reached for snaps and buttons with clumsy fingers.

The sexual conjunction of Thérèse and André, made so very plain by the revelation of Igor's parentage, never ceased to amaze Vincent: Thérèse seemed so unattractive, so asexual, it was hard to picture anyone's wanting her. "Can you imagine," he said to Sarah, "making love to that corpse? You know, once I was at a party where Thérèse also showed up and there was dancing. I had no choice, I had to dance with her once, and it was like dancing with a skeleton. I could feel every bone in her back, moving and creaking: It was one of the most morbid experiences I've ever had, rather like the fourteenth-century Dance of Death in which everyone is a corpse. And then, if you picture them together...!" He paused to reflect. "Actually, if you think about it, it's really comical. She's so bony and he's quite fat—do you suppose her bones leave creases in him? I know that the strangest-looking people have sex ... but still! I should think he would practically smother her, and she must be so uncomfortable to lie on!"

"Well," Sarah answered helpfully, "maybe she sits on him."

Vincent laughed. "It's even worse! The other way, at least he can't see her much; but imagine staring at those absolutely flat breasts! I can picture nothing more anaphrodisiac. Still, they must do it, somehow. Igor is here to prove it."

Thérèse always felt wonderfully liberated after making love with André. Ever since she had surrendered herself to her first lover at the age of seventeen, she had resolutely kept her image of herself as the fearless intellectual, above common customs and prejudices, able to take her pleasure wherever she found it. Of course, it was painful when her lovers left her, especially since it seemed to happen so very regularly, but then she simply became more gruff, more commanding. She might not be very happy, but she was very bright; that was her chief attraction and her main defense; it also made it possible for her to find compensations in her professional life.

Still, as she began to work for André Germain, something had changed inside her. She continued, at least for a while, to have her brief affairs. She still barked at her subordinates; but, for the first time, she came up against a man to whom she did not feel superior. Even better, after a little time had elapsed, she had realized that her relationship with André was deeper, more satisfying than anything she had known before. It wasn't just that they worked well together, although that was important. She was intelligent enough, quick enough to be of real help to Germain. He was disorganized and lived by repeated improvisation; she was orderly, able to carry through long-range tasks by working hard day after day. She kept track of details and figures. More important, however, she understood André's concepts; she had the patience he lacked and without which his ideas would simply wither. Together with Viola, they published what was generally acknowledged to be the best art magazine on the market: alone, neither could have done it.

Very quickly, although she gloried in her position as André's right hand, Thérèse came to feel an altogether deeper satisfaction. Something within herself had been touched. She hardly knew what it was then, and she still wasn't fully quite conscious of it; but people who knew her well did not hesitate to describe it as total, absolute masochism. "There's nothing Thérèse loves more than suffering," Vincent had once told Sarah. "My father exploits her dreadfully. She works fourteen hours a day, seven days a week. I'm sure she's underpaid. She has virtually no life of her own. She's at the receiving end of half my father's fits; but every time she walks out of that office in tears, you can see that it's everything she needs. She's suffering all the time and couldn't be happier." That was before he knew that his father and Thérèse were sleeping together.

At first, André hardly even thought of his relationship with Thérèse as an affair. It seemed so logical: Thérèse did everything else for André; if she could see to it that the plumber fixed a leak in his country house, that the printer had the proofs ready on time, and that the more pressing bills were finally paid, she could also sleep with André. It had started on one of the monthly trips they made to Geneva, where the magazine was printed. When, at the end of the evening, André had followed her to her room and made love to her, she had let him. It seemed no more than an extension of her joyful servitude. Soon, although the actual sex remained infrequent, Thérèse had found a satisfaction much more enthralling than the very best orgasm: Her misery had been significantly deepened.

It was bad enough that André wasn't paying more attention to her as a woman; indeed, he had made love to her much as he would have to a whore; but, more important, she had instantly become a neglected rival, a third-place competitor. After all, there was Viola, so much prettier, more chic, more sophisticated, Viola who would lend Thérèse her dresses and jewelry to make her look a little better, Viola who understood the kind of elegant luxury that meant so much to André, Viola who patronized her. And while Thérèse knew that she had a rival in Viola and suffered accordingly, Viola, on the other hand, was blithely unaware that André had a mistress. Nor did Thérèse hope that André would one day leave Viola. He needed Viola far too much as an editor, as a hostess, as the person who could charm rich clients and keep Pierre-Paul Sanche from pulling out. And so, whenever Viola condescended to her, it was like a knife twisting inside. She couldn't tell Viola the truth; no, she must settle for being always second-best.

Fulfilling as her suffering continued to be, however, Thérèse soon found out that it led her to even greater depths of self-abasement: André was having affairs with still other women and telling her all about them as if, somehow, she didn't deserve even the pretense of fidelity. He still slept with her when they went to Geneva, but this only made her feel even more like a streetwalker, hardly human really, just a convenient body. And it wasn't just that he confided in her: It was her responsibility, every time, to organize the new affair. She must remember to send flowers to André's paramour and to take care of the florist's bill. Since André's schedule was so tight, she had to find time for him to see his new love and do it in a manner that would keep Viola from guessing the truth. Thérèse listened as André told her how attracted he was to his new mistress, how pretty, or bright, or elegant she was. Of course, Thérèse cried long and bitterly afterward. Tears came to her eyes in the office as she remembered that, at that very moment, André was being driven to the meeting she herself had arranged; not even the thought that he was also unfaithful to Viola could console her.

Still, Thérèse knew she had become absolutely indispensable to André. He would obviously never marry her; she would simply continue to be frantically busy, thoroughly miserable, yet perfectly happy. Then came her pregnancy. She said—and it was true—that she had, for many years, thought she was infertile. Who, at forty-two, expected to become pregnant? But she had. (Vincent, when he thought about it, could not help wondering whether it might not be an exotic form of psychosomatic illness. After all, if people can create all kinds of symptoms in themselves, why couldn't a woman control her inner muscles so as to help the sperm reach the ovum?) At first, of course, it seemed as if nothing would change. Thérèse had agreed to say she had been made pregnant by an old flame during a sudden, renewed encounter. It was just another way to suffer.

And, in fact, everything remained the same. Thérèse behaved exactly as if she weren't pregnant, went on working as hard as usual. In good time, she hired a full-time nurse to take care of the child. She didn't even consider staying home. As for André, he pretended that it had nothing to do with him. He was willing to raise Thérèse's salary —after all, the nurse must be paid—but that was that. The baby would bear its mother's name, and the birth certificate would list the father as unknown. It would all be kept quiet. Only, of course, the news had promptly leaked out. Thérèse was a model of discretion, but even she could not help telling a very few friends and the tidbit was too flavorful to be kept secret. In no time at all, people were making nasty cracks all over Paris.

Still, André did not mind. It was, if anything, rather flattering. He was fifty-seven and had the best of both worlds. Everyone knew the child was his, yet he did not have to acknowledge it or incur any obligations. Of course, it might be awkward if Viola found out; but André felt quite sure he could control the situation. Viola, as he put it to himself, knew which side her bread was buttered on. Within a month of the baby's birth, he had launched his affair with Coche del Mancha, forcing poor Thérèse to take up her usual flower-sending duties. What he failed to perceive, though, was that he was no longer the unrivaled center of her life. Slowly, very slowly, she started to shift her loyalty to baby Igor. Some days, instead of lunching with André, Thérèse actually went home; or she would cut short the evenings she normally spent listening to him and leave as early as nine. She even *talked* about that uninteresting little lump of flesh, much to André's exasperation. He didn't worry, though. It was obvious she would soon get over it.

It was time for Vincent to keep that appointment with his father; but, before leaving the house, he tried speaking to Sarah. He had been quite right, though: She was determined to exploit her grievances as fully as possible. It was true that he had shaken her, and he felt deeply ashamed of himself and of the self-pity that had fueled the scene. His shame soon melted away, however, when Sarah went on behaving as if she were the victim of unexampled violence. The very fact that she was making life so unpleasant, and for such a long time, seemed to absolve him. Besides, he was owed some compensation, he felt, for having resumed at once all his burdens. If he could endure his life and not complain, he was owed decent behavior—and he wasn't getting it.

It was already very plain that Sarah wouldn't attend the auction. She had retired to her bed in ostensible pain, pointing out that she was, once again, unable to paint. It was so clearly Vincent's fault, she said. Without that scene, she would be at her easel. Once again, he had stifled her creativity.

Usually, when Vincent was upset about something, he took a taxi: Somehow, the time spent getting to his destination seemed unbearably long. Today, however, Vincent walked the twelve blocks to the Stanhope, where his father was staying. He needed time to repeat to himself that he was being treated unfairly, that he bore an immense burden; and then, too, the whole prospect of the auction appalled him. Now he would be alone with all those people he disliked.

At least, he thought, as he walked into the Stanhope and went over to the elevator, he had scored one little point: Ever since he had moved, his father had asked to see his apartment, and Vincent had always refused. He knew that his father would automatically criticize everything, and also that he minded nothing so much as distance.

When the door opened, their greeting was as cool as usual. "Oh, so it's you," the father said.

"Apparently," the son replied. "Why did you want to see me?"

André smiled and waved to a chair with such good humor that Vincent knew he must have something unpleasant to say; sure enough, it came after the first skirmish. First, André complained about Vincent's insisting on coming to the hotel instead of receiving him at home.

"It was more convenient that way," Vincent said curtly.

"Convenient! I wonder what you're trying to hide from me," André answered nastily.

"You'll just have to keep wondering, won't you?" Vincent said, feeling that he was having the better of the argument.

His father went on: "I had a long meeting with David Copley yesterday."

"Oh," Vincent said during the long pause, his right hand stroking his face.

"Yes. Of course, we talked about all kinds of business; you wouldn't be interested; but then, at one point, I mentioned you. It's very curious, I don't know what it is, but he seems to have something against you. I wanted to bring you over to meet him, but he was obviously reluctant. That's why I decided to see you, to tell you that you had better not try to make contact with him."

Vincent almost laughed out loud. So that was his father's jab: He was meant to feel rejected. "You needn't have bothered," he said, his voice formally polite. "You do business with him, I know. And I have no intention of mixing myself up in your affairs. Of course, I understand why you couldn't wait to tell me. So nice of you."

There was a thunderous silence. André flushed darkly. "Are you trying to make fun of me?" he asked.

"Fun? Me? Why should you think that?" Vincent said, still smiling; then, pleased with himself, he asked, "And how is little Igor?" Before André could answer, the door opened and Thérèse, looking breathless, rushed into the room. She stopped dead in her tracks when she saw Vincent.

"Well," Vincent said, "I see you're busy. So am I."
Nodding coldly to Thérèse, he walked out.

André Germain burst into a rage as soon as the door
closed. "The insolence!" he shouted. "That damned pup
was laughing at me!"

"I'm not surprised," Thérèse said fiercely. "He has no
gratitude. When I think of what you've done for him. He
ought to worship you."

"*Worship* me!" André said in a disillusioned voice. "I'd
settle for a little respect. Do you know, Thérèse, I don't
think he likes me?"

"Well," Thérèse answered, almost purring, "he told me
once, you remember, all about how difficult he found you.
And then there was the time when you decided not to let
him have those Bonnards he was counting on. He was
furious then. I don't know why you even bother with him."

"How can I help it?" André said, thoroughly enjoying
himself now. "He is my son, after all. And I am the most
loving of fathers. God, if I ever get my hands on the little
wretch, I'll teach him something about gratitude, I promise
you!"

"Yes, André," Thérèse said happily. There was a short
silence. "Now, about the auction. You've seen the Renoir
drawing. What should we do?"

"Buy it, of course. It's a masterpiece—but those stupid
Americans will never understand it—the finest still life he
ever did. All they want here is fat nudes. We should be
able to get it at a very good price."

"But, André, what about the money? And who will we
sell it to?"

"The money! The money! That's all you ever talk about!
We'll sell it to the Muttonis, that's who! Or to Walder, in
Zurich."

This time Thérèse was not to be quashed. "Andre," she

said firmly, though tears were glistening in her eyes, "you know we have no ready money at all. You really can't put Pierre-Paul off any longer."

"Oh, can't I, though!" André gave a nasty laugh. "The day when I can't control that limp rag hasn't come yet. I'll just tell him I'll have it transferred to his Swiss account in ten days. Then, in two or three weeks, we'll have the Desroches money and see what we want to do."

"He's coming soon, you know," Thérèse said. "Do you want me to be here?"

"No, better not. After all, I don't want to humiliate him before a woman."

Pierre-Paul Sanche looked nervous and wan as he came into André's room. Everything about him was a little off: His clothes were expensive and well cut, but they didn't quite fit, and they didn't quite match; his dark good looks, his pitch-black eyes looked somehow faded. It always did André good to see it all.

Sanche collapsed into a chair as soon as he had shaken André's hand and launched into his usual catalogue of complaints. The stock market was doing badly, and he was losing money; the painters were taking twice as long to finish his Paris apartment as they had said they would, and he didn't know where he would go when he left New York. No, Zurich was no good either; there, it was the plumbing that was being fixed. And then, he said, he couldn't sleep; he had the most terrible insomnia; he was exhausted all the time. Well, it was no wonder, when his stocks were doing so badly. His broker just couldn't seem to manage his money. In no time he would be ruined. And on top of everything, Nini was being difficult. Well, at least now she was seeing her family.

As usual, André let the flood pour out, nodding, approving; but when Sanche asked about his Degas, everything changed. "I need the money, you know, André," he moaned. "I just don't know what to do anymore. And it is fifty thousand dollars. You said you would pay me now."

"And so I will," André said amiably, "so I will. I didn't want to waste even a day after I received the money myself, so I've arranged for an immediate transfer to your Swiss account. You should have it in all in about ten days."

"Ten days! Switzerland! But, André—"

"Come now, Pierre-Paul, don't whine! I told you the money would be ready about now and so it is. I've even gone out of my way to make it easier for you."

"Yes, André, thank you, but I need it right now."

"Oh, really, Pierre-Paul, you can't tell me you're broke! Pull yourself together! You can get some money here."

Sanche, biting his lower lip, stood up and started to pace up and down, with André watching him. Finally he stopped and turned to André.

"You know," he said with a visible effort, "we must come to an agreement about *Voir*. It's not right for me to be backing both the gallery and the magazine without playing any role at all. Nini is right—"

"No, she's not," André interrupted. "Look, Pierre-Paul, let's face it: You're simply not qualified. You know nothing of either publishing or the art market. And if you think for a moment that I'm going to saddle myself with an incompetent—no, don't interrupt—when I already have more work than I can possibly do, you're very wrong. You can't buy your way into *Voir*, and that's that. Besides, Pierre-Paul, there's nothing wrong with being the money behind a great cultural enterprise. You should be content with what you've made possible. And, between us, I think you should be more forceful with Nini—"

Suddenly, to André's visible stupefaction, Sanche shouted, "How dare you!" and walked out of the room, slamming the door behind him.

"Well," André said aloud to himself, "he must be growing balls"; but when Thérèse answered his summons, it was to face the flood of reproaches André poured on others when he wasn't really pleased with himself.

SIX

Despite the cold steady rain, at eight-thirty that evening Madison Avenue, around Sixty-fifth Street, hummed with activity. Taxis were stopping to let people off, and lines of long black limousines with reflective glass windows moved slowly toward the middle of the block to unload their fragile cargo. This was the evening of Russell and Company's spring auction.

There was no mistaking the event: In the lobby, an international crowd waited for the two small elevators. Vincent, feeling alone and upset, could hear French spoken on his right and Italian behind. There, two rows ahead, David Copley was chatting with Bill Rosenstein as Roberta Boxer listened in. A little farther away was Norman Peters, the California magnate and collector, looking pinched and sullen. The deafening noise of endlessly multiplied chatter made Vincent even more resentful; he put on a look of careful indifference, but, when he saw his father entering the lobby, he quickly redirected his gaze. There was nothing Vincent hated more, really, than this most glamorous of art events. Tonight, as famous paintings went on the block, the prices would soar; millionaires and dealers would vie for the prizes; women in mink and diamonds would try to outbid one another: The art world was giving itself a show. It might be fun, Vincent reflected, inching closer to the elevators, if he were a complete outsider: After all, the sense of excitement was contagious.

That feeling was strengthened when he stepped out of the elevator on the fourth floor. The main part of the auction room was reserved for the elite: collectors, dealers, museum directors, or simply people with a lot of money. Vincent's own seat was all the way at the back of the balcony, and he resented being there. Still, at the moment, the spectacle attracted his attention. Up ahead, all the way at the front of the hall, the mahogany podium was still empty, but already the tables on each side were occupied. Three young women and two young men were sitting behind stacks of papers talking to one another and leaning across to the crowd. Near the side door, two men stood ready to bring in the paintings, and people still poured in under the bright light, chatting, nodding, looking for their places. The hall itself was filled with row after row of carefully marked folding chairs, red velveteen and gilded metal, but already they were disappearing below rows of heads.

The auction was not to start until nine. Vincent, looking at his watch, was appalled to see there was still ten minutes to go. Once again, he felt violently out of place. He started to leaf nervously through his catalogue, but the print seemed too spidery to be read. He looked up again at the crowd still filing in, at the brown velvet on the walls, but without finding relief. Now his arms were crossed against his chest, his right hand clutching his side as if, by squeezing, he could collapse himself, make himself so small that he would disappear; but he was forced to unfold himself as Sophia Lyon walked past and waved to him. He stood up awkwardly, clutching coat and catalogue against his knees; and even as he smiled and chatted and watched the exotic-looking young woman, slim, dark, and large-eyed; even as he was saying that, no, Sarah wasn't coming, she had the flu and, yes, of course, he would convey Sophia's greetings to her; even then he had the feeling that his face, his voice were somehow detached from him. It was as if the conversation were taking place on a stage in front of him, as if he were a kind of screen on which something illusory, a film, were being projected while the real Vincent stood behind watching, saying over and over to himself: What am I doing here? What am I doing here?

Sophia finally passed on and Vincent sat down, his arms folding back across his chest almost automatically, his surface shrinking again. For the thousandth time, he wondered why he was so uncomfortable. After all, he was a dealer. Attending the auction was a professional obligation; it would be an intolerable loss of face if, the next day, he was unable to discuss it with other dealers. Besides, in the second part of the auction, there was one work among the contemporary American paintings on which he must actually bid. Still, he felt as if all this were a party at which he didn't belong. In a world of professionals, he was an outsider. And, in fact, he eschewed both the camaraderie that linked other dealers and their permanent interest in business. The very superiority he felt as a result, his awareness that he knew so much more, had wider interests, understood the world better—all that put him at a disadvantage. Vincent felt he must not let the others see that side of himself; but precisely because he was so much less interested in the art world, in sales, in money than they were, he automatically felt he lacked weight, presence, once he was within their sphere. Always aware that he wasn't a real dealer, and unable to draw on his real sources of strength, he knew himself to be a sham, inferior to all the people attending the auction. At that moment, before the auction started, fiercely, desperately, he knew how much he didn't belong.

Now the auctioneer, his sleek hair shining under the lights, was standing in his dark gray suit behind the podium and reading out in a rapid voice all the rules of the auction. Throughout the hall, people were turning from their neighbors, sighing, coughing, and fluttering open their catalogues. Vincent reached into his inside pocket for his pen and prepared to freeze: This was an auction in which bids would be conveyed by the smallest, least noticeable gestures. There would be nothing so vulgar as hands being waved. At the very most, people would briefly hold their pencils as high as their forehead. The major collectors, the most important dealers, would only nod, almost imperceptibly, scratch their noses, wink. Vincent knew perfectly well, of course, that from his seat in the balcony it would take more than a nod to attract the auctioneer's attention. He was no Norton Simon, whose every gesture would be watched. Still, he would sit in perfect and painful immobility until the picture then being auctioned was sold.

The auctioneer announced that this hall was in TV contact with a similar hall in London, that people there would be bidding by phone; and then the first painting was brought up to the big easel. Clearly, the tradition according to which auctions must be started slowly prevailed: It was a small but exquisite Boudin. Ladies in crinolines sat on the beach at Deauville with the sea in the distance; and a huge, transparent blue sky, with its fleeting white clouds, occupied most of the space. Already the auctioneer, having briefly announced the painting, was lapsing into his rhythmic patter: "What am I bid for this exceptional Boudin? Fifty thousand, I have fifty thousand on my left; fifty-five now. Sixty, sixty near the door, will you give me sixty-five? Sixty-five, on the left again. Seventy-five, seventy-five, all done. . . . Eighty near the door. Eighty-five, eighty-five, ninety. It's against you, sir, at ninety, then. Going, at ninety, at ninety," and, as he banged his gavel down, the two men at his side quickly removed the painting. The auctioneer wrote something down, and the people at the side tables scribbled fiercely away.

Carefully, Vincent wrote down $90,000 in his catalogue, turned the page, and looked up timidly as a new painting passed onto the easel. The auctioneer started again: "Forty-five thousand, fifty, fifty . . ." Already the auction was warming up; it wasn't just the heat of too many people too close together, but a kind of tangible tension, an electricity. Even Vincent, who didn't want to be there, couldn't help feeling the excitement as the paintings changed and the bids went up.

Now the first of the major works was brought out: a big Monet all in blues and greens with purple highlights for the water lilies, and the crowd rustled. "A highly important Monet," the auctioneer was saying rapidly, "the pond at Giverny. We'll start this one at two hundred and fifty thousand. . . . Three hundred. . . . Three hundred and fifty. . . ." Vincent, although he was watching from the balcony, was quite unable to see any signaling. Within two minutes, the bidding had reached five hundred and fifty thousand dollars—where it remained, suspended, for another minute. Then saying: "Six hundred. At six hundred, six hundred, gone," the auctioneer sharply brought down his gavel, and the painting was removed.

A kind of hunger became tangible throughout the hall as the Monet was replaced by a Degas, the Degas by a Pissarro, the Pissarro by a Cézanne. You could feel them almost physically, the huge sums of money, as the bids came and went, lasting only a few seconds. Vincent, writing the prices down in his catalogue, was swept into that great wave beating against the walls as millions of dollars ac-

cumulated under the auctioneer's gavel. All the money in
the world, it seemed, had come that night to Russell and
Company. As canvas followed canvas, the competition
became even fiercer, bids dramatically telephoned from
London competing against those of the people in New
York. A dead silence fell upon the crowd as the last of the
major paintings to be sold that night, a late Van Gogh
landscape, came on the block. Within four minutes it had
been bought by someone, down below in the room, for a
million and a half. For a moment everything seemed
suspended. A million and a half, a million and a half . . .
Vincent could actually see the people repeating the figure
to themselves. Then, suddenly, a loud buzzing broke out
as the hundreds of spectators turned to their companions,
whispering, "A million and a half!" It was a new high, more
money than had ever before been paid for a Van Gogh, for
a post-impressionist. Already the small canvas was being
removed. "A million five hundred thousand dollars," a
man behind Vincent repeated slowly. "Can you imagine?
a million five hundred thousand dollars!"

It was the end of the first part of the auction. Before the
second set of paintings could be offered, the auctioneer left
the podium. After ten minutes, he was replaced by another
man, almost as impressive but perhaps not quite as sleek.
Downstairs, a few people were getting up and filing out,
either because they had come only to buy one of the
nineteenth-century works or because the main climax of
the evening had already been reached: There would be no
more million-dollar sales that night. Suddenly there were
fewer mink coats draped over the backs of the little folding
metal chairs, fewer diamonds sparkling amid the emptier
space. Still, two-thirds of the public was still there, opening
a new catalogue, ready for the first number, a Franz Kline
drawing.

The rest of the evening was devoted to a large group of modern American paintings. Toward the middle, there were some important works: two de Koonings, a Motherwell, a big Frank Stella. Then came a slow letdown until, finally, the auction petered out with Tworkow and Nadelman drawings. Some excitement remained until the major pieces were sold, and then the room began slowly to empty. Still, Vincent stayed. He had a job to do. He had to buy a Partridge.

John Partridge, Olga's lover, was highly successful. Every painting he could turn out was promptly sold, either at his gallery or right at the studio. The fact that his production was enormous, that he painted as much in a year as other painters in a lifetime, did not seem to deter his devoted fans. If, by mischance, however, the very same canvases came up at auction, they suddenly became undesirable and might well sell for as little as a tenth of their usual market price. This, of course, had to be prevented at any cost. A collector who read that a big Partridge had just sold at Russell's for a $1,000 when he had, just three months earlier, paid $10,000 for the same size work, would not be a happy man. Two or three price collapses like that might be enough to kill off the demand since, to outsiders, auction prices make the market.

Partridge was far too shrewd to let this happen. Like many of his colleagues, he arranged for people not officially connected with him to bid on whatever work came up for sale. It was not enough to have his dealer; someone else had to be counterbidding so that the price would rise close to the current rate. The arrangement was simple and effective: If the painting on the block was of the $10,000 size, then John Stuart, Partridge's dealer, and the hidden friend would bid against each other until the price reached about $8,500. Whoever made the bid closest to that sum would officially own the painting while, in reality, it was Partridge's own money that would go to pay for it. As for the painting itself, it would be discreetly taken off the market for a year or two.

Now it was Vincent's turn to help Partridge. A few days earlier, the painter had called him and explained that one of his works was coming up for auction. "Of course," Partridge had said in an unctuous voice, "you of all people understand how important it is to keep the prices up—and since, surely, you'll be at Russell's that night, I would like to ask you for a great favor: Could you bid against John Stuart?" Vincent had naturally accepted.

"What else can I do?" he had said to Sarah. "After all, I have no reason to refuse him."

"But I thought you didn't approve of fixing prices?" Sarah had asked.

"No," Vincent had replied, slowly rubbing his nose, "of course, I don't. It's dishonest. It warps the market, and the collectors—most of whom don't know about these shenanigans—end up as the victims."

"Then," Sarah said in a reasonable voice, "why do you do it if you think it's wrong?"

"You know very well why. If I had said no, Partridge would have assumed I had something against him. It's not that I actually like him, but we're supposed to be friends, and it's awkward because of Olga."

"So, then, you choose to be dishonest," Sarah had answered. Now Vincent wondered. Compromise, after all, was part of any human activity. Besides, anyone who bought a Partridge deserved to have this kind of trick pulled on him; but, as the moment came closer when he must raise his hand, he felt increasingly uneasy. No matter how he looked at it, no matter how widespread the practice might be, still, in the last analysis, it was dishonest. Was he therefore no better than all those crooks, those lying, cheating little dealers, people like Poppea Vlassoff for whom he felt such contempt?

The painting, when it finally came up, was clearly one of Partridge's afterthoughts, another proof that he was producing far more than he should. The colors were garish and ugly, the composition a dreadful mess. The thickly covered canvas looked as if it had had globs of leftover paint thrown at it, then spread with a palette knife. A nasty purple streak collided with an orange zone, only to meet a dirty green oblong. It seemed incredible to Vincent that anyone would ever have bought it; but, as the time came to bid, all thought vanished. Vincent felt gripped by an almost unbearable tension. In the few seconds before the auctioneer spoke up, a thousand fantasies raced across Vincent's mind: What if he didn't bid fast enough and the painting sold for $2,000 or $3,000? What if, in a state of madness, he went on bidding too high, too long, above the agreed $5,000, and Partridge refused to pay the inflated price? What if this were the wrong painting? And just as he was telling himself not to be idiotic, the voice started.

It was all different in the half-empty room. Like his colleague's, the auctioneer's voice fell into the usual sing-song rhythm, but there was no tension, hardly even any interest. "Five hundred dollars," the voice said. "Five hundred. Am I offered five hundred now? Five hundred." Obstinately, Vincent kept his hand down and waited for John Stuart to start the bidding. "Five hundred," the auctioneer repeated with a nuance of finality; then, with a rising inflexion, "Five fifty. Five fifty in the back of the room, six hundred now," as Vincent raised his pen. "Seven hundred. Will you give me a thousand?" Again, Vincent lifted his hand. "A thousand in the balcony. Twelve hundred downstairs, thirteen now . . ." until, slowly, step by hesitant step, the price reached five thousand dollars. The last bid had been Vincent's, and one of the ushers came

up to him with a blank card on which he wrote "John
Stuart Gallery."

When the phone rang, the next morning, Vincent was
fast asleep and alone. He sat up quickly, reaching for the
receiver with one hand and turning off the alarm with
the other. Any remaining drowsiness was dispelled when the
voice on the other end said furiously: "That Magritte
gouache you sold me—Derek Boyle says it's a fake."

Of course, Vincent promptly denied this and added that
he would buy it back that very day; now, on his way to
Poppea Vlassoff's, he was alternately fuming and berating
himself for having trusted her enough to have bought
something from her. As he walked over, he felt an unpleasant chill: If this was a fake, what about the three
Ernsts? They, too, had a Mundberg certificate.

He was all set to confront Poppea and demand his money
back as soon as she opened the door, but he stopped dead
when he saw her: Her clothes were in even greater disarray
than usual, and she had a black eye. At first, in the darkness
of the hallway, Vincent thought he must have made a
mistake; but, as they came into the living room, there was
no longer any doubt, especially since Poppea's left arm was
marked by a huge, dark bruise. Even before Vincent could
speak, Poppea looked at him.

"I'm going to kill him," she said calmly.

"Kill him?"

"Yes, Mark Spence. The shit who did this. He beat me
up, the fucking bastard. He came up here and beat me up,
but he won't get away with it. I'll sue him for everything
he's got."

"Who's Mark Spence? And are you all right? Have you
seen a doctor?"

"Sure, I'm all right," Poppea said darkly, and Vincent noticed that the bruise on her arm was almost arrow-shaped, pointing down to the dark spots scattered on her left hand. "I told you about Mark Spence, that dealer in Boston. He's the one who said the Klee I sold him for a client was a fake."

"And that's why he beat you up?"

"Well, no," Poppea said, looking down at her arm. "It was because I wouldn't take it back. Anyway," she added with satisfaction, "he didn't get away with it. I kicked him in the balls so hard he was doubled up on the floor for at least five minutes. That's when I called the cops. So he heard me phone and went away."

Slowly, Vincent was beginning to see the light. "Poppea," he asked, "that Klee, is it the one you found in Milan? The one I told you was a fake?"

"What if it is?"

"Well, then," Vincent said, "I've got bad news. The Magritte gouache you sold me—you know the one—I'm afraid it's a fake, too."

Poppea stood up suddenly, and Vincent stared at her heavy breasts moving under the thin T-shirt. "So what!" she said.

"What do you mean, 'So what?' It's a fake, Poppea. I'm on my way to buy it back from my client, and I expect you to reimburse me."

Poppea, still standing, laughed. "At least you're not beating me up," she said, and added, "Oh, don't look so shocked. Sure I'll give you back the money, early next week, okay? I'm getting paid for something I sold yesterday."

"All right," Vincent answered, "but no later. And you remember, it was six thousand."

Poppea shook her head and walked over to the plants.

"They all croak on me," she said vaguely; then, brightening, she asked, "So how did you like the auction last night? I hear all the big privates were there."

"Didn't you go?"

"Nah, I got busy at the last moment and then Mark Spence came up."

Vincent looked at her black eye again; the purple edges looked almost like makeup. Feeling a little foolish, he said: "Poppea, except for the fact that, of course, he should never have touched you, he isn't all wrong, you know. I told you in Italy, you have to be responsible for everything you sell. You really owe him his money back."

"I don't owe the jerk a thing," Poppea said shrilly. "Anyway, I wouldn't have let him in, except I thought he was spending the night here."

"What happened, exactly?"

"Well, some bastard told his dumb client the Klee must be a fake because he'd seen the same one hanging at Princeton, so the client asked for his money back. And Mark doesn't have a dime, so he came to me." She stopped to break off a few dead leaves from her plants. "They always croak," she repeated absently. Sitting down next to Vincent on the couch, she added: "It's a shame, because Mark was helping me with my art fund."

"Your what?" Vincent exclaimed.

"Yeah, sure, my art fund. See, I figured if we got in some privates from out of town, it would look more serious, so Mark was going to bring in his client, the one with the Klee, for fifty thousand."

"I don't suppose he will now!"

"No. Also Mark's got a cousin in graduate school who's helping me with the statistics. Oh, fuck it all!" Poppea said savagely. "I never knew it was so hard to be a dealer."

Vincent laughed. "It's not so easy," he said, standing up.

"Look, Poppea," he went on, "I have to go and pick up the Magritte, but I'll be back this afternoon."

André Germain was not the man to forgo any of life's amenities, so lunchtime found him walking into La Goulue, a new, chic restaurant just off Madison Avenue patronized by successful art dealers and rich New Yorkers. He stopped and looked around: In Paris, he often had lunch in a similar restaurant with Thérèse. I don't like it here, he thought. I shouldn't have to walk in alone like this. What I need is a pretty, elegant woman; still, even Thérèse is better than no one. He made up for his mood by stopping at several tables on the way to his own.

"I have to speak to you, André," Thérèse was saying when the waiter came to take the order. She turned to him. "A very underdone steak. No potatoes. And a salad."

"Madame!" said the horrified waiter.

"Yes," Thérèse repeated, "a very underdone steak. You have steaks, I suppose?"

"Yes, Madame."

"You've heard what Madame ordered," André said firmly. "I'll have the fish terrine and the *boeuf en daube*. And bring us the wine list." Then, turning to Thérèse, he laughed. "They're not used to you yet. These New York restaurants! They take themselves so seriously," and, looking toward the door, he waved at David Copley, who was just coming in.

Thérèse stared at him briefly. "You're behaving just as if everything were normal," she said admiringly.

"Of course I am. Just a new kind of normalcy, that's all," André replied, smiling expansively. "You wanted to talk to me about something?"

"Yes," Thérèse said, curtly. She waited as the fish terrine

was set, with a flourish, before André, and went on: "It's about Igor."

"Is he sick?"

"No. But, André, what are you going to do about him?" Thérèse asked, her eyes already filling with tears.

There was a pause as André stared at her in annoyance. She really looks impossible, he thought, watching the chalk-white face with its hollow cheeks, the stiff, straight hair, and the red hands twisting her handkerchief. "Do?" he snapped. "Do? I don't see that there is anything to be done. He has a nurse, doesn't he? What more does he need?" Tossing down his glass of wine, he added furiously, "I thought we understood each other!"

For a moment Thérèse, her face a mask of terror, sat staring down at her empty plate; but, as the waiter, lips pinched, served her bloody steak, she began to recover her courage. This was a public place, after all; André couldn't storm at her in front of all these people who knew him. Looking up at him, she said, "Yes. About his father. What will I tell him?"

André laughed nastily. "Tell him? He's only eleven months old!"

"Yes, but soon—"

"Really, Thérèse," André interrupted, "I thought you were more sensible than that. You know very well that if there's one thing I can't stand, it's a scene in public."

"Yes, André," Thérèse whispered and, lifting her handkerchief to her face, she blew her nose vigorously.

André was not, however, so easily satisfied. "You know very well what the situation is," he went on angrily. Thérèse did not, in fact, know what he meant, and remained silent. "I always think of you as a sensible woman who doesn't fuss, unlike Viola or my first wife, who was always making scenes in public. You're not going to disappoint me, I hope?" he added ominously.

"No, André. I'm sorry," said Thérèse, looking down at her steak.

André relaxed. "I don't know how you can always eat those steaks," he said, to show forgiveness. Thérèse answered, barking as if nothing had happened, "You know I can't digest anything else."

When Vincent went home that afternoon, he found Sarah miraculously recovered and obviously determined to be pleasant. She was sitting in the dining room, drinking coffee, and amazed him by asking if he wanted a cup.

"Sure," he answered, "but don't move. I'll get it myself."

It became quickly apparent that what Sarah had in mind was an exchange: Vincent would admit he had been wrong in the quarrel, wrong to shake her; she would then forget her vendetta, and they would be reconciled. For a minute, Vincent was uncertain about paying her price: Why should he do the groveling? But then, he thought, continuing the fight was hardly worth the trouble; so, sitting across the table from her, he admitted his wrongs.

"All right," Sarah said, "but you have to promise never to shake me up like that again." Once more, Vincent complied. But when Sarah added, "I don't know what to wear for John's party tonight," Vincent was once again overwhelmed with the unreality of their relationship: If their great fight came to an end because Sarah meant to enjoy herself that night at Partridge's party, then nothing had any meaning. The hostility and the reconciliation became a stylized choreography that might do very well on the stage under the lights but could never pretend to reality. Once again, like that time at Kennedy, Vincent looked at Sarah with a new eye; and once again he saw a stranger.

Still, that was all a moment's reflection. Already Sarah was discussing just what she would wear, long dress or

short, her jewelry, her hairdo, and asking Vincent how
he intended to dress. Like Partridge's other parties, this one
was to be glamorous. The women would dress up, but it was
not a black-tie affair. As he thought about it, Vincent felt
his stomach sinking: He hated large, disorganized parties
where either you didn't know enough people and might find
yourself suddenly without anyone to talk to, or, even if you
did, the noise and the crush were such that conversation
was replaced by an exchange of inanities. Then, too, it was
sure to be one of those buffet suppers where the guests
struggle to carry an overloaded plate, a fork, a knife, a
paper napkin, a piece of bread, and a glass of wine to some
low table where, crouching in hideously uncomfortable
positions, they fill up hastily, longing only for a proper
meal.

As soon as Sarah left a lull in the conversation, he said
gloomily: "The truth is, I wish we didn't have to go
tonight."

"Why not?"

"You know how I hate those big parties."

"But it's not like going someplace where you don't know
anyone," Sarah answered. "After all, it's Olga's house as
well, and it'll be full of art world regulars. Besides, you
aways complain beforehand and enjoy yourself once you're
there."

She wasn't completely wrong. Olga and Partridge knew
how to give a party: There was usually just the right mix
of artists, dealers, and collectors so the art world could
indulge in its two favorite subjects: itself and money. This
was leavened with young and pretty girls who came alone
but left with escorts, and unattached men, Some of the
women wore real diamonds; others carried their bohemian
look as if it were a choice and not a necessity. Partridge's
ex-wife would be there, and a number of Olga's ex-lovers.
There would be the usual contingent of gay men, some

looking desperately macho in leather jackets, jeans, and
boots, others wearing beautifully, fashionably cut suits and
Gucci loafers.

"There will be variety in everything," Vincent said
during the long taxi ride downtown, "except the conversation," and Sarah gave him a warning look.

He found some comfort now in looking at his wife. Her
hair was swept up in a complicated chignon adorned with
a Victorian garnet comb Vincent had recently given her;
she had spent almost an hour doing (and undoing) her eye
makeup; and she was wearing a splendid wine-red Turkish
caftan of heavy velvet with gold embroidery and lace edges
they had bought together in the Bazaar in Istanbul. Its
barbaric splendor really belonged to Sarah; her dark complexion and Mediterranean face appeared exotic, and en-
hanced by the sumptuous robe. She knew that everyone
would notice and compliment her. Vincent, too, was
pleased: Making an entrance with a spectacularly beautiful
woman on his arm gave him assurance and security.

The taxi reached SoHo and drew up to the newly
painted building on the Bowery where Partridge had his
studio. The broad avenue looked indescribably shabby;
although it was not yet as bad as it became two or three
blocks farther down, the sidewalk was littered with dirty
paper and broken bottles. Garbage cans gaped wide open
so that, even on this cool night, the stench was revolting;
even the little entrance hall to the building, paved and
walled in murky green tiles, was anything but pleasant. As
they waited for the elevator to come down, Vincent hoped
they would not have to share it with other people
whom they hardly knew or didn't know at all; at last, the
doors opened. Already, as the elevator began to move
up, they could hear the roar of the party.

The babble grew deafening as Vincent and Sarah walked
into Partridge's studio. Their first impression was of a

huge white hall; the eighteen-foot-high ceiling was supported by a row of slender cast-iron columns and pierced by three large skylights. At each end of the big room—it was over a hundred feet long—tall windows crisscrossed with wire and burglar alarms were covered with beige Japanese blinds. Partridge's paintings covered the walls, except for an area on the side where, behind a golden screen, a bed and a table were hidden. Across the room, in front of the open kitchen, a bar had been set up near a huge table covered with food; both were surrounded by a jostling crowd.

Vincent took a deep breath as they stood just inside the door; already Sarah was turning away, so he launched himself forward into the din. Everywhere, small groups of people clutching their wineglasses were shouting at one another.

Even though all the paintings on display were new, no one pretended to pay them any attention so, with a last look at them, Vincent started to search for a familiar face. In no time he was greeting Mrs. Melville, one of Partridge's most faithful collectors, who promptly started to describe her latest acquisition.

"The ground is pale blue," she said busily, "with a red and purple design. You know, Vincent, the funny thing—although, of course, I would never dare tell it to John—is that it fits in exactly with the colors in my living room! So I took away that other painting of his I had there—you remember, the one with the green and yellow—and replaced it with this new one; and it looks so right. And now he's giving me a watercolor for my arts club! We're having an auction, you know, just before Christmas. . . ."

Vincent was nodding amiably when suddenly he saw a gleam appear in Mrs. Melville's eye. "Speaking of the auction . . ." she said, purposefully, but already Vincent was replying that, alas, he never dealt in contemporary art anymore.

At that moment, luckily for Vincent, Iris Johnson walked by. Vincent, calling her name, went over and kissed her. She looked separate somehow from the whole, noisy scene. Continuing what was obviously an ongoing monologue, she said, ". . . And if I closed off the downstairs, I could make it into a special gallery where I would show only very expensive paintings, by appointment. You understand, Vincent, it would be like being a private dealer, only in a gallery."

"Yes, Iris," Vincent answered calmly—he was said to be one of the few people in New York who could keep up with Iris's sometimes cryptic utterances.

Anxious to break the flow, however, he asked: "How's Freddy?"

"Wonderful," Iris said with a smile, "but she misses you."

"Oh, I miss her, too. She looks so beautiful when she flies!"

Freddy was Iris's macaw, a magnificent parrot glowing with color but gifted with a nasty temper. Since it is an established fact that the larger parrots prefer humans of the opposite sex, Iris had bought what she thought was a male bird; but when, a few months later, Freddy produced an egg, it became obvious the pet shop had made a mistake. Since Vincent was a male, and an animal-lover besides, he and Freddy had quickly made friends; he was called more than once, in the days when he worked for Iris, because the beast had waddled down the stairs and was advancing with menacing shrieks toward the frightened bookkeeper.

"Why don't you come and see her?" Iris said. "She's been very bad-tempered," and Vincent, looking down at a large Band-Aid on Iris's ankle, could well believe it; but before he could continue the discussion of Freddy's moods, he felt a hand on his shoulder: It was Olga, her long blonde hair floating down her back, wearing what Vincent recognized as a Cardin dress.

"How chic!" he said, admiringly.

"John gave it to me," she said with a grimace. "Have you had a drink?" and Vincent, answering that he had not, made his way to the bar. The long table was almost impossible to reach through the thick crowd pressing against it. Patiently, Vincent squeezed in as close as he could and, waiting for his turn, found himself next to Lottie Wasserman, who promptly put out her cheek to be kissed. Once again, Vincent braced himself.

Lottie Wasserman was a newcomer to the art world. She was divorced from some unmentioned Mr. Wasserman, well off without being rich, and bored. Art was chic, so she had started going to the galleries and buying cheap little drawings; then, ruthlessly, she had thrust herself forth until she was invited almost everywhere. It was well known she would spend the night with whomever asked her at the end of the evening; and while she made it plain that she preferred young men, rumor had it that she sometimes went home with a woman. Tonight, it was obvious that she had already had a few drinks.

"Vincent," she shouted above the din, "are you doing anything thrilling these days?" She winked obscenely.

"Afraid not. Are you, Lottie?"

"Yes, I'm making films. . . ."

With an apologetic grimace, Vincent, turning away, ordered a gin and tonic, then came back to Lottie. Continuing the conversation, they slowly extricated themselves from the writhing mass around the bar. "Making films?"

"Yes, about artists. I follow them around and shoot everything they do. I'm starting on Partridge next week." Desperately feigning interest, Vincent was suddenly taken over by a fantasy of Lottie, thin legs rising to bloated stomach, in bed with the artist, busily making love as the camera whirred. Luckily, before he could ask if she really filmed *everything*, they were interrupted by John Partridge.

He hugged Lottie and shook Vincent's hand. Muttering, "What a wonderful party!" Vincent pushed on and found himself face to face with Sophia Lyon. He grinned at her with a feeling of intense relief, and they settled down to a long gossip.

It felt as if only a few minutes had passed when Olga, coming through the crowd, announced that the food was ready. Vincent turned around and headed for the table, promptly losing Sophia, who was stopped by a man Vincent didn't know and who, judging from the intensity and fixity of her smile, must be a collector. Looking through the crowd, Vincent could see a number of familiar faces. Albert Applebaum, fierce and bearlike, was holding court in a corner; a little farther along, a young museum curator was engaged in earnest conversation with a ravishing redhead— probably an artist, Vincent thought, looking at her jeans and see-through blouse; next to her stood two German dealers who had obviously come on a buying trip. I should go and talk to them, he thought, and, with a shrug, headed for the buffet table.

Olga had done things well. The long white tablecloth was covered with carefully arranged platters. A whole ham lay sliced between two big baskets of dark bread, each flanked with an arrangement of raw vegetables. There were bowls of dressings, a huge roast beef, and a gigantic carved turkey. Then came the salads, more bread, and stacks of silver plastic goblets surrounding bottles of red and white wine.

Vincent carefully arranged slices of all three meats on his plate; avoiding the potato salad, he then took some *salade niçoise*, mushrooms *à la grecque*, and a few artichoke hearts. He picked up some of the dark bread, filled a glass with red wine, and, stepping back, looked around. It was the moment he disliked most, when a dinner companion would have to be found. Eating by himself would have been a terrible loss of face. Luckily, he spotted in the middle distance an equally lost-looking woman and quickly made his way over to her.

"Kate," he said warmly, "I won't kiss you because we're both holding plates, but will you have dinner with me anyway?"

Kate Weiss was a phenomenon. Short, dumpy, unattractive, her dyed blonde hair jutted out stiffly from her shallow forehead. She was in her late fifties and happily divorced. One had the feeling that she would have been an exceptionally effective Jewish mother if only she had had children; instead, some ten years earlier, she had become an art dealer and turned out to be both shrewd and honest, a rare combination. She never sold anything very expensive, but worked all the time and made, Vincent suspected, spectacular amounts of money. He was fond of her. They did a little business now and again; he liked her unconcealed avidity. She never pretended to love art and despise money —while feeling exactly the opposite—as so many dealers do. Vincent found it endearing that, without fuss, she had managed to build a collection of small modern works of exceptional quality.

Kate now proved as adept at getting a chair as she was usually at finding her provender. As soon as Vincent, holding gingerly on to plate and goblet, had settled at her feet, she turned to him.

"How's Sarah?" she asked.

"She's fine," Vincent answered.

But Kate wouldn't let go. "Why don't you find her?" she said. "Have her come and sit with us."

Vincent began to wonder if Kate was hinting at something and, standing up, he looked around. "No," he answered, "she's busy talking to that man from the Whitney —you know, what's-his-name. I don't want to interrupt them."

The dinner turned out just the way he had expected. Kate talked about the Bergs, to whom she had just sold a Lichtenstein print for their daughter's birthday. She asked Vincent if he had seen their new apartment in Philadelphia: This was obviously a test, and, as soon as he had replied that he had, she launched herself into a room-by-room appraisal of everything that hung on the walls, stopping once, as she mentioned a Kandinsky, to say, "Your father sold it to them."

"Yes," Vincent answered coldly, "so they told me." Kate, continuing her descriptive tour, gave him a shrewd glance.

She was interrupted when Olga walked past and said: "Dessert and coffee are ready. Why don't you help yourselves?"

"I love sweets," Kate said enthusiastically and marched off.

Vincent decided to join Sarah and noticed in passing that Partridge and three other guests were sitting at a real table, eating from real plates. He reached Sarah and, taking her away from the curator, said: "It's too funny. Look over there at Partridge's table. Of course you know who they are?" And when Sarah didn't, he continued, "Mrs. Wentworth and the Dillards: John's step up in society. Mrs. Dillard is Henrietta Basker's sister-in-law—you know, the hostess, the one who was always having Lady Bird Johnson to stay, the one with the foundation. And the Wentworths are related to the Rockefellers. What you're looking at is, I'm quite sure, the result of years of solid work."

"Now you're being nasty," Sarah said indulgently.

"No, I'm not. Just realistic. Everybody knows about John's social ambitions. And the funny thing is, if he keeps at it long enough, he'll probably succeed. People always end up getting what they really want, you know." They turned toward the tall chocolate cake. But before they could sit down together, they were separated again, this time by Olga, who asked Vincent if he had spoken to her friend Gail . . . and promptly whisked him away.

"You'll like Gail; she's very bright, and a writer," Olga said as she brought him face to face with a tall, plain, gawky girl in a rather messy cotton tie-dyed suit. Bracing himself, Vincent prepared to start a conversation.

It was a little after midnight before he finally managed to tear Sarah away from the party. The crowd had subsided an hour earlier; and the studio looked magnificent, its great white expanse of space animated by Partridge's wild colors. Vincent thought how nice it might be to live in such a space; he was saying so now as they waited for the elevator.

"Oh, yes," Sarah answered, "but you don't really think so. For one thing, you'd never live in this neighborhood; and then, you like real rooms, not great open halls." Vincent knew she was right. From then on, the conversation became a kind of postmortem.

"Did you see what Harry was wearing?"

"Did you speak to Sally?"

"I thought the food was really quite good."

"Yes, but Olga had it all sent in; she didn't do any of it herself."

"What about Partridge? How did you like his special table?" Vincent was saying as the taxi passed Madison Square on its way uptown.

"You don't like him, do you?" Sarah said.

"No, I really don't. He's such a bad painter—"

"He's not," Sarah interrupted. "I think a lot of his work has real magic, especially the recent paintings."

"Magic!" Vincent said. "Magic! They look like designs

for Bloomingdale's latest line of sheets. And besides, that social climbing, it's really rather revolting."

"Why should it be?" Sarah protested. "After all, you can be a social climber and a good artist."

"Oh, I don't know. That's at least open to question. I mean, you didn't notice Picasso's dying for a mention in the society columns!"

"You're being unfair," Sarah said. "You just don't like Partridge, so you never give him the benefit of the doubt. And I do like his work. . . ." Soon the conversation went back to the various people each had talked to that night.

Farther uptown, in the bar of the Stanhope, André was having a nightcap with Thérèse. "That dinner was simply perfect," he said smugly. "Of course, really chic people have a sense of what great conversation is like, and I was really brilliant tonight. You should have seen them, the whole table was listening to me. Maybe we really should move to New York," he added. "At east they appreciate me here!"

Thérèse nodded, but quickly interrupted him. "I want to tell you about my dinner with Ercole Fornetti," she said bleakly.

"Well?"

"My steak was medium. I had to send it back." She sniffled vigorously but, noticing the expression of anger creeping over André's face, resumed quickly: "I told him we were interested in working with him, that we have that big Delvaux and those Picabia gouaches, which are just right for his clients. So he said business is slow right now because of all the kidnappings, and that it is all he can do just to reach some of his collectors."

"God," André interrupted, "those Italians! They're always crying poor when they're really making millions."

Thérèse blew her nose with desperate energy, her white face flushing for a moment, and went on: "Well, I let him complain, and then, suddenly, I said I understood he was responsible for the Barolo collection. Naturally, he said that was all long ago, and that Barolo doesn't buy anymore. So I answered that I was aware of that, but thought he should be pleased to have assembled so many good paintings under the roof of one collector. '*Cher ami*,' I went on, 'I must tell you, we've been selling some of the collection, and there is one painting we're not very happy about.'"

André laughed. "I wish I could have seen his face right at that moment," he said with obvious enjoyment.

"Oh," Thérèse answered flatly, "there was nothing to see. He just looked blank and said, 'You surprise me, *chère amie*,' so I went on and mentioned the Chagall, and how curiously stiff it is, and how, since the painting came from him—Fornetti—we wouldn't dream of doubting it. But I said that, if it had come from almost anyone else, we would really have wondered about it and felt it our duty to take it straight to Chagall."

"Bravo," André interrupted, "Thérèse, you've been doing superbly. So then what?"

"Well, he said it was very courteous of us to behave in that way—not, of course, that there was any possible doubt about the Chagall—and he hoped he might be able to do us a good turn in exchange someday. So I said, 'Well, since you're nice enough to appreciate this little favor, perhaps you could make a special effort to sell our Delvaux and Picabias at the top of the market?' And he said, 'But, *chère amie*, what is the top of the market these days?' So then I told him, and he said that was far too high, and I said, 'I can't believe that the man who was able to put together the Barolo collection can't get decent prices,' and he sighed and answered, 'How can one resist a compliment? I will do my best.' So then I told him that we trusted him completely but would be very pleased if he could sell everything within the next two months. He said, 'Anything to please you, *chère amie*,' and he kissed my hand."

André laughed again. "I can just see him, the crook," he said with relish. "You've done a good night's work, Thérèse. Our plan is working superbly." He paused, smiling, and stared at her. "You look charming tonight," he went on. "Let's go upstairs."

SEVEN

"It's my life. It's my life!" The sentence floated before Olga's eyes—even though they were closed, while her legs were open, she was hardly aware that Partridge was making love to her.

After the guests had left, he had walked over and held her close. Then he had started to kiss her and, pressing hard against her, had demanded that she undress. She had complied. A little later, as his mouth danced a ballet around and over her breasts, she began to respond, breathing heavily, kneading his neck and shoulders. She liked it when his mouth traveled down her; when he spread her legs and she felt his tongue flicker, she moaned. Then he was in her, and the sex became secondary. She could feel her pleasure mounting along with his; she could hear his obscene whisper. She started to moan louder and louder, crossing her legs behind his back, tossing her head from side to side. Still, in spite of her climax, in spite of his, in spite of the relaxation she felt all through her body, Olga kept seeing those words obstinately denying her pleasure.

She almost said the words aloud as Partridge settled next to her. She turned so that she could feel the hair on his

chest rubbing against her left arm; it was when he sat halfway up and started to kiss her again that she could no
longer control herself. She turned her head away from his
mouth and said, in a flat impersonal voice, "It's my life,
John, it's my life."

Partridge looked at her in utter surprise. "Your life?" he
said as if he were far away. "What do you mean, it's your
life? Your life is my life, you know that."

But still the phrase hung there, before her eyes. She
shook herself—this is silly, she thought. And when he covered her right breast with his hand, she in turn put her
hand over his. It didn't mean anything. They had just
made love, she was satisfied and sleepy, and she loved him
besides. She snuggled down closer to him. It *is* my life, she
almost said aloud. It was obvious, and right, she repeated
to herself before drifting off: This was her life.

When she woke up again, it was Sunday morning. The
bed was empty, but she could hear water running across
the studio: Partridge was already in the shower. For a moment she didn't move; she was too comfortable. The air
was cold on her cheek, but the sheet, molded through the
night to her body, covered her like a long, still caress. She
stretched slowly, feeling with delight the cooler regions of
the bed. Just then, the water stopped. Partridge, opening
the door, stood looking at her; he was still naked and, for
the first time, she felt absolutely no desire. She didn't want
him to come back to bed and make love to her again;
quickly, before she could think about it, she smiled at him
and said, "I'm dying for pancakes. Let's go out and leave
the mess behind."

She didn't even realize she was angry when they came
back in; but she waited impatiently while he unlocked the
door, and felt somehow out of place, as if she didn't live
there, as if she were just a quick pickup. Even when Partridge started changing into his painting clothes and she

realized he had no intention of helping her with the mess, she still felt strangely composed. She knew the place must be cleaned up; it was just one of her chores. She had been at it a good fifteen minutes before she became aware that Partridge was standing before his big table, watercolors, paper, and brushes at the ready. And then, suddenly, the earthenware dish with its traces of dried guacamole started to throb in her hands. For a moment she stood perfectly still; then, with a piercing, prolonged yell, she threw it as hard as she could against the wall.

The silence that followed startled her just as much as the crash had shocked him. For a minute he just stared at her while she looked at the spot on the wall where the pot had shattered; but then, as she was about to speak, as something within her (she didn't quite know what) almost physically gave way, he said, turning back to his watercolor and adding several rapid touches: "Olga! Darling! What is it? What's happened?" and looking at her now, he added: "Poor little girl! The party was too much for you!"

For Olga, it was exactly as if a switch, long stuck in one position, had finally been released. Now that she knew, it was completely, maddeningly obvious: She couldn't stand it another moment. Buoyed by a peculiar mixture of icy clear-sightedness and absolute rage, she walked quickly to the middle of the big studio and, staring fiercely at Partridge, her voice full of contempt, said, "You selfish bastard, I hate you."

When months, even years, later, Olga remembered that scene, she recognized it as one of the great turning points in her life because, when she told Partridge she hated him, she spoke with a part of herself hitherto submerged; but at the moment, she had merely surprised herself. After all, she still loved Partridge, she still needed him.

Fights had been a part of their normal life—not very frequent, perhaps, but fierce. They would yell at each other, exchange accusations, give themselves up to their rage, so much so that several times Partridge had hit Olga quite hard, kicked her even, his face purple, his whole body convulsed in anger; and Olga, shrieking with pain and anger, had given back as good as she got. But then the scenes had ended, always the same way, in bed; they made love passionately, completely, again and again, sleeping for an hour and waking to renewed desire. Only, this time— when, as it turned out, everything had changed—there had been no lovemaking, no real fight. Before Partridge could say anything, Olga had run into the bathroom; when she came out of it, she announced in frosty tones that she needed to be away, so she was spending the afternoon with her friend Anya, adding that she would be back at six. Partridge, clearly relieved, had nodded agreement. Leaving the shattered pot on the floor, she had walked out of the studio.

It was then, sitting with Anya, that Olga had realized how unhappy she was, and she felt enormously surprised. Until then, whenever she had thought about her life, she had counted her many achievements: She had an interesting job and liked working with Vincent; she was bright, pretty, admired; her lover was sexy, successful, loving. If ever a doubt arose, she had but to look at her life: She saw glamorous people almost every night; Partridge's hard-won social connections had taken to her immediately; he was making a great deal of money and spending it freely; she was well ahead of her friends. And even when she felt depressed and complained about it, to Vincent or to a girl friend, either it was for a good, specific reason, or it was because she felt, in some vague, indefinable way, that she should be doing something more; but she didn't quite know what. Some days, she thought she should be working with children—teaching them art, perhaps, or giving them therapy. Other days she would launch forth, get various university catalogues, and consider some sort of postgraduate course. In the end she always decided that she didn't want to spend three or four years as a student. Sometimes she even thought she would write a book, although she wasn't altogether clear about what it was she wanted to say. Or she believed she might design something. She loved good materials; she could become a textile designer.

The truth was, of course, that she had no time for any of this. She worked four days a week even though Partridge had, long ago, offered to support her; but she was far too independent for that. She would have no self-esteem without a salary; and the rest of the time she was, in effect, doing chores for her lover. He had shows that must be organized, catalogues that must be proofread, mailing lists to be kept current, and mailings to be sent out. There was insurance to keep track of, paintings lent to various exhibitions, and even a large illustrated monograph of his work, which had been in the making for over two years.

In the evenings, there was their social life. Partridge's carefully cultivated connections were an essential ingredient in his success, so there were parties to attend and parties to give. Even the trips abroad took time: Partridge had a studio in London, and a show there every two years; so off they would go for the three summer months while the art business in New York conveniently shut down. All in all, it wasn't that Olga had any idle time during which to ponder her life: She was, on the contrary, always busy, and she liked most everything she did.

Of course, that made it all the more puzzling: She was dissatisfied without knowing why. Partridge had proposed to her several times. She had refused, feeling that she wasn't ready to get married. In any event, she had all the advantages of marriage except for children—but then, she wasn't at all sure she wanted any. In the abstract, it seemed a shame to pass up the experience: Every woman should have one child, she felt, just to live out that part of herself; but when she considered the reality of being pregnant for nine months, of having to take care of a baby, of having to raise a child, she knew full well that she wanted no part of it.

Oftener, of late, her dissatisfaction had centered on Partridge: He took too much of her time, of her attention; she didn't have a minute left for herself. At first, rationally enough, Partridge had asked her what it was she wanted the time for. Did she have a project? And when she admitted she didn't, he made fun of her. Soon, however, he realized that was a mistake, so he insisted: What did she want to do? If only she would tell him, he would help her as best he could. Somehow, that had upset Olga even more. Now it was all up to her. She was free, if only she could use her freedom. At first, naively, she announced she wanted to spend two nights a week doing watercolors; and Partridge immediately set up a table in a little room behind the studio, bought her good French paper, watercolors, and brushes. As soon as she started to produce a little work, he praised it to the skies.

Olga should have been pleased; instead, she was torn. She knew she ought to be grateful, and she was; but also—she tried not to think about it—she hated the fuss he made about her watercolors. One day, he came home with a big package which he gave her. When she opened it, there were five of her works, matted, framed, and ready to hang. Another time, he gathered a small group of friends and showed them her watercolors; he could not possibly do more for her, yet the more he did, the angrier she became until, finally, she abandoned her paints.

For a while, to show her gratitude, she returned to his projects. An exhibition of his oils was to travel to small museums all across the country. The details were number-less: Reuseable crates must be made, and remade along the way if they were damaged; insurance estimates had to be obtained; an inexpensive catalogue had to be put together; an order had to be imposed on the tour so that the route traveled would be as straight—and therefore as cheap—as possible. Then, there was the problem of sales, with the host museum getting a 15 percent commission: Should the painting, once it was sold, travel on? The buyer would not like that. Should it be replaced? And, if so, would the new painting fit into the old crate? And what about the cata-logue? Could it be allowed to list paintings no longer on show while ignoring their replacements? Clearly, some one person had to take care of all this. And since, after all, Partridge had to keep painting, Olga volunteered. Sud-denly, she found herself overwhelmed. She no longer had any time for herself at all and asked Vincent for a month off so she could catch up.

Olga knew she was doing a superb job, that without her the traveling show could never have become a reality; and she made sure that everyone was aware of it. Out-wardly, she took pride in her work, but she began to resent Partridge more and more. Their fights, although they came no oftener, were nastier, more destructive.

When the exhibition was well under control, Olga de-cided to return to California for two weeks: She hadn't seen her family or her college friends in a long time; she needed a change, a rest after all her hard work. The mo-ment she put it to him, Partridge agreed: It was a wonder-ful idea and he would join her for the last weekend, he said. Within a week of their return, she found out that he had been having an affair while she was gone. There was a scene, but he finally explained it all away: He couldn't bear to be without a woman for two weeks, but it didn't mean anything; he didn't care if he never saw the girl again. It made sense, after all; so Olga understood; but having understood, she thought about it and decided it was her turn. The only way to dispose of her resentment, the only way to reestablish her relationship with Partridge on a sound basis was to have an affair herself. Just as she was wondering who the lucky man would be—he had to be attractive but discreet and easily discarded—she received a call from an old lover, a German who was in New York for two weeks. He was the very man she was looking for, but she didn't really enjoy her fling. It was more a matter of principle than pleasure and that made her angrier still: She had paid Partridge back but at some further cost to herself.

Partridge remained quite unaware of Olga's revenge. Like many jealous men, he was always suspicious when there was no need to be at all; but when Olga actually took a lover, she got clean away with it. Still, her dissatisfaction was noticeable, and Partridge set about to cure it. It took a little planning, but one day he returned to the studio with a bolt of beautiful, soft-colored Irish tweed for Olga. He knew she would love it and she did; when she started to talk about fabrics, he told her she should really be designing some herself. Why not start with cotton and go on to linen or silk?

Olga loved the idea; but, she said, it was impractical: She would need a lot of space, vats for dying, tables for stretching the fabric, and, above all, privacy. She would not be able to work unless she concentrated. Here in the studio—with Partridge painting, the phone ringing, and endless interruptions—it was clearly impossible. And that was when Partridge sprang his surprise: He had just sublet a loft a few blocks away, he told her. He had intended to use it for storage, but there was plenty of room. She could set herself up and work in perfect privacy. She wouldn't even have a phone. For a moment, Olga felt all her anger melting away. Partridge really understood her, really cared about her; just when she felt sure he was utterly selfish, he had given her proof of the contrary. Her whole life was opening up again.

At first, she gave herself wholeheartedly to her new work. She spent at least two evenings a week and part of every weekend in the loft, experimenting, designing; but within seven or eight weeks, Vincent, who was following this new development with interest, noticed that Olga returned only the briefest answers to his questions. This became so marked, in fact, that he talked about it to Sarah, who, with her usual acumen, analyzed Partridge's maneuver and pointed out that Olga would never be completely satisfied until she was really independent.

"Independent?" Vincent said. "She'll never leave Partridge, and I don't think he'll leave her either. Besides, she's doing what she wants, isn't she?"

"No, she isn't. She's doing what Partridge wants her to do so she won't make trouble. And I don't agree with you: I think she may well leave him provided there's another man in her life; only, if there is, she'll have exactly the same problem."

"Maybe. But he must be giving her something or she wouldn't stay."

Perhaps it was because her textile phase was tapering off and she was no longer sure of her feelings for Partridge, Vincent thought; but, whatever the reason, it was a great nuisance: Olga had decided that she, Vincent, Sarah, and Partridge should get together for the evening every so often, not for superficial fun, but so that a deeper friendship could evolve. It was impossible to refuse Olga's suggestion; after all, he couldn't very well say that he found Partridge not just unpleasant but a crashing bore.

"The worst of it," Vincent told Sarah, "is that he will probably have some new trick, some new psychological theory he'll want to expound all night; and he's so vague it's impossible to tell just what he's trying to say. Besides, even if one could decipher his ramblings, I doubt it would be very illuminating." Still, the date had been made; Olga and Partridge were coming for dinner, and Vincent made very sure that the comforts of the evening would make up for its dullness.

Everything was in place when the doorbell rang that night: The living room was bright with flowers; the dining room shone softly in the glow of its antique kerosene lamps; and a sumptuous dinner was waiting in the kitchen. With a deep breath, Vincent opened the door, smiled as warmly as he could, and greeted his guests. Soon, the three of them were sitting and drinking, waiting for Sarah, who soon made a spectacular entrance, coming slowly down the stairs in a bell-shaped maroon satin and velvet patchwork skirt and a coral satin blouse with a deep décolleté.

"We might as well plan to sit down at table an hour after they arrive," Vincent had said. "You know how Partridge drinks." Indeed, the painter was already draining the last of a very large bourbon; not even the caviar he had brought along had convinced him to drink vodka. Immediately, he was off and rambling on about Mme. Blavatsky and the way inner and outer worlds could be made to coincide through a more precise understanding of energy impulses. Vincent had decided in advance that, as long as he was stuck, he would do his best to follow and participate, but he realized with a sinking feeling that already he had no idea what Partridge was talking about. He threw a glance at Sarah; perhaps she knew what was going on? When she excused herself and went to the kitchen, Olga quickly followed, leaving Vincent—with a mounting sense of doom—to refill Partridge's glass.

For the moment, at least, the painter was still talking, but he was obviously going to stop sometime soon, and Vincent had absolutely no idea how to respond. Still, he did his best and, when the fatal moment came, he said quickly: "Yes, John, I quite see what you mean; only, I think it's even more widespread than you say. We give energy to our surroundings and they give it back to us, just the way you put energy into a painting." And as he spoke, Vincent was telling himself, that's obscure enough even for him. To his great relief, it worked, and the artist was once again holding forth when Sarah came out to announce that dinner was ready.

The dinner was carefully planned so as to provide compensation for a deadly evening. Sarah, who made superb soups, had produced *bilibi*, a creamed essence of mussel; it stood now, fragrant and pastel-colored, in four Chinese bowls, while Vincent quickly poured some cold Pouilly-Fumé into the left-hand wineglasses. The *bilibi*, as he had known it would, stopped the conversation dead: Sarah was now explaining how she first took a great mound of mussels, steamed open in a little white wine and chopped shallots; then used only their juices, heated with a little saffron; and finally enriched the broth with heavy cream and egg yolks. Vincent looked at her with pride as she talked: She was lovely, competent, fun, and for a minute his heart went out to her. The dinner will be easy, he thought, and concentrated again on the soup.

When they had finished, Vincent, removing the soup bowls, brought on the next course. It was a roast turkey, surrounded on its platter by a cortege of small browned potatoes and accompanied by a purée of lima and string beans. Instead of carving the golden bird the usual way, however, Vincent took his knife and cut it right in two: It had been boned and filled with a veal and pork pâté.

It's rather fun, isn't it," he said amiably. "Such a shock

always to see the knife go right through the middle!" Once he'd served everyone, he poured some Mouton-Cadet.

By the time the dessert—a *tarte tatin*, its apples caramelized to a golden brown—and coffee appeared on the table, the effect Vincent had hoped for was taking place: John and Olga were too full of good food and wine for anything more than desultory chatter; Sarah was telling a story about the road in Morocco she and Vincent had driven down last summer, where, every twenty yards, children were stationed selling hashish at $2.oo an ounce. Vincent now brought out balloon glasses and his prize Delamain brandy; there would be no more of John's deadly, pretentious speculation. When Sarah finished her story, he switched the conversation to Partridge's next trip to London. Still, nothing could overcome Olga's pertinacity; within five minutes she was reminding the others that the evening had a purpose. She suggested a psychological game.

"It's a good way of opening up," she said firmly. "You pick an object and you free-associate."

They all moved back into the sitting room, and Vincent said, in a polite voice, to Olga, "You start."

"No, you start. You're more inhibited than the rest of us," she replied, and Vincent felt nothing but resentment as he looked about the room.

The game, as it turned out, did not produce the intended result: Vincent picked a silver Art Nouveau vase and proceeded to explain, at length, why he liked it, carefully confining himself to its aesthetic properties. For the next fifteen minutes he managed to be interesting, eloquent, and absolutely impersonal—as Olga quickly pointed out. Secretly delighted, Vincent shammed regret and told Olga it was her turn.

Her object was a key that reminded her of the key to her house in California, the one she had mislaid the weekend her father died. She had had to wait and wait outside the house when her parents and brothers had already left for the hospital, and she now talked of the anguish she'd felt before a neighbor finally told her where they were, and of her pain when her father died two days later. It was all very moving, Vincent thought coldly, and, even though Olga was actually crying, completely phony: Oh, he felt sure that weekend had indeed been devastating, but the telling of it had the quality of a set piece, something that had been recounted time and again; all the spontaneity had drained away, and even Olga's tears seemed wholly theatrical.

Still, Olga ended her story, with John hugging and comforting her. "Your turn," she told him, and, taking out his silver cigarette case, he started on an apparent stream of consciousness centered on reflections, reality and image, the reality of unreality. As John's voice droned on, Vincent thought ruefully that at least with Olga he hadn't been bored. Partridge was once again lost in meaningless elucubrations. Vincent returned from his thoughts in time to hear, Partridge referring to the greater substance of the unsubstantial so that, wickedly, Vincent wondered what would happen if the coffee table were to start lifting itself up. He visualized the table floating above them as it drifted across the room, then realized with horror that he was smiling. He nodded quickly several times, hoping they would all mistake this for a sign of approval, and dug the nail of his left thumb hard into his ring finger until his inner laughter stopped.

Partridge went on for much longer than either Vincent or Olga had, but at last, after some particularly cloudy considerations on timelessness, he ceased.

It was now up to Sarah, who promptly said she didn't know what to choose as her subject.

"The mask!' Partridge exclaimed, pointing to a large

Mexican tin mask with obsidian eyes, which hung on the wall.

Vincent handed the mask to Sarah. He stopped paying attention as soon as he sat down again, coming to with a start as he realized Sarah was attacking him. "Reading is just a way out," she was saying heatedly. "He uses it to stay out of our relationship. All Vincent does whenever he has a chance is read; he makes me feel as if I didn't exist. All he cares about is books. He reads here, he reads when we travel in the summer, he reads at the beach. When does he relate to me? Never!"

Aghast, Vincent stared at her. How could she speak like this in front of other people? And perhaps she sensed his shock: With a visible effort she changed the subject and began to talk about spontaneity.

She soon stopped, but, to Vincent's displeasure, Olga was taking up where Sarah left off. "It's true, Vincent," she said, "you hide from people. You're just polite to them as a way of avoiding contact. You don't want to get involved in the real world. . . ."

His eyes glazed, his face blank, Vincent sat stiffly until Sarah interrupted Olga: "That's not quite true," she corrected and went on to defend him; but the evening was clearly over.

In one respect, Olga had been right: Vincent reacted to unpleasantness by withdrawing from the world for a while. Even the next morning, he felt unable to sally forth to do business, so he compromised by going to the office—it was Friday, and Olga was off—but doing no work at all until after lunch; then, slowly, reluctantly, he called Poppea Vlassoff. She was at home, busy, she said, with her art fund.

She looked just the same as usual when she opened the door. Her taut, soiled T-shirt, with *Voulez-vous coucher avec moi?* emblazoned across the front, left exposed an inch of flesh above the jeans's waistband. Her hair was unwashed and hung in streaks around her face. The bottoms of her bare feet were almost black. She didn't bother to hide her left hand.

"I've been working my ass off," she said without a greeting and, before Vincent could say anything, she led the way into the living room. The floor was littered with layers of graph paper on which multicolored lines could be seen crossing; here and there, yellow lined pages were covered with scribbled figures. Flat on his stomach, a bearded young man was drawing yet another line across a graph; like Poppea, he was wearing jeans, a T-shirt, and no shoes.

"That's Jimmy," Poppea said offhandedly. "He's helping me with the fund." Turning slightly, she added, "This is Vincent Germain, Jimmy. I told you about him."

"Good things, I hope," said Vincent feebly, watching as Jimmy got up on his knees.

"Yeah, man, glad to meet you," Jimmy said. Vincent noticed that the young man's fly was gaping open.

Poppea carefully picked her way around the piles of paper. "That's my art fund," she said proudly. "I'm going to make a fortune. I've already got this rich private who's willing to invest a hundred grand, and Jack Griffenbaum says he knows people who want to get out of stocks and into art." Settling down on the floor, she added: "I've been doing research all week, like about this Picasso that was sold at Russell's for sixty-five thousand dollars five years ago; this year they sold it again for a hundred forty, that's more than double, and I'm going to have color reproductions of it to show the privates. It's more impressive that way."

"You're not having it printed?"

"Nah, just color Xeroxes, and even so it's costing me a

fortune. Jimmy here is always asking me for more supplies. I've already spent over three hundred bucks. Anyway, Vincent, you can help me. I've got to tell the privates about paintings that are for sale, so they'll know where their money is going. You told me about a cubist Picasso. Where can I get it?"

"Poppea, you can't just get a painting like that. First, the owner won't let it out of the house until he's been paid for it. And, besides, you don't want it anyway. I told you it was badly damaged and heavily restored. Even if you had the money to buy it, you could never resell it: The owner wants too much for it, and it's been offered all over town. You'd just be stuck with it."

Poppea bent over to study Jimmy's graph, holding on to his jeans's waistband as she did so. "Is that the year's profit?" she asked. Without waiting for the answer, she turned to Vincent. "It doesn't matter," she said. "It's something to show the clients. I can always say someone else got it because they took too long to cough up, anyway. And, even if I bought it, I'd make my money on it first."

"You can't do that, Poppea. If you really have an art fund, you can take a salary or a percentage of the profits, but you can't give yourself commissions on the sly. That's outright theft."

"Yeah," Jimmy said suddenly, sitting up on his heels and stroking his beard. "Yeah, the guy's right, Poppea. You can't do that."

"That's all shit," Poppea answered flatly. "They'll never know. Anyway, it doesn't matter. Can you get me the picture?"

"I don't think so."

"Yeah, well, try. And, you can help me with this. Like I'll bet you can write. You could do up the prospectus for me. Look, when this works out, we'll need consultants. You can be one and make an easy ten or fifteen grand."

"Well," Vincent said, "let's talk about it when it happens. The reason I came over is that six thousand dollars you owe me. You were going to give it to me last week, remember?" He braced himself, expecting either evasion or an outburst. To his stupefaction, Poppea stood up.

"Hold on," she said, and vanished into the bedroom. Within a minute she reappeared holding a check, and handed it to Vincent. He looked at it with amazement; it was for the right amount and made out to him.

"You're sure it's good?" he asked with a smile.

"Sure," Poppea answered and, settling down again, added, "Here, I'll show you about the investment and the profits."

As she went into detail after detail, it became clear that she had indeed been hard at work: She had gathered records of market fluctuations covering the last thirty years. Specific collections had been chosen as examples of the potential profits. Poppea had even compiled comparative figures for stocks, government bonds, and gold which showed clearly that first-rate art had yielded the greatest profits.

"You must have studied economics," Vincent said with a smile, and when Poppea answered that she had, in college, he was tempted to believe her.

It was only when she went on to explain what she would do with her million—she had decided to be content with a mere million—that everything became vague again. The truth was, Vincent realized, that she had not really made much progress since that first time, eighteen months earlier, when she tried to sell borrowed works from gallery to gallery. She still had no sources of her own, no real clients, and, as a result, her whole scheme was a pipe dream. Even if she were actually given that million—and Vincent could hardly believe she would be—she wouldn't know how to spend it. She would buy badly and be unable to resell fast enough to give her investors a profit. Her only choice then would be either to hold on for several years or sell out at a loss. Although he was tempted to say nothing and just nod approval, he couldn't. She had done real work, and she deserved the truth.

As soon as he started to speak, Poppea interrupted him. "Wait," she said, turning to Jimmy. "How about lunch? Here, I'll give you some money. Why don't you go down and get us some hamburgers?"

"Sure," Jimmy answered, smiling. He stood up and, crossing his arms behind his head, slowly stretched.

Poppea looked at him appraisingly. "Your fly is open," she said, and Vincent, who was standing behind her, saw Jimmy wink as he zipped it shut.

"I didn't want to talk in front of him," Poppea said as soon as the door was shut. "You know, he works part-time for Mark."

"Mark?"

"Sure, Mark Spence. From Boston. You know."

"Oh, Poppea!" Vincent said, appalled. "Surely you're not dealing with him anymore. I mean, the man beat you up."

Poppea dismissed this argument with a wave of her hand. "He's got a private for my fund," she said. "Besides, we still have some deals going."

"Did you pay him back for the fake, then?"

"Nah. Well, some. And he can wait for the rest. Anyway, about my fund. That's why we'll have advisers. Jack and Mark are coming in on it with their privates, so it's got to look like I know what I'm doing; but listen, you can get pictures, so I'll just come to you and two or three other dealers, like Pearl, and buy from you, that's all. Anyway, as long as I can resell two or three little things fast, they'll wait for the rest."

Vincent stared at Poppea, noticing that she had once

again positioned herself so that he couldn't see her spotted hand. He felt a wave of sympathy, much like that time in Milan when they had dined with her friend Zaza. "Are you going to run an art fund in jeans and a T-shirt?" he asked, but she ignored him.

Poppea was in a trancelike state. "Anyway," she went on, "you'll give me a dealer's discount, so already we'll have a thirty percent profit right there."

"Only if you resell to a client. But you seem to be working only with dealers, and they certainly won't give you your profit. I'm all for your art fund, Poppea, but if you don't watch it very carefully you're going to get into a lot of trouble."

Just then, the buzzer rang. "Oh, fuck," Poppea said after she had pressed the button, "it's Mark. Don't talk about this in front of him, okay? But don't go, either. I told him all about you and he wants to meet you."

"I'm not so sure I want to meet him," Vincent answered, but he was too curious to leave.

Mark Spence was young, tall, burly. His brown hair curled high over his head; his face, in spite of the cheek-bones, looked fleshy, no doubt because his eyes were so small and round. His shirt was unbuttoned almost to the waist; his skin-tight jeans were tucked into heavy leather boots. "I can't stay," he said. "I came with the van and it's double-parked downstairs. I left Eva sitting in it." Turning to Vincent, he continued, "Poppea told me about you. She says she does business with you, and I want in on it."

Vincent stared. "It depends," he said, finally. "Do you have anything to sell?"

"Sure," Mark said, smiling broadly. "Ask Poppea. She's sold me plenty of stuff; maybe I can sell some of it back to you. Anyway, I got things of my own."

"Oh?"

"Yeah, photographs, Civil War photographs. Look, I got

this client, his old man collected them and now he wants to sell them. He wants a hundred grand for the lot."

"Does he? He's not likely to get it. And I don't deal in photographs. You'd better go to one of the specialists. They'll tell you what to do."

"Yeah," Spence said. "I know. What about the other stuff?"

"What other stuff?"

"Didn't Poppea tell you? I told her to offer it to you," and he shot Poppea a menacing glance.

"She hasn't had a chance, yet," Vincent answered, instinctively trying to protect her. "This is the first time I've seen her for a while. What's this all about?"

"Italian masterpieces," Mark said with a nasty smile. "Poppea's best," and he thrust forth several transparencies.

Vincent immediately recognized the first two, the fake Klee and the Picabia he'd been offered in Milan. "I've already been offered these. I'm not interested." Then he felt as if he had suddenly been punched in the stomach: He was looking at an Ernst oil very similar to the three he'd bought himself. "Where is this?" he asked in a neutral voice.

"In Boston, at my gallery," Mark said. "I can bring them in anytime."

"Well, not now, at any rate. I'll let you know later if I want to see it."

When Vincent opened the door to his office that afternoon, he was only dimly aware of having walked to it. Even though he wanted to believe that his own Ernsts were good—after all, they did have Munsberg certificates, and everyone who saw them loved them—his stomach still ached. The mere question, the what if, was enough: Three fakes would mean a loss of over $120,000; and, since

Poppea would certainly be unable to refund the money, it would be enough to end his career. They *must* be good, he repeated to himself, they *had* to be, there was nothing wrong with them just because they came from Italy. As he walked up the stairs and sat down at his desk, he repeated over and over again in a singsong: "It's a disaster, disaster, disaster." When, finally, he was able to stop, he felt absolutely unable to work. He knew he had phone calls to make, and even forced himself to dial the first number, but as soon as the ringing began he slammed the receiver down. He couldn't even write a letter. He typed "Dear Sonia" and got no further; in fact, that maddening singsong started to play again in his mind, so he left the typewriter and picked up Trollope's *The Eustace Diamonds*, which he had started the day before and had carefully brought to the office: There was comfort in these almost endless volumes.

Vincent spent the rest of that day reading; when he finally went home, he was clutching his Trollope. "I'm exhausted, Sarah," he said, looking into the study where she was painting. "I'm going to bed." As soon as he had taken off his shoes and suit, he reopened the book with a sigh of relief; but even there, he came across problems he would have preferred to avoid. The greedy Mrs. Carbuncle reminded him of Poppea Vlassoff, and Lizzie Eustace's lies about the diamond necklace seemed much too closely linked to the world he was trying to avoid. Still, better this than reality, and he read on until Sarah came in to ask about dinner.

He spent the rest of the evening reading, but books, so long a natural refuge, seemed to help less and less. Reality had a way of pinching him now the moment he lifted his eyes from the page. It always lurked at the edge of his consciousness.

Through all this, Sarah left him alone. A new stage in

their relationship had been reached. While they hadn't quarreled for weeks, they had hardly spoken, either. Silence was replacing hostility. For a while now, they had slept in separate rooms for purely practical reasons: It was better for Sarah's back not to have Vincent's weight pushing one side of the mattress down; and, besides, she stayed up later and got up later than Vincent did. In the beginning they had gone on having sex; now, Vincent realized, it had been well over three weeks since his last, unpleasant attempt. That night Sarah had been reluctant—her back hurt; she wasn't really in the mood. So Vincent had tried hard to make sex work. Carefully listening to her breathing, he used every trick he knew to excite her. When he finally could feel she was ready and had entered her, she had started to complain: He had taken her too soon; her back hurt; he was inconsiderate and thought only of his own pleasure, until, finally, before he had climaxed, she had told him to stop. Now, turning over in his bed, he remembered the frustration and knew he would not try again.

Clearly, the problem was insoluble: He would not go to Sarah again and, in the middle of all his difficulties, was not about to embark on an affair. Even if he felt tempted by another woman, he didn't have the energy to begin anything new. Still, his need to find release was so severe that he began to fantasize about Olga again. Day by day, she was growing more desirable in his eyes. For the next week, Vincent tried unsuccessfully to work up the nerve to approach her, but he was all too aware that the situation was impossible. Olga was fully committed to Partridge and, he thought, faithful to him. Moreover, she was Sarah's friend and unlikely to start having an affair with Sarah's husband. It's either Olga or Poppea, Vincent thought sardonically. Nobody else will have me. Faced with that double impossibility, he felt even more depressed than before.

The rather unreal world he'd been living in seemed to be slipping away now, faster and faster. His marriage, even when it had worked, had been mixed with elements of playacting. He felt as if he were doing what other people did, but only superficially, without their motivation and involvement. Recently, only the suffering had seemed real. Now even that seemed to be happening at a distance from himself. His marriage existed in form only, and yet he was unwilling to leave Sarah. Just to move from his apartment would be more than he could cope with. He was paralyzed, stuck in that empty relationship, incapable of starting a new one.

With growing dread, Vincent felt that business, too, seemed to be receding. Even assuming the Ernsts would prove to be genuine, money was a problem. Sales weren't going through. It seemed that something always happened at the last moment: Clients were suddenly unwilling to sell or demanding impossibly high prices. He was still making the same gestures, had the same contacts, made the same phone calls, the same visits—but his efforts had lost all efficacity. He was already living on the profit from the sale of the first Ernst. What would happen next? he kept wondering. Should he fire Olga and save her salary? Or would she prove to be that connection to reality he so desperately needed?

Then, too, there was his involvement with Poppea. Although Vincent would have denied it if anyone had mentioned the subject, he realized how much the situation had changed since the first time that peculiar young woman had come to see him. The relationship was based entirely on greed; he knew that much. He felt almost physically soiled every time he saw Poppea, but the prospect of an easy gain kept leading him on, and now he began to wonder about his integrity. All his principles were fading away under the pressure to make money. Was he now to deal in fakes? What was left to him except to be a crooked dealer like all the others, only less effective?

"You should be teaching, or writing," Sarah used to say to him. "Or perhaps be a critic." He had paid no attention to her; to him it was all patently impossible.

Now, his regrets were bitter. Briefly, he indulged in a fantasy of success. He saw books and articles winning him acclaim, heard the praise for his audacious ideas; but such fantasies quickly faded away again: It was too late; it would never happen. Instead, he would soon be as contemptible as his father; he too would watch for the next dupe, or plot to abuse some client's trust.

It wasn't even as if he could disentangle himself. He was stuck with Poppea for a while longer yet; he must make money. The goal he was now formulating was to make enough to take a year off. And what would he do with a year off? What would happen with Sarah?

He began to wait greedily for the weekends, when he could hide out from dealers and clients.

No, Vincent repeated to himself, there is no way out. He thought perhaps if he held on long enough his life would improve. He tried to imagine a time when, all their problems having been resolved, he and Sarah might look back almost fondly on their time of trial. And besides, he told himself, I've always been lucky. Something will happen at the last moment.

Vincent was far too proud to admit that things were beginning to slip. He could just hear what people would say if he and Sarah split, if he went broke; and when he thought of his father's joy at seeing him fail, there could be no doubt. No matter how difficult the situation might become, he must hold on.

EIGHT

Whenever Viola Germain returned to New York, it was with a satisfaction compounded of insecurity: Her place, she felt, was only assured as long as she remained a glamorous exile. She loved New York and the fuss people made over her; life seemed simple after all the complications of Paris. Here, she was known and loved by her many friends for herself, she would claim, while firmly believing that if you were unsuccessful even your best friends would stop knowing you. Still, she was Viola Germain, not Mrs. André Germain; her personal success gave her a solidity she never quite achieved in Paris. Besides, she was in greater demand: For her, New York was an explosion of invitations and parties.

Then, too, there was the comfort of American ways. When people asked Viola about France, she spoke warmly about the delights of living in an eighteenth-century house graced, in the 1820s, by Chateaubriand's presence; about the beauty of the city; about the quality of its food. She made it very plain that Europe in general, and Paris in particular, were the only places any really civilized person could live. After all, Viola continued, she didn't have just a "place in the country": Her house rose above cellars built in the time of Joan of Arc. But, with all that, Viola secretly felt that life was easier in America.

It was nice to admire the patina on stone walls centuries old, Viola thought, but that pleasure was more than superseded by the fight to stay warm within them. The endless conflict with her landlord, who lived on the floor below, was one of Viola's best repertory pieces; her pleas for a little heat after nine at night sounded hilarious when she repeated them in a Park Avenue drawing room; they had, however, long ceased being funny to her. Everything was difficult in France. The electricity didn't work properly because the wiring was old and insufficient; the heater with which she tried to remedy the deficiency of the central heating was as likely as not to overload the fuse and cause a blackout. The phone seemed to be constantly out of order; in this *quartier* of ministries, getting a dial tone was always a battle.

Even the servants became a problem: Either they didn't work, or they quit, or they got drunk. Often, when dealing with all this, Viola had visions of a simple apartment with sufficient heat and hot water, stocked with labor-saving appliances, in a city where supermarkets delivered and telephones worked. And so it was always with a feeling of relief and ease that she returned to New York.

In New York, she felt she really had friends. When people gave a party for the Germains, she knew it was a party for herself. She could make a grand entrance and spend an even grander evening. Here, all her talents came to full flower: Her famous charm, her sophistication, her elegance, all were appreciated and valued. For these few weeks every year, the balance in her marriage changed. It was Viola (and André) for whom dinners were given,

Viola (and André) who were asked for the weekend, Viola (and André) whose wonderful magazine their friends kept on the coffee table. The worst of it was that André knew it too, and he hated to take second place; naturally this made him odious. But even he could not spoil New York for her.

This time, as soon as she arrived at the Stanhope, exhausted from her trip, he was raging at her because she had delayed joining him. At first, although she knew it was perfectly useless, Viola tried to reason with him in quiet, convincing tones. "You know very well, André," she said, "that we agreed I was to finish the Munich article before I left; and it took longer because we couldn't photograph in the rain—"

"The rain! Naturally!" André shouted. "When you're directing the photographer, it always rains! Do you know how much money that kind of delay costs? Don't you know *Voir* can't afford your spendthrift habits?" By now he was shouting at the top of his voice.

"Not so loud, André," Viola said, calmly. "This is a hotel room. Other people will hear you."

"I don't care who hears me," André yelled, his face flushed a dark red. "How dare you get here a week late when I need you! Oh, he's doing nicely, your friend Pierre-Paul! Trying to wriggle out of our agreement! I'll show him, the little worm! I'll destroy him! I'll make sure everyone knows just how grotesque he is! And the Bergs, we should have gone to the Bergs!"

"You could have gone without me," Viola answered, but the uncertainty in her voice betrayed her, and André pounced. Once he made her cry, he knew, he would feel much better, so he went on shouting.

"Without you! Without you! And why should I go without you? Do you for a moment imagine I want to put

up with those vulgar idiots by myself?" Seeing the tears
had come to Viola's eyes, he went on, nastily. "I can't afford
to support you, you know, not when you spend money
like water! And if you think, my girl, that I'm going to
see the Bergs alone, you're very much mistaken!" He
stopped pacing and watched his wife with satisfaction:
She was really crying now. "You have to work too, you
know," he said almost amiably, adding, "Why don't you
go put on your face? Thérèse should be here any moment."

"Oh, God, Thérèse!" Viola said with disgust; but before
André could start ranting again, she had vanished into the
bathroom.

By the time Thérèse knocked at the door, Viola had
changed into a hostess gown and made up her face. She
smiled amiably at the younger woman and extended her
hand without rising. "Well, Thérèse," she said, "you must
tell me your impressions. How does it feel to be in New
York for the first time?"

Thérèse scowled. "It's wonderful," she said mournfully.
"Even more exciting than I imagined." Turning toward
André, she barked, "You have to call Copley. Unless he
puts up the money now, we're going to miss that Chardin."

"But can we afford to pay for half?" Viola asked with
surprise.

"We don't have to . . ." Thérèse said, but she stopped
as André shook his head.

"What do you mean, we don't have to? Surely David
isn't putting up all the money himself," Viola said slowly.
Then, stiffening, she asked, "Or is he? Oh, André, what
have you been doing with him?"

The absolute silence that followed was broken by a
knock on the door. André nodded and Thérèse opened it
only to find a rather grubby man standing before her.

"Mr. Germain?" he said. Thérèse nodded toward André,

who came forward. "Here, that's for you. You've been served," the man said, thrusting an official-looking paper into Andre's hand and retreating hastily.

"Served? What does he mean, served?" André asked, looking startled.

"I think that was a process server," Viola answered. "Do look, André, and see what it is."

Thérèse became even whiter than usual as André unfolded the paper.

"It's from the Bergs," he said, handing it to Viola. "Here. You're an American. You'd better see what it is." There was a pause while she held up the document with trembling fingers.

"Oh, my God!" she said. There was another pause.

"Well," André asked impatiently, "what is it?"

"Yes," Thérèse chimed in. "Yes, Viola, what is it?"

Viola looked bleak. "André," she asked, ignoring Thérèse, "André, did you know there was anything wrong with that Chagall you sold the Bergs?" and, when he didn't answer right away, "You knew, didn't you?"

"Certainly not," André answered huffily. "What do you mean, something wrong? That Chagall came from Barolo, as you know very well."

"Well, if there's nothing wrong," Viola asked in weary tones, "then why are they saying it's a fake?"

Women, John Partridge sometimes thought, were really not fully human. They often seemed to him like little animals to be petted and indulged, adorable creatures who could be bought for the right price. Yet, one thing was sure: They were necessary, at night especially, and, while his need for Olga was paramount—it had been for a long time—he hardly saw it as precluding a quick extracurricular fuck. This was, in fact, one of his most constant preoccupations: Every time he saw an attractive, available young woman, he tried to make her, taking great precautions so that Olga would never find out. As soon as he met Flavia Marchetti at an opening, and she told him she was a free-lance publicist who worked out of her apartment, he knew he was in business.

As it turned out, everything happened even more easily than he had expected. Flavia might not know much about art, but she felt proper awe for a successful artist when she was introduced to one. She was perfectly happy never to see a painting from one year to the next, but thought of artists as glamorous bohemians—a not uncommon attitude in New York. Since she was tall, slender, bosomy, and quite pretty, Partridge immediately went to work, complimenting her ravenlike hair and deep, deep eyes, following with an invitation to come to his studio someday, and bring a friend if she liked. That elicited the desired response: She'd come alone.

From the gallery to the Saint-Germain, a little basement bar three blocks down Madison Avenue, it was a quick move. Partridge, suddenly fascinated by the world of free-lance publicity, asked Flavia to tell him all about her work over a quiet drink. He might well need some publicity himself, he told her. (Olga was in Chicago visiting her sister for three days and Partridge knew he would have to find a woman before the end of the evening.)

The artist was not one to spoil his own pleasure. The drinks were followed by a leisurely dinner, the dinner by an invitation to the studio. "Why wait?" Partridge asked, as if suddenly struck by a bright idea. "Let's go down there right now."

Flavia was duly impressed by the huge room, the stored paintings, even the fur cover on the bed. Still, he consulted her quite seriously about his relations with the press. He said he knew columnists James Brady and Liz Smith, but felt that wasn't enough; he needed more exposure. Looking at him meltingly, she told him all about campaigns and media events and her contacts. Finally, he showed her his collection of pre-Columbian objects. She sighed happily when he put an arm around her waist. He then pointed out a little fertility figure, admiring her shape, and said, "She looks sexy, but not half as sexy as you!"

Flavia, visibly melting, answered, "So are you, oh, so are you."

Within two minutes, Partridge was telling her that she had extraordinary breasts; within ten, the fur coverlet had been turned back and they were both naked. Partridge liked sex and treated it seriously; Flavia had never had such sophisticated love made to her. She stretched and moaned and bent again as his mouth traveled over her body, kissing, blowing, gently licking. Her other lovers had sometimes worked to put her in the mood, but Partridge took more obvious pleasure in pleasing her than they had done. She might be a quick fuck; but then, he thought a quick fuck should last a long, long time. When he sat next to her heaving body and gently bent her head toward his loins, she moved forward eagerly and opened her mouth wide.

Partridge had good reason to be pleased with himself that night. Flavia was immensely sexy to look at, very easy to arouse, and very willing to start all over again when he woke her in the middle of the night. The next morning before breakfast, they made love once again, as Flavia whispered frantically, "You're so good."

This affair lasted longer than Olga's absence: Flavia had so much more to contribute than sex. Keeping her away from Olga was a little awkward, of course, but Partridge knew that he would give himself away if they were together; the very fact that Flavia was so attractive made things all too clear. He pretended to be surprised when he found himself mentioned in the *New York Post* and later

invited to be a panelist on a radio talk show. And two large
Partridge watercolors now graced the once empty walls of
Flavia's bedroom.

The best thing about Flavia was that she understood
why she could no longer come to the studio and, in fact,
found it thrilling to be Partridge's secret mistress since it
meant that she was really his favorite; she liked making
love at odd hours and feeling so completely fulfilled, but
Partridge had a new problem. She had learned how much
she could expect those first nights, but now there was Olga
as well and, after all, he was not inexhaustible. There could
be no question of his neglecting Olga—she would never
allow it—but it would have been humiliating to disappoint
Flavia. Now, after some six weeks, Partridge was beginning
to look for a way out; he had had enough of Flavia. Still,
she must be let down gently; perhaps the best way would
be to leave town for a while.

So he told Olga he wanted to go to California: He had
to see his dealers in Los Angeles and San Francisco; and,
anyway, they needed a rest. They might drive up to Big
Sur and spend a few days there. Olga was delighted and
said so. Partridge told Flavia that the trip was an obligation and had been arranged long ago. Still, his last week in
town was especially frantic, quite unnecessarily, too, as it
turned out: Olga already knew all about the affair.

It wasn't just that a good friend had seen Partridge and
Flavia having breakfast together one morning, and
promptly reported it to Olga; Olga was quite shrewd
enough to realize that a sudden burst of publicity doesn't
just happen. So she put two and two together and, much
to her surprise, found that she didn't care. Then she thought
of making a fuss on principle. Partridge shouldn't get away
with it, she told herself, it was just another example of his
lack of respect for her. Besides, there was something faintly
humiliating about the sexual side of it: Olga, who valued

her attractions and her proficiency, felt she should be enough—indeed, more than enough—for any man. And so, two days before they were due to leave, she told Partridge to forget his little game: She knew all about Flavia Marchetti. Partridge was far too clever to deny it all, so he simply minimized its importance—it had begun, he said truthfully, while she was away.

"I see," Olga answered calmly. "So every time I'm away for a night or two, I can expect you to be unfaithful."

When Partridge explained that he had been feeling lonely and depressed; that it had meant nothing; that, besides, they were now going away together—what better proof of his love did she want?—Olga, again to her surprise, accepted his explanations. It didn't seem worth a fight somehow, and, after all, she felt neither very hurt nor humiliated. As for Partridge, he was stunned: None of his more important women had ever taken an infidelity so calmly. On second thought, he even worried a little: Could it be that Olga was tired of him? But then, she went on behaving the same way as usual. They made love that night, and Olga clearly enjoyed it; they were still going to California. As he thought about it, Partridge became firmly convinced he had, at long last, achieved the perfect relationship: He was free and Olga was not.

The trip to California was a great success for Partridge. Olga was pleasant, his dealers obsequious, his collectors hospitable; but Olga went on feeling unhappy without quite knowing why, especially since California usually cheered her up. She still loved Partridge—she felt sure of that since the thought of leaving him filled her with dismay —and yet she felt aimless. She functioned just as efficiently as ever, she knew that, but without gusto; she enjoyed the days at Big Sur, but less than she would have a year or two earlier. Even her sex life, so important to her, seemed strangely lackluster. Partridge was just as good a lover; her orgasms came just as often; the pleasure she felt was just as acute; but somehow the edge was missing.

She had thought about all this long and hard before finally coming to a conclusion and calling Sarah. Their friendship had paled in the last two years, partly because of Sarah's ill health. But she felt that Sarah, as an old friend, was indispensable when it came to discussing these vague feelings of depression and the quality of her life with Partridge. After their confidential lunch, however, Olga felt even worse.

Sarah, she quickly realized, was only pretending to listen, only waiting until she could start talking about herself. "You should leave him," she had said when she heard about Flavia, and then, after a few minutes, added, "But if you'd rather stay with him, you should." When Olga complained that she often felt bought, that Partridge was spending money on her instead of attention, Sarah nodded and answered that she had the same problem with Vincent. When Olga said she felt aimless, Sarah had responded bitterly that she, at least, wasn't married to a man who stifled her creativity. Still, when Sarah asked Olga which aspect of her life she found the most satisfying, Olga, to her surprise, found herself answering that it was her connection to the art world.

Later, Olga tried to dismiss the thought. She knew, after all, what mattered in life, and it certainly wasn't whether you knew a lot of dealers. As for her job, that hardly mattered. Vincent might hope she would bring in sales, but she fully realized how little attention she gave to that particular problem. She typed what had to be typed, did the minimum that was expected of her, and, lately, had spent a lot of time away from her duties. She explained to Vincent that she did this so that he wouldn't have to pay her, since business had become so slow; but that was just a pretext. In fact, she was bored. As long as Partridge was so anxious to support her, she now felt, he might as well do it; perhaps they both needed the commitment. And shortly after returning from California, she told Vincent that she must stop working in order to find herself. Ever practical, she asked to be fired so that she could collect unemployment.

That, she soon found out, was a clear improvement. She made less money but it was still enough for minor, everyday expenses—she wouldn't have liked to be completely dependent on Partridge. Now her time was her own and, conscientiously, she spent most of it checking and reorganizing Partridge's files and his storage space, updating his mailing list, and planning his next career moves. It's all very satisfying, she kept saying to herself. At last, she was fulfilled; she had found her way.

Partridge, of course, happily concurred. He had always felt he should be treated like one of those important artists; if Picasso had people looking after his work and life, busily recording every one of his works, then so should he. There was nothing like being surrounded by a little court of followers. He promptly started a brand-new project, in charge of which he put a specially hired student working under Olga's supervision. Having always felt he would be famous, Partridge had collected photographs of himself, along with clippings of reviews (well, the better ones, at least), mentions in the columns, letters, and other assorted materials. Now this great mass, which filled box after box, was all to be reordered, arranged, and displayed so that an extensively illustrated "life" could be published. An autobiography would have been ideal—Partridge by Partridge; who better could understand his great qualities, his unique talent?— but the work involved was a little daunting. And then, there was the very real satisfaction of receiving praise from someone else, of becoming some other man's subject, the center of his attention.

Indeed, for the next few weeks, it was obvious that Olga had made the right choice. Fiercely independent though she was, she felt that by submerging her personality in Partridge's she was achieving a deeper womanhood; it was all a little like some pioneer wife's looking after her "man," only she had the added satisfactions of New York and the art world. As for Partridge, he was ecstatic and, for the first time, almost forgot that his work was held in contempt by most serious critics and collectors. If he thought about that at all, it was only as a long-defeated general who has at last caught his enemy in a trap.

And it wasn't only Partridge's career that seemed on the upswing; even Olga's dissatisfaction seemed to wane. Whenever Vincent spoke to her—which wasn't very often anymore—she told him how pleased she was with her choice. And Sarah was consumed with envy. As long as Olga had suffered in a difficult relationship, then she, Sarah, could tell herself that it was the common fate of all those who chose to live unconventional lives, leaving the milieu in which they had been raised and venturing into an exciting but alien environment. Now, however, she was alone; so she told Vincent at great length about Olga's happiness and at even greater length about her own misery. He almost agreed with her: Clearly anyone associated with him was somehow tainted with his own difficulties. He wasn't surprised that Olga felt happier: It was further proof that he alone was doing badly.

The emptiness of his office was another manifestation of this. At least, until now, he had sometimes had Olga there. Her very presence had forced him to try for new deals, to push old ones to a conclusion. Now, it seemed, there was no reason for him to make the effort. Just how absurd that feeling was, Vincent knew very well: More and more every day, he needed to make money. After all, even if the Ernsts should turn out badly, they could be made up for by new sales, new income. And besides, this was his chosen work: It would be shameful to sit there, day after day, hiding from his obligations. He should, at this very moment, be calling people and making appointments, writing to out-of-town clients, seeing other dealers. But when he sat in that empty office, he did nothing at all except read a newspaper or a book.

Of course, the relevance of Olga's behavior to his own marriage did not escape Vincent, but when he pointed it out to Sarah she was full of quick answers, the chief of which was that Partridge, at least, had encouraged Olga's creativity, even if it failed to go very far. And then, Partridge was an artist, not just a dealer—well, perhaps not a great artist—although, who was to say—but, still, Partridge's career was something far more worthy than Vincent's. That made it all the bitterer for Vincent, especially since he was convinced that in the short run it was the mediocrities who succeeded. Seeing Partridge rise as he himself sank, while perhaps not surprising in itself, remained most unpleasant—so unpleasant, in fact, that suddenly a new avenue of redress opened up before Vincent. He had just been reading the Pléiade volume of eighteenth-century French novels and was struck by the deliberateness with which various characters sought certain affairs. Apparently, it was common practice to court and bed a woman for revenge; and he thought he would try with Olga.

"But I assure you, Pierre-Paul, André is doing everything he can; you know how highly he thinks of you. Just the other day he was saying to me, 'Thérèse, I wish we could use Pierre-Paul, but we just don't have the time—' "

"And is that why you wanted to see me?" Sanche asked in a low voice.

"Of course, Pierre-Paul, and to tell you that André is thinking about your problem so that—"

Thérèse broke off as the phone rang and Sanche answered. She was even paler than usual. Perhaps because it was so cold outside, her nose and eyes were so red that she looked rather like a depressed rabbit. As Pierre-Paul continued to speak, obviously to his broker, Thérèse got up and paced.

When she sat down again, her right hand plucked obstinately at the hem of her jacket; still, despite the embarrassment she was so obviously feeling, her voice had been as loud, as commanding as ever. Now, as Sanche put the phone down, she straightened her back and glared at him fiercely. Before he could say anything, she went on: "Oh, Pierre-Paul, if only you knew how hard André has to work, how much he does. I realize you'd like to run *Voir*, but really, I assure you, you have to know so much, make decisions so fast, and be there continually—you should see him, sometimes he even works until eleven or midnight. And then, there's the quality of the magazine. But, I assure you, André wishes you could work with him. He needs an assistant very badly. I can't do everything, though I try—"

Thérèse had been staring straight ahead as she spoke, and she jumped as Sanche interrupted her with some violence. "Assistant? Did you say 'assistant,' Thérèse? Do you know who I am? There would be no *Voir* without me, and you suggest I become André's assistant!"

"But surely you don't think you could run the magazine?" Thérèse said in the tone of voice she might have used to an unreasonable child. "After all, running any publication requires technical knowledge, and you must be aware you don't have it."

Sanche stood up, his face pale and set. "Has André sent

you to convince me that I'm incompetent?" he asked
coldly. "Because, if he has, I think you had better go back
to him and tell him to face me himself the next time. I
don't like being insulted by proxy, you can tell him that,
too. Now, Thérèse, if you are quite finished—"

"I'm not," Thérèse answered without moving. "You're
obviously not aware of your good fortune in having André
run *Voir*. You could never replace him. And there is no
question of insulting anyone. I'm just trying to explain
to you—"

"You have made yourself quite clear, Thérèse," Sanche
said, opening the door of his hotel room. "There is nothing
more you can explain to me. And it might be just as well
if you remembered that your salary is paid with my
money."

Thérèse opened her mouth to speak, but Sanche, pinching his lips together, shook his head. As she walked through
the door, Thérèse tried again. Smiling with obvious effort,
she held out her hand as she said, "Let me tell André that
you understand. After all, someone of your caliber—"

Sanche, merely staring at her proffered hand, walked
back into the room and closed the door.

"The office is so quiet without you, Olga," Vincent said
into the phone, "that I thought we should have lunch together; it doesn't seem right never to see you anymore.
Surely you must come uptown sometimes? . . . Yes, an immense amount of work, I can well imagine. . . . Oh? But
how very nice that you got it all settled for him. . . . Yes,
Tuesday, by all means. At one, then? Perfect." He smiled
as he hung up.

When they met that Tuesday, he was all ready to give
his project a try. It would be his revenge on Partridge,
whose success was so irritating; on Sarah, who apparently

thought sex was a favor; on the world at large, which at the moment was treating him so very badly. It was important that he succeed at his revenge: The very last thing Vincent wanted right now was another failure. But it wouldn't be easy.

His technique with women depended a good deal more on their weakness than on his strength. Over the years, he had discovered that words mattered. A seductive conversation could lead right into bed, especially if he left it up to the woman to make the first move. It was easier to be seduced, to appear hesitant and undecided; but that wouldn't work with Olga. It wasn't that she would hesitate to seduce a man she desired, but Vincent was well aware he didn't belong in that category. If he wanted Olga, he would have to conquer her, and not just by being eloquent and available. This time, he would have to fight a well-planned campaign and almost force her into surrender. He would have to make her angry with Partridge—an essential prerequisite—so that she would not hesitate to be unfaithful. Then he would convince her that he wanted her, really wanted her, and push his advantage quickly.

They met at the Hunting Pub, a dark little restaurant on Madison Avenue. It was hardly better than a bar but, Vincent thought, just the kind of place he wanted: Anything more expensive would make Olga suspicious. And since they were now meeting as friends, he could show her more affection: He kissed her on both cheeks, told her how much he liked her dress, and asked her whether she had been outdoors a lot.

"No," she said, puzzled. "Why?"

"Because your hair is so golden, so shining, it makes this whole place look sunny," he answered. The campaign was well under way.

It progressed quickly. Olga usually managed to steer the conversation away from herself; now, she was telling

Vincent all about her work for Partridge—the catalogues, the shippers' lists, even the accounting with various galleries. She was proud of her efficiency and explained at some length how she had reorganized Partridge's whole mailing list.

For the best part of an hour, Vincent listened admiringly. Then, as if he had just thought of it, he said, "Well, Olga, all that's wonderful for John, and he's incredibly lucky to have you. You're just what he's always needed. But what about you? Are you doing anything creative yourself?" Turning away, he ordered two more Bloody Marys.

It only took a second, but when he faced her again, her whole face had changed. "Olga!" Vincent exclaimed in apparent alarm. "What's the matter? Oh, dear, I'm afraid I've said the wrong thing. It's just that, good as you are for John, it never occurred to me that you had given up your own life. Look, I know it's none of my business, but I'm very fond of you, and it would be a shame if you didn't develop yourself." There was a short silence as Olga downed half her drink, then looked up with a determined expression.

"I'm not giving anything up," she said. "I made a deliberate decision. I'm fulfilling myself through John's career."

Vincent noted with satisfaction that she looked quite unhappy and, for the first time, he noticed several little lines at the corners of her eyes. "I can see that you might," he said, "although it seems a shame that you're giving up your own creativity. Still, perhaps, if you expanded what you're doing? . . . I mean, you're a born dealer. Couldn't you do it for yourself and John as well? Work for him part-time, conduct your own business, and make some money? Let's have another drink," he added quickly before she could answer. "This is Old Home Week!" He

turned away once more and then went on: "Also, didn't
you want to work with children?"

Olga shook her head. "Yes," she said, "I want to work
with children, I always have."

Before she could say anything more, however, Vincent
added, "Look, I may be wrong, but it seems as if John's
being awfully selfish. I mean, it's one thing for you to
offer him your time, but it's another for him to accept.
Frankly, I think he's letting himself exploit you."

They ate their meal, and shortly afterward Vincent said,
"Let's get out of here and go back up to the office for a
minute. I have a sensational bottle of brandy: Come and
have a taste before you go back downtown."

Everything hinged on Olga's reply. Normally, she would
be far too busy to accept. If she did come up, he knew he
would have his chance. He watched her intensely as she
thought about it. "It's superb brandy," he said, "and, besides, you look so radiant, you have to come up. The office
needs your sunshine—it's been so gloomy since you left."
He could see that he'd won.

"All right," she said, "I should be going, but I'll come
up for a minute."

As soon as they were out on the street, he smiled. "It's a
good thing you're not coming up at five," he said, and,
seeing her look of surprise, he went on before she could
speak: "How stupid of me! You don't know what a *cinq à
sept* is, do you? Well, at the turn of the century, the period
from five to seven in the evening was the only time people
kept free of social obligations, so that's when lovers met. I
wouldn't want John to think we were having a *cinq à
sept*," he added in mock horror, and she laughed. "Anyway," he continued, "you're safe enough: I didn't bring
my *baise-en-ville*."

"Your what?"

"A little suitcase," he answered as they went up the

flight of stairs to his office, "which you took with you so you had a change of linen after your *cinq à sept*—it means 'screw-out' literally, you know, like 'dine out,' only . . ." and, as she laughed again, he unlocked the door.

He helped her off with her coat and, feeling real desire, realized he was caught in his own trap. "The brandy," he said quickly, taking out the bottle and glasses.

"It's good, isn't it?" he asked as she sipped. "Sarah said you found out about one of John's floozies. I hope my talking about it doesn't upset you, but, really, I think you're being exploited." He looked at Olga. Her hair was a golden halo around her face; the deep blue of her eyes held him. "God," he said, as if he were speaking to himself, "you're so beautiful." Then, apparently remembering her presence, he added, "I hope you don't mind."

"Mind?" Olga answered with a smile. "Why should I?"

"You shouldn't," Vincent said. "It's all your own fault and you must take the consequences. I expect I shouldn't tell you, but you have incredibly appealing breasts."

Olga laughed. "Bullshit!" she exclaimed. "I'm flat-chested. I spent years praying I could be more like other, bigger girls. Anyway, what's come over you?"

"The way you look. I've never seen you so golden, so sexy. And I love small breasts that fit into my hands. I'd love to hold you, Olga," he whispered, putting a hand on her knee. "I'd love to kiss you," and he bent over, but before his lips could touch her she pushed him away.

"Vincent!" she said, standing up. "What are you doing? You're married to my best friend."

"Hardly!" he said bitterly. "I'm sure Sarah told you all about it. Anyway, I no longer have that kind of obligation to her. Oh, Olga, I do want you." Picking up her hand, he kissed her fingertips.

She quickly snatched them away. "You know it's impossible," she said.

"I know no such thing. Look, if we like each other, we're free adults; and you're lovely and sexy and desirable." He took her by the shoulders; but again, before he could kiss her, she shook herself free.

"No, Vincent," she said with finality. "No, I can't. And I shouldn't. We're not really free, either of us. You're my good friend," she added, consolingly. "I care about you. But I won't start an affair behind John's back."

"I understand," Vincent said, visibly making an effort to control himself. "I understand; but, oh, Olga, you're so lovely. Well, let's have our brandies. And remember, if I can ever do anything for you, I'll be right there."

Olga left ten minutes later, kissing Vincent on the cheek; and as she walked out the door, he felt depression closing in. It didn't help when he told himself that, after all, he had lost nothing: He had tried; it didn't work; and, if it came to that, nothing need prevent his trying again one day. He repeated that to himself as he stood, forehead pressed against the window. For a minute, he could see himself becoming a figure of fun as Olga told Partridge and Sarah, but he tried to believe that she wouldn't, that most women wouldn't. Still, that wasn't the worst of it: He felt so desperately lonely, so hopeless, so burdened. At least, he said to himself bitterly, she was solid; an affair with her would have meant renewed solidity, a more direct, more efficacious relationship to everybody else. It might have made all the difference.

Besides, another pleasure had just been withdrawn. Vincent, remembering the early days of his marriage with Sarah, shook his head: Sexual impatience fell on him like a choking need. There was no fighting it, no calming down. Feverishly, Vincent crossed the room and, reaching inside his desk drawer, withdrew a tabloid newspaper, which he quickly opened. He dialed a number, then said in a low voice into the phone: "Samantha? I'm calling about your ad.

Would you be free in twenty minutes? Yes, that's right, one hundred dollars."

When Vincent came home that night, he felt even less connected to reality: He avoided Sarah, rushed into the shower, and wondered, as he washed, whether or not he had caught anything: Later, he sat in front of the television so he wouldn't have to talk. The sickening lust of the early afternoon was gone, but that made Olga's rejection even harder to accept. Anybody could have a whore if he was willing to pay; and, at that, Vincent was aware he should not have spent the money, that one day soon he might not have it to spend anymore. And then what? He could no longer imagine a relationship with a woman, or with anyone for that matter. Sarah asked him what was bothering him, but he answered "nothing" in such an unpleasant tone of voice that she walked out in a huff. "There is no exit," he repeated over and over to himself.

It almost seemed an improvement when Sarah came back in, sat down, and said: "Vincent, I want to talk to you. I can't stand it anymore. I think we should separate, for a while anyway. We've been together too much and we're not getting along."

Vincent straightened up and immediately felt better. A fight was at least something he could cope with; so it was with a feeling of real pleasure that he answered: "Separate? Never. I'd rather have a divorce," knowing full well that Sarah was not ready to go that far. Life, after all, was back to normal.

The scene gave Vincent such energy, in fact, that he decided to tackle David Copley the next day: There was no reason why the dealer should dislike him so, and, if some misunderstanding had angered him, then it should be cleared up: He called and told the secretary that he knew how very busy Copley was, but that he would be grateful if a ten-minute meeting could be arranged; when she came back on the line, to his surprise she suggested the next day. As soon as he put the phone down, though, he began to regret his initiative. After all, he had managed without Copley until now, and there was no sense in inflicting a confrontation on himself. Anyway, what could he say: I know you don't like me? He tried to talk to Sarah about his apprehension, but in vain: She was still sulking, so he went on worrying and finally decided to cancel the meeting although he knew that would create an irretrievable breach. It was a little after six when the answering service picked up; Vincent hung up without saying a word.

It was with a sinking stomach that he rang David Copley's bell the next day: He knew he was making a mistake, and now it was too late to get out of it. Still, he smiled to the young woman who opened the door and walked in as if it were the most natural thing in the world. As he had expected, he was told to wait and soon found himself in the sitting room. At first, he sat down; then he stood up and walked over to the wall with the Tiepolos; he was still looking at them with a pleasure spiked by apprehension when the door opened and Copley came in. His greeting, Vincent thought, was cordial enough. They both sat down and Copley, taking out his snuffbox, said: "Well, Vincent, what can I do for you?"

With a great effort, Vincent, overcoming the parched feeling in his throat, answered: "I'm afraid you may find this visit rather strange; but, to tell you the truth, I heard that you had something against me. I can't imagine what it is and, since I have always looked up to you, I thought it best to see you and ask you what the problem could be."

"Who told you I felt that way?" Copley asked, taking a pinch of snuff.

Vincent hesitated. "I don't want to be indiscreet," he said, "and perhaps I was wrong to mention this at all—"

"No, no," Copley interrupted. "You were quite right

and I'm delighted you came; in fact, I'm surprised you didn't call earlier. I told your father last year I would be glad to work with you."

Vincent's stupefaction must have shown clearly, because Copley laughed and said: "Didn't your father tell you?"

"Actually, he never mentioned it," Vincent answered. "Perhaps, David, I'd better tell you the truth: My father and I are not on the best of terms; and so, if you should find it an embarrassment to be connected with me, I would understand perfectly." To Vincent's amazement, Copley got up, walked over, and patted him on the shoulder. "Your father is not always an easy man," he said warmly, "but that has nothing to do with you. I've always liked you. I'm delighted you came to me. There is no reason why our relationship shouldn't be completely independent of anything I do with André. In fact, perhaps I should tell you that the last time I suggested you come and see me, he warned me that you were not entirely reliable. Of course, I know that's not true—other people have told me about you. Look, I don't have much time now, but come back tomorrow around four and we'll look through the stock together. I'm sure there are things I can give you on consignment."

Suddenly, it seemed to Vincent that he had been saved. Copley would give him paintings to sell; he'd make enough money so that the Ernsts wouldn't matter; his position in the art world would be immeasurably strengthened. He could already hear people saying, "He's very close to Copley, you know." And then, there was the satisfaction of having overcome his father's attack. It was all too much to keep to himself; as usual, Vincent flagged down a taxi.

Although Viola Germain was glad to be in New York, she felt left out this time, ignored by André and even by

Thérèse. She tried not to worry about it. Nevertheless, she had trouble avoiding the recurrent feeling that something highly unpleasant was about to happen. She did not feel reassured by André's speeches: If the Bergs were suing, something must be really wrong. André had pointed out, of course, that the Bergs were notoriously difficult and liked to make trouble; besides, what could be amiss with a Barolo picture? Viola saw his point, but remained unconvinced. So when Thérèse knocked on the door of her room one evening at six and said, "Viola, I just don't know what to do next," it was not altogether a surprise.

"Come in," Viola said, "and sit down. But I can't give you more than a half hour: We're going to a cocktail party, then to a dinner; and since the cocktail is being given in my honor, I really can't be late."

"It's Pierre-Paul," Thérèse said, sniffling. "André sent me to see him about that fuss he's making and he threw me out."

"You mean he wouldn't talk to you? That doesn't sound like him," Viola said. "Are you sure it isn't something else?"

"Well, no, he did talk to me. It was when I explained to him why he wouldn't be any use at *Voir* that he became so angry. I thought maybe you could do something about it because André—"

"Oh, God, Thérèse, now what have you done?" Viola snapped. "I told André not to push Pierre-Paul. Why did he have to send you? Let's face it, Thérèse," she added with a hint of enjoyment, "tact is not one of your qualities. I'm sure you must have enraged the poor man. Well, we need him. I'll have to try and repair the damage you've done." Turning to the phone, she called Sanche.

"Dear Pierre-Paul," she said softly, "it's so long since we had lunch together. . . . Yes, Thérèse—too annoying, yes, I know. . . . Yes, Pierre-Paul, of course. . . . No, no, we'll talk about it . . . tomorrow, then, one o'clock. Good. I look forward to it."

She put the phone down and, turning to Thérèse, who was blowing her nose, she asked: "Do you have a cold?"

"Yes, my sinuses are infected again," Thérèse, who had clearly recovered, barked back.

"Are they?" Viola asked absently, before changing the subject. "What about that Chagall, Thérèse? Why are the Bergs suing? I'm sure there's something André didn't say. Do you realize what this makes us look like? How much damage it may cause? You do realize that if the Bergs win, we'll be finished in America? I must know what is going on before it's too late."

"There's nothing wrong with the picture," Thérèse answered in her usual gruff way. "The Bergs just like to make trouble, that's all; anyway, André would have told you if there were a problem," and, with this parting shot, she went out.

When André came in a little later, Viola mentioned Sanche with great care. She thought André was behaving stupidly, but wanted to avoid the scene that would ensue should she say so. At the very mention of Pierre-Paul Sanche's name, André's face had darkened, so Viola simply said: "Thérèse evidently had trouble with him—he can be difficult, as you know—and she asked me to help. I'll have lunch with him tomorrow and try to smooth his feathers down. Do get changed. We have to leave in a few minutes."

The next morning, the sky fell in when Viola cautiously suggested that perhaps Sanche should be given some sort of position with the magazine. For once she held fast through the explosion, however. "I have to tell him something, you know, and, after all, neither you nor I want him to pull his money out," she said as soon as André had stopped raving.

"He wouldn't dare. That washed-out rag! He only says what Nini tells him to say, but he'll never actually do anything. And there's no question of having him with us. I can't waste time inventing work for him."

"But couldn't we have him do something useful? We could put him in charge of advertising, for instance; he might be quite good at it. And we could give him a flattering title so it would look as if he ran the business side of the magazine."

"Never!" André shouted. "Never! I won't have that good-for-nothing in the office. And if he doesn't like it, let him take his money back. We'll manage without him."

"Oh, André," Viola began—but she was interrupted by the phone. "Yes," she said. "What's wrong, dear Pierre-Paul? . . . Oh, no! How could she? . . . Last night? . . . You must feel terrible. . . . I wouldn't dream of it. Of course, we'll have lunch together and you must tell me all about it. . . . Yes, one o'clock." She put down the phone and turned to André. "Nini has left him for a racing driver," she said with a hint of enjoyment.

CHAPTER

NINE

"I just can't understand why you go on like this. Don't you have anything better to do?" Sarah said angrily when she found Vincent rewriting Poppea Vlassoff's art fund proposal. Although Vincent explained that he was slated to be a well-paid consultant if the idea came off, he knew he was merely hiding from the truth. The art world might be disorganized and haphazard, but he could hardly believe Poppea would soon find herself in a position to dispose of other people's capital. Still, it didn't make any difference. Straightening out the confused mess so that it became clear, convincing, well-written prose was something he enjoyed doing.

Besides, Vincent told himself, stranger things have happened: In a world where persistent mediocrity usually triumphs, there might well be room for a Poppea Vlassoff. Only when he tried to imagine what would happen if she succeeded did he become uncomfortable: He would, after all, be selling his name to an enterprise that was bound— well, almost bound—to collapse. He knew that Poppea would cheat to pay off her debts, that she did not even pretend to be honest. Without quite realizing how it had happened, Vincent found himself associating with crooks.

Luckily, there was Copley, Vincent said to himself as he walked over to Poppea's apartment, text in hand. Now he would have a way out: he was only tied to her because of the Ernsts; once that was over, he could simply cut her off. He'd be selling Copley's paintings, and he'd be prosperous again. It was only as he waited for the elevator to come clanging down that he wondered just how difficult it would be to get rid of Poppea: She was, after all, nothing if not tenacious.

This time, as he came out onto her floor, she was actually waiting for him. "What, Poppea, not on the phone?" he said smiling, and added, "You look wonderful today." And, in fact, she looked better than he had ever seen her. Her short black hair had been washed and carefully brushed around her face; she wore makeup; the nails of her right hand glistened, red and long; and instead of her usual T-shirt and jeans, she was wearing a peach-colored blouse and maroon velvet pants; as usual, she was tottering on enormous heels, but now they looked appropriate.

"I told you I can look gorgeous when I want to," Poppea answered. "You should have seen me when I went to charity balls. Anyway, a private is coming to talk about the fund in an hour. I've been waiting for your text," and walking in, she shouted: "Jimmy!"

"Here," she said to the bearded young man, "get this Xeroxed and put it in the binder." Vincent nodded at him as he went out, and Poppea continued: "Shit, I don't know what I would have done without him. He cleaned up all that stuff you saw the other day and put it in order."

"But, Poppea," Vincent protested, "you might not like what I wrote. How could you send it out without even looking at it?"

"Oh, I'm sure it's okay," she said flatly. "Anyway, there's no time to change it." She paused and looked at the room with satisfaction. "How do you like it?" she asked.

"Like it?"

"Yeah, the room."

Vincent hesitated. It all seemed much the same, but then he noticed that the dead plants had been replaced by live ones; the stack of frames was gone; and there was actually a Riopelle on the wall. "You fixed it up," he said with a smile.

"Sure I did. And I even had a maid come in and clean. Jack said it had to look good for the private. And Zaza and her fiancé are coming over later for a drink."

"Don't tell me you've paid her back!"

"Not yet, that's why they're coming."

"But, Poppea, what will you do? Do you have the money?"

"Nah!" Poppea answered with contempt. "But that's okay. I got a Miró gouache. I'll tell them I made an exchange."

"Did you, Poppea? Make an exchange?"

Poppea laughed. "Of course not," she said, "but they won't know that. And, anyway, once I get the fund started, it won't matter. Look, the private's coming today, and Jack said he'd help me organize a group that'll cough up at least two million."

"What if Zaza won't wait? Can you give her the Miró?"

"Well," Poppea said, settling back with a sigh of satisfaction, "not exactly. I have to return it in three days. But that's okay. I'll tell them I have a private who's reserved it for a week and that I can get them a good profit on it."

Vincent stood up and walked over to the wall. "Nice Riopelle," he said just as the phone rang. This time, he paid no attention to Poppea's conversation. It had just occurred to him that six months ago her little tricks amused him because then she had still been just a curious phenomenon; now, he and Poppea were almost associates, and he was sinking down to her level.

As soon as she put the phone down, Vincent turned back to her. "I think another Ernst may be sold," he said. "I may find out this evening. Poppea, tell me the truth. We could be in a lot of trouble if it's a fake. Were those pictures really part of an exchange with Ernst? I don't care if they weren't. It's just that we'll both be better off if I know their real provenance."

Poppea raked her hand through her hair. "I told you," she said defiantly. "You know as much about them as I do. Look, that private will be here soon and I want to talk to you about something else. Can you come back tonight?"

"No, not tonight," Vincent answered, thinking with horror of what a meeting with Poppea would do to his evening. "Tomorrow morning, if you want."

By the next morning, Vincent felt much better. Sophia Lyon had sold the Ernst he had given her on consignment, and that was reassuring: She was a shrewd dealer and would surely have noticed if there was anything wrong; and, besides, the fact that the paintings were snapped up so quickly was also a good sign. The profit from the sale meant he would have no financial worries for a while. Even Sarah was in a good mood; Vincent began to think he had worried too much too soon.

His new-found optimism began to evaporate, however, immediately upon meeting Poppea. Once again, she was dirty and disheveled when she opened the door. There were mascara smudges under her eyes; her T-shirt, which had "Easy Lay" printed across the front, was full of stains, and the zipper in her jeans was only half-closed, revealing a piece of pink nylon panty.

"God, Poppea," Vincent said in spite of himself, "you look awful this morning."

She didn't answer but simply jerked her head toward the living room. "Damn it," she said as she sprawled down, "I shouldn't have done that. Jesus, am I hung!"

Vincent smiled. "Too much to drink?" he asked.

"That bitch Zaza," Poppea snarled. "I'll get her. I'll tell her precious fiancé about that lover she had in Italy and what she did with him. . . ." And, to Vincent's horror, she embarked on a long, vicious recitation that alternated between Zaza's sexual habits ("She's the biggest cocksucker in all of northern Italy") and the cheapness of her fiancé ("That mean son of a bitch! He's a millionaire and he wants to sue me for six thousand dollars"). Several minutes passed before Vincent could interrupt her.

"Come on, Poppea," he said weakly, "you won't even remember this when you're the head of an art fund." He stopped as she stared at him, her black eyes almost hypnotic.

"You gotta let me have six thousand today," she said as if she hadn't heard him.

"Today? You must be kidding!"

"What's the matter? You got money. Look, that bastard with his high-powered lawyers, he's suing me if I don't give him the money tomorrow morning."

"I'm sorry, Poppea," Vincent said more firmly now, "but there's no way I can lend you the money. Why don't you ask Jack Griffenbaum? I'm sure he can afford it."

Poppea looked at him sharply and bit her lip. "I owe him some money already," she said, "and he keeps asking me to repay him."

"Well, surely you can stall a little longer. We should soon be getting paid for the Ernst. Try calling Zaza, talk to her, tell her you need just a few days."

"Yeah," Poppea said; and, just as if she didn't care, "I'm going to Italy in a week or two."

"To Italy? But what about your art fund?"

"Jack says it'll take time. And I'll only be gone a few days. I've got to see a new lawyer in Milan. My friend Giancarlo says he's fantastic when it comes to suing people."

Vincent laughed. "Come on, Poppea," he said, "who are you suing now? And in Italy yet?"

Without answering, she stood up, and Vincent, who had already noticed that she was not wearing a bra, could not help staring at her heavy, jiggling breasts. She walked to the window in silence, and, with her back to him, she said in a low voice, "I gotta try to get something back for those fakes."

"The one you sold me, you mean?"

"Yeah, and that Klee in Philly. If I don't take it back, Mark is going to ruin me with the fund. He'll tell Jack all about it."

"Poppea, how does he know about Jack?"

Without answering him, she went on: "I'm scared. It's all Mafia. But I gotta get something back and Italian law is very strict about fakes. I'm going to sue that little creep. I'll put him in jail if he doesn't pay me back."

"Can you?"

"Oh, sure. I can prove he sold me fakes. I've got photographs and receipts. All I need is a certificate saying it's a fake, and I've got him by the balls."

"A certificate from Mundberg?" Vincent asked abruptly.

Poppea turned and stared at him. "Why not?" she said.

Vincent had told Sarah about his lunch with Olga (but not about the little scene in his office) and soon found himself under attack. "Why should you have lunch with her?" Sarah asked sharply. It was no good saying that because she used to work for him she might still be useful. Sarah could see through all that, just as she did when he finally said, "Well, she is a friend."

"You know you don't like her," she answered. "You never have. You thought she'd bring sales when you hired her, but she didn't. And you don't even have anything in common." There was no way out of it for Vincent but to be unpleasant, and he was.

Still, it was Sarah who asked Vincent not to come home before seven the next day: Olga wanted to talk to her, alone; and he promptly agreed, although he wondered whether, as in years past, Sarah would tell him all about it later. He thought this time she might keep it to herself, but the secret, which, once, would have been endlessly provoking, didn't seem to matter as much anymore. He wasn't sure whether he had grown out of curiosity or merely sunk into indifference, but decided to think the better of himself for it, and came home at a quarter to eight.

He felt faintly annoyed when he found Olga still there. He had been sure that she would be gone; it was only after he had taken off his coat that he realized the possibilities and wondered whether she had told Sarah about his attempted seduction of her.

"What time is it?" Olga asked when he walked into the room. "Christ, I'm late. I was supposed to meet John fifteen minutes ago." Immediately, she was gone.

Vincent walked over and poured himself some scotch, then went back to Sarah. "That was a long meeting," he said. "You must be dead. Do you want to go out to dinner?"

When they were settled in the restaurant, Sarah, in a provoking tone, remarked that she and Olga had a great deal in common: They were both miserable; but when Vincent failed to rise to the bait, merely looking blank instead, she went on to say that Olga had talked for hours.

"Oh?"

"Yes," Sarah said, unable to resist so rich a subject. "She can't stand living the way she does. She thought that it was her fault she wasn't getting along with Partridge, and so she decided to take on all that work she's been doing, to be everything to him—a secretary, an organizer, a hostess, not to mention his mistress. But it's not working, and she's very unhappy. She says she can't stand it anymore."

Looking happier than usual, Sarah sat back as the waiter put down her *potage Saint-Germain*. Vincent, who knew his duty, filled the time with elaborations on Partridge; but, as soon as she had eaten the last spoonful, Sarah continued.

"I told her it was all wrong for her when she started it. She should have her own work, something with children maybe, or some creative project. She won't be satisfied if she doesn't express herself. Anyway, she said she was going to stop working for Partridge. It's either that or she'll leave him."

"No!" Vincent exclaimed. "Do you think she might?"

"Well, not right away; but she's certainly closer to it than she's ever been. Anyway, she still wants to save the relationship, so I suggested we run an art therapy class for children together. We could do it in the apartment."

"In the apartment?" Vincent said, horror-struck.

"Yes, upstairs in the study. It would just take a little rearranging, and then, the second year, we could rent our own apartment." And soon the evening went the way of most others: Sarah accused Vincent of not taking her project seriously, of not believing in her. By the time coffee was brought to them, they were sitting in sullen silence.

Vincent, though he might deny it, had expected that nothing would come of the project, and, as the days passed, he could tell he had been right. He carefully refrained from asking Sarah, who was painting again, and in a better humor, about the idea. But he noticed that she never mentioned it: so it was not without a delicious feeling of having been right that he asked her one evening about six weeks later whether she had heard from Olga recently. Sarah, who was painstakingly filling in a small area of color, looked up and shook her head.

"You haven't heard the news, then?" Vincent asked, smiling broadly.

"The news?" said Sarah absentmindedly.

"Yes. About the business." And as Sarah suddenly stared at him, he said, "She's becoming a private dealer. By herself. Starting this week."

Sarah put down her brush with a decided movement. "How can she?" she said angrily. "She doesn't have a stock. And where will she work from? Partridge's studio?"

"Come on, you know her better than that. No, no, she has it all arranged. Partridge is buying her an apartment."

"What!"

"Yes. He had some money to invest and she needed a place. So he's buying a one-bedroom apartment on Seventy-fourth and Park. That way, she'll have an office and a way to be apart from Partridge whenever she feels the need."

When Vincent visited Copley the next day, he was shown into the living room and asked to wait, but now he was able to enjoy the paintings and drawings hanging on the walls. He smiled with pleasure when Copley came in; walking quickly over to him and shaking his hand, Vincent said: "David, this is like the Frick, only nicer because it's private."

Copley smiled back. The compliment had obviously pleased him; and they spent the next twenty minutes walking around the room, looking and discussing. Vincent felt right, at last, because he could use his knowledge professionally; compliments were exchanged, Vincent praising the pictures and Copley Vincent's erudition. They were equal, for a time, sharing in the enjoyment of what they saw. When Copley finally said his time was short and they must see what Vincent would like to have, it was in tones of great amiability. As he preceded him through the door, Vincent knew he had finally arrived. The rest—sales, money, more sales, more money—all that was a foregone conclusion.

The huge room they walked into, at the back of the maisonette, was lined with racks; at the table in the middle sat Copley's secretary, with a consignment sheet in place.

"Well now," Copley said cheerfully, "let's see what we can give you." Moving briskly, he pulled out a small framed drawing. "Could you sell a Degas?" he asked. Vincent answered, yes, he thought he could, and Copley handed it to him. It was fine enough: The nude combing her hair had all the grace and life of a good Degas, but the face had gone dreadfully wrong. It was so misshapen that it gave the whole work a sinister cast. But Copley promptly named a consignment price which he might have expected for a perfect drawing.

This was followed by a difficult, dark Corot landscape; by a very pretty Cézanne watercolor that had, unfortunately, faded; by a Renoir red chalk drawing of a woman not merely plump but grotesquely fat; by an early Braque landscape that looked like a Derain but was priced like a Braque; and by a ravishing but very tiny Boccioni gouache. Every time Copley produced a new work, Vincent smiled and said, yes, he'd like to have it. The secretary gave him the consignment sheet, and Copley shook his hand, telling him his man would deliver it all the next morning.

Vincent still felt good as he walked out the door and found himself in the sunshine on Fifth Avenue. The trees in Central Park were beginning to take on that peculiar chartreuse green of early spring; people were strolling briskly; it was all a new beginning and he actually wondered why he was feeling nervous. It was only after he sat down in his office and unfolded the consignment sheet that he began to worry.

The pictures came the next morning, right on schedule. Vincent lined them up along the wall and, as he looked at them, then at the prices, he realized with a sinking feeling that, while Copley might be well disposed toward him, there was a price to pay; in fact, the dealer had given Vincent pictures so difficult to sell that he couldn't bother to do it himself. The glow faded now, and a new failure loomed ahead; it was entirely possible that Vincent would not sell even one of the Copley pictures.

For a moment—a long moment—Vincent saw that prospect from one angle only: his father's triumph. The relationship with Copley would obviously depend on how well the consigned works sold. Vincent thought that Copley's friendliness was motivated, at least in part, by resentment of André; and that would hardly be enough to sustain this new relationship. The possibility was so unpleasant that he did not even stop to realize that Copley would not tell his father about their connection. As he sat there, it all came back to him bitterly, painfully: the past in which he had fought his father for survival and barely avoided defeat.

"You're going to fail," his father would always tell him in a satisfied voice. "I have to tell you because you're my son, and if I don't, who will? Of course, I wish it weren't so; but I see your shortcomings far too clearly not to warn you that you can never succeed."

Now the taunting words were coming back after a long period of silence. "I have tried," Vincent muttered to himself, "and I have failed." Then he shook himself and stood up, as another voice replaced the first. "He did all he could to make you fail," Sarah had often said, "and look at how well you've been doing." Looking up, he laughed out loud, conscious of the theatricality of his gesture, and thought

Sarah wouldn't be so supportive now, but he began to feel better anyway. So he sat down at his desk, called his photographer, and asked him to come over: He needed color transparencies of the new pictures.

Everything changed again before the end of the day. Vincent was almost inclined to think it was his triumph over depression that, in some mysterious way, had brought him better luck: Sophia Lyon called to say that she would have a check for the Ernst within a week. Obviously, Vincent thought, he'd been a fool to worry. The picture must be real: It had been bought by a well-known Ernst collector who, surely, would not have touched a dubious picture. And, if this one was all right, so were the others. Soon, Vincent would be getting the third one back from the framer's, and that one, he promised himself, he would sell alone: Why share the profit with someone else? He even began to believe he would do well with the Copley pictures —not easily, perhaps, but he would manage. The point was not to make a lot of money, but to show Copley how competent he was; then, he felt sure, more paintings, less difficult paintings, would come his way. By the time he left the office, he was feeling positively jaunty, and his luck held: When he said to Sarah, "Let's go out and have a really good dinner tonight," she agreed enthusiastically and went in to change.

It was only when they had reached the main course—a trout mousse with the lightest, most delicate sauce—that Vincent noticed how unreal the situation had become. The food was indeed delicious, the restaurant pleasant; but to Sarah, who for once was dressed and made up, he had nothing to say. He wasn't angry with her, nor she, he supposed, with him; he simply felt estranged, awkward, as if all the good cheer was nothing but pretense. Still, they could hardly sit in silence: With great effort, he kept up the conversation and even went so far as to tell Sarah, in considerable detail, that she looked beautiful. Although it was true, he felt just the way he did when he was obligated to praise a painting he didn't like: It was hard, unpleasant work.

By the time they returned home, Vincent could see that his efforts had had their effect: Sarah was behaving the way she had at the beginning of their relationship. With a stirring of interest, he realized what her improved humor probably meant, and, sure enough, she soon put on some music and said she felt like dancing. From then on, deprivation took over: He wanted her so badly that nothing else mattered; and she was responding. Soon, they stopped dancing, went upstairs, and fell on the bed, mouths open and hungry; but when the feverish caresses stopped, when Vincent had entered Sarah, who was moaning deeply, his head became clear again: He knew he needed a climax desperately, but also that he was only using Sarah. It was as if a curtain of lust had suddenly been drawn; the act of love had become a mere hygienic necessity. He wasn't surprised when Sarah, a little later, answered his words of insincere endearment by saying: "It has nothing to do with you and me. I wanted sex so badly I would have enjoyed it with anybody."

David Copley felt a twinge of pleasure when he decided to give Vincent a few pictures: At least, in a small way, he was getting back at André; he even smiled to himself as he remembered a conversation, some two years ago, in which André had calmly explained that he preferred not to work with Vincent. The pleasure faded quickly, though. André was still blackmailing him, after all. In fact, he was coming back that very afternoon. For a moment, Copley thought of canceling the meeting; then, squaring his shoulders and reaching for his snuffbox, he decided to go through with it. The man must be faced, at least until he could be neutralized; and Copley suspected that once he really started searching, a handle would not be that hard to find.

Besides, despite what André claimed, Copley knew he could not afford to carry through his threats: After all, no dealer would trust someone who had ratted in this particular way. Even if André were to move to New York, thus evading the French tax authorities for good, he would be unable to function in a world where he would be universally shunned. No dealer could afford to do business with him, for fear their transaction might not stay secret; and Copley knew that André did not have the clientele, in America anyway, to survive without the dealers. In the end, the danger was not as great as it seemed, although it would grow. André's position must be made clearer to him—a task Copley did not relish. He almost regretted now having agreed to provide the funds for the Chardin himself: Although he often bought major paintings alone, this time he was committed to sharing the profit—or at least some of it, he thought, resolving that he would report a low sales price to André. Still, André's demands would probably grow; the only question in Copley's mind was whether or not it would be better to quell him now or to wait. And knowing what he knew, Copley decided he would wait, for a few weeks at any rate. Other people might well do the job for him: The Bergs, he had been told, were already complaining loudly, and Nini Sanche had been entertaining her many friends with Pierre-Paul's coming pull-out from *Voir*.

Thoughtfully, Copley took another pinch of snuff. He couldn't help regretting the alteration in his relationship to André, who represented just the kind of European sophistication he yearned for. There, he felt, was a man who had always lived well; who understood decoration, and travel, and food; a man of real culture, who ran a magazine and enjoyed a reputation as an intellectual—something he, Copley, only yearned for. He always felt American, in the Jamesian sense, in André's presence, as if André Germain belonged to an older, finer, lusher world, as if he understood art better. Even Copley's undeniably greater talent for making money appeared, when seen from that point of view, almost a failing. When they were together, he always found himself impressed by André, as if the older man's very presence brought him a step farther down the road to that desirable state of aristocratic detachment.

When André came to see him the very next day, it was obvious to Copley that he had been right. André had bought the Chardin, he said, for $1,200,000. It was all settled; the payment was to be made immediately; and the Chardin would be picked up by representatives of *Voir* as soon as that was done. It could then be shipped to New York: If Copley would write a check, the transaction could be concluded within a week. Copley nodded and went out of the room, stopping to ask where the money was to be transferred. When he came back, the conversation continued as if nothing had happened to mar its harmony.

Nothing could have stopped Partridge from attending the opening at the Guggenheim that night. It was a place where a successful artist owed it to himself to be seen; and since the sculptor being shown was safely dead, there was no reason to feel jealous. The fact that David Smith, if alive, would have been scarcely older than Partridge, and that his sculpture was universally admired, bothered the painter not at all. When it came to artistic rivalry, Partridge knew whom he feared, and his rivals were all too alive. Still, the occasion was not as satisfying as it should have been. True, there was the colorful, dressed-up crowd swirling up and down the great spiral ramp. He himself was conscious of looking his best; he thoroughly enjoyed greeting all the people he knew, waving to acquaintances in the distance, praising—oh so selflessly—the work on display. But he also knew that he would have to keep repeating that no, Olga wasn't there that night, the poor darling had the most terrible cough while, actually, the darling in question was simply waiting for him to come home so that she could continue the scene interrupted by his departure for the opening.

Even as he talked to people, Partridge was acknowledging to himself that he had made a mistake: He should never have offered Olga that apartment.

That, he felt, was what had started the trouble. He was aware, of course, that he and Olga had had some pretty severe fights before there was ever any question of the apartment, but, then again, he expected conflict. As it was, Partridge thought, he had always been generous: As long as he had his way, he was willing to spend money. It all made perfect sense: His women gave him sex and allegiance; when, as was true of Olga, they belonged to a superior category, they even furthered his career; and, in return, he presented them with exciting nights and a lush life-style. But this time he had slipped.

It was really a question of outfoxing himself. He had been more anxious to keep Olga than practically any of his other women: partly because, within his limits, he really loved her; partly because she had proved such an asset to his career. When she kept insisting she must have her own life, he had cooperated in ways he well knew were altogether safe. Because that first move to a separate studio had been really successful, he had let himself slip into getting her the apartment. At first, it had seemed to make sense. Life had been wonderful when Olga was giving all her time to promoting his career, but he realized even while it was happening that such an ideal situation was not likely to last forever.

Naturally, he had protested when she said she wanted to make money: It was quite unnecessary; he was always willing to give her anything she wanted. It was when she went on to explain that she wanted to become a private dealer that the light had dawned. Partridge could never have enough dealers selling his work, and Olga would be a welcome addition, someone completely loyal to him who could provide him with yet another source of income while earning money herself. And on top of that, he could strengthen their relationship by behaving generously; so he promptly offered the apartment and a supply of works on paper with the understanding that she would develop her own clients in a way that would not compete directly with his New York gallery. Olga had been thrilled, of course, and he had congratulated himself on his own cleverness.

Only now it wasn't working at all the way he had intended, he reflected glumly, while pretending to admire a large, shiny steel sculpture. Instead of continuing to depend on him, she had created a completely new direction in her life: His interests were actually coming *after* her goddamn business. And even now, he was so distracted that he was not putting his all into making this evening a success. He was so conscious of the problem with Olga that, instead of going home, he stopped for one drink, then another. The crisis, he knew, must be carefully managed. Olga's refusal to accompany him to the opening heralded a new stage in their relationship. Obviously, he could not afford much more of this: Continued success did not allow for any distractions. But he felt he actually loved Olga—to his surprise—and wanted to keep her. Partridge had traversed many crises in the past, but they had been either professional or legal: pictures that didn't sell, galleries that didn't cooperate properly, ex-wives who wanted too much alimony. Then, too, there was the permanent wound, the fact that, although he was so popular, critics either ignored him or put him down; but the problem with Olga was a new emergency altogether, one he had never encountered before. When his other women proved too much trouble, he dropped them. Now he did not want to lose Olga.

That there would be trouble when he finally got home, he knew all too well: Their earlier fight had been unusually nasty and, in the height of his rage, he had actually kicked her, hard. Obviously, that would have to be paid for. Still, there was a remedy: So he went to the all-night florist at Fifty-seventh and Lexington and bought a huge, spectacular bunch of tulips and irises with which he hoped to appease Olga's anger. He therefore felt he had a real grievance when his flowers were greeted, as he was, with scorn and contumely.

"You can't buy me off with flowers this time," Olga said as she refused to take them. "In fact, I don't want any more gifts from you"; and she paced to the other end of the studio. Safely, since her back was turned to him, Partridge allowed himself a grimace: It was going to be a long evening. Much to his surprise, though, Olga came back to him after a few minutes, and said in serious but not unpleasant tones, "I want to talk to you; we can't go on like this." And to his horror, he found that there was to be neither a scene nor a reconciliation. He tried to be loving and abort the discussion, but Olga would not let him touch her.

He told her he loved her, that she was his little bird, and he would do anything for her, but she simply answered that that wasn't the question. And when, smiling, he asked what the question could possibly be, she said sharply: "Don't patronize me, John. I'm very serious."

Partridge now thought the time had come for a good

fight, and he started to reproach her for having stayed home that night. Perhaps she'd been meeting some other man, he said heatedly. It was clear she didn't care for him if she refused to accompany him on such an important evening. Refusing to get angry, she merely answered that perhaps he was right and that they had better discuss it.

For a moment, he was tempted to use his tried-and-true technique for disposing of unwanted women. He never said he didn't want them anymore; on the contrary, he was eminently agreeable—when he was there. The thing was, he was scarcely ever there. Slowly, the woman would find out he had a new mistress and would herself suggest a break-up. He would then amiably, regretfully, agree. But he knew that he was not ready to lose Olga or replace her. He still wanted her.

With the utmost reluctance, he settled down for a long, unpleasant exchange and found himself faced with something so new, so unexpected, that he hardly knew how to react. He was being asked by Olga to step into new, frightening, unfamiliar territory. She was saying that she had put him first for years, but no longer could; that their relationship would only endure if she had real independence, if her own aims took precedence, if at long last the priorities were shifted to her. "We fought earlier tonight," she said gravely, "because you complained I was spending all my time at the apartment and only paying attention to my own work. Well, you were right. But that's the way I want it to be. I can't sink myself into your career, your social life, your needs anymore. I have to have my own life. And that means I won't be around here nearly as much from now on. I want to see *my* friends, not go out with you to visit people for whom I care nothing. Maybe that's not possible; in that case, I'll have to move out."

He could feel the blood leave his face as she spoke. After a moment of panic, however, he negotiated, slowly and painfully. When Olga announced that she planned to furnish the new apartment so that she could occasionally spend nights there, it seemed they had come to an impasse; he knew he couldn't spend a night alone. But Olga finally agreed that, for now anyway, and although she would buy a bed, she would stay with him at the studio every night. Still, it was understood that he could no longer expect her to share all his social obligations, that she would devote weekdays to her own work, and that he must get himself a secretary. Then, after he had agreed, she calmly added, "And don't ever kick me again."

The truth was, as she told Sarah the next day, that she still loved Partridge and didn't want to leave him, but she so enjoyed her business and making money, she so needed to recover her old, independent personality that she could not have survived any longer without a change.

"I suppose that means other men," said Vincent with a smile.

"No," Sarah answered, "well, not yet anyway. She likes being taken seriously and running a business. I asked her how she was doing and she wouldn't say, exactly; but she's making plenty of money, obviously, she's already bought at least ten thousand dollars' worth of drawings. Of course, I wanted her to take my work, but she said she had no clients for it. Some friend!"

"It's the money, I suppose," Vincent said, carefully ignoring Sarah's last words. "You know, Olga says that all she cares about is self-expression, but I have the definite feeling that, for her, being rich is a very satisfying way of fulfilling oneself. I'd watch out, if I were Partridge; in fact, if I were he, I'd entrust her with some capital."

Sarah laughed grimly. "Why don't you entrust me with some?" she asked.

*   *   *

That was exactly Viola's question, the same day, to André Germain. "I don't understand you," she was saying. "Why can't I have a salary and a bank account?" Quickly, before André could answer, she continued, "Yes, I know, you've told me that I can't have a bank account in Paris because I'm an American, but what about here? Why can't you pay me a salary here? I just can't stand having to go to you for every penny I need. After all, I work for *Voir*. Why should I be the only unpaid person on the staff?"

André looked at her warily. "I can't pay you here," he said, obviously making an effort to control himself. "You know very well that France has currency regulations. I couldn't change francs into dollars every month. Besides, you only have to ask me if you need money."

"Then why can't I be paid out of the dollar sales of the gallery? It wouldn't have to be every month, it could just be every three or four months."

"I've just told you it's impossible," he said, standing up. And as soon as Viola had said, "But André," he exploded. It was a familiar speech: He had quite enough worries without Viola's causing further complications and, anyway, she spent far too much money. Her clothes alone . . .

"You know very well you told me to get a suit at Saint-Laurent," she said firmly. "You said I would need it on the trip, that it's good for business if I look elegant."

"I never said that. I never said that," André shouted frantically. Pounding on the bedside table, he went on screaming. "How dare you contradict me! How dare you!" and looking wildly about, he rushed out, slamming the door behind him.

It was a shaken Viola who made her way to her lunch with Pierre-Paul Sanche. Of course, she had known what André's reaction would be, only it had been even worse. He had never been easy, certainly, but lately he had become even more bad-tempered, more unwilling to answer any questions or consider anyone but himself. Viola felt useless. At the beginning she had been associated with all the major decisions at *Voir*. Her contacts with most of the famous European painters had guaranteed that articles often appeared under her by-line. But now she was deliberately pushed away, encouraged to stay in the country or do nothing at all, and it was immensely depressing. Much of Viola's self-esteem depended on visible achievements; as those became fewer, she had begun to feel worthless. And a lunch spent appeasing Sanche wouldn't make her feel much better.

She looked for him when she walked into the Polo Room. He was late, naturally, so she went on thinking about her life. She couldn't leave André, she said to herself bitterly: How would she live if she did? She had no money of her own and few illusions about the help likely to be extended by her friends. She had nowhere to go, nothing to do. And as for working on a magazine here in New York, it would be almost impossible. For one thing, she was not at all anxious to take on a nine-to-five job again. At least, if he'd been paying her, she could have been saving money, she would have a cushion: As it was, she was stuck in a life that, she realized more clearly every day, made her terribly unhappy. No, she couldn't leave André; but she wasn't sure she could go on with him, either. She sighed. And now Sanche was coming to her for comfort when she needed it so badly herself.

When Pierre-Paul finally arrived, he looked properly desperate. His face was dead white, his eyes puffy, his whole body bent forward, and he answered Viola's greeting with a moan. Having apologized for being late, he went on to explain that he hardly knew where he was, that the shock had been so great he was still reeling from it.

Viola listened with obvious sympathy and finally said: "I know, Pierre-Paul, how painful it all is for you, but if you think it would help you to talk about it . . ."

Holding back nothing, Sanche poured out the story of his married life, adding pitifully, "Of course, I know I wasn't exciting enough for her."

"Nonsense, Pierre-Paul, of course you were," Viola answered firmly.

"Well," Sanche said, "you may be right; it wasn't just me." He interrupted himself to order eggs Benedict, and then went on: "After all, you know, if André had not been so impossible, she might not have left. She was longing to be involved with *Voir;* it was my doing nothing she couldn't stand. And I can't see why André was so obdurate. After all, it is my money and he could at least have made an effort. And then, sending me Thérèse—that was so insulting. When I told Nini, she was livid—"

"But, Pierre-Paul," Viola said quickly, "you told me she had run off with a racing driver. Are you quite sure? It doesn't sound like Nini; I mean, she did care, as you were saying, about her position."

Pierre-Paul gave a loud groan. "He's not just a race-car driver," he finally said. "He's an Italian prince who likes to race. He has a palace in Rome, a house in Paris, and an apartment here." He paused and looked at Viola with tears in his eyes. "I've really lost her now," he went on. "My cousin Claudia, who knows him, says he's very handsome. She'll never come back to me, and I simply can't bear it. I can't live without her, I just can't do it."

For the next hour, Viola was busy trying to reassure him that he could manage. When finally they parted at the restaurant door, she saw her chance for revenge. "Well, Pierre-Paul," she said, "the only thing that'll help you now is work: You wouldn't feel so miserable if you had something to do. I'll talk to André about it; surely he'll see your point, although, as you know, he can be difficult; but I'll do my best and you must keep after him." And Sanche, nodding gratefully, promised he would.

It was not without a certain feeling of pleasure that Viola returned to the hotel. If Sanche did indeed work at *Voir*, André would be forced to treat her better if only because she would be a necessary go-between; and if Pierre-Paul concerned himself with the magazine's finances (after all, what else could he do?), then she would be in a strong position to suggest that she was entitled to a salary. She almost rubbed her hands together: This time, she would beat André at his own game.

A little later that day, she proceeded with her plan. "Of course," she told André, "he moaned and groaned and lamented. He's lost Nini for good, apparently, but, you know, he hasn't changed in one way. He blames you for his sorrows, and he's determined to work at *Voir*. In fact, he sees it as a compensation for what he's enduring; and he still wants to show the world that he's not just one of the idle rich. I suspect he hopes Nini might come back to him if he can be seen to work on the magazine. In any event, you might as well be prepared: He won't take no for an answer. He says he wants to run the financial side of things. And why shouldn't he, after all? It's only a burden for you."

She wasn't surprised when he exploded once more; only, this time, she could see that he was genuinely worried.

TEN

"I have money for you," Vincent said, smiling, as he walked into Poppea Vlassoff's apartment later that week. "Aren't you pleased?"

Poppea laughed. "I'm fucking ecstatic," she answered, reaching quickly for the check, but frowning as she read it; and in a flat voice, she went on: "You're short. Five grand short."

"No, I'm not, "Vincent said as he sat down. "Remember the discount I gave? We agreed about that long ago," and, watching Poppea as she stood there biting her thumb, he added, "What's the matter, you don't look pleased."

She wasn't surprised when he exploded once more; only, window, she said, "I needed that money for my trip to Italy. I mean, I'm broke without it." She stared at her new plants, which were already turning brown at the edges.

"How can you be?" Vincent asked. She didn't respond. "Look," he said earnestly, "you're making ten thousand dollars on this. And surely the rest of the money gives you leverage. You can just refuse to pay for this Ernst and that will make up for the fakes, so, really, you don't even need to go to Italy."

Poppea finally turned to him and, for the first time, Vincent thought she looked embarrassed. "It's not that easy," she said slowly. "I owe that money to Jack Griffenbaum. See, I had to pay for the pictures, and I couldn't; so I borrowed from him, and now I have to pay him back. And the rest I owe my janitor."

"Not again?"

"Yeah. I had to give Zaza some money, so I told him I had a great investment for him, only I have to give him a thousand profit, and I still owe rent for this month."

"Well then," Vincent said, "don't pay Jack back. Or don't give him the whole amount. Just tell him you're still owed money."

Poppea shook her head. "He knows you're paying me," she said glumly, but soon brightened up. "Wait a minute! I could tell him to call you and then you could tell him you only got part payment. He'd believe you. Yeah, he would."

Vincent froze. "No, Poppea," he said, "I'm not going to lie to him; and, besides, what I pay you is strictly between you and me. I'm afraid you'll have to think of something else."

There was a silence, but just as Vincent was getting up to leave, Poppea stopped him. "Maybe you can lend me the money," she said, "just for two or three weeks. Look, when I get to Milan, I'll get my money back and I'll be loaded. It'll only be three weeks, a month tops. I mean, we do good business together. You can trust me, right?"

She hardly looked surprised when he refused and she went on as if nothing happened.

"Maybe you could buy my car?"

"Your car?"

"Yeah. Last year I exchanged a Poliakoff for a Triumph. It's pale blue—"

Vincent laughed. "Really, Poppea!" he said.

"Well," she continued, "it's that creep who's marrying Zaza. I had to give him two grand to stop him from suing me, and I'm supposed to give him two more next week. Why should he care? He's got all those lawyers on retainers sitting on their asses doing nothing. Shit, I'd never win."

"Poppea, I don't understand why you're so broke. After all, you are doing business. You must be making commissions. Every time I see you, you've just sold something and you never have a penny. What do you do with it?"

"It's those fucking fakes. I mean, I'm just starting out in business, and already I own two paintings, but right now they're not worth shit."

To his surprise, Vincent realized he actually felt sorry for her: She was incompetent, greedy, dishonest, and getting no more than she deserved, and yet he could not help sympathizing. Her resourcefulness seemed somehow admirable: She was surviving in spite of all those fakes; she was managing, coping with her debts and creditors. There was something appealing about it all—although, he quickly thought, not appealing enough to gain his help. Still, he wanted to show his goodwill and asked about the fund.

Immediately, Poppea cheered up. "It's going great," she said. "God, I put everything together, all the documents and charts, and it really looks professional. I gave three copies to Jack so he can show them to his investors, and I've kept another one for an old boyfriend of mine, he's a big investment banker. I called him and told him all about it. I told him we're starting with five million—"

"Five million! Poppea!"

"Yeah, five, well, I thought ten, but Jack said no and—"

Vincent laughed. "Poppea," he asked, "where on earth are you going to get five million dollars?"

She stared straight at him; he looked uneasily into the darkness of her eyes before turning away.

"The more we have, the more we make," she said grandly. "You buy a million-dollar painting, you can resell it right away for a million and a half. Anyway, Jack's friends are so rich, a million doesn't mean anything to them. I told my ex-boyfriend not to talk to me about anything less."

"And what did he say?"

"Oh, he had to consult his associates," Poppea answered, "but he should be good for at least a million. Anyway, I'm going to get it all set up soon, I told you, I'll make you one of the advisers so you can really make money too."

There was a brief pause before Vincent said: "Do you realize how few million-dollar paintings there are and how difficult it is to get them?"

"So? You know all those rich privates. You can get us the pictures."

Vincent's sympathy was quite gone now. "I have to leave," he said, and, turning back at the door, added sarcastically, "but let me know as soon as you've got your millions."

It was all a great nuisance, André Germain thought. In fact, as usual, life was unfair to him. It was bad enough that he should have to struggle so hard when other, less deserving people had money simply thrust upon them; that he should have so little recognition when he was so much more intelligent and cultivated than most everyone else around. Just as he was beginning to rectify this ghastly situation—the Chardin Copley had financed would, he reflected, make a solid difference—there were more complications.

The fake Chagall, he now realized, would not prove as convenient a tool as he had hoped: If the Bergs really went on with their suit, they would probably win in the end, and that would make him look bad. He didn't really want to be a subject of gossip for a year or more, with people saying he sold fakes. He flushed as he imagined just what would happen. The question was how long it might take to have the Fornettis—who, after all, had sold the painting to Barolo—reimburse him for the picture. That they ultimately would, he did not much doubt. After all, they were about to open a gallery in New York: They could hardly want scandal at this point. Still, it might take a while, and the Bergs would be squawking in the meantime. Then, too, he was losing his tool. He had thought the Chagall would give him a handle, allowing him to use the Fornettis pretty much as he saw fit; but now, if he forced them into buying back the Chagall (and, of course, they would do it just because of Barolo), then they would be free of him. It really seemed sometimes as if fate were conspiring against him, constantly raising undeserving mediocrities and leaving him in the lurch.

As if things weren't bad enough, now there was also Viola. Silently, André cursed Thérèse for not having held her tongue. It just needed a few firm denials, he thought to himself; Viola was pretty credulous. With a twinge of satisfaction, he remembered the time he had sold her Matisse drawing—a work she had bought herself before they ever met—and told her it had been lost in the move from one apartment to another. She had believed him, of course, and he was now the richer by several rare, superbly bound first editions. Then, there were his affairs: Viola never had a clue. Even Coche, he thought: All Paris knew, but Viola didn't. Shaking his head, he came back to his current problem.

"How could you!" Viola had hissed scornfully. "And with Thérèse! It's not even as if she were pretty! Besides, your own assistant! It's like sleeping with the maid. And when I think of how I've helped her through the years! The worst of it is the way you both lied to me during all those months of her pregnancy. How can I possibly ignore being made a fool of all this time!" And before André could say anything, she had added: "You'd better leave me now. I can feel a headache coming on and, besides, I'd rather not see you for a while."

At least, he had given Thérèse hell; that was something; and he would do it again. She'll cry, all right, he thought with pleasure. She'll cry for a long time; she's going to repent at leisure. And angrily dismissing that delicious prospect, he decided that, as usual, Viola would have to lump it. It might take her a little while to get over it, but he would see to it that she did. Already he had told her that, as far as he was concerned, the whole situation simply didn't exist: It was Thérèse's problem and she could cope with it as she chose. He wasn't giving it another thought, and neither should Viola.

That statement, when he made it, had been greeted with bitter laughter. "Not give it another thought!" Viola had repeated. "As if that were possible now! You don't seem to realize, André, that you have been lying to me all this time. I can never trust you again. Now I'll always wonder what new blow is going to fall, what other catastrophe you have concealed from me. How can I ever believe you again?"

It seemed to Viola, as she remembered the beginning of that afternoon, that the blow had been all the heavier for coming at a time when, finally, the future seemed a little more promising. She had been congratulating herself about her lunch with Sanche when she returned to the hotel: At last, she was manipulating André instead of just helping him. Whether he liked it or not, he would be compelled to let her have her way; and once she was paid a salary, it seemed to her, everything would become possible. She had been feeling so good, in fact, that, upon meeting Sheila Mockridge in the hotel lobby, she had been particularly amiable. She had even kept her smile when Mrs. Mockridge, true to her reputation as the nastiest gossip in New York, had asked how Thérèse's child was and added that it must be quite a thrill for André to be a father again.

"Oh, Sheila, honestly!" Viola had answered, laughing, "you are the limit: Of course, it's not André's child." And, with mock severity, she had added, "Now, you're not to go on saying this. Poor Thérèse. Just because she isn't married is no reason to make wild guesses. I'm sure you're far too kind to go on spreading this sort of thing."

She really believed it was all nothing more than malicious gossip, so much so, in fact, that when Thérèse had come in to ask about Sanche and Nini, Viola had recounted the little incident to her. "You must admit," she had said, "people are impossible, saying that Igor is André's child. What next, Thérèse, what next!" And then, much to her surprise, Thérèse had burst into tears.

As Viola remembered her naiveté, she clenched her fists in rage. She had really thought that Thérèse was distressed by the gossip, so she had consoled her, telling her that no one paid attention to what Sheila Mockridge said, that Sheila would no doubt drop the whole thing. Even when Thérèse, choking with sobs, had shaken her head in violent negation, Viola had insisted that there was really nothing to be upset about, that Sheila was simply hopeless. When Thérèse had mumbled, "It's true," Viola had misunderstood and answered, "She really is, and I'm sure she's already on to a tastier tidbit."

Her whole face flushed in shame as she relived the humiliating moment when Thérèse, the tears running down her cheeks, had managed to blurt out: "No, no, Viola, what she said is true. Igor *is* André's child." For a few seconds,

Viola thought she had misunderstood; but then Thérèse, unable to contain herself, had burst forth.

"Oh, Viola," she had sobbed, "I wanted to tell you long ago but André wouldn't let me. It's been so humiliating for me, pretending I had just slept with an old lover when I knew you'd understand if I told you the truth. Every time I wanted to talk to you, André would forbid it, and I just didn't know what to do. Igor is André's child, and I just couldn't bear pretending he wasn't. God, I even had to put 'father unknown' on the birth certificate, but I'm so glad now—"

"Get out," Viola had said in a whisper. Thérèse looked up, startled, wiping the tears from her eyes.

"Get out," Viola had repeated, a little louder. "Now."

"Get out? But, Viola, I don't understand . . ." and she jumped as Viola, seizing her firmly above the elbow, pushed her toward the door.

When Thérèse stood in the corridor, Viola had added, still in a low voice, but with a look of disgust: "I never want to see you again. I never want to talk to you again," and slammed the door in her face.

That, at least, Viola remembered with some satisfaction. She had not allowed herself to show anger or hurt but had behaved the way she would if a servant had offended her in some way: You would simply dismiss them without further discussion. And she would make it plain to André that she had meant every word she had said.

In fact, she almost looked forward to the confrontation. Here, at least, was one occasion where she was so plainly in the right that she could compel André to listen, then to admit he was guilty. After all those unprovoked scenes of which she had been the victim, this was a fight in which she would have the upper hand. Still, she set her stage carefully. When André returned, the curtains were drawn and she was in bed, holding an ice pack to her head.

"What's the matter?" he asked nastily as he closed the door. "Don't tell me you have one of your headaches again!"

Viola waited a full minute before answering; then, with a dramatic movement, she turned to him and, sighing deeply, simply said: "How could you?"

André looked at her. "You don't have to be so dramatic," he answered. "What if the Chagall is a fake after all? We'll give the Bergs back their money, that's all, the dirty parvenus."

Viola gave a start. "Oh, no," she said, "not that as well! I should have known, I suppose. No, André. Thérèse has told me everything."

"Everything! What, everything! What are you talking about?" André asked prudently; but his face was already drained of color.

"As if you didn't know! Igor, of course! Your own assistant, a woman to whom I have shown nothing but kindness, having an affair with you behind my back—and now the child! It's so sordid! And those endless lies, the way you both lied to me all these months!"

"Well," André said reasonably, "you would just have been upset if I had told you."

With that, Viola, who until now had contained her rage, exploded. "Upset! Upset! How dare you! I have every right to be upset, and more than upset! When I think of what people are saying behind my back! Just today, Sheila Mockridge asked me how the little bastard was, and I told her she was all wrong. Oh, she's having a good laugh now, you can be sure. To think that everyone knew except me. Liar! Liar!"

André flushed. "I forbid you," he said in a tight voice.

"You! You forbid me!" Viola shouted with a theatrical laugh. "That's a good one! You have a sleazy little affair behind my back with Thérèse. You produce a little bastard.

And you have the gall to forbid me! God, André, it's not just all the lies, all the deception, but Thérèse! That skeleton! If she were attractive, at least, I could see why you did it—"

"Stop it!" André shouted, stamping his foot in rage. "Stop it! Don't you dare talk to me like that!"

"Dare? What should I do? Smile happily and say I'm glad you're sleeping with your secretary and have given her a child? Should I ask you to go on lying to me? And what else have you been lying about, I wonder? You might as well tell me now, I'd rather find out all at once!"

André, making a visible effort, said more calmly, "Look, Viola, I can see why you're upset; but none of it really matters. After all, Thérèse was just a convenience. As for the child, well, he was an accident. But it makes no difference. He's just hers, that's all. You know very well that the birth certificate says 'father unknown'—"

"I wonder!" Viola interrupted. "That's probably just another lie."

"Oh, for God's sake; I'll have Thérèse show it to you, if you like. It doesn't matter, any of it, it changes nothing—"

"Show it to me!" Viola answered dramatically. "Do you really think that Thérèse is in a position to show me anything? I told her I never want to see her or talk to her again, and I mean it. I will not have her in the same room with me."

"Oh, really, Viola, do be realistic," André said in the tone of a man who forces himself to be patient. "Of course, you'll see her. How could you not, when we all work together? If you'd rather not have her as a guest for a while, I understand, but obviously as far as the magazine and the gallery go—"

"The magazine! The gallery! I don't care if they both close tomorrow! God, André, don't you have any decency? You haven't even said that you were sorry, that you understood what I'm going through! Don't you ever think of anyone except yourself? No, I told her and now I'm telling you: I will never see her again. And if you can't understand that, then I don't want to see you either."

"That's enough, Viola," André said violently. "There's no question of that. And obviously you have to see Thérèse again. You're simply not being realistic."

For a few minutes, they remained silent, but Viola looked as if she were choking. When she spoke, it was in an icy voice. "I mean it, André," she said. "I've had enough of all this. You can go back to Paris without me."

Even though André, back in Paris, was safe from the Bergs and their lawyers, somehow the relief seemed incomplete; and yet, on the surface, everything was back to normal. Viola had indeed stayed on in New York; but while the issue of Thérèse was still undecided, it was now understood that, in some four or five weeks, Viola would join André in France; and, characteristically, she took care of appearances by inventing several justifications for her continued presence in America. As for the bone of contention, Thérèse was back at work, sniffling louder than ever.

It was actually a relief, André realized, to have Viola stay in New York. It spared him a great deal of unpleasantness and freed him for his renewed pursuit of Coche del Mancha.

Of course, while he argued that Thérèse didn't really matter, he kept Coche quiet in spite of a strong temptation to use her as a concluding argument: You can see how little I really care about Thérèse, he almost said, since it's Coche I'm really interested in. But he prudently decided to forgo the argument. Who knew what Viola thought about Coche?

It was immensely convenient for him, back in Paris and

alone, to pursue Coche. Because of the servants, she still couldn't spend the night at his apartment; they'd be sure to tell Viola and that would be an unnecessary provocation. But there was nothing to prevent his sleeping at Coche's, or his taking her out to dinner as often as they were both free. It was really ideal: Thérèse organized everything as usual; Viola was actually doing useful work in New York; and he was left to enjoy himself.

It therefore seemed to him both annoying and unfair that he was unable to relax; he could not determine what was bothering him. The Chagall would be taken care of when he saw the Fornettis at the end of the month. The Chardin was well on its way to being sold, which meant that very soon the money would pour in. Pierre-Paul Sanche was, temporarily at least, out of action. All should be well, he kept thinking. It finally became so puzzling that he decided his was a case of insufficient self-indulgence; so he told Thérèse to reserve a table at Maxim's for the next evening— Thursday, the dressy night—and invited Coche.

He had obviously been right, he told himself the next day, as he adjusted his black tie. He was just in the mood for this kind of festivity. Coche, when he went to get her, looked particularly elegant in her pink brocade Saint-Laurent dress. After a few minutes dancing, somewhere between the crayfish Nantua and the pheasant *en papillote*, André knew the world was finally going his way. The red velvet banquettes, the Art Nouveau mirrors, the pheasant on his plate, the Lafite '67 in his glass—all combined to give him a sense of well-being.

"You know," Coche said, "I was talking about you the other day to Laure de Goldschmidt." André listened to this with rapt attention. Since one of Coche's main attractions was that she was the Baroness de Goldschmidt's closest friend, Coche was his key to those glamorous parties at Ayville, the Goldschmidt château near Chantilly, his entry into the world of multimillionaires. If he, André, could become part of that tightly closed inner circle, then nothing would be beyond his reach. Not only would his social position become unassailable, but he would also have access to the most prestigious of private collections. And now Coche was telling him that Laure found him charming and entertaining; that she wanted to see more of him; and that she would call him soon to invite him for a weekend.

The pheasant was delicious; Coche said so and André quite agreed. But he was far too euphoric to taste it properly, far too busy striking the right balance of pleasure and nonchalance with Coche: She must be encouraged but not allowed to realize just how much she was doing for him. Ayville! He would soon be spending a weekend at Ayville! Already he could see himself descending the famous staircase with its banister of chased silver and the suite of Gobelin tapestries woven specially for Louis XV and bearing the royal monogram. He could hear himself dazzling Laure at dinner as the goldplate shone on the table and gradually all conversation died down so everybody could listen to him, André. Nothing could stop him now; and, in his impatience for the promised invitation, he was almost annoyed when the silver salver set down before him yielded a mere hazelnut soufflé. He told Coche that she had never looked more beautiful, and was soon dancing with her again.

Much later that night, after Coche had fallen asleep, he realized that, of course, everyone would know if he went to Ayville with Coche. It would get back soon enough to Viola, who wouldn't like it. At that, he almost laughed out loud. Who cared now what Viola thought? He would soon have the Goldschmidts behind him; Viola would become altogether unnecessary.

Coche, turning over in her sleep, reminded André that

he, too, should be resting, but he didn't care. Always prone to insomnia, he felt no discomfort, no wish to drop off. There was far too much to think about. For it was becoming obvious to André that his life would soon assume a whole new alignment. It was time to leave the plateau of these last few years and proceed to new peaks. Viola had, in her time, advanced his career. Now she could be jettisoned and replaced by Coche, who would finally bring him everything he had always wanted. He could see himself a year from now, divorced and remarried, a frequent guest at Ayville and in the Goldschmidts' Paris house, part of that golden circle to which anyone with social ambitions aspired.

Then, too, the money would be flowing in from that Chardin and from his new contacts. He would soon be able to live on a much more spectacular scale; already he could see himself selling his country house—which he had always thought lacking in glamour—to buy something much larger, a small but exquisite château, in fact. As for the Paris apartment, that would have to be changed. After all, he would be giving large, envied parties. And then there was Coche: She must dress only from couture houses. He even wondered for a while about whether she should go on accepting Laure's spectacular—and hardly worn—dresses and decided it might be all right as long as no one knew about it. And when, briefly, Thérèse intruded upon his thoughts, he knew she would be no problem: She could go on working as always and raise the child herself.

Olga Kourakin, in her New York bed, was sleeping no better than André Germain, but for very different reasons. Far from seeing a future imbued with a rosy glow, she was beating her head against a wall: She needed her freedom more every day, and yet she could not leave Partridge.

She loved him still, she was sure of that, but also she was terrified of what he might do if she told him she was moving out.

She felt miserable and unable to endure much more. There was her career; she looked back with amusement on those days when she thought Partridge would be her full-time occupation. Oh, she told herself patronizingly, she had been right to try it; after all, every woman must at some time harbor the illusion that she can live entirely through her man. Now that she had her own business, she could see what really satisfied her. The success she achieved must be her success; the money she made, her money. Besides, she enjoyed the hunt for material, the give-and-take of bargaining, the search for clients. It was fun to sell, to convince a hesitant collector that this—whatever it was—was the one item he could not do without. And she loved keeping up with the collectors until they were ready to buy again, forcing their attention and their respect. The satisfaction of making money was much greater than she had expected; she had become addicted to success and wanted a great deal more.

Of course, she said to herself, with another man, it might have been possible to have all that *and* a relationship; after all, there were a number of successful women dealers who were married as well; but, with Partridge, the conflict was unending. He wanted all her attention and most of her time; even when she made it very plain she had other occupations, he would skillfully create a little crisis so that she would feel obligated to help him. That very day, he had called her at the end of the morning: The shippers were coming in three hours to pick up the paintings for his Los Angeles exhibition, and there was neither list nor insurance record. Yes, he had thought of it ahead of time and tried to reach his part-time secretary but she must be out of town. No, he couldn't do it himself, he would be glad to if only he had the time. ("Liar!" Olga said to herself.) And there was still so much to be done. Some of the stripping had been knocked off, and he was having trouble with three of the stretchers, so could she please drop everything and come right down. He knew he was putting her out, but there was no other way.

Fuming, Olga had come down, done the work, and rushed back uptown to keep a key appointment—she was showing a $50,000 Noland. She sold the painting, as she knew she would, but felt angry because of the hours extorted from her earlier in the day, because she had had to rush back to the apartment, because she had felt flustered. Most maddening of all, perhaps, was the fact that Partridge evidently didn't understand why she was upset.

"But, darling," he said, "I had no intention of lousing up your day. It was just an emergency." He evidently did not see that he was no longer entitled to this kind of devotion.

No, Olga said to herself, it can't go on; and yet, I love him, I'm sure of it. They had been together for many years now. What would she do without him? Besides, he was still an exciting lover. Silently, she got out of bed and walked through the dark studio into the bathroom; for a moment, she stood motionless, holding the door handle, feeling completely paralyzed; then she opened the door and, sitting down on the closed commode, she burst into tears.

She was lucky, she thought as she got up the next morning, that it was a weekday; she desperately wanted to be alone. She told Partridge she had an early appointment and, dressing quickly, she went out without stopping for breakfast, but when she found herself in the apartment, she knew there could be no question of working. Again, she felt paralyzed and the feeling was almost unbearable. All her life, she had taken pride in her efficiency, in her ability to face and solve any problem. There was nothing she despised more than those dithering, incapable women who spent their lives drifting; yet, here she was, doing precisely that.

As she sat, the agony grew more unbearable. After a while, she stood up and started to pace. There must be a compromise, she thought. Of course there must. She could talk to Partridge, set up rules so that she could function on her own and yet go on living with him. It could be done. But she could foresee that no rule that Partridge felt *forced* to accept would ever work. It would be just like yesterday: Something would always happen at the last moment to break their agreement, until finally it was dropped altogether.

For a moment, she imagined what life would be like without Partridge. The thought of sleeping with another man was strangely unappealing; and, although she knew that she was already earning more money than she would need to live on, she was afraid of having to fend for herself. Besides, she said to herself wildly, what if everyone drops me because I'm not with John anymore? Even in the midst of her panic, she could see that that was not very likely. Still, she feared it, and once again the tears came pouring out.

After a little while, she stood up and went to wash her face. This wasn't like her, she thought. Perhaps talking to her friends would help. For the next few days, she spent long hours reviewing the situation with six of her most intimate friends. It didn't help when the first of these, a liberated woman who wrote scandalous books, simply asked: "Is he a good fuck?" and concluded, "Well, as long as he is, give him the night and keep the day."

Olga was far too sensible to be satisfied with this rather summary prescription. She went on talking, complaining, wondering aloud until another exhausted friend said: "Stay with him and try to work it out; maybe he'll change. Anyway, you're obviously not ready to leave him."

That conclusion, it seemed, was unavoidable. One after the other, all six of Olga's best friends agreed, for a variety of reasons. Even Sarah told her that, while she should undoubtedly strike out on her own, she wasn't yet ready. She was even likely to have a breakdown, Sarah predicted sagely, if she left Partridge now. She had better stay for a while longer and free herself little by little. "Give it a year, even two," she said. "Make sure you go on with your business as much as possible, and stay away from him whenever you can. Don't accompany him when he goes to England. Try visiting friends out of town and look for another man to whom you can switch at the right moment." Olga demurred. She didn't want a new lover at all; that would just be an unnecessary complication. No, she just wanted her freedom, but she wasn't ready for it.

So there was a consensus: She couldn't yet be on her own. Olga, who was nothing if not thorough, went a little further and consulted Dick Steinberg. He was, after all, one of her dearest friends, an editor, a poet, whose mind she respected and whose judgment she felt she could trust because he was gay and liked Partridge besides. He would be especially generous with advice, as Olga had helped when his lover had left him. Dick listened—with a more intense kind of understanding than any of her women friends, Olga felt, as she explained everything. She even cried a little, something she hadn't allowed herself to do in front of anyone else. It was all very satisfying, but the result was much as before.

"Olghina, darling," he said, his voice full of concern, "you mustn't leave a man you love. Believe me, you'd regret it all your life. Of course, you must stick up for yourself and make John face his responsibilities. After all, he loves you, too; you must help him to see that if he wants to keep you then he's got to be more flexible, less demanding. I'm sure he'll understand."

Olga wasn't so sure, but she did feel much better. At least she had talked out her depression and decided that compromise was possible. So what if Partridge was egocentric? People change when they want something badly enough, and surely she was that something.

Still, she postponed the confrontation. There was no rush now that she felt better; and it would be so grave, so decisive that she needed to work up to it. She knew that a difficult time was coming, and so she made special efforts to be pleasant without realizing that she was leading Partridge into a fool's paradise.

Since her behavior had changed so markedly, he had concluded that he had been right, that there was nothing wrong with his demands. Olga had just been going through a typically feminine depression. All women did now and again; it meant absolutely nothing, he thought. She might even be secretly glad if he made it so difficult for her to conduct her business that she would have to give it up. On the other hand, she obviously needed to feel loved, so he spent more time with her, was more ardent sexually, more affectionate, more flattering. He also behaved as if she had nothing to do but help him. It was when he suggested they go and spend three months in London that Olga realized she would have to talk to him.

She tried to start gently. "I'd love to go to London with you," she said amiably, "but, John, how can I? I'm in the middle of several deals. I can't just drop them, and my clients would think I'm not serious if I just vanished for three months in the middle of the season."

Partridge leaned over and kissed her. "Oh, that silly old business," he said. "You can always pick it up again. Everybody knows we're together, so they'll understand why you wanted to come with me. Besides, I couldn't be away from you for three months. I love you." Smiling, he went and replenished her drink.

Olga could feel herself flushing with irritation. She was determined to stay calm, to work things out as all her friends had agreed she should. So, patiently, saying that she loved him too, that she didn't want to be without him all this time, either, she tried to explain that she still had her own life to lead, her own career to pursue, and that her very identity depended on it.

Partridge looked pensive. "It's money, isn't it?" he said. "You want to have your own income. Of course, I understand; but look, you've done so much work for me, I owe you money—"

"You don't understand, John," Olga answered sharply.

"Hush, hush. It's nothing to be embarrassed about. You know I can well afford to give you a big allowance. How about this: I'll pay all your bills and give you five hundred dollars a month for petty cash? Perhaps that's not enough— no, it really isn't. Let's make it a thousand."

Finding it increasingly hard to control her anger, Olga tried to explain that it wasn't a question of money, that she didn't want an allowance; she wanted to prove herself. Still, John failed to understand.

With a placating smile she recognized instantly, he told her that she had no need to prove anything. Why, he said, everybody knew how bright, how charming she was.

There was a pause, and, just as Partridge was congratulating himself on his deft handling of a difficult situation, Olga burst out.

"How can you be so blind?" she cried. "Don't you understand anything? I need to live my own life, not be like some limpet attached to you and your career. I don't want to sell your work or organize your shows. I want to work for others, for people who take me seriously as a professional. I'm fed up with being your camp follower. Damn it, John, can't you recognize the existence of anyone other than yourself? Oh, what's the use?" she went on, "now you're going to start shouting. We'll have a scene and everything will be just the same."

"Oh, no, we won't," he said, obviously stung. "You're hysterical and I won't answer in kind. In fact, I refuse to continue this discussion until you're calmer. I don't think you really know what you want; but one thing I can tell you: When I get on that plane to London, you'll be right there with me."

More than ever, it seemed to Viola Germain, the future was closed before her. Now that André was gone, she felt calmer but even more depressed. Quite obviously, he was not going to fire Thérèse. Aside from what she could see was the impossibility of throwing out the mother of his child, she knew full well that he could not function without Thérèse. Yet, Viola felt that she couldn't go back on her word. She had said she would never see Thérèse again, and she must stick to it.

For the first time, staying in New York failed to cheer her. She still saw her friends. She still went to chic dinners and glamorous parties. She was still recognized and respected as the editor of *Voir*, but it no longer mattered. She was miserably unhappy.

For a short time, she toyed with the idea of talking to Vincent. They had once been great friends, but, in the last few years, she had taken André's side and the closeness was gone. She felt certain that he must resent the whole Thérèse situation, but she didn't quite know how to go about resuming her relationship with him. She had at one point, and rather halfheartedly, called to ask him and Sarah for a drink, but he had said they were busy that night, so she had just given up.

The worst part was always having to pretend. It wouldn't do to let people see there was anything wrong.

Although prompt to remind herself that she had many friends, Viola had few illusions about their real feelings. Sheila Mockridge was worse than most, but they would almost all be glad enough of any trouble as long as it made for some juicy gossip. There was no choice: She must go on seeming to be successful and happy. But now the stress of keeping up an appearance so thoroughly divorced from reality was becoming almost impossible for her to bear.

There was no way out, that was the trouble. Although André had abandoned his old custom of calling her from Paris almost every day (he's afraid, she told herself), she knew he would never agree to a fair divorce settlement— he would want to keep everything. On the other hand, she really didn't see how she could retain her self-respect if she went back to him. Still, where else would she go? She could hardly stay at the Stanhope forever. All her things were in Paris. She had nothing to do in New York once she finished her current work. She had no life of her own.

Then she thought of fighting him. Suppose she waged a real battle and used her knowledge to defeat André. If she convinced Pierre-Paul Sanche to pull out, if she were to speak out about André's business practices, she could ruin him. That wouldn't make much sense, since, after all, she depended on him; still, it might work as a lever. Then she realized André would see through that right away. What was it she actually wanted? A divorce? More power within her marriage? She really didn't know; and besides, how would it look if she ruined the man with whom she had lived for so long? It seemed impossible, after all those years of keeping up appearances, to start speaking the truth.

Once again, she wondered about Vincent. Together, they might achieve more than she would by herself. She had just seen David Copley, and he had told her, with a peculiar smile, that he was dealing with her stepson. Something was obviously going on, and, knowing André, she suspected the truth. She phoned Vincent again but was reluctant to say anything specific. Vincent, unaware of her real position, took her mention of a lunch with Copley as a taunt and remained aloof. No, she could see there was nothing to be done. She would go back to Paris in a few days and, eventually, have to eat her words. Still, she found it deeply depressing. It wasn't just a question of pride, though that was bad enough; simply, basically, she realized, she could no longer bear her life.

Olga, who had allowed several days to pass since her inconclusive discussion with Partridge, felt much the same way. All the advice, all the time spent listening, had been for naught. Partridge was impossible. He wanted everything his own way and she could no longer accept that. Still, the thought of leaving him made her almost dizzy with fear. Despairing, she tried a violent scene, hoping that would get through to him better than reason. So she provoked a fight and really let go; she told him he was a monster of selfishness who never considered anyone else's needs and especially not hers; that she bitterly regretted ever having come to live with him; that his self-indulgence, his blindness to everyone else, would soon lead him to disaster; and that she would no longer lift a finger to help him. The result was the same as usual except that, she noticed with wry amusement, he didn't try to lay a hand on her. This time she made sure there was no reconciliation in bed. Of course, late in the night, he tried to make love to her, but she wouldn't let him; and, to her surprise, she found she really didn't want him. Her resentment was so deep, so present, that she couldn't relax.

The next day, she tried coldness. In the morning, she announced that she would be busy all day and dining with her friend Pomona. She wouldn't be back until very late and maybe not at all. She had an early appointment the next morning and might just sleep uptown. At that, Partridge became visibly upset; but she refused to listen or pay attention, said she was late, and walked out. A little later, when the phone rang at the apartment, she deliberately didn't answer. She had no doubt it was Partridge.

Still, she refused to sink back into her old depression. She went to work setting up appointments, writing letters, calling other dealers. She was beginning to feel like herself again when the doorbell rang. A client, she thought, although they didn't usually come without an appointment. When she opened the door and saw Partridge standing there, she froze. Before she could say anything, he had pushed her aside and walked in.

"This apartment belongs to me, you know," he said menacingly. Pacing up and down, he recited a long list of her misdeeds, culminating with her announcement that she would not sleep at the studio that night.

He had never before been so nasty to her, never shown her such contempt, rhythmically punctuating his denunciations with "you little bitch." She was, after all, nothing more than his creation, he said. The people she knew were his people. She only worked because he had given her paintings to sell, and as for her so-called artistic endeavors, like that grotesque dyeing, well, her art was just a bad joke. It was time she shaped up, he said, and showed some gratitude. He'd had enough of her self-centeredness. Let her realize how lucky a no-talent like her was to live with an artist of his caliber. Of course, he expected her back that night. She could start out by canceling her dinner date; and he had a good mind to take the key of the apartment back from her, although he might allow her to go on working there if her behavior warranted it.

There was a good deal more, but Olga hardly heard it. She

sat, paralyzed, and watched Partridge as he paced before her, wondering when he was going to hit her, certain that he would. She said nothing, but simply stared and waited. He never touched her. Finally, after repeating she had better be at the studio by six, he left, slamming the door. Even then, it took her nearly an hour before she collected her wits; and then the tears came. After a while, she called Dick Steinberg and asked if he could come over and see her right away, but he couldn't leave his office. Sobbing, she told him what had happened, asking again and again, "What shall I do, Dick? Where shall I go?"

Partridge was quite pleasant, that evening, when she showed up at the appointed hour. He took her out to dinner, behaving as if nothing had happened and pretending not to notice the woodenness of her responses. When they finished eating, he ordered a brandy, then a second, then a third, and still he talked. When he was finally through, she followed him home mechanically, and complied when he started to make love to her; but this time she simply felt dirty. Even then, that was only the beginning: All through the night, as if to prove a point, Partridge used her. Once he noticed that she wasn't responding and asked her what the matter was in a tone of voice that prompted her to feign pleasure. The worst of it wasn't the actual intercourse. I'm just like a whore, she thought as he raised himself to her mouth, "only I'm not getting paid." The phrase kept coming back to her all through that long night.

It was obvious, the next morning, that Partridge was in a state of euphoria. He felt he had won in every way, on every level; Olga showed nothing. As soon as she could, she announced that she had a dentist's appointment. Under Partridge's watchful eye, she walked out carrying nothing except her pocketbook. As soon as she reached the first phone booth, she called Dick Steinberg. "Is it all right if I spend a few nights at your place?" she asked.

Later that day, she called Partridge and told him she needed time to herself. She wouldn't be back for a week. He said in that case he was coming over to get her. With great satisfaction, she answered she was staying with a friend, not at the apartment. When he called her a slut, she said she was at Dick's; she knew he wouldn't dare behave like a bully in front of a man with so many connections. She meant to go back to Partridge, of course, she explained to her host when he got home. She still loved him. But now, for a week, she would be free.

ELEVEN

There's more to modern art than meets the eye, Vincent said to himself with a smile as he walked down the street, and he began to enumerate: legs, eyes, hair, breasts—a lot more. He slowed down a little: There was no rush, this time; no need for a taxi.

It was a long way to his office, but he enjoyed every step—not because of the beautiful late spring day, or the fashionable crowd, or the tempting shop windows. For the first time in many years, he felt cheerful, optimistic, full of energy. And it was all his own doing.

Just a few days earlier, it had occurred to him that enough was enough. He didn't care anymore if Sarah was angry or Olga distant. He was sick and tired of dealing in what he described to himself as dead art, paintings that came from hands other than the artist's. He remembered with longing his work at Iris Johnson's. At that point in his career, he had visited young artists every week to find new material for the gallery. He had been in touch with art as it was made. Now, suddenly, he came to a conclusion: He would represent two or three young painters. The very decision made him feel better. He called his friend Peter Passarolo and made a date to go and see his latest paintings.

Now, much to his surprise, it became easier for him to do his other work. As soon as he put the phone down, he started on a series of enthusiastic letters to out-of-town clients about the Copley pictures, even offering to fly in and show them anything they wanted to see. And, to his amazement, he found himself typing a letter to Max Ernst and enclosing slides of those worrisome pictures. The suspense must be relieved, he told himself, once and for all. If they were fakes, then it would be better if he were the one to find out and correct his error; if they were good, then he deserved the peace of mind.

The next day, when he had finished looking at Peter Passarolo's work, he knew even better how right he had been. The young artist was still unrepresented by a gallery, but Vincent had no doubts about his talent or his future. His canvases showed an understanding of color that reminded him of the great Venetians Veronese and Tiepolo. The structure of the paintings was complex and subtle. The seemingly spontaneous array of lines and fields and dashes was revealed, on close examination, to be the result of precise planning. He noticed a remarkably subtle balance between surface activity and openings into deep space, between painterly qualities and a feeling for design. "You're a damn good painter," Vincent told Passarolo, "perhaps a great one." Then, carefully pointing out the difference between his office and a gallery, he offered the young man a show.

It would not be the same as a normal exhibition, Vincent explained; while he would keep the office open as if it were a gallery, they would not have the same traffic as a street-level space. The magazines might review the show, but not *The New York Times*. And while he would, of course, send announcements to all his clients, they were, most of them, out of touch with contemporary art. Still, it was surely worth a try and Passarolo agreed.

"It will be so much more alluring than showing in a gallery," he said with enthusiasm. "Only the happy few will come, so they will have the feeling that this is something special, something so good that it is reserved only for them." Passarolo urged Vincent to stay a little longer: Donna Frankel, a girl who wrote for *Arts and Artists*, was coming by in an hour: Vincent could meet her and tell her about the show.

The moment she walked in the door, Vincent was attracted to her; she had a freshness, an immediacy that was enormously desirable and made up for her lack of special beauty. So he paid great attention to her, and was himself stimulated by her obvious admiration. His life before Sarah was coming back to him, that time when his foreign, sophisticated quality had made him attractive to a succession of girls who, though they now lived in Manhattan, had come from the outer boroughs. "You're so charming," they would invariably tell him, "so really French." And now he looked with pleasure at Donna's glowing complexion, at her full mouth, at the round breasts under the tight sweater. She wasn't very tall and her ankles were thick; her brown hair was a little mousy; but none of that mattered: Her figure was good and her enthusiasm obvious.

They looked at the paintings together and Vincent dredged up all his art-history vocabulary. It worked; Donna was impressed, and that encouraged him to even greater flights of fancy, to more daring metaphors. When they moved out of the studio to go and have a drink, he sat looking at her. Vincent felt something snap within himself: This was one girl he was going after. He could, he realized, wait and let her make the moves—she was certainly behaving as though she might; but he didn't want that. This time, it was to be a conquest; he would take what he desired, in a bold move. When they had finished their drinks, Vincent asked Donna if she could come by his office to see some paintings she might enjoy. She agreed, and they were off.

He did show her several of the pictures when they got to the office, but then, very quickly, the atmosphere changed. At first, Vincent asked questions. "Tell me about yourself," he said softly. "I know you have a good eye, but now I want your history just as if you were a painting: the story of Donna's provenance." He paid close attention to her answer. She came from Brooklyn, she had gone to City College, she loved art, she had traveled, but never to France. "What!" Vincent exclaimed. "You've never been to Paris!" He told her about the city's atmosphere. "You must go," he went on, "a pretty girl belongs in Paris. Isn't it funny, it's such a cliché, but it's true. Paris is the city of love, a place to hold hands and kiss in the shade of a plane tree on the bank of the Seine, a place to look deep into someone's eyes and have a taste of his lips. You'll go, Donna, and soon; but, for now, let's have Paris right here," and he bent forward to kiss her.

As soon as his mouth touched hers, her lips opened and he felt her tongue searching for his. With immense excitement, he prolonged the kiss, moving his head a little to cover her lips better. Standing up, she locked her hands behind his head and he could feel her breasts pressing against his chest. With a low, involuntary moan, he broke the kiss and outlined her mouth with his thumb. Looking into her eyes—they were a very light brown—he just said, "Kiss me again."

Almost without a word, they went on, for what seemed like hours, just kissing. Vincent felt an excitement that, although it contained desire, was completely unlike the painful need that had driven him to visit a whore. He knew he would eventually find himself in bed with Donna, but he was in no hurry; the moment was far too enjoyable. It wasn't just Donna's mouth, or the beating of her eyes under his lips, or her fingers weaving through his hair. It was a sense of power, of freedom. He had stepped forward and made a choice, reached out for something he wanted (it was only much later he realized he had done that, in fact, when he had offered Peter Passarolo a show). Donna's breasts were pressing against his chest, and the world glowed full of promise.

Finally, Vincent stepped back. "You kiss pretty well," he said with a look of serious appraisal. "I had to make sure!"

Donna laughed. "That was a double French kiss, I guess," she said softly. Vincent, looking in her eyes again, saw that they had become very bright. "Why don't we get into something more comfortable," he said with a smile, "like your apartment. Where do you live?"

Worrying a little in the taxi on the way down to the Village, he told her he was married, though not very, but she simply shrugged and kissed him; and right then, as he felt his tongue twisting around hers, he knew again that he wasn't anxious for the conclusion: They had all the time in the world and every second was bliss. The walk through the lobby, the wait for the elevator, everything gave him pleasure. As she opened her two locks, with some difficulty, he simply put his hand on her waist, feeling the curve of her warm flesh.

When they walked in, he noticed the apartment was full of wicker and plants; but soon, they were in each other's arms again, then undressing. She had a surprisingly white skin with a very fine grain and very dark nipples. For a second, his palm flat against her hip, he just looked at her. Then he lowered himself on the bed and found her mouth again. Soon his lips were moving down to the little hollow at the base of her neck, and then tracing a circle around her right breast. She moaned a little and arched her body, her fingers once more in his hair.

It was all his way. Her caresses waited for his and followed them; her touch was infinitely exciting, her fingers light and provocative, but he set the pace and she obviously liked it. When he finally raised his head to kiss her again, his right hand, which had wandered all over her body, came gently to rest between her legs. She was ready, he could feel it. "I want you, right now," he whispered. Without a word, she kissed him and opened her legs wider, but he broke the kiss as he entered her and, licking her earlobe, told her how good she felt. She responded quickly and soon stiffened, then relaxed; within a minute, she was moving again, forcing groans out of Vincent. "Now," she said, "now." Without answering, he moved faster and then, with a long shout, finally stopped. For a while, they just lay on the bed, catching their breaths; then, lifting himself, he brushed her lips with his and said: "Darling, that was pure heaven!"

A little while later, Donna got up and went into the bathroom. Vincent, still not moving, felt intense gratitude. She had demanded nothing, he thought. She had simply given herself, and he could not remember feeling such pleasure or such relaxation. He had made no effort to arouse her but just followed his own feeling of her body, and she had liked it. With amusement, he thought of a comedy in which the lover kept asking, "But did the earth move for you?" I don't have to ask, Vincent said to himself with satisfaction.

When he left Donna, a little after six, they had a date for the next day. "Can you come in the evening?" she asked. "They won't like it at the office if I disappear during the day again." When Vincent said yes, she looked a little surprised. "Doesn't your wife care?" she exclaimed.

"She probably doesn't," he said, "but I'll tell her I have to meet a client." There was no reason, really, why he shouldn't tell Sarah he was having an affair. After all, she had refused herself to him. But the thought of her anger and of the fuss she would make was enough to stop him. If he went on seeing Donna, as he surely would, then Sarah would eventually realize he was never home: Kissing Donna good-bye, he didn't care. Once more, her mouth opened under his; it felt as sweet and exciting to him as it had earlier in his office. "I'm hooked," he said to himself with satisfaction as he waited for the elevator.

André Germain would not have been amused if he had been told about his son's affair. Only someone as hopeless as Vincent, he might well have said, would take a mistress who provided him with no advantage except sex; as for himself, he knew better than that.

Although he had very little doubt about the conclusion of the affair with Coche, at first, some four months ago, he had been careful. Thérèse did notice that he was willing to devote more time than usual to his new flame, that more flowers were sent, more meals arranged, more phone calls put through. It was only a few days after his return from New York, when she saw his bill from Cartier's, that she realized how serious it had become.

It seemed so incredible to Thérèse that, marching into André's office, she barked, "There must be another Germain," as she slammed the bill down on his desk. Even when he curtly told her to pay it, she was unable to believe it was for Coche. "You're buying Viola a present?" she even asked. In the explosion that followed, she was told, first, that it was none of her business; then, that he, André, had no need to give Viola jewelry to keep her in line; and, finally, that she had better get used to his sending

Coche presents. Relenting a little, he added: "By the way, we're going to Ayville next weekend, so you'd better be here early on Saturday." And Thérèse, whose tears had been flowing right along, walked out, clutching her moist handkerchief.

That André felt nervous about the forthcoming visit could hardly be denied. He knew he must be a success and, although he thought highly of himself, the world of Ayville was a little daunting. Then, too, there would be further trouble with Viola. On the whole, that probably didn't matter. He had pretty well decided to dump her in favor of Coche. As it was, he could have spared himself both the anxiety and the decision: Everything had been settled, just a few days before, by Laure de Goldschmidt.

The baroness had invited Coche for lunch that day; but when the butler, opening the door to the green sitting room, had announced, "Mme. del Mancha," there was no one there except the hostess.

"Where is everybody?" Coche asked as she walked in.

Laure answered, with a serious look, "We're having lunch *en tête-à-tête*. I must speak to you seriously."

At first, Coche thought the baroness was having a new affair, or that her husband's current mistress had become difficult; but in no time she found herself under attack. "Darling," Mme. de Goldschmidt said, looking utterly serious, "it's time you settled down. There's nothing wrong with living from day to day when you're young, but, now that you're over forty, what you need is a solid marriage that will establish you in Paris. You have a position because everyone knows you're my best friend; but it's time you had your own house and some stability; besides, you're beginning to have a bad reputation. People are saying you're little better than a kept woman, and I see their point: After all, you've had three lovers in the last year alone, and they've all been married."

Coche, aghast, stared at her friend. "But, Laure," she said, "surely you don't believe—"

"Of course not," the baroness answered impatiently, "but that's not the point. It's time you made people respect you. And you have just the right man in hand. Look, darling, we both realize just what André Germain is like; but I think he's exactly what you need. First, you'll have no trouble getting him. Everybody knows what a fearful snob he is; he'd leave his wife just to get to Ayville, so that's easily managed. He has some money and he can make a lot more; if he knows the right people, that gallery of his could be a very good thing. And there's *Voir* to give it all glamour. I really don't think you can do better. Between the two of us, we can see to it that he lives in the right style and is invited by the people who matter. I mean, he is perfectly presentable."

There was a brief silence as the baroness lit a cigarette. "Well?" she said finally.

"But, Laure, it's impossible. He never stops talking and you have no idea how unpleasant he can be. Why, if it were not for Viola—"

"You're sleeping with him, aren't you?" Mme. de Goldschmidt said coldly.

"Yes, darling, of course I am, but that's just for now. It's not like being married to him."

Impatiently, the baroness crushed her cigarette and stared at Coche. "Have you had a good look at your face, lately?" she asked. "I can tell you. I'm your best friend. You're beginning to age. How much longer do you think you can choose your lovers? And what will you do when you can't? No, no, you must take what's available. André Germain may be difficult, but at least we can make him marry you, and that's more than we can do with the others. Tell him he'll be invited to Ayville next weekend. I'll treat you like a couple and, if he doesn't propose, I'll talk to him myself. Now," she went on as the butler opened the door and announced that lunch was served, "we can consider it settled and have a good gossip."

The invitation was duly offered and the following Friday, at seven, André and Coche drove past the gatehouse and down the long tree-lined *allée* that led to the Château d'Ayville. So far, it was all very familiar to Coche, but when she saw her friend waiting in the huge hall, she realized that there was no way out: It was most unusual for Mme. de Goldschmidt to greet any but her most exalted guests when they arrived. Much to André's pleasure, the baroness was amiability itself.

"I've put you together, of course," she said, smiling benignly. "You have the blue room, Coche, and you, André, the Saxony room right next door. We dine at nine, so there's plenty of time to change. Come and have a drink with me first and tell me all the news." To Coche's stupefaction, she led them to her private sitting room.

That evening and the rest of the weekend, it seemed to André that he was finally living his dream. By the time he reached his bedroom, his luggage had been unpacked and his evening clothes laid out. A bath was drawn in the marble-walled bathroom, and four bottles of Floris bath oil stood in line on a shelf while a thick, soft terry-cloth bathrobe rested on a warm stand. Everywhere he looked, he saw not just luxury but habit: The Goldschmidts had been very rich for a very long time and it showed.

The bedroom itself, all Victorian, was a nest of fabrics, double curtains, petit-point carpeting, a paisley cashmere counterpane, velvet table rugs and sofas. Lined up on silk-covered shelves were Meissen figures: shepherds and shepherdesses, dancing courtiers, fantasy Chinamen. It was utterly charming and, as André quickly reflected, worth a fortune. Then there was the famous staircase with its chased silver banister, which he presently descended with Coche;

and the pink living room with its brocaded walls and Fragonard's series depicting the months of a year, and the small dining room with its delicate rococo paneling, made for Louis XV's retreat at Meudon. Then, too, there was the table, with its old lace tablecloth; the gold forks, knives, and spoons; the Sèvres plates. There could be no doubt: André was just where he wanted to be.

"This is only a small, intimate weekend," Mme. de Goldschmidt had told him, "just our dear Coche and you, and a very few friends"; but, as André said to himself, what friends! There was Achilles Oresteion, the Greek shipping magnate; the Duke and Duchess de Ruvigny, whose titles dated back to the Crusades; the current Minister of the Interior; the pretender to the throne of Tuscany; and the Ogilvies, whose Texan fortune was, according to rumor, in excess of three billion dollars. In all his dreams, André could not imagine greater glamour. Best of all, he was treated like a perfect equal. Laure de Goldschmidt often called on him to hold forth; he was brilliant and he knew it. Coche looked dazzling, and everyone behaved as if she were his wife. He clearly belonged in this most rarefied of atmospheres. By Saturday night, it had come to seem natural that his sheets had lace borders threaded through with ribbons, and that invisible servants washed, pressed, and returned everything he had worn. He, too, should live like this; and while he yet had sense enough to realize that he couldn't, that he probably never would, still, there was the prospect of numberless weekends at Ayville and in other houses like it; and he owed it all to Coche.

The point was made manifest for him on Sunday morning. Flatteringly, Mme. de Goldschmidt had sent her *femme de chambre* to him with a message: Would he like Madame la baronne to give him a tour of the château? She would meet him in an hour. And, indeed, Laure had shown him all around, passing from the great ballroom to the blue living room, from the summer dining room to the huge winter garden built onto the side of the house in the 1880s. She was a good guide but frequently interrupted her explanations to tell André how much she and M. de Goldschmidt (who, alas, had to be in Argentina this weekend) cared about Coche; how anxious they were to see her settled; how important her happiness was to them—so much so, in fact, that her husband must also become one of their closest friends. She went on to say that she was about to break a confidence, she knew, but she simply couldn't resist telling André that Coche found him too wonderful. "We're so pleased to see you together," she concluded as she left him; and André understood.

When he drove Coche away that afternoon—it was a well-known tradition that weekend guests always left Ayville on Sunday after tea—André was ecstatic, although he tried very hard not to show it. Still, he could barely contain himself and, for once, had almost nothing critical to say. He told Coche about his tour that morning and raved about Laure de Goldschmidt's elegance, about her intelligence, about her qualities as a hostess. By the time he had stigmatized the Ogilvies as typically vulgar Americans, he was in seventh heaven. Coche pushed him a little further: She had had a long private chat with Laure, she said, whose best friend, after all, she had long been. And while, perhaps, it was indiscreet to tell him so, Laure had said she found André even more brilliant, more entertaining, more likeable than she had expected and had added she hoped he would become part of their circle.

"We had a very serious talk," Coche went on. "You know, Laure thinks you could go far. There are people you should know better, she said, since you are an art dealer. That's why she invited Oresteion. I need hardly tell

you about his collection. Besides, she feels that Wildenstein has ruled the market too long. It's time for new blood,
and a closer connection to certain people could do wonders
for you. I'm sure you won't be offended, dear André, if I
tell you that Laure can do a great deal for you if she
chooses; and she seems very taken with you at the moment.
Only, there's a problem. You must swear never to repeat
what I'm about to tell you. If Laure knew I had broken
her confidence, she'd be simply livid; but I think you ought
to know. You do promise, André?" Looking at him, Coche
thought that, for all his vaunted intelligence, he was no
harder to handle than a simpleton.

"Well," she resumed after he had duly sworn himself to
silence, "Laure says the only thing preventing you from
assuming a position of real importance is your personal
life."

"Personal life?" André asked, so startled that he almost
hit the car in front of him and had to brake violently. "But,
darling, I don't understand. She can't mean you!"

Coche laughed. "Me? Dear André, how could I ever be
a hindrance? No, no, it's the very reverse. You see, although
she stretched a point this weekend, Laure really doesn't like
having unmarried couples. Now that divorce has become
so easy, she says, there's really no excuse for that anymore.
And then, in the strictest confidence, she doesn't really like
Viola. She can't very well go on inviting you alone when
Viola comes back from New York. Of course, I told her it
wasn't fair to hold you back just because of her personal
dislikes, but, still, I thought you should know."

André nodded. "I'm not a bit offended," he said. "In
fact, I think it shows what a perceptive woman Laure
really is. Viola and I have really had nothing in common
for a very long time. But you know how it is: One allows
oneself to drift; and besides, one can't help feeling some
compassion. Still, an end must come. As long as Viola is in

America, I think she had better stay there, and I'll tell her
so tomorrow."

"What, dear André? You're thinking of a divorce?"
Coche asked carefully.

"Yes, of course, a divorce."

"But won't it be very expensive? One always hears about
those American women getting such a lot of money, and
Viola is co-publisher of *Voir*, isn't she?"

André laughed with real enjoyment. "Don't worry," he
said. "I screwed my first wife—she didn't get a penny—
and I'll screw Viola."

Coche stared at him for a second, then appeared to think
better of it. "How nice," she said in a toneless voice. "You'll
be a free man again. The world will be open to you."

"Darling, what could the world mean to me without
you? You know how much I love you. The only question
now is whether you are prepared to become Mme. André
Germain."

"I'll stay for a week if I'm not in your way," Olga had
told Dick Steinberg when she moved into his apartment.
"I really need the time to think things through." Now the
week had passed. Dick would soon be home; and she was
just as confused, but less upset than a few days earlier.

Partridge had behaved precisely as she had expected. Far
from making scenes or demanding her immediate return,
he had called up and thanked Dick Steinberg for his kindness. "I feel so much better," he had said softly, "knowing
that Olga is in the care of a good friend like you. She's
upset, poor darling, and she needs a rest. I was a little worried. She's been so nervous lately. Oh, and if Olga wants
to speak to me," he had added in a very offhand tone, "perhaps you could put her on for a minute." But Olga had
shaken her head violently, and Partridge simply sent his

love. During the next few days, he had called several times, asking how she was but never speaking to her directly. Now the time was up and Olga dreaded what might follow.

Then, too, there was her business. She was far too scared to work at the apartment; so she had bought an answering machine and, in Dick's company, had set it up. It informed all callers that Olga was unavailable for a week and would return their calls later. Now those calls must be taken care of. Olga was not about to give up her success.

She had thought about it all, day after day, and there was no other way: She must go back to Partridge and somehow work things out. It couldn't be a complete loss since she still loved him; in fact, she was pretty sure she would be glad to see him again. That morning at breakfast she thanked Dick effusively. Later in the morning, she called the studio and told the answering service to let Mr. Partridge know that Olga would be home by five.

She wasn't willing to go back to work yet. Things must be settled first and, besides, she didn't want to be surprised by Partridge at the apartment; so she spent the afternoon baking. When he returned home, Dick Steinberg found two loaves of bread and a mound of cookies "with love from Olga." For a while after leaving her message with the answering service, she had thought Partridge might call her back, but the phone remained silent all day. Now it was four-thirty. She forced herself to put on her coat and take her bag; then, with increasing difficulty, she went out, locked the door, and put the key in an envelope, which she clutched anxiously. The ride in the elevator seemed very short, the doorman far too eager to take the envelope and get her a taxi. Then, as she was driven downtown, she went over her decision once more: She loved John and would tell him so while explaining he must leave her free to run her business. It was very simple, really; New York was full of people who lived out this very arrangement. No doubt Partridge, too, had taken time to think things out. There was really nothing to worry about, she was sure.

Still, she waited for the elevator as if it contained some awful threat. By the time she was ready to let herself into the studio, her hand was trembling. She paused for a minute before inserting the key; then it was in, and she turned it very slowly, but in no time the door was open. Standing outside, she took a deep breath and walked in.

She was all ready to walk up to Partridge and kiss him, but when she said, in an uncertain voice, "John, I'm home," no one answered. "John? John?" she repeated. With a pang of anger, Olga realized there had been no need to worry, after all. Partridge wasn't even there.

It was all immensely awkward. She was back but didn't want to behave accordingly until she had talked to Partridge and worked things out. She felt like an intruder, a thief almost, and she didn't know what to do. Taking off her coat, she picked up a book and sat down; but there could be no question of real concentration, and time passed unbearably slowly. Every thirty minutes, carefully restraining herself, she looked at her watch to find that only five minutes had actually passed. Soon, she stopped feeling awkward. "He should have been here to meet me," she said aloud to herself. "It shows how much he cares. He doesn't even bother coming home to see me," and felt very angry. When Partridge finally came in, smiling and amiable, over an hour later, she blurted out: "John, I can't live with you anymore."

For a minute, there was absolute silence. Partridge looked shocked and Olga herself could hardly believe what she had said. After all, she had been determined to try all over again; but then, suddenly, she felt a tremendous lift inside herself and knew she had said what she really meant. She looked at Partridge, who had stepped back in shock, and said more calmly: "I'm sorry but we have to separate."

His face tensed, but before he could answer, she burst into tears and added, "Oh, John, I love you so much but I just can't make it anymore."

She saw him relax; and then, encircling her in his arms, he said: "You poor baby. Of course, I understand, and I love you, too," while she sobbed peacefully. "It's all right," he kept repeating, "it's all right." Finally she calmed down; letting her go, he moved over to the liquor cabinet and poured two stiff bourbons. "Here," he said, handing her a glass, "you need this." He paused for a sip. "Look," he went on, "I understand. Of course, I didn't expect it, but I think you're right. Things have been just too difficult between the two of us lately. Naturally, I'll miss you; but I agree it's best for both of us."

Still in shock, Olga started to cry again. "Oh, John," she said passionately, "I didn't want it to end. Really, I didn't. It just came out of me. What will I do without you?" And for the next two hours, Partridge was at his best. As Olga was to tell Dick Steinberg when she came back to his apartment later that night, he had behaved so well that she felt sorry he was leaving him and almost wondered whether it wasn't all a terrible mistake. But then she remembered how she had suffered going downtown, how depressed she had been for months. Obviously a separation had to come. No sooner had she said it, however, than she started to cry again. "I really love him, Dick," she sobbed. "I do. I'm going to miss him all the time. God, I can hardly bear it. Why did I have to do it?" It was hard to believe, Dick told her, that it was actually she who had left him.

"Well," Vincent said to Sarah with satisfaction, "she's finally left him. She says she's devastated, but, if you ask me, she'll be recovered in no time. Not to mention rich, of course."

"Money!" Sarah answered with contempt. "That's all you ever think about! You don't understand anything. I talked to her this morning and she cried through the entire call."

"But she's working again, isn't she? Actually, it's just as well. Business will drive Partridge right out of her head. I wonder how she does it?" Vincent went on dreamily. "She's still using the apartment, you know, even though it's his. You'd think he'd mind. After all—"

"Some men are generous," Sarah said pointedly as she walked out of the room.

Yes, Vincent said to himself, and so are some women, thinking with gratitude of his two weeks with Donna.

It wasn't just, he realized, the sex, though, God knows, that was the best he had had in a very long time; nor was it the companionship. Donna's very sincerity, her lack of complication, her simplicity were all very pleasant in small doses, but he knew full well he wouldn't be able to bear them for a minute if they were actually living together. No, in those two weeks, Donna had come to represent a different kind of life for him, one in which he actually made the choices instead of enduring impossible situations. She remained linked to his new direction; on the same day, he had broken out of two ruts, and now he not only looked forward to Peter Passarolo's show but to an active sex life coupled with daily doses of approval.

Life looked a little grimmer, though, when he did his accounts. In his cooler moments, Vincent realized that not many of Passarolo's paintings were likely to sell, and, even if they did, their prices were so low that it wouldn't matter much: At $150 for a watercolor and $700 for a medium-sized painting, a 33 percent commission didn't amount to much. He would be lucky if the show paid for the announcements, mailing, and advertising; covering the rent was obviously out of the question.

Nor did the Copley paintings help. In spite of his enthusiastic efforts, they were simply not moving. There had, in fact, been one offer for the Degas, but it was a third too low and Copley had turned it down. Right now, he had a bite on the Cézanne watercolor but he suspected that, if the collector actually came through, it would be at a price that would eat away most of his profit. Still, he told himself, that didn't matter. If the Cézanne sold, it would be replaced by something else on which he could make money; and if he maintained his new, positive attitude, then the world would come halfway to meet him. Anyway, the Ernsts would keep him going for a while longer yet.

Of course, only part of his new energy went into work; Donna took up the rest, and Vincent wondered how Sarah could manage not to notice the change. It wasn't just his mood, but also the fact that he was hardly ever at home anymore. Surely she would realize it wasn't like him to stay out on business night after night. Shaking his head, Vincent prepared to leave the house, muttering to himself, "If she doesn't want to know, so much the better," when his phone rang. At first, he thought there had been a mistake: The voice on the other end was sobbing hysterically and utterly unfamiliar, but just as he was about to say that the caller had the wrong number, he realized that he did know the voice after all. It was Viola's.

At first he stiffened. Viola and he were hardly on friendly terms these days. But something was obviously dreadfully wrong and even while he was saying, "Dear Viola, try to speak a little more slowly. I haven't understood anything you've said," he thought perhaps his father had died. Then, he began to understand.

"On the phone," she was saying in a voice still racked

with sobs, "he told me on the phone, Vincent, just like that, just as if he were making plans for the weekend. He called and said he had decided he wanted a divorce and I was to stay over here. What am I going to do, Vincent? What am I going to do?"

"Dear, dear Viola," Vincent said, "it can't be as bad as all that. I mean, you weren't that happy with him. You'll probably do much better on your own. Besides, he can't be serious about your staying here. All your things are in Paris, and you can't live at the Stanhope forever. No, no, you must go back."

"He doesn't care," she said, a little calmer now. "He wants to get married again, so I have to be out of the way."

"Married? To whom?" Vincent asked, unbelieving.

Viola laughed bitterly. "To Coche del Mancha. Oh, I knew they were having an affair, but I thought, 'After all, this is France and we've been married a long time,' and, besides, it made him less bad-tempered, so I closed my eyes even though I knew that Laure de Goldschmidt and her little circle were all gossiping about it. But now he wants to marry her. Why, Vincent, why? She doesn't have any money and she's certainly not beautiful. She dresses well, of course, but her clothes are all Laure's castoffs. And when I asked him what I was supposed to do, since we could hardly go on working together after we were divorced, he said I could be *Voir*'s American correspondent and that, since I was so anxious to have a salary, now I would be earning one. So I asked how much and he said ten thousand dollars a year. How can I be expected to live on that? And what would I do here? There's no real work for me."

"That's obviously absurd," Vincent said. "He's probably only taking a bargaining position; still, I must say, I don't see how you can avoid going back to Paris—"

"Bargaining! I thought you understood André better than that," Viola said, with anger now. "He doesn't want me anymore, so he'd rather have me out of the way and, of course, he won't spend any real money for someone he's discarded." She paused and started to cry again. "Oh, Vincent," she went on, "I can't just can't settle down here and live on a tiny income."

"Of course you can't," Vincent replied. "Look, maybe if I talk to him, it'll help. After all, if he thinks he's going to look bad to everyone, he'll make an effort. I'll call him if you like. And why don't you come and have dinner with us tonight?"

When Viola arrived that night, she looked absolutely ravaged; but, while distraught, she was also very angry, and for a while Vincent and she exchanged horror stories about André's behavior. Sarah, who had tactfully retired to the kitchen, reappeared just in time to hear Vincent say, "I'm afraid you're right about that ten thousand dollar income. I talked to him this afternoon, and he was even more odious than usual, especially since I told him at some length that he was behaving very badly. Of course, at first he assumed I'd be on his side; then he understood and told me only an unnatural son would defend a stepmother, so I pretended ignorance. You should have heard him! Anyway, he said he would send you your clothes and some furniture as soon as you had found yourself a place in New York. So I said, 'Not on ten thousand dollars, she won't,' and he answered that you'd have to manage. That's all we said, really, except that I repeated he was behaving shamefully."

Viola sat back in tragic triumph. "Can you believe it," she said, appealing to Sarah, "after all those years and the work I've done for *Voir*?"

"He wouldn't get away with it over here," Sarah answered fiercely. "If you were to divorce him in New York, he'd have to give you half of everything. I suppose it's different in France."

"But is it?" Vincent asked cheerfully. "And anyway, what about the business he does over here? Viola, you had better see a lawyer as soon as possible. I'm beginning to think you may end up getting a great deal more than you hope."

Vincent never got to tell Donna about his father's divorce. At first, although anxious to pass the story on, he put it off: It required too many explanations and would take too long; after all, they had better things to do. And then Donna started asking about Sarah: She didn't mind Vincent's marriage, she explained; she just wanted to understand the situation because she cared about him. So, reluctantly, Vincent described the evolution of their relationship, complaining, as he did so, that it was bad enough having to face it at home without talking about it as well. Donna sympathized, of course, but then she asked Vincent why he stayed married. "If you really don't care about her anymore," she said, hitching herself up on the pillow, "and she doesn't seem to like you much either, why don't you split up?"

Vincent shook his head. "It's not as simple as you think," he said. "Besides, I probably can't afford a divorce; and then, think of the complications, dividing everything, having to move." He laughed. "Maybe she'll leave me instead," he added.

"Maybe," Donna answered seriously.

"You know, I almost wish she would. Anyway, why do we have to talk about it? I can think of at least two subjects I'm much more interested in," and, laughing, he uncovered her breasts. "The trouble is," he went on, "I don't know which of the two I should choose."

"Take both," said Donna, arching. "Two for the price of one." They made love, but, even so, their earlier conversation kept haunting Vincent. Perhaps he should tell Sarah he was having an affair, he thought, and offer her a divorce. It would be better than lying and pretending all the time; but then he remembered what she had said about his father's affair with Coche and wondered whether he was simply behaving in the same heartless way. Of course, he had no intention of marrying Donna. They had come together by chance and, while he found her very attractive, he certainly wasn't in love with her. Still, he had almost decided to tell Sarah the truth without asking for a divorce: There were many marriages where husband and wife each went their separate ways, although, he admitted to himself, he felt a very unpleasant pang when he imagined Sarah in another man's arms.

He was sitting in his office a few days later, thinking about the whole problem again, when the phone rang. He answered it with annoyance. When he heard the tone of Sophia Lyon's voice, his mind went blank. "No," he finally said, "no, absolutely not. That's impossible. It's not a fake. . . . No, Sophia, I told you . . . directly from the artist. . . . Yes, of course, I'm sure. . . . Oh, come on, you loved it. . . . Who said it wasn't good, anyway? . . . Oh, him! Well, what do you expect? He's jealous. . . . No, we shouldn't reimburse the client yet, just because he panics for no reason. . . . Look, Sophia, if you don't calm down, we're not going to get anywhere. I sent Max the photos just ten days ago, as it happens. Look, I'll call him myself. I suppose your client will take the artist's word. . . . Yes, of course, I'll have him endorse the photos. . . . Okay . . . okay. . . . Yes, I'll get back to you as soon as I reach him."

For a moment, as he put the phone down, Vincent felt nothing. He just sat, his hands flat on the table before him, staring straight ahead as if time had stopped; then, slowly, the room went out of focus. Whatever he had said to Sophia, he really had no doubt that the Ernsts were fakes;

his stomach started to sink. Slowly, he began to recognize the familiar sensation of impending disaster. It seemed outside himself, a symptom recognized in the abstract, except that it was accompanied by an almost physical pain. "It's such bad news, it must be true," he said aloud, and the sentence hung in the air before him.

Idly, he watched his hands on the table as they curled up, came together, entwined, gripped, and twisted. He had spent all those weeks pushing the possibility away so successfully that he had sent off the photographs without worrying. Now, even before receiving the answer, he knew the truth. The protective wall had collapsed. Everything he had ever felt about being a dealer was flooding in on him. Right down to Poppea Vlassoff's level, he thought. There it was; he had finally reached his place. All those years of unreality, those deals happening in spite of himself, the disdain he had felt for his job—everything was coming back to him, a cargo of irony. It was true, he was no dealer; but this time he was less, not more, than his despised colleagues. He was just one of those little fly-by-night crooks who sell fakes.

I should call Poppea, he thought idly, but there hardly seemed any point in it. He knew all too well what she would say. Still, he tried. To his surprise, her answering service said she was out of town, so he simply left an urgent message. He still wanted to talk to someone, however. He should have been able to count on Sarah, he mused bitterly, but it was too late for that. Sarah wasn't interested in a disaster; she had no support to give, would feel no concern. He could predict exactly how she would react and, having done so, felt just as hurt, just as indignant as if it had actually happened. Was there no help anywhere? Briefly, he remembered Donna; she might give sympathy, but she was so much on the periphery of his life that it wouldn't mean much. No, the collapse was all his own. He could hear people asking what had happened to him. "Oh, Vincent Germain?" they would answer, "well, you know, he sold fakes, and they caught up with him. I haven't seen him in ages"; and twisting the knife, he added to the imaginary conversation: "I hear André was really shocked!"

Perhaps that made the difference. Suddenly, he sat up straight and, reaching for the phone, dictated a telegram to Ernst with a prepaid answer. "Self-pity!" he said to himself in disgust, and, vowing to fight, he decided to go home and wait for the answer; then, he remembered Donna, but to his surprise he simply didn't feel like seeing her, so he called her and said he had a crisis to deal with and would talk to her the next day. As he walked home, biting his lower lip, he decided he would go on no matter what: Nothing would prevent him from showing Passarolo's work or enjoying Donna.

Sarah was painting again when he walked into the apartment, and paid him no attention. Finally, he said, "I'm home."

She looked up and nodded. "Didn't you have a late meeting tonight?" she asked indifferently. "Or was it tomorrow?"

"Tonight," Vincent answered quietly; then, seized by an irresistible wave of anger, he added, "Not that I can see why you should bother asking."

"It's true," she said, "I really don't care." Turning back to her canvas, she added, "and I don't see why you should, either."

Suddenly, Vincent exploded. "Not care! Not care!" he shouted. "You're my wife, aren't you? The person I live with? Maybe if I tell you I'm ruined, you'll condescend to listen? Ruined, do you hear! Ruined!"

"What's the matter?" Sarah asked calmly. "Did your Ernsts turn out to be fakes, after all?"

For a moment, robbed of his effect, Vincent froze in stunned silence. "That's right," he finally said in a strangled voice, adding, to his own surprise, "well, probably."

"You mean you aren't even sure?" Sarah said with disgust. Picking up her brush again, she went on, "Don't tell me about your problems, Vincent. I'm busy. If you sold fakes, then you'd better unsell them; but don't bother me with it."

For a minute, Vincent looked at her in disbelief. "How *can* you?" he asked with passion.

Sarah laughed. "Look," she answered, "just because you have business problems doesn't mean our relationship has changed. Let's just behave the usual way: You work out your crisis and I'll take care of myself. In case you didn't notice, I've been painting every day, and I'm not stopping to give you emotional support."

There was a silence. Vincent, feeling beaten, stood paralyzed. Sarah was right, of course; they no longer had anything in common. But, as he watched her quietly filling in a little area of color, he felt something give within himself. Even as the words came to his lips, he knew he was being foolish. Although he would regret what he was about to say, he couldn't stop himself, and, very stiffly, he went on: "How right you are. It's a good thing I have someone else."

Sarah looked up quickly. "I thought you were lying," she said.

"Lying?"

"Yes, when you kept telling me you were working late. It really wasn't like you and, since we've stopped having sex, I figured you must be having an affair."

"I'm glad to see you are taking it so calmly," Vincent said with a little bow. "You see, I didn't tell you because I was afraid you'd be hurt, which evidently shows how naive I am. Perhaps you'd like to meet her, while we're at it. A little dinner for three, so civilized."

Sarah dropped her brush into a pot of turpentine and stood up. "Yes," she said, "you would try to be nasty. You're the one, you know, who's done something wrong. Not that it matters," she went on, "because I was planning to leave anyway. I thought I'd put off the disruption because I'm painting so well, but you really leave me no choice. I'll move out as soon as I've found a studio," and she walked out of the room, leaving Vincent speechless.

For a while, not knowing how he felt, he just stood in the middle of the room without moving. After all, it was true that his marriage had died long ago, that he had sought out Donna, and that he shouldn't care; but he did. Perhaps it was because it came on top of the fakes, he said to himself. That must be the reason: It was all too much at once. And, for a moment, he visualized a huge earthenware pot being hit by a hammer: As the pieces all fell apart, he tried and failed to catch them; and, just then, Sarah walked back in.

"Please leave this room," she said. "I work here. You can use the rest of the apartment." Almost mechanically, he started to walk out, but then she stopped him. "We have to talk about money," she said. "I assume we'll split the furniture, paintings, and objects, but I also need money for the first year or so."

Vincent felt the blood rush to his head. "I wouldn't give you a penny if your life depended on it, you bloody bitch," he screamed, and rushed out of the apartment.

By the next morning, they still hadn't spoken. Vincent had spent two hours the previous evening walking around the city, unable to understand what was happening. It's very simple, he kept saying to himself, I've sold fakes which I can't afford to buy back and my wife is leaving me because I told her I was having an affair; now I have to take the consequences. But the words seemed curiously void of meaning. When he tried to think of what he should do next, he came up against a blank wall. The situation was beyond hope. After all, he told himself reasonably, he could neither authenticate the paintings nor stop Sarah from leaving. For a moment, he thought of going home and humiliating himself. Perhaps if he begged enough, Sarah would stay; but he didn't, not so much because his pride stopped him as because there seemed to be no point in it. The thought of divorce was acutely painful. He didn't care about keeping Sarah, but he couldn't bear to lose her. And in the same way, while he certainly wouldn't miss being a dealer—he couldn't imagine continuing to be one if the paintings were fakes—he didn't know what else he could do or how he would earn a living. He thought he would have to cut back severely, take a small apartment, live very modestly. He shuddered. Somehow, it seemed as if his life-style mattered more than anything else.

At last, he walked to a phone booth and called Donna, but she wasn't home. He thought for a while of ringing a friend, but he couldn't, and then he remembered Olga. He dialed. The phone rang, and, much to his surprise, she answered. "I'd like to talk to you," he said, and, oblivious to his tone, she answered joyously, "Oh, I have news for you, too. Why don't you come over?"

Their conversation, when he remembered it the next day, struck him as a model of unreality. As soon as he walked in, she announced that she had reached an agreement with Partridge. She had expected, she said, their parting would be stormy; but, on the contrary, he had been really generous. He was selling her the apartment for half its price and giving her three years to pay it off. She would, of course, keep everything he had given her, and they would be friends.

"What, his paintings, too?" Vincent asked.

"Yes, everything!" Vincent congratulated her, prudently keeping to himself the rumor he had just heard about Partridge's new affair with a well-known critic. "Yes," Olga continued with satisfaction, "I've already moved in. I'll live and work here; it's everything I want." But her face suddenly changed its expression. Tears came to her eyes. "But, you know, I miss John so much. I really love him still. I'll be doing something and then I'll remember him, and I start to cry."

Marveling at himself, Vincent sympathized, encouraged, praised . . . until, finally, Olga asked him what he had wanted to talk about. "Oh," he answered, "it's nothing important. It's getting late, it'll wait for another time." When he came home, he found Sarah's door firmly closed; so whatever he felt—and by now he really didn't know what it was anymore—he must keep to himself. Still, he had trouble sleeping.

He woke up the next morning to the insistent noise of the alarm and, still half-asleep, he tried to stop it, but it kept ringing, and he realized it was the phone. With an effort, he sat up in bed and picked up the receiver. "Yes?" he said.

"Is this Mr. Germain?" a nasal voice asked him.

"Yes, it is."

"I have a cable for you, Mr. Germain. It says, 'Paintings definitely fakes. Please send details. Ernst.' Do you want me to mail you a copy?"

"No," Vincent said tonelessly. "No, operator, that's not necessary."

TWELVE

When Vincent, a year later, looked back to the morning of the Ernst telegram, it never really came into focus. He knew, all right, that it was the beginning of the end, but his feelings that day and later remained confused and inchoate. Always he saw, in his mind's eye, a sort of maelstrom whose dark and oily waters rushed in all directions with a deafening noise, carrying the broken pieces of his earlier life. As it collapsed slowly and painfully around him, he watched each fresh disaster and suffered accordingly, but with a feeling of utter impotence. He waited for events to take their course without being able to influence them in any way. Soon, a sort of numbness set in: Humiliations that he would once have thought unendurable now simply washed over his head, leaving him breathless but alive.

At first, he tried to minimize the disaster. There was no ignoring it, of course; and his first taste of the months ahead came when he had to call Sophia Lyon. That the conversation would be unpleasant, he well knew; and he felt almost incapable of saying the words: "It's a fake."

Postponing the confrontation, he tried to call Poppea. This time, when her service said she was out of town, he asked if there were some address where she could be reached, explaining that he had a most urgent need to be in touch with her. After being asked to hold, he gave his name again.

"Oh," the woman said, "Mr. Germain! Why didn't you say so? Miss Vlassoff left a message for you. She's gone to Milan on business, but she'll be back in a week and she'll call you as soon as she returns."

When Vincent asked where Miss Vlassoff was staying in Milan, the operator said she didn't know. Curiously, the very difficulty of reaching Poppea came as a relief. It meant postponing the call to Sophia, of course. While there was nothing Vincent could do to make the painting real, he could at least try to find Poppea. Settling the pillows behind his back, he called the international operator, asked for Milan information, and proceeded to call the three hotels where he had known Poppea to stay; but not one of them had a reservation in her name. For a while, his mind a blank, Vincent simply sat in bed. Telling himself he could hardly deal with Sophia on an empty stomach, he went downstairs and made himself breakfast; but once the bread was toasted and buttered, he found he couldn't eat, so he went back up with his cup of coffee.

Hoping that Poppea would call him, he did nothing at all. Later that day, when he thought about it, he wondered what good it would have done him to reach her: After all, the Ernsts would still be fakes, and he knew full well she couldn't pay him back no matter what she promised. Still, at the time it seemed mysteriously as if Poppea might have a solution, as if the fakes could be replaced by real paintings. Perhaps her trip would be successful; perhaps she could pressure Francesco Tevere into replacing all the fakes he had sold her. He called her New York number again and said he needed to speak to Miss Vlassoff the very moment she was in touch with them, no matter where she was.

For a minute, Vincent thought of putting the whole problem off. He would do nothing until tomorrow and pretend that today was just an ordinary Tuesday, but then he remembered Sarah and realized he could have no peace even if he hid from Sophia. Besides, he would only make the situation worse by postponing things. What if Sophia's collector was also in touch with Ernst and had the same answer? Then it would look as if Vincent were deliberately trying to hide the truth. No, the sickening mess must be faced; with leaden fingers, he dialed Sophia's number.

Her secretary answered and asked cheerfully how he was; Vincent dutifully told her he was fine, asked how she had been doing, and finally, feeling curiously breathless, said he must speak to Sophia. "Well," the secretary replied, "you'll have to call back. She's with a client right now, and she has a pretty busy morning. How would this afternoon be?" Vincent was tempted, but then, dutifully, he answered that it was very urgent, Sophia had better call him the moment she was free.

As soon as he put down the phone, he realized how little he wanted to wait. He tried to think of the interval as a respite but he couldn't: It was simply a prolonged torture. He tried to read but, of course, was unable to concentrate. Even the adventures in Trollope's *The Duke's Children* failed to distract him now. Angrily, he put the book down and rubbed his palms on the sheet; they had been sweating steadily and unpleasantly. He thought of washing and getting dressed, but the effort was too great; so he simply sat, waiting for the phone to ring and dreading it at the same time. Then, finally, the call came and he almost leapt on the receiver.

"Well," Sophia said cheerfully, "is it good news?"

Vincent swallowed hard. "I'm afraid not," he said. "Apparently, we've all been fooled. I just received a cable this morning."

There was a brief pause. "Are you sure?" Sophia asked in a tight voice.

"Unfortunately, yes. Ernst says they're fakes—"

"Oh, my God! I knew it!" Sophia shouted, interrupting him. "This is the end, the end. What will I tell my client! It's all your fault, Vincent. I never liked the wretched picture in the first place, and now, of course, I have to give him his money back. . . ."

Sophia's ranting was just what Vincent had expected. When she finally slowed down a little, he said, "Look, I know this is very unpleasant, but it's happened to every dealer; and we did have those Mundberg certificates."

Sophia gave a theatrical laugh. "Mundberg!" she said. "As if that meant anything."

"Well, I admit I made a mistake," Vincent answered, "but so did you, and everyone else. And he is an expert. Look at his books—"

"Oh, God, Vincent, haven't you heard? He's been selling his certificates. In the last month alone, I've heard of at least three fakes, all surrealist, with Mundberg certificates."

"No! Have you?" said Vincent, interested despite himself. "Do you suppose he knows what he's doing?"

"That," Sophia answered, "is not the point. How soon can you give me a check? Make it any time today. Even if I'm not in, Claudia will take it."

Vincent, who had been leaning back, sat up straight. "I'll pay you back," he said tightly. "You don't have to worry. But today is out of the question. I don't have that kind of money just sitting in the bank. You may have to wait for a week or so," Patiently, he listened to Sophia's renewed hysteria.

As soon as the call was over, he lifted the phone again. In a way, Sophia had been easy to deal with: He could at least react to the scenes she made. But now, he had to tell Charles Morgenstern that he, Vincent, had just sold him a fake. At least, he thought, it was a good thing that Morgenstern had only bought it as an investment and agreed to have it offered for sale as soon as it was framed. Since the profit was to come only then, Vincent, if he could recover the cost of the painting from Poppea, would not lose any money. Still, the thought of telling his client about the fake was so unpleasant that he felt it best to get the whole business over as quickly as possible. As it turned out, Vincent found it even more painful than he had expected.

He told Morgenstern the painting was a fake and complained about the Mundberg certificate. Even before Morgenstern could ask, Vincent assured him he would be repaid in full; it would just be a matter of a few days. But his client's politeness made him blush with embarrassment. When, finally, the call was over, Vincent gave a great sigh. Biting his lips and shaking his head, he felt a wave of disgust come over him. It was as if he had just been splashed with some evil, fetid, foul-smelling mud. It wasn't just that he looked foolish, that he had lost prestige in the eyes of a man who had trusted him: That particular discomfort would come later; nor was it the probable loss of a backer thanks to whose capital a great deal of money might have been made. As for the financial disaster involved in paying everybody back, that, too, would have its day. No, at the moment, Vincent simply felt soiled; he disgusted himself. Slowly, he understood that the guilt and despair over what he had made of himself was the real cause of his suffering.

Still, he realized he could hardly keep on sitting in bed, feeling upset with himself. There was an almost endless array of unpleasant tasks to be faced, and he decided to start with the easiest. Knocking at Sarah's door, he went in, said good morning, pretended not to notice her silence, and said amiably: "Sarah, I have to talk to you. I know we have a number of disagreements and you're perfectly free to leave if you want to do so. I just want to ask you to wait for a few days. The Ernsts are fakes and I'm having some awful complications as a result."

Surely, he thought as he planned his little speech, Sarah would agree to the delay, and that at least would be one less problem to cope with; but, to his horror, Sarah shook her head.

"Oh, no," she said, "I've had more than enough of always coming after your current problem. This time, I'm looking after myself first."

He pointed out that they could live completely separately while sharing the same apartment, that nothing could be arranged anyway since he no longer knew whether he had any money at all, and that he simply had neither the time nor the energy to get everything settled. But Sarah would not relent. "Well," he said finally, "do what you want, but don't count on me for anything," and started to walk out.

"Wait," Sarah said, in the coldest of voices. "I'm willing to stay, but you'll have to get out of here. You can just live at your office for a while."

Vincent shook his head. "You know that's impossible," he answered. "There's no bed, nothing to sleep on."

"Then go to your mistress."

"I can't do that either, Sarah."

"You mean she's already fed up with you? I'm not surprised. Well, take a hotel room."

"Goddamn it, Sarah, don't be absurd," Vincent said angrily. "I have to be where I can be reached. If you want to be alone, you go to a hotel; but don't count on me to give you the money for it."

There was a brief pause while the two glared at each other. "Very well," Sarah said, her face set. "I'll leave."

"Where will you go?"

"That's none of your business. Please get my suitcases down for me so that I can start packing."

"Get them down yourself," said Vincent, feeling thoroughly childish, as he walked out of the room.

For a while, he stood considering what he should do; then, remembering that he owed over $100,000, he decided to go to the office and see just what his financial position was; but once he sat down at his desk, he felt paralyzed. He knew there was no time to waste. Even if Charles Morgenstern waited for two or three weeks, he knew that Sophia Lyon would be calling several times a day.

When the phone did in fact ring, he answered it reluctantly. To his relief, it was a client and, by the time the conversation ended, he had sold the Cézanne. Quickly, he called David Copley and told him the news, feeling a tremendous lift. A little calmer now, he knew he was only making $750, but he didn't care: It wasn't the money that mattered, but the sign that life might begin to improve after all.

Still, he had to face his problems. By the time he had finished his calculations, the situation was all too clear. Using everything he had in his bank accounts, he could reimburse Sophia immediately. He hadn't yet paid Poppea for the second Ernst and he could still get his $15,000 profit together. Of course, that would leave him broke. Even if Morgenstern gave him a little time, he would have to be reimbursed by Poppea before he could in turn pay his client back. Quickly, he made a list of all the art he owned. Even if he sold them all, he would only get around $10,000 out of them; he would still be short $40,000. There could be no question: Poppea was his only hope. Perhaps, if he put enough pressure on her, she would rob someone else to pay him.

He looked at the figures again and came to a decision.

He would give Sophia a check for $55,000 of the $65,000 he owed her. That would enable her, at least, to reimburse her client; keep her quiet for a week or two; and still leave him some ready cash. And he *must* reach Poppea. He tried calling her number once more, and was again told they didn't know where she was. There was, apparently, nothing more he could do. The day stretched empty before him. He could take a check to Sophia and send his client a bill for the Cézanne. He contemplated juggling one sum against the other: He could tell Copley his client was paying him in thirty days, and use the money he had to reimburse Morgenstern, but the thought of facing Copley stopped him. Besides, he told himself, that would actually be robbery, and he hadn't sunk quite that low—yet. Reluctantly, he typed out the invoice for the watercolor. It was still only a little after twelve and the day gaped ahead of him. "Well, at least," he muttered, "Donna is expecting me tonight."

When he rang the door to her apartment, it seemed as if nothing had happened. He was back in the heady atmosphere where he controlled his own life. Donna, when she opened the door, was as fresh, as sexy as ever. They kissed and Vincent considered pretending everything was just the same; but then, he thought of making love and realized he simply wasn't interested. Perhaps talking to Donna would help; so he said he had had a rather bad two days and would tell her about it over dinner. It was a long story and she listened carefully. He noticed that, when he told her about his split with Sarah, she didn't suggest that they move in together; and, while he was explaining to her how the Ernsts had turned out to be fakes, it struck him that he wished she had offered—even though he wouldn't have let her come to live with him.

Even when Donna tried to comfort him, Vincent thought, she wasn't very convincing. She was right, of course, when she said that Sarah and he had nothing in common anymore; that he would be better off alone; that now he had a chance to rebuild his life. Again, he missed any note of joy. She was sure, she said, he would overcome the problem of the fake Ernsts. Clearly, she meant well, but Vincent stopped her rather roughly by saying she didn't understand the full extent of the disaster. When, after coffee, Donna said, "Of course, you're coming up," Vincent felt sure their affair was ending: Before, she wouldn't have asked the question. Donna was still the same woman. He still enjoyed her, and she seemed, if anything, more amorous. Throughout it all, however, he had the feeling he was being given a last night to remember. He had intended to spend the entire night with her. Yet, at midnight, he said he should go home. Donna made no effort to stop him. In the taxi going back uptown, he felt, to his surprise, a tear roll down his cheek.

He wondered, as he started to unlock his door, whether Sarah would still be in the apartment. At first, it seemed so quiet he thought she must be gone and, to his surprise, minded it a great deal. Then, he saw that her door was closed. There was a note on his pillow. Quickly he picked it up and gave a great sigh of relief. It said simply, "Call Poppea Vlassoff at the Hotel Splendid, Milan." Without hesitating, Vincent dialed the overseas operator; it was a little after six in the morning in Italy, but Poppea richly deserved to be awakened with the bad news just as he had been that morning.

It took a while for the call to go through. The night watchman was obviously still manning the hotel exchange, but finally he heard Poppea's unmistakable voice saying, "Pronto." As soon as Vincent spoke, she answered, fully awake: "Oh, God, I'm so glad you've called. I spent the whole night trying to reach you. You weren't at your office, and your home phone didn't answer so I told the operator to keep ringing, and then your wife answered. Is there something wrong with her? Well, anyway, I need you to come right away."

"What?"

"Yeah. I got this fantastic new lawyer and we've been going after Francesco Tevere, but I need you here as a witness that he sold us fakes. In Italy, you have to present evidence in person. In exchange, I think I can get some real pictures out of him."

"He owes more than you know," Vincent said grimly. "The Ernsts are fakes."

There was such a long silence at the other end of the line that Vincent said, "Poppea, can you hear me?"

"Yeah," she answered, her voice gone quite flat. "I can hear you. How do you know they're fake?"

"The artist says so. Look, I'm in a lot of hot water over here. It's a good thing I wasn't paid for the second one yet," Vincent went on mendaciously, "but you owe me the forty-five thousand I paid you for the first one, and I have to have it right away."

"You know I don't have forty-five grand. Shit, I'm in the hole for a lot of other stuff already."

"Can't you return them?"

Poppea laughed. "Sure," she said, "like I can return this. Look, you really better come over."

"How can I? Poppea, there's no way for me to leave New York until I've paid my client back."

Again, there was a silence. "What if I can get you fifteen grand?" Poppea asked. "Then you could give it to your client and come to Milan. See, if you're here, then I can get other paintings and I'll be okay."

"Well," Vincent said reluctantly, "I'll tell you what. You get me twenty, not fifteen, and I'll try to come. How long would you need me to stay?"

It was agreed that she would get him the money within three or four days and that he would then fly to Milan and stay for as long as two weeks, if necessary.

Vincent slept very badly that night; as soon as he stopped worrying about the fakes, Sarah's impending departure came back to haunt him. No matter where he looked, he said to himself bitterly, he saw only misery. The thought of work made him feel sick. He began to feel that perhaps the fakes were a warning. Then, the image of Donna would surface, and he would lapse into wondering whether or not he would ever see her again. He had no grounds for complaint, he knew that. They had come together by chance, and there was no room in their relationship for the kind of crisis he was now enduring. Still, his affair with Donna had been an essential part of his new life, and it was already ending. Briefly, Vincent wondered about Peter Passarolo: He didn't think he could afford the show anymore, and didn't see where he would get the energy for it: Another part of his life was dying away.

Sarah kept flitting in and out of his mind. Again, he had no legitimate complaint—except that a divorce would be humiliating and would, no doubt, please André, always so alert to evidence of his son's failure. It was curious that he minded losing her; they had really had no marriage for quite some time. It was only because it was happening at such a bad time, he told himself; otherwise he'd be glad to be free of her; but he failed to convince himself.

Then, there was the trip to Milan. At this point, Vincent hardly felt up to seeing Poppea day and night. When he thought of the negotiations with Francesco Tevere, he actually felt sick. It was fastidiousness, really: He didn't want to deal with all the cheating, all the dishonesty. He reminded himself he had put up with it quite happily when he was buying the Ernsts. He laughed aloud at himself when he remembered his superior tone, his disdainful statement that he would do nothing without a Mundberg certificate. When Vincent went to sleep that night, his dreams were full of anxiety, and he kept waking up. He opened his eyes for good after dreaming of a long pursuit through thick, clinging mud. The waking reality seemed so much worse than the dream, however, that he said aloud: "God, I wish they'd got me."

"I'm going to sue the shit out of him," Poppea said darkly. "I'll ruin him. He'll have to sell his collection to pay me. Nobody will publish his books or pay for his certificates once I'm through with him."

Vincent, listening to her with half an ear, asked: "Mundberg, you mean?"

"Who else? Anyway, it's a good thing you came. Francesco will be here soon, I told him you were coming, and that your evidence would put him in jail. Look, he thinks you're very rich and, if you shout at him, he'll really get scared and bring some real pictures."

"Don't be silly, Poppea. He's much too shrewd to do anything like that. What about your lawyer? When are we seeing him?"

There was no hurrying her, it seemed. To Vincent, every minute spent in Milan was wasted. He had come, lured by the desperate hope that perhaps Poppea could recoup her losses and pay him back, and with the proviso that he wouldn't stay more than a week.

"That'll be enough," Poppea had said. "As soon as Francesco sees that you're here, my lawyer can talk to him and he'll realize he's got to make good."

Vincent took the last sip of his double espresso. "Well," he asked, "when do we actually see him? And, by the way, it's pretty obvious that the story about the Ernsts' being given directly to his father was a lie."

"Oh, sure," Poppea answered as if it were the most natural thing in the world. "I knew it all along."

Vincent drew himself up. "I see," he said. "You knew. Then why did you lie to me?"

"Well, you had to have a provenance, didn't you?" she answered matter-of-factly. "I didn't want to put you off. Come on, I made an appointment with a dealer I just met. I want to make an exchange with him. I'll give him one of the Ernsts against some American paintings he says he has."

"You don't mean . . . But, Poppea, you know they're fakes. Aren't you in enough trouble as it is?"

Poppea laughed. "It doesn't matter," she said. "They all sell fakes here anyway."

By the end of the day, Vincent began to realize with a sinking heart that he had wasted both time and money in coming to Milan. The American paintings touted by Poppea were real but unsaleable, mostly works of unfashionable second-generation abstract expressionists, like Hartigan and Goldberg. During the meeting with the lawyer, it became clear to Vincent that he could have given testimony in New York just as easily: He would simply have had to go to the Italian consulate and take an oath in front of one of the officials.

When Francesco Tevere showed up at the hotel in the late afternoon, Vincent began to get the feeling that he and Poppea were in cahoots again, and so he said very little except that he had seen the lawyer and was ready to be a witness against Tevere at any trial. The young Italian had seemed frightened but, to Vincent's more practiced eye, his fear was tinged with playacting. Still, he had promised to come back with a big Rothko, so perhaps there would be a way out after all. Vincent wanted to believe him, but he was pretty sure that something would simply be wrong all over again.

It was more than he could bear to have dinner alone with Poppea, so he said he was tired from the journey and would have a sandwich in his room. Before going up, however, he asked in a last desperate effort whether or not she had seen any collectors.

"Oh," Poppea said, laughing, "sure, I could see the Sardine, only he's in jail. They convicted him for embezzling money from his firm. He got three years. But there's this new private I met who's got this villa with a big collection outside Florence—only he doesn't want anyone to know about it, so I told him you were my business partner, and so we can go there anytime."

"What does he have?" Vincent asked wearily.

"Well," Poppea said, "he wouldn't tell me. He says he's afraid of being robbed—"

"Honestly, Poppea!" Vincent answered with a gesture of dismissal. "I'll see you in the morning. Call me when Tevere gets here."

As soon as he was alone in his room, Vincent began to feel restless. He thought of going out, but he didn't really want to. He realized he had come to loathe Milan: Everything was tainted by Poppea's presence. He tried to tell himself that it might be a long time before he would return to Italy, that he really should take advantage of these few days, but nothing made any difference. He began to wonder bitterly whether Poppea would always remain associated with Italy in his mind, thus spoiling one of his favorite countries.

When the phone rang the next morning and Poppea said Francesco had arrived, Vincent's heart sank. Resisting the impulse to hide in his room and say he was ill, he went down to find Tevere talking away at a great pace. There was no sign of any painting. Nodding to him coldly, Vincent turned to Poppea. "Where's the Rothko?" he asked.

"Francesco can't get it until tomorrow," she answered, but he has this huge Picabia—it's too big to move—and he says we can take that if we want."

"Where is it? And where does it come from?"

"At his girl friend's place. It belongs to her. She's a big model. But she'll give it to him so he doesn't have to go to jail."

"All right," Vincent said wearily, "I suppose we'd better look at it."

Francesco's girl friend, if the apartment was indeed hers, lived in luxury. There were furs on the sofas and thick carpets on the floor; the furniture was modern, Italian, and expensive; the walls were covered with silk; and, leaning awkwardly against a chair, was the painting.

"Who does this actually belong to?" Vincent asked suspiciously. "It obviously doesn't usually hang in this apartment." In spite of Poppea's voluble explanations—it had just come back from the framer's but Francesco's girl had owned it for years—it occurred to Vincent the painting must be either fake or stolen. That impression grew even stronger when Francesco explained that Elena had bought the painting a very long time ago—well, last year—from a collector who had owned it since the twenties but was now dead; and, since that collector had bought it directly from the artist and had not owned anything else of importance, there was really no way to check. With admirable gravity, Francesco offered to guarantee the painting himself.

For a moment, Vincent felt as if he were back during that earlier stay in Milan when he had bought the Ernsts: The painting was convincing enough; he need only take it and hope for the best. Only this time, while the painting was probably real, it was also probably stolen. Ignoring Francesco, he turned to Poppea and said coolly: "Look, do whatever you want; but if you handle this painting, you'll have to do it all on your own. It's no joke to have a hot picture and I, for one, would rather not end up in jail." As he turned and started to walk out of the apartment, Poppea joined him.

"Even if it's hot, how would anybody know in New York?" she asked. When Vincent had finished telling her about Interpol and the lists circulated to dealers and major collectors, she looked uncharacteristically abashed. "Francesco says Elena owns it," she said finally, "but I don't believe him." As they made their way to the lawyer's, she started to describe the Rothko they would be seeing, and asked Vincent what it would sell for in New York if she had to get the money quickly. Had it not been for the shining copper plate on the door saying "Avvocato Curzio Atrabile," Vincent would have thought him simply another one of Poppea's acolytes.

At least, Vincent mused when he was once again alone in his room, there was something to be said for being away from New York. Here, once he got rid of Poppea, he enjoyed a kind of peace. He was suspended in a no-man's-land where his problems almost ceased to exist. He thought briefly of the money he was spending; but since he was charging everything, he dismissed the worry. Feeling almost jaunty, he went down to an English bookstore in the Galleria; then, returning to his room, he ordered dinner with great care. The evening was his to enjoy.

By the next morning, the nightmare was back in full force. When Vincent went downstairs, he saw that Tevere had brought the Rothko; but, even from across the room, it looked singularly unattractive. Nodding to Poppea and Francesco, he moved closer until, stopping some six feet away, he said: "That's the ugliest Rothko I've ever seen. You'll have a lot of trouble selling *that* in New York." Tilting his head, he added, "Anyway, there's something wrong with it. It's too shiny. Rothko always has a matte surface. Maybe it's been badly restored." While Poppea was busy translating this to Francesco, Vincent moved closer and carefully felt the surface of the painting. "That's funny, I don't think it's varnish," he said. Suddenly, almost as if he had been stung, Vincent lifted his finger from the painting's surface and examined it closely; then, in a sepulchral voice, he announced: "Well, Poppea, Francesco is even more obliging than we thought. Look, the paint is still wet. He must have had this Rothko made just for you."

Without waiting, he walked out and returned to his room. He had barely finished reserving a seat back to New York on the afternoon plane when Poppea knocked and came in.

"Man, did I give it to him," she started to say, but Vincent interrupted her.

"Look," he said, "there's obviously no sense in my staying here any longer. I'll be glad to go to the Italian consulate in New York anytime you need my deposition. But you might as well face it: Francesco is incapable of coming up with a genuine painting. And I think we'd better settle up our own business."

So far, Poppea had been remarkably still, but when he explained that he expected to be repaid in full for the outstanding fake, her face changed. "Like hell I will," she hissed. It occurred to Vincent that this was probably the first time she hadn't put on an act for him. He stood horrified as, with a great outpouring of profanity, she explained that there was no reason why she should refund anything; that he was just as responsible for the fakes as she was, since he had chosen to buy them; that the $20,000 Jack Griffenbaum had given him in New York was just a loan. With a sinking heart, Vincent suddenly understood the ambiguous letter he had received and the word "loan" on the check itself. "You owe that twenty grand, not me," Poppea added with satisfaction.

At that, Vincent lifted his hand. "He can't collect it, you know," he said quietly. "I never acknowledged that debt."

"What about the check?" Poppea retorted venomously. "Jack's lawyer says that's as good a receipt as any."

"Of course, Poppea, you realize that if you take that position, I can sue you for selling fraudulent merchandise; besides which, obviously, I won't lift a finger to help you over here," Vincent said in an even voice. There was a brief silence.

"All right," she said. "I'll pay you back half when I can. But half of it is your own debt, and you're still responsible to Jack." At that, the fight between them again broke out, and, by the time he stepped onto the plane, Vincent knew he had no bitterer enemy than Poppea Vlassoff.

"Can you believe," Viola said indignantly, "that he's even trying to keep things I owned before I ever knew him?"

"Yes, all too easily," Vincent answered. "But, surely, he can't get away with it? What does your lawyer say?" Viola launched into a long discourse on the differences between French and American law. Although Vincent was altogether on her side, he paid scant attention to her explanations. His own life was already more than he could cope with. Perhaps Viola noticed his absent look; at any rate, she soon changed the subject and asked Vincent about his own difficulties. When he answered her, the picture he drew was so depressing he could hardly bear to go on.

When he thought of his life now, what he saw was a very, very slow earthquake. The earth trembled on and on; the buildings swayed, cracked, and collapsed, sending up great clouds of dust and crushing him as they fell; but unlike the real thing, his cataclysm seemed to go on endlessly. There was Donna, of course. Vincent had had the satisfaction of the final gesture, at least: The day after they said good-bye, he sent Donna an enormous bouquet of splendid red roses with a note that simply said: "Thank you." The fact that the florist's bill remained unpaid only added irony to the situation.

Then, there was his business. He still had the office, but the lease would run out at the end of the month, and he would be unable to renew it; as it was, he couldn't even pay the final month's rent. Not one of his frantic efforts to sell a painting had succeeded; after the Cézanne, everything had stopped. The remaining paintings were going back to David Copley, who had been surprisingly nice about everything and told Vincent he was quite right to cut down on expenses. "Call me," he had even said, "if you're ever looking for anything in particular."

Even the answering service was disconnected; and it was just as well since most of the calls came from Poppea. Vincent and Poppea were suing each other, with Jack Griffenbaum lingering menacingly in the background, so that she had become a permanent nightmare. Vincent's lawyer had told him several times that Poppea didn't have a leg to stand on, that he had nothing to worry about. Still, the pretrial hearings kept multiplying and Vincent felt utterly soiled by the sordid wrangle. Coming out of the courthouse one morning, he had found himself rubbing his hands as if he were washing them. He thought of Pilate and of Lady Macbeth, repeating to himself, "Not all the perfumes of Araby . . ." But he knew that this was no joke, that he had allowed himself to be contaminated by Poppea's blind greed. He hadn't cared whether the Ernsts were real or not so long as they brought him money. When he looked back, it seemed incredible that he had not at the very outset sent the photos to Ernst. Whatever the outcome of his fight with Poppea, that mud would not wash away.

Business, like a receding sea, had withdrawn from him. At one time, deals had come to him unbidden. Now that he had disturbed his own equilibrium by reaching out for money in a blind and grasping way, he had lost whatever quality it was that made him different from the other dealers. And, since he lacked their persistence, their monomania really, he could no longer function. Now and again, he felt a brief measure of relief: He was freer, in a sense, than before; he no longer had to perform all those odious duties.

Even that comfort was fleeting and quickly dispelled, however. There was, after all, the trouble with Poppea; he was utterly broke; and, almost worse, he had had to sell his collection to repay Charles Morgenstern. Naturally, since he was in a rush, he had been unable to get full value for his drawings and prints. As he offered them to other dealers, and although he did his best to seem nonchalant and uncaring, he felt sure they could see right through his pretense and knew that he was liquidating his every possession. He thus endured burning humiliation. At least, he kept telling himself, he was doing the honorable thing by repaying Morgenstern. He had nothing to be ashamed of, but the whole process remained enormously painful.

Chief among the losses he dwelt on was the Passarolo show: Just remembering it was a recipe for instant depression. It had seemed like such a good idea and would have led him so far. He could see himself as another Kahnweiler to Passarolo's Picasso, becoming rich and famous with the artist he had backed. It wasn't just making money, either: All profits came from the early recognition of a major talent; they were legitimate. Disregarding all the difficulties that would have, in actuality, been inherent in organizing the show, Vincent did not cease to mourn the death of his stillborn career as a patron.

For a very brief moment, when he felt that losing his apartment would be the final blow, Vincent considered appealing to his father for help. He was stopped by the thought of the pleasure André would take, not just in refusing, but in making a lengthy speech revolving around "I told you so." Nevertheless, of all Vincent's losses at the time, the Passarolo show was perhaps the most immediately painful to him. Suddenly, Vincent could no longer pay the rent nor even claim he needed the space. Sarah had left, taking her belongings with her. Far too much stuff remained, however, to fit into Vincent's tiny new studio apartment, so most of it had to go into storage. He felt more deprived than ever. As he mourned the consequences of his move—no more dining room, no real kitchen, no possibility of inviting people—he realized that all those unbearable changes had, in fact, concealed one essential fact: He was no longer married.

It was something he never mentioned to anyone: How can one say that one minds losing one's apartment more than one's wife? Still, it was true. The agony of dismantling shelves and closets, of rolling rugs and packing plates, silver, and saucepans left very little time to think about the divorce. Sarah, now that she had reached her decision, had become quite pleasant. They worked together, dividing their possessions with very little friction. It was the last night, when only the beds were left in place, that Vincent fully realized that his marriage had gone down the drain with everything else. By then alone in the stripped-down bedroom, he felt seized by the most violent panic. It was like being a lost child with no hope of being found, a loneliness so vivid, so intense that he walked into Sarah's room, sat down on her bed, and said with a forced smile: "I think we've just done a lot of good work together."

"Oh," Sarah answered bleakly, "it's always easier to dismantle. If we were fixing up the apartment, we'd be fighting."

"But would we?" Vincent asked, his voice unnaturally bright. "I wonder. It's not too late, you know. We don't have to split up just because we're giving up the apartment. After all, we've had some good years together. . . ."

Sarah, who had been reclining, sat up suddenly. "Don't be stupid," she said. "The only reason it's been going so smoothly is because of the divorce. I certainly don't want to live with you anymore; I don't want to live with anyone. And I don't think you do either."

Vincent stared at her in silence and nodded. She was right; but once he was alone in his room again, the panic returned, just as violently as before.

Of course, moving into the new apartment turned out to be intensely depressing. It seemed terribly small by comparison with his previously generous space. All the amenities were gone: It had neither a real kitchen—only an alcove with a stove, a sink, and a half-refrigerator—nor a dishwasher. Although the new building had a doorman, and his studio's ceiling was high, there was no air conditioning. To Vincent's jaundiced eye, it looked like a prison cell.

Then, too, a living had to be earned. Much to Vincent's surprise, a friend called and offered him a translation job. On top of the still unpacked boxes, there sat a history of French architecture to be turned into English, and Vincent knew that, for the next three months at least, he would be able to manage.

When he considered Olga's career, however, jealousy took over. He forgot how much he had disliked being a dealer, and simply envied her. That she had found her true vocation was beyond question. In the last three months, and in spite of the usually slow summer season, Olga had become an established, successful dealer. Now that she was free of Partridge, her talent for attracting people and making money could flower unhampered. Already, she was talking of selling her apartment and buying a larger one. She still sold Partridge's works—they paid the rent, she said— but now they were eclipsed by Picasso drawings. Vincent did not find seeing her very pleasant. It wasn't just that he envied her, but that he also felt subtly patronized. The tables had been turned. Now it was Olga who had money and influence.

Only when she complained about missing Partridge did Vincent find the old Olga again. Success notwithstanding, she did miss him. She cried when she thought of him, she still said, and when Vincent answered, "Surely you realize you'd never have done this well if you were still with him," he was treated to the classic disquisition on the heartbreaks of a career-woman. And yet, he noticed with amusement, Olga had resumed her old habits: Men came and went, very much at her whim. She might still long for Partridge, but she had set forth on her own, independent course, and Vincent suspected that she would never look back.

THIRTEEN

It was spring again. Once more the buds were opening along Fifth Avenue and the florists' shops were gay with tulips and peonies. As Vincent walked down Madison Avenue that evening, he felt wonderfully light. For the first time that season, he had left his heavy winter coat at home; there was no weight on his shoulders, no burden to carry. He swung his arms freely and faced into the warm breeze.

He was on his way to Viola's new apartment and smiled to himself as he remembered that anguished meeting about the divorce, almost a year ago. We have crossed the Styx, he thought, and found life on the other side. He felt great satisfaction as he entered the large living room of Viola's new apartment. His father had been defeated in more ways than one.

With pleasure, he remembered his many meetings with Viola's lawyers, the information he had given them, the suggestions he had made so that André could be forced to behave a little less indecently. For a while, conditioned by the past, he had thought Viola's a lost cause—only to be astonished by the toughness, the resourcefulness of her lawyer. At the thought of André's rage, he smiled with pleasure. There had been the day when his phone had rung and, to his surprise, his father's voice had greeted him. Apparently unaware of the frost in his son's voice, André had asked amiably: "So you're divorcing?"

"That's right," Vincent said tightly.

"Quite right. Quite right. I always thought Sarah was the wrong wife for you. Well, if you're going through a divorce yourself, you must understand how difficult it can be. Vincent, you know I've always been your best friend," André continued, ignoring his son's denial, "and now it's time you did something for me. Poor Viola, of course, doesn't realize what she's doing, she never had any common sense, but her lawyers have just put an embargo on all my American business—"

"Embargo?" said Vincent, feigning ignorance.

"Yes, all my funds are frozen and, between us, it's really inconvenient, because David Copley owes me a great deal of money and now he can't pay me. So I want you to go and see Viola. Explain to her how wrong this is. Tell her it will only harm her in the end, and have her order her lawyers to lift the embargo."

"Well, but should I also tell her to live on ten thousand dollars a year?" Vincent asked. There was a brief silence.

"I don't see why she should have more," André finally answered, "but I've always been generous. Tell her she can have fifteen if she lifts the embargo."

"I'll convey your offer," Vincent said in a perfectly straight voice, "but that's really all I can do. Frankly, I think she'd be a fool to accept it."

There was another pause, and then André thundered: "Which side are you on? Don't forget that she's nothing to you, and I'm your father! I expect you to tell her exactly what I want."

Vincent laughed. "I was wondering when you'd go back to normal," he said. "I think you'd better let your lawyer

talk directly to hers: He might be more convincing."
Vincent could hear his father breathing heavily all the way
from Paris.

"I warn you," André finally said, "if you don't do as I
ask, I will disown you."

"Then I considered myself disowned," Vincent answered
and hung up the phone. When it rang an hour later, and
André was once again on the wire, Vincent refused to continue the conversation. "I think we'd better disown each
other," he said simply as he put the receiver down.

As it turned out, that offer was only the first of a series;
and now Vincent was having a drink with Viola to cele-
brate the signing of the settlement agreement: After much
squabbling, Viola was to receive half of everything owned
by André.

They were celebrating. "I have wonderful news," Viola
said as soon as they sat down.

"You mean you're getting both halves of the property?"
Vincent asked, smiling.

Viola laughed. "That'll be the day," she answered. "No,
I had a most productive meeting with Pierre-Paul Sanche
today. As you know, he's been thoroughly involved in
this whole mess since the lawyers had to find out what
André was really worth. That led to a lot of questions about
Pierre-Paul's own funds. I don't know whether André
simply spent the money on himself, or what, but already
Pierre-Paul has found out a dozen ways in which he was
being cheated."

"I'm not surprised," Vincent interjected, "but I suppose
he'll just go on suffering as usual."

"You couldn't be more wrong," Viola answered with
satisfaction. "I've been listening to him, of course, and
sympathizing. The thing is, he does want to work. So we
have come to an agreement: He is pulling out of *Voir* to
start a new magazine over here. He'll be the publisher and

run the business side; and guess who will be the editor-in-chief?"

"Not—"

"Yes," Viola said, "that well-known journalist, Viola Germain." And lifting the bottle of champagne, she eased out the cork.

The last issue of *Voir*, Vincent thought as he leafed through it, clearly reflected André's disarray. He wondered what the next one would be like. Surely, the magazine would find another backer; still, he could imagine André's fury when he heard that Viola was starting her own publication.

"I wonder whether he'll still want to marry Coche," Vincent said to Viola. "He must feel distinctly sour about the noble estate of marriage!"

"Why should he? After all, it was because of her that he divorced me," Viola answered. "And besides, you know what he's like. She's still the key to Laure de Goldschmidt's good graces. I hear he spends practically every other weekend at Ayville."

Had she but known it, Viola's information was a little out of date. It had been well over two months since André had received one of Mme. de Goldschmidt's coveted invitations. At first, Coche had explained the silence away: It really would be better for André's ultimate social position if he were to lie low while the divorce was in its most virulent stages. People were already gossiping far too much as it was, and frequent visits to Ayville would only aggravate the problem. Laure would say she missed André but, alas, he was busy, and so people would realize his position was as solid as ever.

André had not been quite convinced: It was all too obvious that Coche was beginning to have second thoughts.

André found that infuriating, of course. Luckily, there was always Thérèse, handkerchief at the ready, and she was made to bear the consequences of his situation. He was far too shrewd to think that his marriage would still take place if he lost *Voir*; but that possibility never entered his mind. He merely kept telling Thérèse he would screw them all in the end.

As for Coche, she was now almost sure of the outcome. "You know, Laure," she told her friend, as they sat together having their hair done, "he's becoming increasingly unpleasant. I mean, I knew he was bad-tempered, but the other night he made quite a violent scene for no reason at all."

"Oh, well," Laure said indulgently, "it's the divorce. I hear that Viola is being difficult—"

"Difficult! She's demanding a huge settlement. André keeps complaining that she's trying to ruin him. Frankly, Laure, I wonder if she's not succeeding."

The baroness, disregarding the ministrations of M. Hubert, turned her head sharply and looked at her friend.

"You don't think . . . you mean he's going broke?" she asked.

"Yes," Coche answered, "and I'm willing to bet he'll lose *Voir* before it's all over."

"Oh, well," Mme. de Goldschmidt said with a deep sigh, "it looks as if we put up with him for no reason after all. Still, darling, do be careful. You never know how these things may end; don't dismiss him yet."

André himself clung to his coming marriage: It was the one bright point amid his difficulties, the one possibility he could think of with pleasure. Even so, it was hardly enough to counterbalance all the other disasters.

True, he had finally taken back the Chagall and returned the Bergs' money, but, before he did so, they sued him in Paris as well as in New York and went around to all the

French dealers complaining about the fake they'd bought from André Germain. For a while, his favorite leitmotif had been: "Why haven't those goddamn Fornettis paid up? They said they'd buy the Chagall back!" Thérèse, always willing, had made three trips to Milan to demand restitution. At least, there was one consolation: The Bergs did not know the Goldschmidts; but André had told Coche, who told Laure, who found the story amusing and passed it on to a few friends, as, in turn, André soon found out. And, now that the Fornettis had bought it back, his whole scheme based on blackmailing them had collapsed.

None of that, however, was nearly as bad as what followed. Copley had sold the Chardin, and André had counted on that money, blocked now by Viola's embargo. It now failed to appear. He was unable to do business in the United States, and, although reduced to desperate financial straits, he was far too busy with lawyers and accountants to do much business even in Paris.

Still, André struggled on, but things became more difficult every day. Now that competent accountants were looking through his books—he had resisted opening them as long as he could—all sorts of discrepancies were being brought to light. There was an avalanche of long overdue bills, but the money with which to pay them had somehow vanished. Little by little, his transactions with Pierre-Paul Sanche revealed a consistent pattern of fraud. Deny it all as he might, André became painfully conscious that he was being exposed. And to make it all even more infuriating, Thérèse now claimed she could no longer work every night, because she wanted to spend more time with Igor. Igor was a delicate subject and, rather than discuss it, he let it go.

Needing to vent his rage on someone, he turned on Coche and became painfully aware that his behavior was doing him no good at all. Day by day, she was moving away from him. All of a sudden, there were invitations he didn't share and evenings when she was too tired to see him. Clearly, a solution must be found, and fast.

As it turned out, André was waiting for Coche one day when he received a letter from Sanche's lawyer that brought down the full thrust of his thunder on Thérèse's head. She had innocently walked in to ask about an article in the next month's issue, only to be told that she was an idiot, that there would be no next month's issue, and that she might at least know enough not to bother André with futilities. Sobbing away, she was still desperately looking for her handkerchief when André thrust the letter at her, saying: "See for yourself. This is the end." He spent the next month desperately searching for another source of capital, but it had become all too clear that anyone who was willing to buy *Voir* would also run it, and would therefore have no need of André. The same was true of the gallery: There was nothing left to do but liquidate.

In a last, desperate attempt, André even asked Coche to feel out the Goldschmidts: If only they would back him, everything could be saved after all. This time it was Coche who created the scene. She accused André of caring only about business. Refusing to hear his attempted vindication, she announced, in sad but firm tones, that their relationship must be considered at an end.

Like a wall that has been struck by a wrecker's ball, André's way of life quavered but continued to stand for a few days. The final crumbling came when both magazine and gallery closed their doors. There was no help for it, now, no salvation. The debts incurred by the magazine had all fallen due; since they had, according to the books, been paid long ago, they became André's sole responsibility. He lost not only his offices, but also his apartment, for that was "attached" also.

Throughout the cataclysm, Thérèse stuck by him. Day after day, she stood meekly before his desk as he ranted and raved. Industrious as ever, she helped expedite the myriad tasks connected with closing down the business, and still she was pale and obedient. It was only when they moved from Paris that everything changed. In his very worst nightmare, André Germain could not have imagined a more painful situation. His country house, mortgaged as it was, was all that was left him. He suddenly had no income, and so the domestic staff consisted of a lone cleaning woman who came for three hours twice a week. There he was, isolated from Paris, its glamour and society, living with an increasingly dour Thérèse whose preoccupation with Igor never ceased to exasperate him. There were no more gourmet meals. Thérèse reluctantly did the cooking, but her competence was as limited as her diet. Worse, she even behaved as if she expected to become Mme. Germain. André, who could imagine vividly what people would say if he sank so low, produced one of his finest scenes. Still, he was stuck, bored, and unable, even, to go on having affairs: There was no one around but Thérèse. And always, little Igor, who was constantly underfoot, almost monopolizing the attention that was due him, André. His one consolation was that the child would never bear his name and he knew how much Thérèse minded that; but such consolations didn't help much. The thought of one son tended to remind André of the other; and when he pictured Vincent in New York, conspiring with Viola and gloating over his father's discomfiture, it was almost more than he could bear.

André was not altogether wrong: Whenever Vincent thought about his father's plight, he felt distinct pleasure.

For once, the villain was getting his just desserts. Vincent had cut himself off from André so thoroughly that only Viola reminded him of what had become a closed chapter.

Other memories were not so pleasant. Vincent still shuddered with disgust when he remembered the two-month "eternity" during which his fight with Poppea had sent him downtown day after day to stand around in courts and answer lawyers' questions. For weeks afterward, he went on feeling soiled and guilty, wondering sometimes whether she didn't have a point, whether he shouldn't bear the entire loss himself. But then the question became academic. Poppea withdrew her countersuit because she could no longer pay her lawyer, and Vincent, who could hardly afford his, desisted on the grounds that, even if he won, he would be unable to collect.

On the whole, he realized, even that loss was a relief. Somehow, during the past months, Poppea had come to represent everything he hated about his days as a dealer: the greed, the suspended honesty, the contact with people whose hands he would have preferred not to shake. Every time he thought of her, it was like reopening a wound. He wondered if he would ever be able to return to Italy without being haunted by her ghost; and he dreaded running into her on the streets.

Now, as he looked back on those months of drift and uncertainty, they seemed to be one long nightmare. The translation he was doing kept him alive, just, and he didn't know what he would do next. As he came closer to finishing it, he sank into an even deeper depression. It wasn't just that he had no idea how he would earn a living, but that he was a man without a task, without a goal. The only thing he knew for sure was that he never wanted to be a dealer again; but was he competent to do anything else? One day, an English friend who was passing through New

York sat him down and, looking him straight in the eye, asked him what he was going to do with himself. To his shame, he was unable to answer her: He didn't know, he couldn't imagine.

Over two months passed, after the end of the lawsuit, before he could see his way. At first, he had withdrawn: Even seeing a friend was too great an effort, and, besides, he had learned early that friends forget you when things go badly. Now, to his surprise, people called and invited him places. Acquaintances in whose homes he would not before have dreamed of staying asked him for the weekend. He was a guest at dinner after dinner, and wondered at all the kindness.

Most curious to him in this new life was his taste for solitude. Even though he went out, he lived quite alone and found great solace in it. All his life, until now, he had made sure he would always be with someone. Now he reveled in the lack of company; living with a woman again became intolerably burdensome. He also noticed that many of his old needs were falling away from him: Luxury no longer mattered, nor did travel, nor did appearances. In one way, he remained unchanged: He still loved reading more than anything. And because, financially and psychologically, he now supported only himself, his new circumstances took on a clearer meaning.

He realized what was happening to him the day when, looking around his studio apartment, he suddenly felt contented. The prison had become freedom; and smallness, liberty. He realized that, like porcelain, he could come through the fire and be transmuted into a harder, more resilient substance. Then, quickly, he reproached himself for his smugness.

He avoided Olga: He knew she would not agree with him. She had moved to larger quarters and was overwhelmed with work; but her voice left no doubt as to the satisfaction she felt as a consequence. She always asked what he was doing, of course, but she sounded different. It was obvious that, to her, Vincent was sinking just as fast as she was rising.

Still, it was through Olga that Vincent heard about a part-time job. She phoned one day to announce she was getting married to another dealer. She loved him, he was good to her, and while they would do some business together, each would keep a separate place, a different clientele. With a brief pang—after all, he was alone—Vincent, who knew her fiancé, realized that she was right: She had at last found the right man, and he had the vision of a fifty-year-old Olga, many years hence, very happy, very successful, and very rich.

"And by the way," Olga went on after she had made her announcement and been duly congratulated, "I have a friend who's been teaching part-time—art history at City College—and she's leaving town suddenly. Maybe you could replace her."

"Well," Vincent said, "it's nice of you to offer, but I don't know. I mean, I've never taught and—"

"You can do it," Olga interrupted, "and you need a job." So it was arranged. Vincent went, was interviewed and hired, with the warning that they would let him go at the end of the term unless he enrolled in a doctoral program.

He only had a week to prepare for his first lecture— on Giotto—and it was hard work. Then, when the day came, he repented his acceptance. At the thought of those thirty students awaiting him, he felt something very close to panic. Still, he had no choice; the class must be faced. With dread, he walked in, greeted the students, and made the usual announcements. As the lecture progressed, he found to his relief that he never bothered to look at the thick pile of notes he had brought with him. He understood Giotto and could discuss him clearly, easily. It was a revelation.

Suddenly, his life had changed again. He still had no money, but it mattered even less than before because he derived such pleasure from lecturing, from communicating his knowledge. It was all far too wonderful to keep to himself, so he called his friends and told them. He visited Olga and expressed his gratitude to her. "I always knew you were the academic type," she said. He agreed, but said that it had been a great surprise to him. "The thing that matters in life," she said, "is knowing when you're in the right place. What you really need always comes to you; the trick is to seize it," and Vincent agreed.

It was pure pleasure, he said, to see at last where he was going. He would start on his doctorate in the fall and had already applied for a scholarship; he would go on teaching in order to manage financially, but otherwise, he didn't care about the money. "In fact," he said, "I almost feel I should be paying them to let me teach!"

Olga laughed. "That wouldn't be a very good precedent," she said. "Oh, by the way, guess who I've just heard about?"

"I don't know. Partridge?"

"No. Well, yes, I mean. He's still living with that critic of his. No, someone you'd want to know about."

"I give up," Vincent said. "Who?"

"Poppea Vlassoff!"

"Not really?"

"You'll never believe what she's doing now," Olga went on with satisfaction. "My friend Zita was in Great Neck the other day. You know, she's a dealer. Well, she passed a shop that said "Poppea Vlassoff Fine Arts" and had a big banner across the window with OIL PAINTINGS FOR $10 AND UP, so she went in, and there she was—the dreadful Poppea in person, standing behind the counter."

Vincent laughed. "Speak of being where you belong!" he said.

He should have been delighted, he thought as he walked home, that Poppea had been humbled. Surely that would quell her ghost forever; but he found he didn't care very much. He soon dismissed her from his mind. There were too many other matters of importance.

Flinging down his raincoat as soon as he walked into his apartment, he sat at his desk and took out a yellow pad. Within a few minutes, he had set down a rough outline detailing time, income, expenditures. His future stretched before him: the part-time teaching; the three years—perhaps four with the dissertation—spent studying; the small, barely balanced budget. It would mean a lot of very hard work on very little money—a straitjacket, almost. But, looking at all his obligations, he lifted his head, smiled to himself, and said in a clear voice: "I have never been so happy."